WEST OF APOCALYPSE

West of Apocalypse

Bill Blume

Time Killer Publishing

For Sheri

Contents

"Life can walk upon most worlds,
but there are places the living should never go."

Kristian Basten,
Basten's Warning

PART I

The Town

1.

The knight stabbed her dagger into the dirt and watched the way its shadow fell. She'd planted the blade next to a leaf-barren husk of a tree. The dagger had a better chance of growing.

The two shadows didn't line up right, a little off.

Summed up this world. Ayleen had sensed it the minute she emerged from the dark energy tunnel. Even fifty feet beneath the planet's surface in the keyhole's cave, that thin sense of wrong had marched up her legs and pricked at the length of her spine.

One of the Thirteen was here, and her sword whispered sweet promises to her from within its black wooden scabbard, eager to bathe in blood. Its hungry voice had lived in her thoughts ever since her forging ceremony.

She'd never visited Griffin, at least that was the name on the battered, metal sign back in the keyhole chamber. Couldn't call it a "welcome" sign, because the planet's name was all it offered in black text on what was once a white field. It hung at an angle. No one felt a desire to hammer out the dings or wipe off the layers of dirt. The only light to read it came from the yellow glow of the "keyhole," the sphere that allowed entry and exit through an interstellar tunnel from one world to another.

Griffin matched its sign. The land beyond the mouth of the key-hole's cave wore more cracks than blades of grass. Hot air baked Ayleen beneath her thin, pale green poncho. The frayed garment concealed most of her weather-worn uniform. Her brown, wool hat with its three-inch brim did nothing to shield her retinas from the harsh orange light of the sun, eager to drown in the horizon.

A narrow post fashioned from black steel stood in the direction her dagger's shadow pointed. She pulled the blade free from the parched land, adding a fresh wrinkle to Griffin's face. She wiped the blade on her pants leg and slid the dagger into its sheath on her right thigh, below the scabbard for her sword.

A yellow sign with black letters attached to the top of the pole pointed into the darkening east: *Midchron 17 clicks.*

The other three directions on the post only had the shredded remains of whatever yellow signs once belonged there. She'd seen the like on dozens of worlds since she'd started her search a little less than two years ago.

The Thirteen.

Any world they touched devoured itself, snakes feasting on their own tails.

The whole galaxy had lost its way. Like her dagger, nothing about Ayleen lined up with the worlds she walked.

She'd lost everything but her sword. Now, she only wanted the lives of those thirteen souls who'd taken more from her than any other.

She gripped the leather-wrapped hilt of her sword. The weight of the weapon, concealed in its scabbard upon her right hip, sang to her for release. Instead, she pulled her water pack's drinking tube out from beneath her poncho. The plastic tube infused the warm water with an artificial aftertaste she hated. That didn't stop her from taking a long draw.

Returning the drinking tube to its resting place on her back, she followed the yellow sign towards Midchron.

She glanced over her shoulder at the sun. No chance she'd reach Midchron before sunset, but for the chance of a roof with a bed beneath it, she'd push on in the dark.

For revenge, she'd walk the rest of her life. No place darker than that.

2.

Ayleen followed the remnants of a road to Midchron. Bits of blacktop covered the landscape, akin to a skin infection on the world's dry surface. Firelight outlined the curve of the horizon against the night sky.

Her first view over the hill of Midchron disappointed. It consisted of only two intersecting roads. A few lanterns burned atop their mounts and lined the streets.

On her way into town, she passed the remains of brick walls, the rest of their structures long lost. The first to take note of her arrival staggered down the right side of the street towards her. The short man wore a black hat and vest over a white dress shirt covered in a collection of stains in various shades of brown. A dagger rested in a sheath on each hip. Glassy eyes leered at her from beneath the shadows of his hat, its brim so wide it almost matched his height. His stench of hot piss and cheap alcohol forced her to the opposite side of the street. He laughed and muttered something as if sharing a joke with an invisible ghost.

The offensive wails of a harmonica led Ayleen to a tavern, planted on the far left corner of the intersection. Light spilled out the front windows of the first floor, stretching out in long, bright teeth across the covered porch to gnaw into the dirt road. The front door hung open, the only inviting thing about the place as she strolled inside.

Her heavy leather boots announced her arrival with loud thuds and creaks from each step along the sawdust-covered floor. Half the conversations in the tavern stopped. The space was filled with round tables, most with mismatched legs. Only half of the tables were occupied. She counted more than twenty people, all human-oid in appearance. A woman eyed her from behind the bar. She wasn't the only one studying Ayleen, who offered plenty to grab their attention. Ayleen wore the dust of Griffin's desert on her face, most of it on the bridge of her nose which bent to the left, a souvenir from her training in the Knighthood. The real grabbers came as benefits from her dual heritage. The straight, blue hair she inherited from her Pleiaderean father spilled out from beneath her hat and down to the middle of her back. Her Cygnian mother had gifted her with deep purple eyes. The only patrons not distracted by her were focused on a card game at the table by a crackling fire.

The middle-aged woman behind the bar scowled at her, adding to the wrinkles from too much sun and too many cigars. Her face resembled the land so much, she might as well have been named Griffin, too. "What can I get you?"

"What have you got?"

The bartender pointed behind her to the shelf lined with tall, narrow bottles. "Drinks, food, and rooms." She planted both hands on the bar so her torso filled the knight's view. "Just no charity."

Ayleen wondered if she looked destitute or if the Midchron wel-coming committee greeted every stranger in such fine fashion.

"First three will do me well." She reached into the small leather purse, attached to her belt on her left hip. The gamblers across the room noticed the silver she placed on the bar. "Won't need the latter."

After a bit of haggling, the bartender placed a short glass in front of Ayleen and filled it a third of the way with an amber liquid that was supposed to be brandy. While it might have had alcohol in it, its relationship to brandy ended there. The taste curled her lips, but given the look of the town, a glass of water might leave her shiting tidal waves. Her dinner was risk enough. Heavens only knew what kind of beast these desert dwellers were passing off as snake, especially if claiming it was a reptile sounded more palatable than the truth. She considered her doubts justified given her drink.

Using the mirror behind the bar, Ayleen studied the room. Everyone took a turn sneaking a look at her for signs of where she was from and why she was here. They tried to figure out her sword, but the only part visible was the hilt. Its brown leather wrap couldn't have been plainer. The wrap had once included engravings of stars, but repeated use had worn them to smudged impressions.

Halfway through the leathery strip of snake on her plate, Ayleen got the answer she'd been trying to see in the mirror: which of these locals would approach her first.

A young man with blond hair stood from the card players' table and swaggered up to the counter. He placed his empty glass on the bar and waved the bartender over for a refill. Judging from the loose way he moved, he'd already had enough of the cloudy green liquid the bartender gave him to build a fine buzz. "Thanks, Sarane."

The bartender answered with a thin smile. No money exchanged hands, and Sarane didn't linger in anticipation.

The stranger had his drink but didn't leave the bar. He smiled at Ayleen and offered his hand. "Name's Cerris."

She kept her hands occupied with her knife and fork. She never looked away from her plate. Around a mouthful of snake, she said, "Torr."

"That a first or last name? Or do folks from your parts just settle on the one?"

"It's my last name." She paused to sip her drink. "You don't require the first."

He must have noticed her wince from the brandy hitting the back of her throat. "I prefer the absinthe." He raised his glass, giving the green contents a swirl. "Tastes smoother." He leaned a hip against the edge of the bar and placed the drink closer to her. "Try it."

"Don't tell me what to do."

He shrugged off her rebuff and sipped his absinthe. "Just trying to be friendly."

"No, you're being nosy." She cut off his protest. "You've got my last name. You know I'm rude. That's plenty enough for you to gossip with."

She pointed with her knife back towards the table with the card players. "Get."

With a little bump of his hip, Cerris pushed away from the bar, but he didn't walk away. "As you like, but word of advice...don't be wearing that sword in town. You keep showing it off long enough, someone'll decide to find out if you know how to use it."

"You always give advice you don't follow?" She sawed off another bite of snake before popping it in her mouth. When he didn't respond, she pointed with the knife at the sword on his left hip. The left side of his vest also sagged in a way to suggest he possibly had another blade there, but she couldn't be certain.

"I'm deputized." He tapped his forehead with his hand in a polite bow and walked back to his table.

Using the mirror, she tracked his movements. His swagger suggested confidence, but even an ignorant buffoon who believed himself invincible carried bravado. More telling was the way the room responded to him. A few savored the view, one woman more openly than the others. Some waited, as if to hold their breaths, until Cerris sat. A drunk man grabbed his glass of liquor, downed it, and somehow walked a straight line out of the tavern with an obvious effort to not look at Cerris.

No one disturbed her for the rest of her meal, such as it was. A handful of people came and went, but while they took their turns staring at her and her sword, no one other than Cerris and Sarane said anything to her.

That worked fine for her. She took her time to study everyone there while she finished her drink. She didn't know the face of every member of the Thirteen. Rumors suggested all but one had carried a sword like hers. Knights wore a certain demeanor that no years nor dress could hide. They'd also been traitors, though, and nothing of their betrayal had confessed itself in their walk, salute, or sword swing. Not until a blade kissed a sister or brother's heart.

Did she really believe she could spot the Thirteen so easily? She remembered the one who killed her father. He'd chased her and the group of squires in her charge into the bowels of the Citadel in Mount Hawkken. The memory of so many children cut down steps from the safety of the keyhole shook her hand. She grabbed her glass and took the remaining swill in a single shot.

The way Ayleen slapped the empty glass back on the bar spoke her need. Sarane answered by pouring more brandy.

Finishing her second round, Ayleen climbed the stairs to the small room she'd rented for the night. A rickety ladder-back chair with uneven legs and a thin chest of drawers with a wash basin atop it occupied the left side of the room. A narrow bed for one took up the right side. That left enough room for Ayleen to breathe and little else.

She locked the door and shoved the back of the chair up beneath the door handle. She marveled her rough handling didn't break it into a pile of splinters. The chair wouldn't stop anyone from getting into the room, but it would give her a couple of seconds to get her sword and greet them with a single-edged "How do you do?"

She pulled off her poncho and her pack, dropping them to the floor. A glimpse of her reflection in a cracked mirror above the wash basin made her jump. She didn't recognize the woman who glared at her. Was she still nineteen, or had she crossed into her twenties? Hopping to worlds not charted on her map had turned time into something vague and cruel. She'd check in the morning if Griffin was on her star chart.

Her uniform's reflection filled her with shame—its poor condition worth more than a hundred lashings. Only no senior officer existed to deliver her punishment.

She slid off the jacket. Guilt stopped her from tossing it to the floor. She placed it on the foot of the bed. The sword belt joined the jacket, but she dropped it closer to the headboard. Not bothering to remove the rest of her offensive clothing, Ayleen collapsed onto the bed. She pulled close the sword still in its scabbard, cradling it against her as a child clung to a doll. The sick odor of cheap tobacco and cheaper sex from previous occupants clung to the paper-thin mattress.

The alcohol caressed her mind. She welcomed its vulgar touch as the room spun. Anything to keep her from puzzling over how to find the traitor here in Griffin was a blessing.

A familiar voice from the thickest grove of shadows in her head offered the tempting solution to kill every fucker in this dying pit of barren dirt.

Kill them all, and there won't be any doubts, her sword whispered to her.

She mumbled curses, both at the sword's unwelcome advice and the unpleasant memories that haunted her until sleep claimed her.

3.

The next day started with blinding light. Ayleen rolled away from the thick beam of sunrise flooding into her room. She'd overlooked the lack of a curtain last night when the sky was painted pitch.

Awake and close to sober, she decided to wash the desert from her face. A drowned bug with seven splayed legs floated in the wash basin. She tipped the bowl, sending the bug over the edge atop a wave that splashed loudly onto the floor. The heel of her boot crushed the bug on the off-chance a little life remained in it.

When she emerged from her room, she looked respectable enough to only deserve double-digit lashings. After a detour out the back for the privy, she came back into the tavern to find someone new behind the bar. The girl wore her black hair in a tight bun held in place by a dull brown clip. The collar of her tan blouse hung open by all of one button, showing off a little of her neck that some small, prudish towns might consider scandalous. The room held onto a little of the night's chill, but it wouldn't survive the sun's ascension.

"Morning to you," the girl said. Ayleen guessed she couldn't have been much more than sixteen years. Her big smile and round eyes belonged to a life of simpler hardships and innocence not yet lost.

Ayleen nodded, pausing by the front window to see if anyone milled about the streets. The most she saw was a pair of wagons at an open air market. A skinny, grey-skinned beast of burden swatted at a fly on its back with its narrow, pink tail. Despite its long legs, the creature reminded her of a giant rodent with its thick neck and head narrowed into a pointed nose. If memory served, it was a pilcho. She wasn't sure and didn't bother to ask the girl at the bar for confirmation.

The girl stared at Ayleen with obvious fascination. "I'm Mirla."

"Coffee?" Ayleen asked.

"Sorry, miss?" Mirla's eyebrow raised in embarrassed confusion. "Is that your name? Don't think I quite caught it."

"It's a drink. Guessing you don't have it." Little surprise. Out of the handful of inhabited worlds she'd run across in her two-year exile, she'd only found coffee on one of them.

The girl boiled some water for tea. The sensation of steam from a mug taunted Ayleen. If the scent offered any indication, the beverage would taste bitter once it cooled enough for a sip.

Mirla rested her chin on her hands with her elbows on the bar. "You really came from the keyhole?"

Ayleen rubbed her temple, hoping the girl would let it go. The lack of other customers did nothing to help matters.

Her sword whispered as it had the night before. *Kill the perky thing now. One down, the rest to go.*

Ayleen was grateful only she could hear her sword. "Yes, I came from the keyhole." She lifted the mug to blow at the steam, hoping to hurry things along. "Why do you keep the town so far from it?" Given the opportunity for trade provided by the keyholes, towns surrounded most of them, even on the most eroded of worlds.

"Sand demons."

That got her attention. "What are those?"

Mirla held her hands apart as if measuring out five feet. "About yea wide with four legs and two arms with claws that'll snap a man in half. Suckers burrow into the ground. Their backs look a lot like the ground out that way. Used to be you'd step on one, and they'd pop out." She jumped up while performing a snapping motion with both her hands. "Ate you right up with their two heads. Sure would." More snapping motions with her hands. "Chomp! Chomp! Chomp!"

"Would?" She risked a sip of the tea, which singed her tongue. The reddish brown liquid was bitter as expected, but with a strange tang.

"Once the town made some money off the mine, the sheriff hired a posse and led them into the desert. Wiped them out. No more chomping for those beasties. Got the mayor talking about expanding the town closer to the keyhole."

Ayleen grunted her limited interest and took another sip of her tea.

"So what brings you to Midchron?" Mirla leaned against the back of the bar. "You looking to stay?"

Ayleen's eyes narrowed and hardened at the girl's question. Sure, she might just be making conversation, but Ayleen wouldn't put it past one of the Thirteen to use someone with Mirla's disarming manner to pull information out of a stranger. "I'm just passing through."

"Not planning to stay long?"

"Just enough to rest." The knight glared across the bar. "You got any other questions?"

The girl stepped back, taking a deep swallow before she said anything. "Sorry, don't mean to offend, if I did, but..."

"What?"

The girl answered with her eyes. Grey irises went direct to the sword resting on Ayleen's right hip.

One down, the rest to go.

Ayleen silently told her sword to shut it. She stood, planting her hands on the bar, much as Sarane had done to her the previous night.

"What?" She smiled in a most unkind fashion to Mirla. "You aching for a look at it?"

"Was just curious. Sure, folks'll carry daggers around here, but most no one wants to be caught dead with a sword on 'em. The mayor calls it an open challenge to authority."

Ayleen rested her hand on the hilt, not to draw it, but more to make sure it stayed put.

"Hear me right. My father always said a sword should only leave its scabbard for one of two reasons. One is to train. The other, to kill." She picked up her mug of bitterness. "I'll be taking this outside so you won't see something you might regret."

The porch in front of the tavern was covered, but that didn't stop the heat from sneaking into the shade. The hot tea warmed what the air couldn't touch. She pulled off her poncho and slung it over the railing, which doubled for her seat. She'd anticipated losing the poncho today, so she'd left her uniform's jacket in the room upstairs. That left her in a simple black vest over a faded red, button-down dress shirt. The few people on the worlds she'd seen in the past few months hadn't talked about the Thirteen with any affection, and since most of them had once worn the same uniform as hers, she figured it best to keep her past to herself.

Leaning against one of the porch's wooden posts, she watched the town wake. Much of the foot traffic traveled north, men and women armed with pickaxes and shovels. They all wore or carried hard hats, some with big round lights attached to the front. Ayleen wondered what they mined here, what could possibly have enough value to give these people work, especially when nothing she saw suggested they traded with anyone.

She avoided conversations with any passersby. Some nodded to her. She answered any man who leered with a hard look.

Ayleen watched for one thing—a hint of the traitor among them. She didn't really expect any of the Thirteen to live like this. Those knights didn't turn their backs on their Way to hole up in dust bowls, work in mines, and screw their brains out making babies. If one of those bastards had landed in such pathetic situations, she'd be tempted to leave them be. To find her enemy in such a state would be awful considerate of the Galaxy, and if her life and knighthood training had taught her anything, the Galaxy never dealt in consideration. The Great Bitch took what she wanted and rained falling stars on the rest.

A girl of about ten years walked onto the porch long after the morning commute. One look at her made it clear she also understood the Way of the Galaxy. She hugged herself in the manner of a person who knows no one else will. Her big, brown eyes offered a wide view to all the shite she wanted to burn.

Ayleen got tired of the girl staring at her. "What?"

The girl didn't blink, even though Ayleen had barked the question at her.

"You staying?" Her voice sounded dry as the cracked land.

"Passing through."

"When you leave," she hesitated. Her half-starved features reminded Ayleen of a feral cat. "I wanna go with you."

"No."

"Midchron's not safe for me."

"The space by my side won't be better." Ayleen glared at the child. If she took it for threat or warning made no difference as long as she recognized the advice was the gods' truth.

The girl didn't move. "You gonna be here tonight?"

Ayleen looked away from the girl, dismissing her. "Maybe."

"If you are, you'll understand why you're wrong."

Ayleen sipped her tea.

The girl's footsteps assured Ayleen she'd driven her off, but as the small feet reached the bottom of the front steps, the girl said one thing more. "My name's Dara Ercanna."

Ayleen turned to tell Dara to get lost, but the child was already walking away. She wasn't hugging herself anymore.

4.

With her mug emptied and her patience shredded, Ayleen left the mug on the railing and strolled to find answers. She stopped in front of a shop with a large, cracked window. A deactivated android with its head removed and the neck's melted innards on silent display wore a yellow dress meant to show off an impressive amount of cleavage the android's makers had not endowed it with.

A wooden sign reached out from the corner of the building near the front door to identify the business as "Faye's Fashions."

Ayleen fingered the worn end of her rolled up sleeve. She rarely wore them down these days. Overuse had worn holes into the elbows. Now made a fine time to get a new shirt and, if the Fates wove their webs in her favor, possibly some insights into Midchron.

The Fates' weave led Ayleen to some fine irony. Faye's proprietor was a woman named Viv, which was short for Vivalandraysa.

"Belonged to my mother-in-law, may her soul rest well and trouble me none again." She laughed.

Viv was dark of skin with long, silver hair piled up top to show off her slender neck. In both hands, she held a pale, thin tape of what was once yellow with black marks on it. Using the tape, Viv measured Ayleen and noted the numbers on a small chalkboard she left on a table. Ayleen didn't recognize the thin characters with sharp, short lines Viv used. The entire process made Ayleen twitchy, having removed her hat, which rested on the hook of a nearby rack.

The rambling tailor appeared oblivious to Ayleen's discomfort.

"Married her only child, I did, and Faye never forgave me for it. Never mind I gave the ungrateful ol' skeleton the grandson she dearly wanted. About the only time I saw her smile in my direction, and the once was enough." She laughed again as she took a step back from Ayleen to study her. "Only reason I keep her name on the shop is because I'm not from around these parts. Don't want to discourage customers by reminding them."

Ayleen couldn't fake a laugh, so she didn't try. A smile worked fine, though. Viv seemed the type who needed only another's ear and sufficient oxygen to carry a conversation…the ear, optional.

Ayleen glanced towards the window, which faced north. "Your husband work in the mine?"

"What's that? Oh, yes." She smiled at Ayleen. "Mayor says the mine will save the town. Digging to find our Way."

"What are they mining?"

"Gemstones of some sort. Already brought in folks looking for work." Viv added under her breath. "And other types."

"Other types?"

"Thieves, dear." Viv filled the word with venom. "Our Sheriff Javo does fine hunting them down, say it sure."

Javo… The "yah" at the start of the name gave it an Ohmejan or Sahyitarian sound, neither of which had any business in this end of the Galaxy, assuming she'd correctly identified Griffin on her star chart this morning.

She wanted Javo's name to draw at her memory, fit some name from the Knighthood, but her efforts failed. She'd get a look at the sheriff soon enough, the sheriff and all the rest in this town.

Viv, returning to the task at hand, sorted through a pile of all color and fabrics. Most of the material on the table looked too small to be anything but remnants from larger stock Viv had scavenged. "You've lovely hair, but I think you should go with something to bring out your eyes. Here. What say you to this?"

Viv tugged free some purple fabric and held it up against Ayleen, covering most of her torso. "Take a look in the mirror."

Ayleen avoided the mirror and looked down at the material, rubbing it between her fingers. The fabric felt sturdy and was textured with endless lines in the shapes of diamonds. A shirt made from this material would be dark enough to hide blood stains.

"It'll do."

"You say sure? I've plenty of other options." She stood like a statue, stopped short of searching for more expensive fabrics on the table.

"I'm sure." They haggled, and for all her inane chatter, Viv proved a tough negotiator. The tailor had the added advantage of the poor condition of the shirt Ayleen already wore. She could hide the holes in her sleeves but not the sweat stain that had soured the edge of her collar from vibrant red to dark brown. Ayleen hoped Viv sewed as well as she talked.

"Check with me tomorrow morning." Viv shooed Ayleen out the door. "Good chance I'll have it finished."

Ayleen put her hat back on as she stepped into the sunlight.

Three men in the middle of the street walked past her. They carried a long beam of wood to the center of town. Didn't take long to learn why.

5.

Near sunset, the townsfolk gathered around the middle of Midchron. Ayleen leaned against a post on the front porch of the tavern.

Dara Ercanna was one of the last to arrive. She took a spot on the ground, right in front of Ayleen. The crowd stood shoulder-to-shoulder, but they granted this child a berth reserved for lepers.

Dara glanced over her shoulder at Ayleen. Eyes like that chilled even in this desert.

No one spoke.

A boy carried a long pole with a burning wick on the end of it and lit the street lights. He stopped with only the nearest lanterns. The rest didn't matter. No one would leave until the show was done.

The wooden beam stood in the center of the intersection. Three unlit torches on slender poles, stabbed into the ground, surrounded it. A short chain with a metal collar dangled from halfway up the pillar of wood. Its long shadow stabbed into the approaching night, a giant sundial to mark an end.

When the sun vanished into the western hills, the boy lit the three torches. The doors to the church on the opposite corner from the tavern pulled open. Five people emerged. Deputy Cerris and an older man, whom Ayleen took for another deputy, escorted what was once a man. To call him anything resembling a human only mocked him. They'd stripped him, not even the dignity of a loin-cloth to keep his privates just that. A thin straw rope bound his wrists behind his back, and a red rag was shoved into his mouth with a thick layer of shiny, grey tape wrapped around his head to keep it in place. Blood and bruises covered him. Swelling reduced his eyes to slits. He fought in vain against Cerris and the other deputy.

Two more followed. The man stood out among the citizens of Midchron. He was tall with muscles that bulged beneath his white shirt, without wrinkle or blemish. Most notable was that he looked well-fed, a term Ayleen wouldn't apply to anyone else in town, most of whom carried a sunken-in appearance as a token of their citizenship. A leather, bandolier wrapped across his chest, from right shoulder to left hip. A sword hilt peeked up from over his shoulder like a cross resting on his back. The mayor, most likely.

The woman next to him wore a copper star on her belt. Not as well-nourished as the man, but every aspect of her warned she could take on any person in this town with no weapon greater than her hands and bury them all. The broadsword in a leather sheath on her hip might be there for decoration, but Ayleen suspected this woman knew how to wield it.

Either of them could be a former knight, one of the Thirteen. An air of military training infused their march to the prisoner. Was it unreasonable to think they might both be members of the Thirteen?

Her sword's voice in her head taunted her. *Leave no one, and you leave no doubt.*

Deputy Cerris punched the naked prisoner in the stomach. The blow knocked the fight out of him long enough for the deputies to fasten the collar around his neck, chaining him to the wooden beam.

The deputies surrendered the "stage," with Cerris disappearing back into the church. The mayor stepped into the intersection and spoke in a deep voice that reached every ear without the need to yell.

"We've suffered more than our share of dark seasons. Some of us still remember when the signs still pointed to New Hope and Karavelle. Nothing left in either direction now.

"The Lord didn't find them fit. They lost their Way.

"I know temptation's call. We all do, but Midchron doesn't answer to that. Not when the Drought of Aurillion's Constellation dried up the river. Not when the armies of the Riyans and the Dromedans dropped their bombs on each other and those souls caught between. And, sure as sunrise, not when the nomads threatened to take our children."

He took his time, walking around the pole, each step turning him in closer to the prisoner.

"We didn't lose our Way. We could have. Could have kept our good fortune to ourselves, not welcome others into our town.

"Midchron suffered plenty, but we're still here." He stopped in front of the prisoner and glared into his swollen face.

The mayor spun to face the crowd with his finger pointed like a hungry dagger at the prisoner.

"Teskin Ercanna, you are here because you lost your Way."

Ercanna... Ayleen looked from the prisoner to the girl in front of her. If there was any resemblance to be found between Dara and Teskin Ercanna, the mangled condition of his face hid the truth.

"This outland scum stole from the mine! He stole from Midchron!" His voice lowered to a rasp. "He stole from every single one of you."

The mayor took in the crowd with a slow turn. Ayleen felt certain he hesitated in her direction, but whether his attention locked on her or Dara was impossible to know.

"Teskin Ercanna, you took from Midchron, and now Midchron shall take its due from you."

Deputy Cerris returned with a steel pitcher and bowed his head as he offered it to the mayor. Tipping the pitcher over Teskin's head, the mayor covered the prisoner in an amber, semi-clear liquid.

"We will offer a prayer for better fortune in your next life." The mayor handed the empty pitcher back to Deputy Cerris. He jerked one of the torches out of the ground and thrust its flame towards the small puddle at the prisoner's feet. "A prayer of fire."

Flames erupted from the land and raced up Teskin's body. The rag in his mouth and the layers of tape muffled his screams until the flames chewed them off.

Some of the townspeople shouted curses at him. Others looked away. A man moved his hand over his face to wipe away tears and snot before others noticed.

Dara didn't move.

Long after the people of Midchron had slunk to their homes and about a half dozen others into the tavern, only three remained. Ayleen stared past Dara's back at what was left of her father. He wasn't the third remaining soul. Whatever ephemeral life had been in him had left around the time his intestines spilled in a blood-smoldering pile among the charred remains of his feet. A putrid odor akin to copper tainted the air.

From the opposite side of the intersection, Sheriff Javo stood with one foot mounted on the church steps. Her left hand rested on the steel pommel of her broadsword. Unlike the mayor, no question existed who the sheriff watched. Ayleen answered with a thin smile, the kind a prowling wildcat offers before she makes the kill.

6.

The lamplighter failed to light any of the other lamps along Midchron's two streets, as if Teskin Ercanna's execution had met the town's nightly quota for firelight. Ayleen opted not to share the thought with the dead man's daughter. Nor did she waste her breath on useless offers of comfort.

Instead, Ayleen asked a single question.

"Why'd they really kill him?"

The mayor had turned the execution into an event. Justice didn't require a showman. Tonight served more as a warning for the rebellious and a reassurance to the loyal and gullible, who drank from the same well.

After Ayleen went to her room to retrieve her jacket and green poncho, Dara led them into the desert.

The night tilted from hot to chilly with frigid close behind. The two orphans walked out of Midchron into a sky of naught but stars. Ayleen wondered if Griffin had a moon. She muffled her laugh at the thought that harkened to more peaceful days before the Knights of the Way were wiped from the star chart. Father joked he'd mapped so much of the Cat's Paw, they should call it Ayleen's Pa instead. She pushed away the thought, because any memories of her father only led to the last time she saw him and the blood covered end of a crystal sword thrust out his back.

With the dim glow of Midchron two hills behind them, they reached Dara's home. The shack was built from a patchwork of flat material the sands of Griffin hadn't claimed. The front was constructed from a handful of metal sheets, four different types of wood, a large yellow sign with "Karavelle 32 Clicks" in black, bold letters, and a divided window frame with cracked glass in all but one of the frames which was covered with black plastic.

The front door, a flimsy aluminum frame with screen mesh, screamed its high-pitched protest as Dara opened it. A spring pulled the door shut with a slam after they entered.

Dara fumbled in the dark until she lit a dirty oil lamp set on a small, round table. The floor was formed from six wooden pallets nailed together. Two large, plastic tubs of water sat in one corner, next to a small wood stove that included a pipe running up out the roof. Two cots ate up most of the space, one with a wooden frame with thick legs. Ayleen had wondered, more than once, what had become of Dara's mother but decided she didn't want to know.

Dara pointed to the cot with the larger legs, specifically one of the legs at the foot of the bed. Ayleen turned the bed onto its side, the mattress and blanket slid to the floor. The bottom part of the bed legs were fatter. Ayleen grabbed the bottom of the leg Dara had pointed to. It slid off to expose the hollowed-out interior and the rolled-up, leather book hidden there.

Ayleen's breath caught as she unrolled the book and recognized the symbol burned into its cover. The same image of a sword cutting down the middle of a spiral formed from two long arms and two shorter ones also decorated the upper left side of her uniform's jacket.

"He found it in the mine," Dara said.

Ayleen peeled open the cover. Not simply a book, but a journal.

The aged-yellow pages within felt brittle as she turned through it. The orderly jumble of letters and glyphs drawn from the language of the Fates taunted her. She remembered seeing a journal like this during her childhood. Mother was one of only five mage generals in the Knighthood's Science Regiment.

"This is a grimoire." Ayleen's hand shook as she ran her fingertips across the page. She glanced over her shoulder through the screen door. Holding one of these, an actual mage general's journal of forbidden science, left her with the irrational fear of monsters creeping up her back. "These are supposed to be burned upon a mage general's death. This shouldn't exist."

Then a more obvious contradiction entered Ayleen's mind. "This is still here." She turned to Dara. "How did they know your father had this if they never found it?"

Dara took the journal from Ayleen. "They didn't know about the book." The child opened the journal and turned halfway into it to a sketch of a crystal shaped like a rectangular box, except for the pyramid-like shapes on the two smallest sides. "They found out he had this."

"Heaven's cunt," Ayleen whispered as her stomach hollowed out into an icy void. "What color was the crystal?" She knew. Only one color would have damned Dara's father, but Ayleen needed to hear it.

"Like gold."

Ayleen nodded. Her mother had said the shade of the crystal was more often described as amber, and it's why they were called ambrosia crystals. Without one of those, almost everything in the grimoire was worthless. "Where is it?"

Dara shrugged. "Sheriff took it."

"Tell me exactly what happened."

The next half hour was spent in a stop-and-go conversation with Ayleen interrupting Dara's tale with questions to clarify things. The story boiled down to some simple but important facts.

Teskin Ercanna and a few others found an ancient building buried in the mine. If Ayleen had to guess, they'd found a long-buried knight outpost that doubled as a crystal farm. The crystals the town had found and started to mine were the wild growth of this lost outpost. Those crystals formed the basis for all of the Knighthood's weaponry and served as a natural power source for most of their facilities. No one gave the uncovered building much interest, but Dara's father returned after his shift had ended to dig through the remains. That's when he found the grimoire, which was only half full of writing, and gave it to Dara to draw.

A child drawing in a grimoire! *Gods above and below!*

The day before the sheriff and deputies came for him, Dara's father had taken a photograph he found in the buried outpost to the sheriff.

"Why would he do that?" Ayleen asked. "Were they friends?"

Dara shook her head. "There were people in the picture, dressed like soldiers. One of them looked like the sheriff. He figured it might be an older relative of hers, so he thought she'd want it. When he came home, he said we needed to hide everything that came from the mine. Sheriff and her deputies searched the house the next day.

They found the amber crystal and a bunch of blue ones that Pa hadn't taken."

They'd come here, planning to plant the blue crystals to frame him for theft. Damn fool hadn't hidden the ambrosia crystal well enough, though. Would they know its purpose, what made it special?

"Dara, you saw the photograph?"

She nodded.

Ayleen took off her hat, placing it on the upended bed and pulled off her poncho, giving the girl a good look at her uniform. "Did the woman in the picture wear a jacket like this?"

Dara nodded and took a few steps back. She must have seen Ayleen's rage flare.

One last thing to put the nail in the coffin.

"The sheriff," Ayleen's voice shook with anticipation, "does her sword's blade look like this?"

Ayleen drew her sword. The plain leather wrapping of the hilt ended with no guard. Only a simple steel button drilled into the crystal kept the wrapping in place. The slightly curved, single-edged blade of blue crystal glowed almost green in the dim, yellow lamplight. The flickering of light through the blade exposed a hint of motion within it, energy flowing like blood.

Dara nodded again and moved back more from Ayleen and the living weapon in her hands.

"I'm not going to hurt you." Ayleen smiled, but the way Dara stayed back suggested it wasn't the friendliest of smiles. "I'm no friend of the sheriff."

Ayleen shoved her sword back into its scabbard. She felt its silent howl at having been drawn without taking blood. Oh, she'd make up for that soon enough.

"I've only one more question." Ayleen slid her poncho back on and donned her hat. "Where does the sheriff live?"

7.

The nighttime glow of Midchron had faded with most of the night gone. She'd left Dara at her house, ordering her to stay put.

"What if you don't make it?"

The girl assumed Ayleen would let her leave Griffin with her.

"I'll come back for you after I've gotten satisfaction for my mother and both our fathers." She rolled her eyes once she had her back to Dara and the collage-constructed house. Yes, gods help her, she planned to come back for Dara…assuming she was alive to do it.

Ayleen cursed to herself as she passed Faye's. Before leaving the shop, she'd paid the tailor half the cost of the new shirt, which she couldn't pick up until the morning. Odds favored she'd have to flee Midchron before sunrise. It wouldn't take long for one of the deputies to find their boss dead in her bed. Best to place Midchron to her back long before that happened.

The church came into view. According to Dara, the sheriff lived in a room above the jail, right next to the church. With any luck, the traitor was hard asleep. Ayleen would slip into the sheriff's home, interrogate her, take the ambrosia crystal, and kill her far faster than she deserved.

A few lanterns still burned in the tavern. She needed to retrieve her belongings before going after Sheriff Javo. If things didn't go well, she'd be hard-pressed to waltz back into the tavern looking a bloody mess and not draw someone's suspicion. That assumed she wouldn't have the sheriff two steps and a sword swing behind her.

Fine, she decided as she climbed the tavern's front steps. She'd wait for the bastards in here to drink their fill and then make her move.

Before she walked inside, she noticed the absence of music. The momentum of her march took her the next step inside where she counted more than twenty people, all armed with swords. They sat at tables, drinking and playing cards in a half-hearted fashion that made it clear neither the booze nor the game was their reason for being here.

Only one person was at the bar.

Sheriff Javo put her glass of tequila down and turned from Ayleen's reflection to set her eyes on the real thing.

"Join me for a drink, girl."

Just like that, all of Ayleen's plans fell into a deep hole of shite.

8.

As ambushes went, Ayleen gave Sheriff Javo's a solid eight out of ten. The absence of music should have caught Ayleen's attention sooner. About the only major move not played was a few hired swords on the front porch to block her exit. Didn't mean there wasn't anyone outside, hiding in the shadows. Of course, the only grading scale for this ambush that mattered was whether Ayleen walked away from it.

She could run now, but something told her if the sheriff really wanted her dead, she'd have gone for a more discreet attack. Likely, that would have involved a late night visit along the lines of what Ayleen had planned for Javo. No, the sheriff wanted to chat before the real fun started. Given the show of strength, Javo hoped to cow Ayleen into a bloodless surrender. Well, bloodless for everyone but Ayleen.

What exactly had Javo seen across the intersection tonight to make her this concerned?

Slower than she should have, Ayleen ran through all those considerations and her options for escape or attack. No one moved, all waiting to see her response.

Reaching up to the front of her hat, she tilted it back with a single finger and flashed a smile to the other girls and boys at their tables as if to say *'All this for little ol' me?'*

Ayleen noticed the absence of a bartender. Sarane must have opted against being here or was told to stay home. Either way, it suggested the sheriff expected things to go poorly.

"There a problem, sheriff?"

"Depends." Sheriff Javo refilled her glass from the dark, stubby bottle on the bar and poured a fresh one for Ayleen. "Here."

They tapped their glasses together in an amiable fashion neither felt nor showed in their eyes or lips. The sheriff downed her glass. Ayleen feigned a sip, opting not to risk the drink might be poisoned. The brush of it against her lips left a familiar scent, sweet and potent.

"Ohmejan Tequila?" Ayleen's mom had affectionately referred to this brand of tequila as "the Good Stuff."

"I like to keep a little taste of home close. Keeps my heart warm." The sheriff poured more of the Good Stuff into her thirsty shot glass. "Speaking of home, where are you from?"

"Somewhere else." Ayleen's snark lacked any bite, given every sword in the room but her own was itching to scratch her.

The sheriff didn't share the same difficulty with bravado. "Shouldn't you already be on your way *somewhere else*, if you're just passing through?"

"I bought a shirt at Faye's." Ayleen rubbed the dirty collar of her red shirt sticking up out of her poncho. "Won't be ready until morning."

"Kind of you to add some coin to the local economy. Viv does mighty fine work." The sheriff rested a hand on the hilt of her sword. "Be a shame to see it get messed up by overstaying your welcome."

Nothing subtle about that.

Ayleen shifted her gaze towards the sheriff's posse. Most of them looked too twitchy to be well-trained with their swords. Only six of them, Deputy Cerris included, looked like they spent more time with their swords than digging for crystals in the mine. Of course, sharp objects had a way of landing on a target, even in the most inept hands.

The preamble marked the worst part of any fight. Whether in a training circle or a blood and mud covered field of combat, the unknown left Ayleen's stomach twisting and empty except for the small but dense ball of dread rolling around in it.

She slid off her hat and placed it on the bar.

"So you aren't from around here?" Ayleen tapped the edge of her glass, still full of foreign tequila.

"No, the mine brought me. The money that's gonna come from it? Also gonna bring in a lot of trouble. These folks needed a fine sword for that." Her voice lowered, the threat in her eyes the equal of any lioness. "You got a point?"

"I'm getting there."

The sheriff arched an eyebrow. "If you think you have that kind of time to spare, you're a hell of a dreamer."

"Guessing I've already overstayed my welcome."

The lioness smiled at the promise of a fine kill. "The night you arrived, don't you think?"

"Suppose so." Why couldn't this lousy bitch have gone to bed?

A few chairs scraped against the floor as the sheriff's posse stood.

Ayleen knew the sands of her hourglass were about to run out. If she wanted to be certain about the sheriff, now was her time to confirm it.

"Before we do this," Ayleen said, stepping back from the sheriff, "grant me a last question."

"Girl, you got titanium petals on you." She put the stopper back on her tequila bottle, pounding it in place with her fist. "What are you dying to know?"

"It's about my boots."

Oh, the look on the sheriff's face… That certainly wasn't the direction she expected this to go.

"You used to wear a pair like them, so what I want to know…" Ayleen pulled off her poncho and tossed it over a barstool. "What was your name before you walked away from your knightly oaths?"

Lines of confusion formed on the sheriff's face as her eyes went straight to the small, silver engraving on the front of the jacket, the spiral with a sword through it.

The closest members of Javo's posse paused in their approach, not sure what final act was playing out.

"Who are you?" The sheriff's question fell off her shaky tongue on a wave of denial and rage.

"My name is Ayleen Torr, daughter of Aydrene and Se Rulian." She put her hat back on, the front leaning low. "Field Knight of the Perseus Legion, and a Knight of the Way."

"That's not…" The sheriff abandoned words and punctuated her sentence with her sword.

Ayleen parried the sheriff's attack. Their blue, crystal blades met with a loud chime, as if the swords sang their owners' mutual hatred. Neither weapon cracked or shattered. Only the wielder's death could destroy a crystal sword.

Four of the other swordfighters pressed in on them with the rest of the room not far behind. Their drawn weapons belonged to the metal variety—cold and lifeless. Their overeager lunges pushed Ayleen back and out of the sheriff's reach.

She had to get out of this tavern. If they cut her off from the door, then math and blood loss would end her.

Ayleen grabbed one of the barstools and swung it at her attackers, letting it fly into the one closest to the door. The bar stool swept the man's legs. He plummeted chin-first to the floor, blood spitting from his mouth.

The rest of the room swarmed her, but the fallen man created enough of a barrier against his comrades for Ayleen to run out onto the porch.

She used the door frame to her advantage. With swords drawn, only one at a time could pass through it. That kind of arithmetic worked in her favor.

The first to chase her through the door—a man with a rust and dirt covered saber—lunged at her. She knocked the blade off course, drew her dagger from its sheath on her right thigh, and slit his throat. The follow-through to the swing of her dagger drew a long, thin line of blood on the outside of the tavern. He collapsed to his knees and dropped his saber with a gasp as he grabbed at his throat in a fruitless effort to stop his life from bleeding out.

A stocky woman with a short and wide, double-edged sword was forced to step around the man bleeding from the throat. She and Ayleen traded swings as the mob shouted from inside the tavern. One of the impatient and more drunken men shoved into the stocky woman's back. Both paid for that misstep. Ayleen's sword thrust through the woman's chest, out her back, and into the drunk's stomach. With a vicious twist to make the wounds worse, Ayleen jerked her sword free. The woman gritted her teeth and glared through tears at Ayleen, but she was done. The drunk screamed as he scrambled back into the tavern.

Ayleen's sword, invigorated by the blood of her enemies, hummed in her thoughts.

Two more brutes shoved the drunk aside and stopped the woman from dropping, using her as a shield.

Ayleen slashed through the dying woman's waist. The crystal sword's enchanted edge split her body in half. The severed legs collapsed to the left as the torso's innards spilled onto the porch. The abrupt change in weight sent the two men holding the woman stumbling forward into Ayleen's next attack. Their bodies joined the growing pile.

The mob paused. Whether they feared Ayleen more than the prospect of walking through the tangle of limbs and viscera of their peers didn't matter. They'd overcome their fear soon enough.

Several others had already run out the back of the tavern. Some might have lost their nerve and chosen to flee, but odds favored they meant to surround her.

She surrendered the porch.

The sheriff's orders to her mob chased after Ayleen as she sprinted down the street. Another voice chastised her. This one belonged to a dead woman—her academy's head trainer.

Never let the enemy define the rules of engagement. Captain Tratella's ashy voice shouted in her memories. The dead instructor had once slapped the back of Ayleen's head with the flat of her sword to make sure she'd never forget her words.

Each time her pursuers neared, Ayleen turned and traded swings. One fool with a sword in poor condition lost an eye when Ayleen's sword shattered the blade, flinging shrapnel at his face.

The lamplighter had left most of the street lamps beyond the intersection dark. That didn't hide the growing trail of bodies leading to the mine.

Something whispered past on Ayleen's right. Too fast for a thrown dagger. Someone had added a crossbow to the fight. Judging from the angle of the bolt sticking out of the ground, the one holding the crossbow was in the direction she was running and perched high.

Ayleen dashed for the side of the street from which the arbalist had fired. Placing herself up against the side of the buildings would make it harder for them to get another shot.

More of the mob came in behind her. The closest were a man and woman with matching flat noses and blond hair that suggested they were siblings. Ayleen split open the sister's chest. The brother grabbed Ayleen's sword arm and pinned it against the brick face of a general store. Before he could thrust his sword into her, Ayleen sliced open his wrist with her dagger. He let go and jumped back. His sword dropped, its blade scraping against the bricks in a shrill cry its owner matched.

Of Sheriff Javo's original mob, only four of her toughs remained. None of them held their swords with skill except for Deputy Cerris. Ayleen couldn't restrain an arrogant smirk, because he no longer stared at her like a lay to take down. He wore the dread of the hunter who's discovered his prey is the predator.

Two of the remaining four toughs wore the glassy, red-eyed stares of drunks, one with hands big enough to wrap around Ayleen's throat. The fourth had tied her hair into a braid that reached down to her waist.

Then there was that fifth bastard with the crossbow. If they had any brains, they were relocating to a better vantage point.

The sheriff brought up the rear. Her smile shined in the shadows. She was throwing these dogs at Ayleen to exhaust her, and the ache in her left shoulder warned the plan was working.

She'd finished most of these toughs in one or two swings. A few required more. Each victory revealed more of her technique. Save for their initial swings at the bar, the fight had exposed nothing of Javo's fighting style. All Ayleen knew was that she was right-handed, and she'd known that from the scabbard on Javo's left hip.

Sheriff Javo pointed at Ayleen with her sword. "Finish her!"

The four remaining swordfighters came at her. Ayleen ran for the mine. She needed to put some distance between her and her enemies. Given they were all upper body strength, the chase would probably tire them faster than her.

The road descended into a man-made canyon. A chain-link fence with its gate chained shut blocked off most of the canyon's nearest side. The gate protected wagons that didn't require beasts of burden. There were also rusted monsters made of wheels and gears with huge mouths to lift and spit out large amounts of dirt. Dozens of dark yellow and brown hills, vomited up by the mechanical land lifters, stood beyond the fence line to the right. The left side of the fence was interrupted by a large warehouse. That's what she needed.

Ayleen slashed the chain on the gate with her sword. The fence parted.

She'd slowed her pace about halfway here when her pursuers had stopped running. They assumed she'd backed herself into a deep pit with no exit.

A soft, blue glow caressed the seams of the large doors to the warehouse. A smaller door intended for the workers stood off to the right of the larger set. Her sword sliced through the lock to open it.

Crates covered the floor of the warehouse. None were stacked. A memory of her mother reminded her why. *Never place an untamed crystal higher than you're willing to let it fall.*

The crates closest to the large doors sat with their lids removed. Each was filled with sand to prevent the crystals from moving against each other.

She returned her dagger to its sheath and dug around in a crate for a smaller crystal, but no such luck. Everything her fingers found in the dirt was too big. Time wasn't in her favor.

Ayleen pulled a crystal from the crate, long but as slender as her fingers. She positioned it across the top of the crate to brace it. The blue light glowed with an explosive hunger for release as she placed the edge of her sword on top. Crystal craft had claimed more of the Knighthood's magi than combat. This required delicate, skilled hands like her mother's. Unfortunately for Ayleen, the genetic lottery had favored her father. For all his years exploring and charting other worlds, Dad's best drawn maps made one question if all of his fingers were broken.

She angled her sword to match the tip of the crystal. If her sword didn't match the angle right, the blast would kill her. The only consolation was it would likely set off every crystal in this warehouse. She'd get Javo and the other four. Darkest demons… the blast radius would consume Midchron.

Sweat soaked the inner band of Ayleen's hat, making its grip on her forehead tighter. For a split second she questioned this course, but she needed an edge.

She whispered to her sword. *"Suaret."* A vibration rippled through the hilt into her hand as the lattice of the crystal blade became thinner than paper.

No time to waste. The enchantment would hold only a moment. If it snapped back midway through the cut…boom.

She sliced her sword through the untamed crystal.

9.

Ayleen hid behind one of the mechanical land movers as Deputy Cerris and the other three toughs passed through the gate. They found the warehouse door Ayleen had cut open. The deputy and one of the drunks entered the building. The woman with the long braid and the man with the big hands looking for a neck to crush searched outside.

Concealed by the shadows, Ayleen slipped around one of the giant wheels on the machines. She grabbed the woman's braid from behind. The yank threw her off balance, and the red line Ayleen drew across her throat made certain she'd never find her footing again.

The man with the big hands launched at Ayleen. His sword, a long metal bastard, cleaved through the space she'd occupied. She jumped back, saving her legs from dismemberment. The brute's form drew on one technique: swing as hard as he could. If he connected with her, he'd shatter her bones. They danced, with Ayleen in retreat. She didn't dare block his attacks, lest he fling her sword from her hands. She waited for the best opening. In his frustration, he swung so hard to his right that he exposed his entire left side. Her sword hissed into the opening, cutting deep into his stomach. He grabbed at the hole in his gut to stop his organs from spilling out. Ayleen toppled him with a swing that severed his left leg at mid-thigh. He dropped onto his face, and she plunged her sword through his heart.

The whistle of something flying fast offered a split second of warning before the crossbow's bolt slammed into her right arm. The impact knocked her down.

She whimpered to hold back a scream. Forcing herself back up, she spotted the short arbalist on the opposite side of the fence.

The boy's panicked eyes rounded into balls as she charged him. He scrambled to reload his crossbow.

Half the distance to him, Ayleen dropped her sword. She reached into a pouch on her belt and pulled out her stolen piece of untamed crystal. She threw the shard towards him. He panicked and pulled the crossbow's trigger before he aimed.

The crystal shattered against the ground at the fence.

Light flared from the impact. Heat and pressure rushed against Ayleen, blowing her hat off and the boom dulled her ears. A large hole marred the fence with the tips of the chain link burning bright orange. Smoke spiraled up from the hole in the ground.

She ran back for her sword. The deputy and big man raced out of the warehouse.

Brilliant pain radiated from her upper right arm. She'd have sworn the tip buried in her bicep contained a squirming porcupine.

With her healthy arm, she drew her dagger and flung it towards the bigger target. The blade missed the brute's torso, her intended target. Instead, the dagger flew high to stab into his open mouth. He dropped to his knees, gagging against the thin steel buried in the back of his throat. His hands shook, reaching for the dagger's hilt but too scared to grab it.

She snatched up her sword as Deputy Cerris reached her. She blocked his attack and kept him to her left, so he couldn't target her injured arm.

The dance ended with a slice across his torso, starting at his right hip, then gliding up through his rib cage, and into his heart. The sword's tip pulled free of his flesh near his left shoulder.

Ayleen's heart pounded as she struggled to calm her breathing. She stalked over to the man with her dagger lodged in his mouth. She slit his throat with her sword and yanked her dagger out, wiping the steel blade on his shirt before she slid it back into its scabbard on her right hip.

Through the fugue of bloodlust, she heard the song of celebration within her sword. If the melody had lyrics, the refrain would have been simple enough.

Midchron's mob down; one to go.

Slow applause mocked her sword's cheer.

Sheriff Javo walked through the hole in the fence.

"Your parents would be proud," she drew her sword, "but only for a little longer."

10.

Ayleen retreated with slow steps, never daring to turn her back to the sheriff.

Javo knew she had her trapped. Aside from a smudge of dirt on her face, the sheriff looked as fresh as when the battle began.

"You never answered my question," Ayleen said, her attention divided between keeping her distance from her foe and whether to pull the bolt from her arm.

"Mera Kaillavo." She spoke the name as if blowing the dust off buried memories. "Let me guess, trained by Tratella?" She laughed at the answer in Ayleen's grimace. "Yeah, she always loved that sword-and-dagger, Bek form."

The sheriff narrowed her eyes. Ayleen felt certain the woman was looking for an answer to another, unspoken question. Whatever troubled her, she wasn't sharing, and looked ready to attack.

"What did you do?" Ayleen asked. If she kept the sheriff talking, she'd buy more time to recover her strength. "What did the Thirteen do to the Galaxy to ruin it in two years?"

The sheriff stopped her march towards Ayleen. "Two years?" Her features shifted between amusement and frustration. "How are you here? How are you still alive after all this time?" She stabbed the point of her sword towards the ground to punctuate her demand.

"Been taking keyhole after keyhole to hunt down you traitors." She started down the path to the mine. She kept her feet in the tracks worn into the road by the giant wheels of the machines above.

Cold fear curled around Ayleen's spine. She was cornered, but that wasn't what scared her. It was Javo's question, the visible panic behind it coupled with a building rage of dissatisfaction with Ayleen's answer.

"It's been more than eight hundred years, girl. How are you here? How did you cheat the Fates?"

The sheriff's temper bested her wish for an answer. She attacked, forcing Ayleen back with no time to process the impossibility Sheriff Javo had declared.

Their swords slammed into each other. The crystal blades produced a war song from their cacophonous chimes. Soft glows of joy emanated from the swords and painted the sheriff's face into a gruesome mask of murder.

Pain raged in Ayleen's right arm. She'd opted against ripping out the bolt to limit her blood loss, but parrying the sheriff's attacks demanded both hands on the hilt. The burn in her arm dulled to numb agony.

Two years—*eight hundred?*—to find one of the damned Thirteen. She didn't want to die without dragging at least one of these traitors to the grave with her.

The road snaked its way to the bottom. Halfway down, the terrain became less stable. The gravel shifted beneath their feet, but for all the cards hidden up the sheriff's sleeves, she stumbled first.

The sheriff barked in panic as the gravel slid beneath her left foot. Ayleen struck before her enemy could regain her footing. She advanced and cleaved her sword through Javo's throat.

Ayleen's teeth chattered as she fell to one knee. The sheriff dropped in two pieces, head and headless.

In that moment—that brief second of false victory—Ayleen discovered how eight centuries made sense.

11.

The first warning came from the sheriff's sword. The crystal didn't crack, as it should have, with the passing of its soul bearer.

The weapon rested on the ground but still within the sheriff's hand. That was the second warning.

The third and most disturbing thing was the lack of blood, not a drop spilled from her head or decapitated body.

Instead, the blade of Javo's broadsword glowed bright blue.

Wind howled and kicked up the gravel. Then the sword's glow passed into the sheriff's body. Light like fire flared from the top of her neck and the base of her head. The sheriff's eyes snapped open with the same glow obscuring her irises.

The head flew back atop her torso. Javo screamed as her entire body launched through the air and slammed back into the wall of the pit.

She dropped to her feet but then collapsed to her knees. Her body, arms and legs splayed, left an imprint in the wall of the pit that should have been comical, but only heightened Ayleen's fears.

The glow to Javo's eyes lessened as she glared up at Ayleen.

"Been a long time." She stopped and coughed, a hoarse hack that ended with her spitting out a few pebbles caught in her throat. She slammed a fist on the ground. Rage made her eyes more fearsome than the now-fading glow had. "A long time since anyone managed to catch me on the end of their sword."

The sheriff stood.

"You won't get that lucky again."

"What are you?" Ayleen stumbled back, torn between trying to kill the sheriff again or running for it.

"I'm immortal." The sheriff sprinted up towards her. "And judging from your reaction, I'm guessing you aren't so blessed as I."

12.

Immortal she might be, but the decapitation and resurrection cost the sheriff something. The force behind her swings lost some of its vigor. The second Ayleen recognized that truth, she pressed the advantage for all its worth, forcing the sheriff into a retreat. Their swords shrieked against each other in a horrid melody.

They reached the bottom of the pit. The opening to the mine glowed in bright shades of blue. The light cast the sheriff as a silhouette as Ayleen pushed her back into that bright maw.

Beams of scavenged wood held the mouth of the cave open.

Sweat dripped from Ayleen's brow, threatening to fall into her eyes and blind her. She needed a little longer.

She roared her defiance calling on the deepest wounds to her soul for strength. *"Father! Mother!"*

The last push placed them more than a dozen feet into the mine shaft, past three sets of wooden beams.

The sheriff laughed as she pulled back to catch her breath. "Damn, you make them proud."

Ayleen didn't answer. She turned and fled from the cramped hole with her sword raised. The crystal blade ravaged through the support beams, and gravity did the rest.

The sheriff screamed. She chased after Ayleen, but it was too late. The mine's entrance dropped with a reluctant groan that drowned out Sheriff Javo's protests.

The face of the mine entrance collapsed. Smoke flooded the base of the pit.

Ayleen ran along the path leading up from the cave.

With the sheriff's sword no longer chasing her, Ayleen's mind worked through the impossibility she'd learned.

Two years for her.

Eight hundred for the Thirteen.

She paused when she found her hat on the ground and put it on. Taking a deep breath, she grabbed the crossbow's bolt in her arm and ripped it out. Her agonized shriek and the whimpers that followed echoed across the desert.

Stumbling back towards town, her weary mind sought the memory of that last day—the day the Knights of the Way ended, the day her quest for revenge began.

13.

The squires Ayleen's father had left in her charge followed her deep into the mountain. A sphere leading to Regan Five waited there. She knew if these traitors had planned their attack so well—one that had already claimed the lives of the best members of the Knighthood, including her parents—the other end of the dark energy tunnel would be guarded.

She and the three dozen children following her would be forced to fight their way out. Only a handful of knights guarded their backs.

Whoever the traitors were within their ranks, they'd caught all here unprepared. An explosion had ripped through the upper levels where Ayleen's mother had been. Blood flowed down stairs in waves, life taken with no discrimination for age or species.

The oldest of the squires, a boy of fourteen, ran with his metal sword in hand. None of these children had earned their crystal yet. Their weeping offered all the explanation needed for why they weren't ready to harvest an untamed crystal and marry it to their souls.

They reached the keyhole's chamber, a large space of white brick walls and grey marble floor. Bodies of fallen knights littered the room. Three rebels guarded the entrance to the DET. Ayleen ran at them. Her sword added these invading dogs to the pile of corpses on the floor.

Shouts echoed from the stairs and through the passage behind them. If the Thirteen's army had finished off the remaining knights, she and the squires were all that remained.

Before the eldest boy in squire grey could run into the glowing wormhole, Ayleen grabbed him by the front of his jacket. "No! All these bodies? No way those three I finished off did this. More are probably waiting on the other side of the keyhole. Give me a moment to fight them back."

But then the first of the invaders appeared from around the bend. He wore the uniform of a captain. Ayleen couldn't recall his name, but she'd never forget his green, slit eyes nor the strength that rippled beneath his yellow, reptilian skin.

"Dammit!" Ayleen knew these children couldn't fight a Khymeran. Better to take their chances with whatever was waiting on Regan Five. "Into the keyhole now!"

She ran into the light. The cosmic tide lifted her body, but the flicker of peaceful nothingness that normally followed was disrupted by a tsunami that ripped apart her essence, replacing light with darkness.

Ayleen woke on the other side. A cut to her forehead ached, scabbed over with flakes of blood running down her nose. The wound threatened to spill more blood if she scratched it.

The keyhole cave where she'd landed wasn't Regan Five. A sign that hung over the passage to the surface proclaimed this world as Atterson. The name held no recognition for her. The floor of the cave was naught but dirt. The only blood on it belonged to her. No one else came through the sphere. She hid at the edge of the sphere of light, ready to slice open the Khymeran or any of his traitorous filth who followed. None did.

Fearing all of the squires had been captured or worse, she finally went back into the keyhole. The normal, peaceful pull she associated with DET travel lifted her along the way to the next keyhole, but where she emerged wasn't the corridor beneath Mount Hawkken. She found herself on another unfamiliar world—the first and second of many places off the map her father had helped the Knighthood create.

Every world that followed was in ruins. Word of the Thirteen and their destructive taint on the Galaxy was all that remained.

The Knights of the Way were lost, and Ayleen began her long walk for vengeance.

14.

Ayleen stared out from beneath the brim of her hat at the mob's bodies littering Midchron's streets. No one had emerged to recover the dead, not even grieving loved ones. Ayleen stayed to the shadows.

She retrieved her belongings from the tavern, going in and out the back.

From there, she searched Sheriff Javo's home. The effort was fast and fruitless. If Javo had known where the rest of the Thirteen might be, she didn't write it down. Worst of all, the ambrosia crystal the sheriff had taken from the Ercanna home wasn't there. No telling where it was. Odds favored Ayleen had buried it in the mine along with the sheriff. Without a grimoire, the ambrosia crystal would do the sheriff little good anyway.

Her last stop before fleeing Midchron was Faye's. Ayleen banged her fist on the back door which, unlike the front, had no window for anyone to see who was knocking.

The door cracked open, a hint of candlelight revealed a single eye, red from tears, staring out from beneath a wave of Viv's silver hair.

Ayleen braced the door with her foot. She snatched a handful of Viv's faded orange nightgown and pointed her sword at her throat.

"If it's ready, I'll be taking my shirt."

Viv's husband didn't appear. Odds favored Ayleen had left his corpse in the street, so she kept Viv alive, not wanting to add the tailor's son to the Galaxy's long list of orphans.

She decided not to dirty her new shirt until she'd cleaned herself. She wore the blood of more than two dozen.

As she walked across Griffin's barren surface with Dara Ercanna in search of the next keyhole, the same thought played through Ayleen's head.

None down—none who matter.

Thirteen still to go.

PART II

The Fate

1.

Ayleen didn't recognize the hills of grey sands. She'd seen only five types of animals, none familiar to her, since she and Dara emerged from the dark energy tunnel's sphere. Most of the tiny horrors skittered away, burrowing into the cover of dead land beneath a colorless sky of clouds. The planet offered little flora, mostly the rare pile of desiccated vines with dried up, six-pointed leaves and thorns. The terrain lacked any discernible roads or paths, shorn away from the constant assault of hot winds.

She might have assumed this was a new world. Well, new to her, but then she found the mountain.

Barren, black rock reached up towards the sea of clouds, its tips devoid of snow as would be proper. Waves of heat mottled Ayleen's view of the peak. Man-made right angles were carved into the lower half of the mountain. In ancient times, archers patrolled the parapet that circled the mountain like a thick belt. Empty windows that once gazed out on thriving villages and long slopes of blue grass now gaped at what little remained.

Though naught but a skeleton without a grave, it was beyond any doubt Mount Hawkken.

Ayleen was home.

2.

The dried up thorn bushes provided fuel for a fire. Ayleen and Dara only started it for light. Even the nights here were hot.

When they'd begun traveling together four months ago, Ayleen had taken to teaching Dara each night how to fight with a sword. They found Dara's gladius in the dried up remains of a city on Griffin. It wasn't a good fit. The short, fat blade rested in a scabbard next to the slumbering child. The weapon weighed too much for her reed-thin arms, and the hilt wasn't big enough for her to hold it with both hands. If they could afford to stay in one place more than a day, Ayleen knew she could help the girl build up her upper body strength, but she was impatient to find a way to destroy the Thirteen. If nothing else, the weeks of constant walking had built up the strength in Dara's short legs, and to Ayleen's surprise, the necessary footwork for sword fighting came naturally to Dara.

While Dara slept, Ayleen flipped through the pages of the grimoire Dara's father had found in Midchron's mines. She cracked into the book most nights, but she'd yet to decipher the language of the Fates. She wanted an explanation for how the Thirteen became immortal, but most of all, she needed a way to destroy them. With any luck, the answers she needed were in the grimoire.

Midchron was only a small example of what the Thirteen were doing to the Galaxy. People seemed to have given up in most places they existed. The desire to rebuild was burning out of existence. All that drove anyone was a yearning to destroy: genocide by suicide.

Anyplace people had resisted the urge for self-destruction, the Thirteen had long ago moved in with their own army and done the killing as they had here on Teikorium.

She resisted the urge to caress the hilt of her crystal sword. The blade moaned for blood whenever her thoughts turned to the Thirteen.

Thirteen to go.

"Be silent!" Ayleen's harsh whisper to her sword didn't stir Dara.

She closed the leather-bound book and ran her fingers across the symbol of the Knights of the Way burned into the cover.

This grimoire held all manner of spells and chemistry to affect the universe. Little good that did Ayleen. Half of the grimoire contained writing, but she could only read what was on two pages.

The first page displayed an ornate cursive text written in a dark brown "ink" that Ayleen knew would have come from the veins of the grimoire's original owner.

Mage General Honor Deus Zahn

Ascension Date: 62.Major Axis +58.Minor Axis -35.960323.Month of

Fuyem.13

"The Way is an Arrow as true as Time"

All text after, written in the mage general's ornate scrawl (in black ink, not blood), belonged to the language of the Fates. Upon their promotion, a mage general spent a year with a Fate to learn the complex order of letters and glyphs. Such had been the way with Ayleen's mother.

The coded writing ate up half the book. The pages beyond that unintelligible script contained more than a dozen disproportionate, coal drawings. The young artist slept on the other side of the fire. In spite of herself, Ayleen smiled at the girl. Dara's poor artwork came close enough for Ayleen to recognize a person or two from her stop in Midchron. She certainly recognized Sheriff Javo, more from the star-shaped badge on her belt than the generic effort at a face.

Dara's handwriting littered the last page.

Up and down and in and out.

Bird of fire meets cold of night.
Neither wins; both dearly lose.
Thus they end in ebon light.

The lines tickled at her memory. Part of a nursery rhyme? She spent most of her life in the mountain learning to fight. Her reading belonged to scientific and arcane principles, military strategies, and history. No one expected any different from the daughter of a mage general of the Science Regiment and an explorer knight of the Stellar Cartography Regiment.

Her skill with a sword had saved her in the fight with Javo back in Midchron, but to put down that monster and the rest of her traitorous ilk, Ayleen needed a way to make their deaths stick. She needed someone who could read this book.

That meant finding one of the Fates.

3.

Ayleen forced herself to slow down. Her usual pace meant her short-legged companion needed to jog to follow. Impatience made Ayleen eager to get inside the Citadel.

The road they traveled rolled around the base of the mountain. Ayleen had started by ignoring the paved path and climbing straight up to the wide mouth that had once welcomed all into the Citadel with the glow of artificial light. Didn't take long to realize climbing up the side of the mountain saved no time. The climb challenged her and proved impossible for Dara, so they followed the winding road. Each revolution of the mountain brought them closer to the entrance, a dark sun pulling two lives into a decaying orbit.

"You walked this every time you came here?" Dara asked.

"I lived here, so I didn't come and go much. When I did, it was usually in a wagon or on the back of a takert."

"What's a takert?"

"A large reptile." Seeing the skeptical pinch to Dara's brow, Ayleen worked her hands as if to force a description into shape. "They've got two long legs and two tiny arms with talons. Also have long necks. I had a yellow and green striped one named Ziggy."

Dara laughed at the name.

Ayleen had missed the beast plenty, and not just because of all the walking she'd done. She was five when he hatched. He'd adored her, always rubbing the long bridge of his snout against her chest.

"Down that way," Ayleen pointed towards a depression south of the mountain, "herds of them would migrate here each summer and gather around Lake Kurter."

"What's a lake kurter?"

The question wiped away Ayleen's smile, because the lake no longer existed for her to show it. "A lake is a large body of water. Lake Kurter was its name."

With half the day gone, they reached the entrance to the mountain and an end to simple questions with simple answers.

4.

The Citadel's entrance opened into the stables, a large space that now housed only dust and bones instead of beasts of burden. Rays of light cut in at steep angles from the windows.

The far doors, hidden in shadows, opened onto the top of a large amphitheater.

Ayleen headed towards the stairs that led to the upper levels which housed the offices and private quarters.

The distant sound of movement brought Ayleen to a stop. She pressed a hand against Dara's chest to stop her.

"What is—?"

Ayleen cut her off with a stern look and a finger pressed to her own lips.

Whatever she'd heard had stopped moving. She drew her crystal sword from its scabbard. Bringing the blade close to her face, she whispered, *"Terastrant."*

A glow filled the blue, crystal blade, providing light to see most of the stables. Only a handful of stall doors were shut. Some doors were ripped off their hinges with vicious talon marks on their insides. Ayleen smiled at Ziggy's door. It was among those ripped open from within. He'd fought.

Nothing moved that Ayleen could see. Whatever had made the noise was gone.

5.

Like most of the Citadel, the stairs were carved out of the mountain's black rock. Repeated use had worn the steps in the main stairwell to where they were smooth with a slight dip in the center of each one. Unlike the stables, the stairs included larger windows to permit natural light. Some of the glass had survived, but most panes were shattered or missing. One landing was covered in shards from where something had smashed in the window.

Near the top, they reached a red door with a black plate screwed onto the door at eye level that identified this floor in bold white, blocky letters as the Science Regiment.

Ayleen's mother had an office on this floor. She remembered the year her mother was away, learning the language of the Fates. Ayleen had turned thirteen during those twelve months and had blossomed. Mother looked shocked when a young woman ran up to her office on her first day back and grabbed her in a hug. The shock lasted for weeks. Every so often, she caught her mother staring at her face. After several weeks, her mom had smiled and said, "You just remind me of someone I used to know."

Ayleen forced the memory aside and pushed open the door. It creaked, a low guttural jerking noise.

Her sword still aglow, Ayleen entered the darkness that hid sweet and bitter recollections. Dara kept her grounded in the present, the girl's body pressing against her back.

"Not so close." Ayleen didn't look behind her as the girl pulled back. "Remember what I taught you?"

In a steady voice, Dara spoke the instructions Ayleen had drilled into her. "Watch our rear, keep my sword ready, and stay outside your sword's reach."

"Done well." She resisted the urge to pat Dara on the back. Instead, Ayleen kept her distance and focused her attention forward.

Three numbers were painted down the right side of each door in the corridor. She stopped when she reached 813. The numbers were white but looked blue in her sword's glow. The surface of the numbers' chipped paint felt rough beneath her fingertips, and the sensation broke something in her. She'd known her parents were dead—that the whole damn galaxy had gone to shite, but this made it real in a way that all the rotted worlds of the past two years never could.

This was her mother's office.

She took a deep, steadying breath. Her tears would get their day when her sword whispered, *Thirteen down. None to go.* Then her eyes would pour out waterfalls of joyful vengeance fulfilled.

Dara's big eyes stared up at Ayleen with a question that required no words. Ayleen nodded she was fine.

Ayleen grabbed the door handle and turned it. The door was unlocked but refused to open. When it became clear one hand wouldn't suffice, she sheathed her sword and wrapped both hands around the handle. She shoved the door with her shoulder. It shuddered within its frame but still didn't move. She screamed as she kicked the door several times, tiny progress with each strike. On the last kick, the door flung open. She grabbed the door frame before she fell through it. Had she face-planted, the floor of her mother's office wouldn't have been the problem. The floor no longer existed. A large hole reached several stories down into a black abyss. If she had to guess, it went as far as the amphitheater, if not deeper. The hole also consumed the two neighboring offices. The damage reached up at least two more levels.

"What happened?" Dara looked around the edge of the door frame, her duty to watch their back forgotten.

"Looks like an untamed crystal exploded." Her mother's office must have been the origin point for the blast. Little wonder the Thirteen would have taken her out first. She was well-known for her skill in combat, both with her sword and her dark science. On that day, Father had said an explosion came from up here, as if to apologize for Mom's mortality.

Dara didn't say anything else. She understood. After all, she'd also witnessed her father's murder.

Hopefully, the damage didn't go deeper than the amphitheater. If it did, the pile of rubble might cut them off from the DET to Regan Five. She'd planned for them to take it to the next world. The

Knighthood chose this location as their base of operations, because the combination of Teikorium and Regan Five served as an ideal launching point for most missions. The spheres on both worlds connected to the most strategic planets in the Galaxy at the time.

Her next thought went to the water pack on her back. It felt too light. They needed to find Dara one of her own. They'd been sharing water from the same pack, and the heat on this world had forced them to drink more over a shorter distance. She doubted what they had left would last long enough for them to reach another DET sphere.

Her eyes shifted to the back of Dara's head as the girl continued to stare into the dark. A part of Ayleen, the coldest part that lived within her crystal sword, knew she could make it on the remaining water. Alone, she'd do fine. All she had to do was leave Dara behind or give her a little push and test how deep this hole went. Ayleen punched the wall as she willed her sword's advice to silence.

Dara jumped back at Ayleen's strike against the wall.

"Let's check through some more of these offices." Ayleen didn't look at her as she said it.

The other doors—the ones not locked—didn't offer the same challenge to open them nor the same peril. Ayleen sliced open the rest with her sword. All Ayleen and Dara found was ash. Whether the traitors and their followers had committed the arson or perhaps the mage generals, in order to protect their secrets, made little difference. Anything she hoped to find here that might lead her to a Fate was long gone.

6.

They returned to the stairs and descended until they reached one of the residence floors. Only the highest ranking members of the Knighthood were granted homes within the Citadel. Her mother's position within the Science Regiment had secured their space.

The corridor lacked any natural light except for what spilled in from the stairwell behind her and the other stairwell at the opposite end.

"I hear something." Dara's warning brought Ayleen to a stop.

She waited, but she heard nothing. "What was it?"

"A tapping noise."

"Where?"

Dara shrugged. "Don't hear it now."

Ayleen knew her family's apartment was the next door to the left, about a third of the way down the hall. Like most of the doors they'd passed in the hallway, the front door to her apartment sat ajar. She pushed it all the way open with the point of her sword. Its light helped her see what had become of her home. More ash. She wanted to believe the Knighthood did this, a last gasp to tell the Thirteen they could fuck themselves, but she knew better. The damage looked too consistent, as if done by the same hands. The Thirteen had burned the knights from the Galaxy for good.

"Stay by the door, little squire." She knew Dara liked it when she called her that, but she did it now out of guilt for her earlier thoughts. "Keep an eye on the corridor. Let me know if you hear anything."

"Say true, I will."

Ayleen shook her head at the girl's reply. She could hear the smile in her answer.

She searched for anything that might have survived, something of her mother's leading to a Fate. The den failed to meet her need, so she moved on to her parents' bedroom.

Dark grey soot marked the walls, floor, and ceiling. She held her sword low to the floor and knelt to run her fingers through the ash.

She brushed against something hard and smooth buried within the remains of the bed. Wiping away the ash revealed a metal safe box. It looked about a foot long, five inches wide, and two inches deep. It required a combination to open it. Her parents might have nothing but old pictures or their marriage papers in this, but mayhap there was more.

"Ayleen!" Dara's loud whisper startled her. "There's something moving in the hallway."

She grabbed the safe box and ran back through the den to Dara's side. Grey daylight from the stairwell they'd taken backlit the silhouettes of strange shapes along the walls and ceiling, bobbing up and down along their respective surfaces in jerky motions.

Ayleen raised her sword for a better look at what was heading their way. Then she wished she hadn't.

7.

The creatures hopped closer to Ayleen and Dara. To say they resembled large frogs didn't account for how dreadful they were, only for their shape. Their skin looked shiny, mottled in shades of brown and dark red. They each had a single, massive eye, some carried it centered on their face above their wide mouths while others wore their single, slit eyeball to the right or left. When they blinked, they did it twice, their eyelids shutting from right and left and then up and down. Dark, thick liquid spurt from their eyes and lips, leaving a slimy trail along whatever they touched.

When they opened their mouths, firelight danced within the back of their throats. One shot its long tongue out, the thick appendage snapping like a whip. Ayleen jerked back in time to avoid the fiery tip. Its spit splashed onto the wall and floor, burning where it landed on the stone surfaces.

One of the frogs stopped hopping towards her. It issued a series of hacking sounds that shook its entire body until a large fireball hit the floor. Flames erupted along the walls, floor and ceiling, every spot the slime from their eyes and their drool had collected.

With the hallway now alight, Ayleen finally saw the source of the clicking noise, the suckers at the end of their feet each wore a long, razor-sharp nail.

The fire revealed something worse. The fire hoppers were also bounding towards them from the opposite end of the corridor. They were surrounded.

One of the frogs with a centered eyeball lunged at them. Dara ducked back into the apartment. Ayleen swung her sword, splitting the ugly beast down the middle as its tongue shot out. The creature gulped as the crystal blade sliced into it and then popped like a bubble, flinging its flaming guts in all directions. If Ayleen hadn't already been pulling away and into the apartment, the living grenade would have covered her in fire. Dara slammed the door shut once Ayleen was safe inside and threw the bolt in place.

Firelight glowed around the edges of the door. Dara ran to the apartment's window. "Can we climb out?"

Ayleen considered their chances of surviving the climb along the face of the mountain to another window. "No, it's a straight drop and there won't be any handholds." Time might have worn cracks into the surface of the mountain, but nothing guaranteed there would be enough to get them up or down to another level.

Flames erupted from beneath the crack in the door as the fire hoppers' eye spit flowed into the room. Ayleen jumped back before the fire reached her feet. The clicking noises shook the door. One of the frog's talons burst through. Then more slashed through the steel barrier, bathing the apartment in lines of firelight. Their angry croaks demanded entrance.

Dara held up her sword, for all the good it would do.

More talons slashed through the door. Through the widening holes, fire spit shot at them. Ayleen moved as far from the door as she could get, dropped the steel safe box to the floor, and shoved her sword back into its scabbard. She pulled out her gloves and stuffed her hands into them.

"Stay back." She drew her sword again, wrapping both hands around the leather hilt with the weapon pointed down. *"Attadior!"*

The blade flared brighter, more white than blue. Ayleen winced at the heat flowing from the crystal.

She stabbed it down, but it didn't make it far enough. She jerked it free.

"Attadior! Attadior! Attadior!"

With each shout, the sword grew hotter and brighter. Despite the hilt's leather grip and her gloves, the sword's magic threatened to bake her hands. She screamed, forcing herself not to let go. This time it slid through the floor as easily as gelatin. The frogs' croaks grew louder and more insistent as Ayleen carved a circle. As soon as she finished drawing its circumference, the severed chunk dropped with a crash into the room below.

She cursed as she dropped the sword. The crystal blade clattered into the room beneath them as Ayleen fell to her knees. Smoke circled up from the palms of her charred gloves. Any longer, and it would have been her flesh.

Dara grabbed her by the arm to pull her back up. "They're coming through!"

The fire hoppers' tongues shot through the holes in the door. Their fiery spit landed inches from Ayleen and Dara's feet.

"I can't jump that far." Dara pointed into the hole.

"We jump or we burn." The drop must have been at least ten feet, which didn't sound like much until you stared it down. Gods, she hated heights. She whispered an entreaty and stepped into the hole. She landed without breaking an ankle or anything else. The room she found herself in was another apartment of the same layout as the one above and just as ash-covered.

"Your turn!" She gestured with her arms in a promise to catch her. Then she remembered the box she'd found in her parents' bedroom. "Wait! Grab the box I dropped!"

Dara disappeared from view. More fire hopper tongues cracked back-to-back as the girl screamed.

"Dara!"

Ayleen's call went unanswered, but something dropped through the opening above her. The safe box clattered to the floor at Ayleen's feet.

Dara came back into view. She shut her eyes and dropped through the hole. The catch didn't go as well as planned. The hole wasn't big enough for Dara's small frame to do more than step into it and plummet like a missile. The catch turned into more of a tackle with both of them on the floor and Dara on top. Fresh pain from grabbing Dara out of the air seared through Ayleen's singed hands.

Dara struggled back to her feet. "That was fun." Her grasp of sarcasm shamed most adults.

Ayleen tried, without success, to get up without using her hands. The whip cracks of the fire hoppers' tongues from above gave her enough incentive to plant her hands on the floor and push herself up with a scream.

The overload of pain—equal to thousands of tiny needles stabbing into her fingers—numbed her hands enough to grab her sword. The crystal had gone dark again. She whispered *"Terastrant,"* and the sword's earlier blue glow returned, which now looked dim compared to the heat enchantment.

"Grab the box!"

Dara snatched it up, and they ran into the hallway, which was blessedly free of fire hoppers or any other beast left on this dead world.

They reached the stairwell. By then, the fire hoppers had chased them through Ayleen's hole and leaped after them in a growing trail of amphibian napalm. Most of the frogs pursued them with short hops down the steps and along the walls. Their eye spit slid down the carved rock, dripping into growing puddles of fire. An over-eager hopper plunged past Ayleen and Dara. With a shrill croak, it splattered in a loud blast that coated the entire surface of the next landing ahead of them in burning frog guts.

"Run through it! Don't stop!"

Dara went first, taking a sharp turn in the thin layer of burning frog entrails. She slipped. Ayleen grabbed her by the back of her shirt, stopping her from falling flat into the flames. She reached over the edge of the railing to drop Dara to safety on the next step.

The frog's remains dripped down the stairs. Ayleen dashed through the fire without slipping. Flames licked at the bottom of her boots. They winked out by the time she made it to the next landing.

When they reached the main level, Dara went straight for the door leading to the stables.

"No!" Ayleen shouted. "Down to the keyhole!"

Dara hesitated. Her face full of the doubts and fears Ayleen had already considered. As soon as they continued down, another fire hopper dropped and exploded into a fireball, blocking the door to the stables.

The stairs had no more windows past that point, leaving Ayleen's sword and the fire hopper puddles as their only lights.

More than once, Ayleen made certain Dara had the safe box. A stab of fear cut her, fear that the box would prove worthless, nothing but legal documents or photographs. She cursed herself for that. *How far have you lost your Way when you believe a picture of your family holds no value?*

Glancing over her shoulder, Ayleen spotted the growing flames of the fire hoppers at the bottom of the stairs. All they needed to do was round the next corner and plunge into the yellow sphere to take them to Regan Five.

They didn't find the sphere around the corner, though. A tall pile of black rock blocked their path.

8.

Ayleen cursed. She spun around to fight the fire hoppers, but too many of them were coming down the long corridor. Killing them would eventually burn her to death.

"There!"

Dara's shout drew Ayleen's attention away from the frogs and to an opening in the bottom left corner of fallen rock where the light from the keyhole was visible. Dara dropped onto her stomach, pushed the safe box ahead of her and crawled through.

Ayleen turned back to the corridor. With nothing to slow them, the fire hoppers were closing the distance.

"I'm through!"

Ayleen got down to her hands and knees. The opening looked too small. She wouldn't have thought it possible for Dara.

She pushed her way into the narrow gap and halfway through, she got stuck. Her water pack was hitting against the top of the opening.

The tapping of the fire hoppers' talons warned they were close. She backed up, flung off the water pack and dove back into the hole. Once on the other side, she reached back through for the water pack. She snagged one of the straps as a fire hopper pounced on it. Ayleen jerked the pack free.

"Let's go!" Ayleen shouted. She held her water pack by the strap in her right hand and her sword in her left. Liquid fire and the hoppers' excited croaks trickled through the narrow opening in the pile of rock.

Fresh fear choked Ayleen as she stared into the same sphere that had set her so off course eight centuries ago. Was the tunnel somehow damaged? Would they end up flung farther into the future?

Dara jumped into the sphere of light, and Ayleen followed.

9.

Ayleen flung her water pack to the ground. The fire hopper that pounced on it before they escaped had punctured it. Even worse, the damn thing emptied out before she noticed.

Dara waited, crouched against the wall of the cave. Ayleen didn't need to ask what had her scared. The child was riding out Ayleen's tantrum. The realization calmed her rage.

She marched over to Dara and snatched the box out of her hands. The box required a four-digit code to open. She tried various combinations, including her parents' birthdays, their anniversary, her birthday, favorite holidays, all zeroes, all ones, and so on. None unlocked the box. Finally, she threw it to the floor, drew her sword and struck the combination lock with the blunt side of the blade until it opened.

Five strikes later, the box spilled out papers and a few trinkets that looked of little or no importance in a universe that had lost its Way.

Ayleen recognized the documents of promotion making her mother a mage general, signed by Chief Knight Carliana H. Higgins. She found her parents' marriage papers, a document for her birth, a small purse filled with gold and silver coins, and photographs of people Ayleen didn't recognize, but given they resembled her mother, she assumed they were related to her. He hands shook as she pulled an old, standard issue star chart.

She unfolded the star chart. Her father had left a note to her mother wishing her safe travels. Hope warmed her chest as she slid her fingers across the map looking for any notes on it by either of her parents. Only there was nothing to indicate if her mother had used this to guide her to one of the Fates. No planets were circled or paths highlighted between the different worlds.

Dara placed a hand on Ayleen's back. Despite her frustration, Ayleen managed a smile to her squire. She folded up the map into a fat, rectangular shape and handed it to Dara. "I'll show you how to read it later."

They split the coins in the purse between themselves. Ayleen needed to find a way to earn more money and soon. The more they came across populated worlds, the more expensive travel became. One town around a keyhole they'd taken a couple weeks ago had required them to pay a travel tax.

Ayleen glanced up at the white granite sign with "Welcome to Regan Five" carved into it. Someone had taken blue paint, crossed out "Regan Five" and replaced it with "Hel."

She tossed aside the empty box and stuffed the documents into her pack. The Knights of the Way had ended eight centuries ago, so it was possible some fool historian or antiques dealer might buy the promotion certificates, assuming those professions still existed.

Dara rolled one of the coins between her fingers. She smiled when she noticed Ayleen watching her. "A trick my pa taught me."

Ayleen wondered what became of Dara's mom. She wouldn't change that today. For now, she wanted to find the next keyhole and a way to find the Fates.

She pointed to the graffiti. "Let's go see how accurate that is."

10.

Upon realizing their only water pack was broken, Ayleen expected the Galaxy to answer with another dry world. Instead, their need was met with irony.

Cold rain poured. She thanked her father for the hat, one much like his. He'd given her this hat as a graduation gift, the day she officially became a knight. The hat's wide brim kept the falling water out of her face. Didn't spare the rest of her, though. Her clothes were soaked.

The next keyhole was a week's walk away, and the rain poured the entire way. Shelter was limited. Their first night, they used an abandoned carriage that had lost all of its wheels. Natural shelter proved difficult to come by, though they found a few caves. One night, they pushed on, because no shelter could be found, and neither of them was going to manage any sleep in the open.

A cave they later found permitted a long, hard sleep. Her mother said a person couldn't catch up on sleep, but Ayleen did a fair job of it that day.

They used a small pile of dust-covered wood in the cave for a fire. The warmth was glorious. Ayleen also found a fat, floppy-eared gorder living in the cave and killed it for their dinner.

"Do we have to go back into the rain?" Dara whined.

"Eventually, yes, but we can rest a little longer."

An uncomfortable silence fell on them. Ayleen wasn't sure what had Dara quiet, but for her part, Ayleen was building up to the question she'd been meaning to ask for a while now.

"What happened to your mother?" Ayleen hated to ask, but they'd walked too many clicks together to justify any distance between them, especially if Dara was going to fight at her side.

Dara shrugged, staring at the ground. "Pa always told me she died giving birth to me, but I also overheard him at this past Amuvia festival telling Jamen's pa that Ma had abandoned us. Never found out which was true."

Ayleen cursed herself for asking and vowed to never bring up Dara's mother again. She scooted over to sit next to Dara and pulled out her map, a more road weary version than the one she'd given her squire. "Pull yours out. Let's give you a lesson in dark energy tunnel travel."

They kept the maps opened next to each other. "Most planets contain five keyholes. Here's where we are." She pointed to the yellow medium-sized dot. "The color and the size indicate the atmosphere and the gravity respectively. See this line?" She ran a finger along the dotted tunnel charted on her map until it landed on a large, green dot.

"So that means this world," Dara hesitated as she leaned in for a better look at the tiny print, "Lynax Three has its keyhole underwater and its gravity is too strong for us, right?"

"Half right. The keyhole is underwater, but a large circle means its gravity is much lighter. When it's a planet with stronger gravity, the dot is smaller, because that represents the way gravity crushes things."

"Okay, so does that mean all of Lynax Three is underwater?"

"Not necessarily. Only means all of its keyholes are." There were some circles carved up like slices of pie with each slice a different color. "Black keyholes mean there's no atmosphere on the other side. Could be a cave-in and easily fixed, but sometimes, it's because the planet doesn't have an atmosphere at all."

Ayleen pointed back to Regan Five. "See this line? That's the next keyhole I'm taking us to. We should reach it tomorrow."

That part of the map was near the message Ayleen's father had written to her mother, next to the spiral and sword symbol for the Knighthood. She ran her fingers over his handwriting.

Safe travels, my love. Come home to us soon.

Love,

Se Rulian

"Was your mother gone for a year or was it longer?" Dara's question shook Ayleen out of her memories.

"What do you mean?"

"You said she stayed with the Fate for a year, but how long was she actually gone?"

Before Ayleen could answer, she realized Dara's point. "She did stay a full year, and she was gone twelve more weeks than that." She placed her map on the ground above her mother's old map. "She started her trip by taking the keyhole to Regan Five."

"So twelve weeks." Dara started running her finger across the map, tracing various routes from this world. "That means the trip there took about six weeks."

Even with the time narrowed to such a short period of time, they spent the next few hours going over the various potential routes.

"There." Ayleen pressed her finger down on a yellow medium-sized dot that on her map was black and small. "It's three keyhole hops away."

"What is?"

Ayleen leaned in for a better look at the text. "Says it's Lycaenidae Nine."

"Your map, the more current one, marks it as a dead world."

"Yes, but my father gave this map to my mother." She ran her fingers back over his handwriting as she worked it out in her head. Knights could modify their maps, make adjustments to them to reflect changes to a world or a keyhole's status. "The knowledge about where the Fates live wasn't exclusive to the mage generals. My father was one of the Knighthood's most respected cartographers. If anyone knew it outside of the Science Division, then the chief cartographers would."

She looked over the map again and ran the math in her head. Closing her eyes, she forced the numbers into an answer.

"Four weeks," Ayleen said it as much for herself as for Dara. "We can be there in four weeks."

"So, the timing fits, but that's also assuming it's actually there." Dara scowled. "What if it's black on your map, because there was a catastrophe?"

"We'll know as soon as we see the keyhole. If it's yellow, it's safe."

"Safe?" Dara crossed her arms. "The keyholes for this world and for Teikorium were yellow. The one to Griffin, where my father was executed, is yellow. You call those safe?"

Ayleen didn't waste her time arguing the semantics, especially since Dara was right. "When we get to the next world, we'll start your sword training again. Need you prepared for those 'safe' worlds."

That at least put half a smile back on Dara's face.

11.

The next hop deposited them into a cave with a floor of grey, hexagonal bricks. The people of this world had carved out the cave to give it four smooth walls and painted them burgundy. Dozens of paintings hung on the walls. The space resembled a museum more than a cave.

Some paintings depicted battles. Others offered panoramic-style images of cities Ayleen suspected no longer existed on this planet, given how pristine and spectacular the images appeared.

Dara knelt before a painting of a vast canyon at sunset. The frame must have been eight feet wide and three feet tall.

"Do you think I can touch it?" she whispered.

Ayleen shrugged. Her focus went to the carving above the door frame. The planet's name, Lagoon VII, greeted them in fat, bold characters.

Dara took in a sharp breath. Ayleen turned towards her, hand reaching for her sword, but she stopped short as she saw the girl running her fingers along the beveled frame of the painting.

"No dust." Dara wiggled her fingers to show they were clean. "There must be people here."

Ayleen wondered what their odds of sleeping under a ceiling tonight were and in a proper bed?

"But why is no one here?" Dara asked.

"It's not wise to stand too long in the light of a sphere. The Knighthood kept guards posted in the corridor beneath the Citadel, but they rotated those staying closest to the sphere so no one remained directly in its light for more than four hours."

Dara glanced over her shoulder at the floating, yellow sphere. "Why?"

"People start to see things that aren't there. Their grip on reality slips. The mage generals believed it's the dark energy the spheres tap into, that it slowly breaks down life around it. That's what it does to get us from one planet to another, breaks us apart and re-assembles us on the other end." Ayleen stepped back towards the sphere, making certain not to get too close lest its gravity pull her back in to Regan Five. "My dad said it's echoes of the lives that have touched the sphere. Some mystics meditate in the presence of a sphere, thinking it brings them closer to spirits."

Standing close to the keyhole didn't trouble Ayleen as much as the paintings. She circled the room. The images captured in the paintings struck her as innocent enough. These people wanted to welcome visitors with a preview of their world from its days of glory. Then she saw it.

One of the battle-themed paintings showed a small group of warriors, armed with swords standing atop of a hill. A sun backlit the group, rendering them into little more than silhouettes. Below them, an army of knights fell back. Many of them were armed with crystal swords, shattered to mark their deaths. The victors numbered thirteen.

Ayleen pulled open her pack and grabbed her green poncho. She slipped off her hat and flung the poncho over her head so it would conceal her jacket.

"What is it?" Dara asked. Ayleen took a small amount of pride in seeing the girl had her hand on her sword's hilt, ready to draw it. She was learning to think like a knight.

Ayleen answered by pointing to the painting of the Thirteen. "Whether it might be good or ill, best we don't let these folks get wind of this." She tapped a finger over the spot where the symbol of the Knighthood was engraved onto her jacket, now hidden from view.

Dara's eyes shifted back to the walls. "Thirteen."

"I know." Ayleen's eyes narrowed. "Figured I'd made that plain enough."

"No, count them," she pointed to each wall as she turned. "Each wall has thirteen paintings on them."

As Ayleen counted the paintings, the sensation of an invisible threat coming up behind her kept her looking over her shoulder. Did the Thirteen know about her yet? Surely not this quickly. Sheriff Javo might have dug her way out of the cave on Griffin by now, but word could only travel so fast. That didn't guarantee they were safe here.

"Mind your words on this world."

Ayleen stared up the passage leading from the keyhole to the surface. Torches secured in sconces provided enough light to make out the lines of the narrow space.

"Let's move." Her body flinched as she took her first step into the tunnel. The urge to curl into a ball and hide pressed in on her. This path led to open sky, but her instincts screamed they were crawling into a serpent's throat.

12.

A midday sky greeted Ayleen and Dara as they emerged from the tunnel. A large, stone courtyard filled with people deafened them as vendors shouted the bargains they had to offer. Dozens of customers, chattering to one another added to the cacophony.

A tall pole stood in the middle of the market. Ayleen nearly dropped to her knees and threw up. A rectangular flag of horizontal lines fluttered: six white, six black, and one fat, red line ran through the middle.

The flag of the Thirteen occupied a space of honor for these people. After what they'd seen in the keyhole cave, Ayleen knew it shouldn't shake her, but the last time she'd seen it was outside the Citadel as their army spilled through the open gates.

That these people walked in this flag's shadow with smiles and laughter sickened her.

Her sword screamed their rage, eager to fly free of its scabbard and draw Ayleen's fury in the flesh of these damned traitors. *Kill them all!*

"It's okay," Dara said. "She took ill on the last world, walking through all that rain. Ain't quite right yet."

Ayleen's gaze landed on an orange-skinned humanoid. "You're a Corsairan." She couldn't hold back her surprise. Her father had told her about them. They were a genderless race known for their deep connection with the land wherever they lived. The antennae on their heads could track the invisible lines of life that ran above and below worlds. Those same stalks also served as their means to hear and smell, because they lacked any ears or noses.

The Corsairans did have a mouth much like most humanoids, though their teeth were more plentiful and pointier, which made this being's nonthreatening smile disconcerting.

"These days I think of myself as more of a Lagoonan, but yes." Their voice trilled, giving their words a musical quality. "If I am not mistaken, you must be part Pleiaderean?"

Ayleen wished she and Dara had chosen false names, but too late for that. She hadn't paid attention to what her squire might have told this stranger, so she didn't dare risk contradicting her.

The Corsairan bowed their head so far that their antennae pointed down. "I am Quior, child of Quaestra, Treybell, and Spran."

Ayleen's squire answered before she could. She held out her hand, offering it in a shake. "I'm Dara."

Quior grinned and took Dara's hand in a slow shake. "And you?" they asked.

"Ayleen." Instead of a handshake, she bowed to the stranger.

"May I inquire what brings you to the town of Kasegal?"

Kill them! Ayleen resisted the advice of her sword, but she shared its suspicions. No matter how friendly this Corsairan might present themselves, they stood under the Thirteen's flag.

"Just passing through." Try as she might, Ayleen couldn't muzzle the edge to her words. It was "good people" like this timid Corsairan who killed all she loved. Either they joined the mob or stepped out of the mob's way.

Quior didn't seem to notice Ayleen's buried hostility. Their gaze centered on Dara. "Is that a Griffin gladius?"

"I," she hesitated, eyes darting from Quior to Ayleen for some guidance, "don't know."

"It's a gladius." Ayleen placed a hand on Dara's shoulder. "We found it a few worlds back."

"May I see it?" Quior's antennae bent inward as their brow furrowed.

Ayleen answered before Dara, pulling her back a step. "Depends on why you're asking."

Quior placed a hand to their chest and bowed again. "I am a blacksmith."

Ayleen nodded to them but directed her words to Dara. "Let them have a look."

Dara pulled out the gladius and offered it. Quior turned the sword over in their hands, grunting as they considered it.

"This sword is in acceptable condition, but barely." They turned the sword so its hilt faced Dara, who took it back. "If I may be so bold, even if its condition was pristine, I suspect it would still be ill-suited for you."

Ayleen could already see where this blacksmith was taking things. She crossed her arms. "We only have so much coin and time, so let's cut straight to your offer."

"I am willing to make a sword better suited to her for 20 silvers." They raised a hand to halt the protest on Ayleen's lips. "I would be willing to take the price down to 15 silvers if you gift me the gladius."

"No." Ayleen's abrupt protest received a whimper from Dara. "We can't. Not for that price. Sheath your sword, and let's go."

"Ten silvers," Quior said. "I can go no lower."

"Please?" Dara whispered, not that her reaction was remotely hidden from the blacksmith.

Quior wanted the gladius, and while she agreed with their assessment of the blade's condition, Ayleen suspected the sword held more value than they were sharing. Otherwise, she didn't think they would take the price for a new sword down to ten silvers. In a galaxy where quality swords were as rare as faithful spouses in a brothel, the twenty silvers would have been a bargain.

"How long will you need to forge it?" Ayleen's question provoked a squeak of anticipation from her squire.

"Eight days."

Ayleen knew that wasn't unreasonable, but eight days... She glanced at Dara and the way the gladius sat heavy on her hip, close to pulling down her britches.

"I'll consider it." Ayleen held up a hand to forestall her squire's wide-eyed plea. "Give me some time to ask around. If your reputation sits well, I'll seek you out. Where can we find you?"

They exchanged the necessary details. Before they parted, a loud horn sounded. Its noise vibrated through the ground and into Ayleen's feet.

Every voice stopped. Those who had been sitting now stood, and all turned to face the flag flying at the center of the courtyard.

A second blast of the unseen horn shook the town. This time, all the people dropped to both knees and prostrated themselves towards the fluttering symbol of her enemy.

A few heads tilted in question at Ayleen and Dara, because neither had followed the locals' example. With a jerk of her head, Ayleen directed her squire to mimic the pose of the townsfolk. Dropping herself to her knees, Ayleen spared a second to glare up at the flag before lowering her head.

Burn it! Burn all of it!

As she held her pose, Ayleen wished for fire to honor her sword's demand.

13.

Ayleen and Dara settled into an inn not far from the marketplace. The innkeeper and a few others at the bar upheld Quior's reputation as a blacksmith, so Ayleen made the deal. They'd be down to a few coins by the time they left, but at least Dara would finally have a decent weapon to fight with.

They kept to their room for most of their stay, since the best way to avoid saying something they shouldn't was by saying nothing in front of anybody. That didn't stop them from venturing out of their room for meals. The food here was the best either had enjoyed in years. They had coffee, which spoiled Ayleen. She knew she'd suffer later for the indulgence of so much caffeine, but she didn't care.

Ayleen and Dara checked in on Quior five days later to see their progress. Their small shop was close to the market. The shack looked cobbled from borrowed scraps of wood. Its front was mostly a set of double doors left open to vent the heat from the forge.

Quior had fashioned a thin, double-edged thing of beauty. The blade reached farther than the gladius but weighed half as much.

"You do fine work, blacksmith." Ayleen slid a finger along the flat of the blade to admire its smooth surface. The experience of watching a sword being born made her smile. "It'll make an excellent weapon, as good as one could hope from a sword not made of..." She caught herself short of saying it would make an excellent sword despite not being fashioned from a crystal. Forcing out a laugh at her stumbling words, she looked towards Quior. "It's fine craftsmanship. Much thanks to you from us both."

"The hilt will be a simple thing." They gestured to a few other swords hung on the shack's back wall. Most were long and wide to attract passersby with their size. "It will be made from umbraewood and wrapped in leather. A carpenter I have commissioned many times will assist me."

Dara danced in place. More than once, Ayleen had regretted her decision to stay here this long, but Quior had made it worth their wait.

14.

The most difficult part of their stay was whenever it came time to sleep. Their room offered a view that included the marketplace. The townsfolk pulled down the Thirteen's flag each night to secure it, but seeing the tall pole where it lived during the day was enough to fuel Ayleen's anger. No amount of exercise or alcohol could exhaust her mind enough not to venture down the dozens of paths of vandalism and murder she wanted to commit.

Among her distractions, she reached for the grimoire. Though it was in vain, she tried each night to make sense of its jumbled content. She held it close and far away, focusing her vision and sometimes letting it roll out of focus. Nothing brought any sense to the shapes drawn on the pages.

Their last night in Kasegal, Ayleen once again flipped through the pages. Dara, on her bed along the opposite wall, turned to stare at her.

"Thought you were asleep," Ayleen said without looking at her.

Dara let out a long breath. "Keep thinking about my new sword."

Ayleen couldn't hold back her smile, but it lasted less than a mayfly's childhood. "I've been thinking…"

"I'm still going with you."

Her squire's firm reply drew Ayleen's gaze. "I've no love for these people, but this place is the most civilized I've seen since…"

"They killed my father." Dara stood and walked to their open window. A cool breeze floated into their room. "The Thirteen, I mean. I know the mayor did the deed, but the sheriff set up my pa. She did it, because what Pa meant as a kindness threatened her secret. I won't bow to that flag again."

They'd made a point of not getting caught in public when the midday horns sounded, nor when the flag went up or down. People were expected to prostrate before it all three times.

"You've a right to want satisfaction, but the road I'm walking is more likely to get me killed than lead to anything good. Here and now is as fit a time and place to get out, if you want to."

Dara didn't turn from the window. "When I watched the fire take Pa, the first thing I thought was how I was finally free to go my own way. I'm not proud of that, but I couldn't stay in Midchron. Don't think there's anywhere my feet can rest that won't leave me staring back at him, so..." She paused and bowed her head. "I'm gonna keep walking, like you. Don't reckon it's safe for either of us to go it alone, so together seems better."

Ayleen didn't question her decision. Dara didn't sound like a ten-year-old ought, but sometimes age was measured in hardships.

"Well, at least we ain't wasted our money for a sword then."

"I wanna pick a name for it." Dara turned to look at her. "I was thinking of going with Fang."

Ayleen nodded. "I like it."

"Does yours have a name?"

Ayleen's throat clenched and she faked a cough to recover herself. "Shyritas," she said. "It means truth."

Her sword screamed at her answer. Ayleen managed not to flinch this time. It screamed one word repeatedly until they doused the lamps to go to bed.

Liar!

15.

After they picked up Dara's sword from Quior, they put what was left of their coin to good use. They found two olive green water packs at the marketplace. Like most everything in the market, the packs had the look of having had many previous owners.

Their walk through the wilds of Lagoon VII took more than a week. Each night, before they stopped to sleep, Ayleen trained Dara with her new sword. She'd picked up many things while working with the gladius, but she learned faster now that she was armed with a weapon suited to her size. She wasn't a match for any knight —not yet—but she showed promise.

After her nightly lessons, Dara drew fish scales on her water pack with some ink she'd purchased during their stay in Kasegal. She offered to draw something on Ayleen's pack, but she declined.

Their water packs proved their worth on the next world. The keyhole to Helix One dropped them into a wasteland of volcanic rock with no drinkable water or vegetation. If any life existed on this world, they never noticed it. A long trail of smoke drifted overhead from the east, the direction they were headed. The top of a volcano, the source of the smoke, appeared not long after they started their walk. Anytime the land shook, the volcano darkened the sky with more ash.

The biggest delays came from the long canyons and the fissures filled with boiling water that occasionally burst upward in fireballs of noxious gas.

To Ayleen's surprise, they avoided any lava flows during their journey. Their walk to the keyhole took approximately two weeks. The days and nights were unusually short here, though, making it difficult to estimate time.

Low on water and food, they reached the coordinates for the next keyhole a few hours before dusk. That placed them near the start of the steepest slope going up the side of the volcano. Ayleen held her sword, pointing down. The crystal blade glowed, indicating she was directly above the keyhole. Only one problem.

"I don't see the way down." Ayleen slid her sword back into its scabbard. "But this is the spot, without doubt."

The ground shivered, giving the impression the volcano was laughing at their predicament.

She took off her water pack and sat on the ground. Dara didn't sit with her, not right away. The little girl stared up at the volcano's peak and the smoke issuing from it.

"Can I draw for a bit?" Her eyes went to Ayleen's pack.

Ayleen hesitated, but then pulled out the grimoire. Dara didn't understand Ayleen's objection to using the blank pages for her drawings. Her father had already allowed her to draw in it plenty. Something about giving a child a weapon as a toy felt profane, an acknowledgment of the Knighthood's end.

Dara sat beside her. She pulled a stick of coal from her pockets and drew the shape of the volcano. Her picture included the black clouds and smoke pouring up into the atmosphere.

Drawing didn't make Dara smile, but it took away the dread that tightened her features and coated her fingertips in coal.

Despite the intermittent tremors, Ayleen dozed a bit while sitting there. She came to shortly after sunset. The unseen lava within the crater atop the volcano cast the black smoke above it in an eerie, orange glow.

Dara had also fallen to sleep, curled on the ground with her poncho folded for a pillow. Ayleen let her be. No telling how much she'd slept, and less certain was how much they needed for what came next.

She picked up the grimoire, which was resting next to Dara. Before putting it back into her pack, she looked at the drawing of the volcano. Looked finished, and was one of Dara's better drawings. She'd included the two of them standing at the base of the volcano, staring at its summit.

The sun had set, and with nightfall, the first sign of how to find the keyhole cave appeared.

16.

Fissures and holes riddled the land around the volcano. Gods only knew what maze existed beneath them, formed from centuries of lava flows. By the light of day, they could search for weeks and possibly never find the keyhole. The night offered something much more helpful: contrast.

A crack in the ground started to the south and offered a faint glow that couldn't possibly be from the lava. Ayleen followed the path of the glow, and the light grew fainter the farther she moved from where her sword had pointed to the keyhole.

"You forget something?"

Ayleen turned to find Dara standing behind her. The girl had Ayleen's dagger in her hand.

"Glad to see you got my message." She'd left it pointing in the direction she'd gone. Ayleen took back her dagger and slid it into its sheath. "You got all your things?"

Dara nodded. "Maybe next time just write a note so I don't have to suss the meaning?"

Ayleen nodded, preferring not to argue over the potential profanity of ripping out a page from a grimoire for a note. "Thinking I've found our way to the keyhole, so seems a fine time to get out of here." The land answered with another tremor as if to say, *"Don't let the door hit ya where them ol' gods split ya."*

They followed the glowing fissure. Eventually, the split in the land grew into a ravine with lava spilling into it, flowing out of a hole on the far side. The lava tube continued on their side, but the split in the land prevented any lava from reaching it. They climbed down to the lava tube on their side using several naturally formed landings along the ravine's wall. The fissure that had led them to the lava tube's entrance ran above their heads as they neared the keyhole.

Shortly after the crack running along the top of the tube vanished, they reached the keyhole.

Ayleen lifted her hat to wipe her brow as she got a good look at the sphere. "Shite."

"So, black means there's no air. Orange is a gas planet. Green is underwater, and yellow means it's what you like to call safe." Dara heaped on a healthy serving of snark as she ran through her keyhole lessons. "So what does red mean?"

Ayleen glared into the crimson ball of light. "Not a damn clue."

17.

The early explorers among the Knights of the Way lived short lives. Never mind all the fools with swords in need of law who refused to take their lessons. The mechanics of early keyhole travel left too many questions. The idea that the color defined the environment and that the size of the sphere indicated the strength of the other planet's gravity only came from trial and error.

She knelt in front of the sphere. The change in angle didn't really improve her view of the situation. She was stalling.

At least the sphere was medium-sized, suggesting wherever it went offered an acceptable level of gravity.

"Never heard of a red keyhole." She said it more to herself than to Dara. Her mother had taken this tunnel, though. She must have, but what if Dara was right? The Galaxy takes roughly 225,000,000 years to make one whole spin. Eight centuries shares more with a nanosecond next to that, but it's still plenty of time for a world to drop into the crapper.

"So any guesses?" Dara kept her distance from the sphere.

Ayleen shook her head. As close as she was, she could feel the slight pull of its gravity. That same tug had saved a few explorers. Her father said he once came out on the other side of a gas planet, and the pull of the keyhole eventually dragged him back to safety. Called it the longest hour of his life. Only reason he'd survived that long was because he'd been wearing an exploration suit. Those things covered a person from head to toe. The round helmets looked big until you put one of them on. Pity the soul who hates confined spaces and ends up in one of those.

They didn't have an exploration suit, though. Certainly not two of them.

Ayleen stood and stepped back from the sphere. "Time to make a choice." She turned to Dara. "You can always go back to the other keyhole, the one that brought us here."

"Not much of a choice." Dara pointed to the sword resting on Ayleen's right hip. "I don't have one of those fancy, crystal swords to guide me if I get lost. Not much water left either. Used most of it to get here."

Ayleen turned back to the sphere. The red seemed appropriate—the color of blood. She'd come this far for one reason. She wanted to kill the Thirteen. Those traitors had taken all that mattered to her, and thanks to her run-in with Sheriff Javo back on Griffin, she knew a simple swing of the sword wouldn't cut it. The grimoire might hold the answers she needed, but without the knowledge of a Fate, she might as well let Dara keep it for a sketch book.

"I'm going," Ayleen said. "If you mean to join, that's your choice to make."

Dara stepped up beside her. Good an answer as any.

They took the last step, the curved light embracing them in its kiss, pulling them in and flinging their essence from this world to the next.

18.

A warm, thick fog obscured Ayleen's view as she emerged from the sphere. She could breathe, gods be praised, but each inhale plunged sticky heat down her throat.

"My clothes are sticking to me." Dara said to Ayleen's right. She sounded close, but Ayleen couldn't see her. Even the DET's yellow sphere was obscured. She only knew she was close, because of how bright the fog was at her back.

"Reach out towards my voice." Ayleen flailed with her right arm until her hand slapped against what she assumed was Dara's hand. "Good. Now, hold my hand until we clear this fog."

"What if the fog never clears?"

"We only go as far as the sphere's light reaches. Don't want to lose our way back to leave this world."

Going by that, they wouldn't get far. The fog turned more grey than pale yellow after a few steps.

The land was sloped. The DET spheres were always underground, so it was normal to travel uphill upon exiting a tunnel. Only, in this case, the land went down.

"Mind your steps." Ayleen tightened her grip on Dara's hand.

The glow of the sphere degraded to the point where the fog was more black than grey. As Ayleen was about to turn them back, the mist cleared, beginning at her feet and working its way up.

Her first unobstructed view of Lycaenidae Nine revealed they were walking down the side of a hill. The DET had delivered them at the hilltop. The path they walked down was wide, but with a steep drop off on each side.

"Never seen a DET sphere that wasn't underground." Ayleen stopped to look back at what she assumed was a cloud.

Dara let go of her hand. "Is that why the sphere on the other side was red?"

"Possibly," Ayleen shrugged. "Can't be sure until we come across another red one."

The further they moved away from the hilltop, the easier it was to see the top portion of the sphere shown above the cloud. They'd also emerged into night, and save for the one cloud atop the mountain, the sky offered a tapestry of colorful stars and two small moons.

The surface of this planet was black, jagged rock. If Lycaenidae Nine contained any life or water, it hid it well.

This world reminded Ayleen of a skeleton. She decided against sharing that with Dara.

One thing offered Ayleen hope regarding her theory of this world's connection to the Fates. The path they walked appeared constructed. At times, it ran through a valley with tall, smooth walls on each side. At other places, the path formed a narrow bridge granting passage over canyons. The surface of the path was smooth, and not the kind frequent use could explain. The path never split.

The last part of the path brought them to the wide mouth of a cave. The entrance, sitting at the base of another tall hill, removed any question as to whether the cave was a natural formation. While the top portion was natural enough, the half-lowered door wasn't. Made of the same black rock as the rest of this planet, the surface of the door was perfectly smooth. Every few feet, a part of the door jutted down a little farther like teeth with matching holes in the ground for them to bite into. A familiar, blue glow emanated from beyond the cave's entrance.

"Crystals." Ayleen rested a hand on her sword's hilt, its song bitter at the restraint her soul placed on it compared to its untamed sisters within the cave. "Might be another abandoned farm, like the one the folks on your world were harvesting." She hoped that explained the size of the door, something designed to allow large transports to travel in and out of the cave for loading crystals and unloading supplies.

"What do the Fates look like?" Dara asked.

Ayleen shook her head. Like most all about the Fates, the knowledge was forbidden. "They're called the Great Weavers, said to be as old as the Galaxy itself."

Dara leaned forward, peering into the dark and light beyond the threshold. The door was raised high enough for Dara to enter, if she chose, without the need to bend over. Ayleen would need to stoop.

"If you'd rather stay out here, that'll be without any shame, little squire."

The girl shook her head. "Dark that," she said, borrowing a curse she'd picked up during their stay in Kasegal. "What if there's a keyhole to leave in there? No sense in splitting up."

"Fair enough." Ayleen drew her crystal sword and whispered the command to make it glow. *"Terastrant."*

Drawing a breath, Ayleen ducked under the door and entered the cave.

19.

A musty smell pervaded the cave. Patches of untamed crystals offered a minimum of light, but would have hardly sufficed if not for the enhanced glow of Ayleen's sword.

The source of the smell revealed itself a few steps into the darkness. Ayleen's foot landed with a splash that startled her both for the noise and the way her foot took six inches longer than expected to reach the ground.

She lowered her sword. The water's surface reflected the light. Nothing moved in the water, only the ripples formed from where her foot broke the surface. From what she could tell, the water covered most of the cavern floor, enough to amount to a shallow lake.

"Mind your steps." Ayleen turned to look at Dara when the girl didn't answer. The child stared in wide-eyed fascination at the water, likely more than she'd ever seen in a single place with the exception of the constant rain on Regan Five.

Steam wafted along the surface of the underground lake. Ayleen preferred the warm sensation of the water invading her boot versus the cold it could have been.

Ayleen made a mental note to find Dara better boots. The tread to the child's shoes was worn thin, especially after her near-spill weeks ago in the exploded fire hopper guts. They'd need to get some more coin, too, but those problems would keep for now.

The cave narrowed on them, three meters wide and curved. It led them deeper into the planet. Clusters of jagged crystals became more frequent as they descended. They avoided touching the volatile crop.

"Think that grimoire might have anything on how to make a sword for me like yours?"

Dara's request reminded Ayleen of when she'd asked her mother if she'd be the one to bind her to her sword. Mom had responded with a horrified shake of her head, as if Ayleen had suggested she slice off her only child's limbs.

"Perhaps." Ayleen hid her own look of horror from Dara. "Let's not start collecting crystals until we know for certain if we're going to do that. Wouldn't do to survive all we have and then trip and die from shattering a crystal with our arses."

"Fine." Dara's vexed reply mirrored Ayleen's long ago response to her mother. At the time, she hadn't understood what it meant to carve off a part of a soul and marry it to a weapon. All the training they endured as children went to testing their spirit's discipline and resolve.

In the dark of the cave, Ayleen wondered if she could do it. If she had the skill to perform the magic, should she bond this girl to a crystal sword? They both wrestled with the loss of their parents and a desire for revenge, but Ayleen received her sword and training before the Galaxy lost its Way. Dara was born into the shitestorm that followed.

The narrow tunnel emerged into a tall grotto. The larger space, roughly the size of a stadium, offered much more light. Not only did untamed crystals stab down from the tall ceiling, but more clusters of crystals pointed up out of the water like tiny, glowing islands.

The water on the path came up an inch compared to the half a foot of water in the tunnel. The slightly-submerged bridge across the grotto narrowed. Ayleen nearly spilled into the pool but caught herself in time. Staring into the water, she noticed more crystals glowing down there. Some seemed to move, but it was difficult to tell if that was simply the ripples in the water tricking her eyes. She wondered how deep the water went. Might only be a few feet, but it could easily be ten times that. Better, she decided, not to fall in and find out the hard way.

She lifted her hat from her head to wipe her brow on her sleeve. Everything about this planet screamed with silent threats. Why she'd ever expected it to be welcoming struck her as foolish now. With so much in the Galaxy having turned for the worse, she'd hoped the Fates would be resilient to what plagued everywhere else. Perhaps they were, but that didn't suggest they'd ever been the kind to embrace a visitor.

The bridge they walked on split in three other directions, leading out of the grotto into other corridors.

"That way." Ayleen pointed with her sword towards the path to their right. The glow of the light looked a bit more green than blue. She wanted to see why, and a small hope formed in her. If not for the fear of falling off the path into the water, she would have run.

The short tunnel felt narrower than the one that led them into the first grotto. The path they walked upon ran down the middle of the passage with space aplenty on either side to fall into the lake.

The passage led them into a space about ten meters in diameter with no other exits. More blue crystals lined the walls and bit up from the water. At the far end of the small space, the reason for why the light from this passage looked different shone bright. Amber light emanated from a circle of crystals sticking out of the wall.

"Ambrosia crystals." Ayleen stared at them. The spells contained in the grimoire weren't worth a takert's droppings without one of these. At the end of the path, which ended about a foot short of the far wall, she reached for them with her free hand, fingers shaking. Mother had kept hers in her office and had forbidden Ayleen from touching it.

"Ayleen." The warning tone in Dara's voice snapped Ayleen from the distraction of the ambrosia crystals.

Dara's eyes weren't focused on the wall of ambrosia crystals, nor on her. The girl stared up.

Ayleen had assumed the room didn't have any crystals in this chamber's ceiling, but as she looked more closely, she realized they were there, but something subdued their glow. She raised her sword, letting its light reveal more of what was hidden above.

Nothing there moved, but a thick weave of silken thread formed a massive, open cocoon with nothing in it.

"What is that?" Dara asked.

Fear pushed aside the sweltering heat and covered Ayleen in goosebumps. "That's a nest."

"For what?"

Ayleen made her choice. She grabbed one of the ambrosia crystals, ripping it free from the cave's wall. The amber light glowed brighter in her hand. As she shoved the crystal into the pouch on her belt, the rush of displaced water echoed through the grotto, coming from behind, where Ayleen and Dara had entered this chamber.

Before she could turn, Ayleen already knew two things. One: she'd found one of the Fates. Two: given the amount of water being thrashed about, the Fate was huge.

The limited bits of mythology and science the Knights of the Way had taught her about the Fates didn't prepare her for what she found between her and any hope of escape. The first thought to enter Ayleen's mind as she stared into the Fate's face was her mother's words to her from long ago.

"You just remind me of someone I used to know."

Now Ayleen knew who her mother meant.

20.

To describe the Fate as a giant spider didn't do justice to the creature blocking the way out of this chamber. Her eight legs hooked up above her torso and then back down into the water. Their tips defied the pool's surface tension to let her stand atop the water without the support of the path.

Blue crystal coated the bottom half of each leg. One leg—one of the left ones—bent at an odd angle as if lame. It didn't quite touch the water like the others. Crystal covered more of that leg, three-quarters of it.

Some of the crystals Ayleen had seen beneath them in the water, when they first entered the cave, had seemed to move. The Fate had lurked beneath the water and followed them from the moment they arrived. No water dripped from her massive body as if she rejected the pool's embrace. Or perhaps the water rejected her.

Her exoskeleton, what wasn't covered in crystal, resembled onyx. The legs appeared spiked with bits of fur, but given how the hair didn't move, Ayleen assumed they were thin barbs formed from the same material as the rest of the spider's body.

Her torso contained two parts, as any spider's would. The rear abdomen made up the majority of the body. A giant bubble of water floated atop the back of the spider with slender threads circling it to maintain its shape. Small fish, large sea caterpillars, and a human infant all floated within the bubble, each wrapped in the same silky webbing that covered the ceiling.

The Fate backed away from Ayleen and Dara towards the entrance. Her back half climbed up the wall to block their escape.

All that made for more pleasant matters to occupy Ayleen's mind. Anything was better than its head. Four pairs of eyes covered the smaller part of its body. Six of the eyes were small, round, and glowed the same color as the blue crystals. The largest pair of eyes were closed but blinked open three sets of eyelids to reveal an amber light. The placement of the eyes formed a flat, mocking smile along the topmost edges of the head, crowning a large pair of black, stubby fangs.

What disturbed Ayleen most was the crack in the spider's head. Something had shattered part of the exoskeleton along the top of the head. From that gap, long blond hair spilled out, and the left side of a human face with a violet eye watched. Though the hair didn't match, the face floating in shadow within the spider's fractured cephalothorax was without doubt Ayleen's twin.

Dara shouted as the Fate tilted her head down to focus on the smaller of her two guests. As the head shifted, water spilled from the crack and rejoined the pool at Ayleen and Dara's feet.

Touching Dara's shoulder to move her, Ayleen placed herself between the Fate and her squire. She debated on putting her sword away, but if the raised weapon hadn't drawn this ancient creature's attack yet, she decided not to risk that lowering it might.

"You knew my mother?" Ayleen stepped back as she asked the question. Her fear made the path feel twice as narrow.

One of the rear legs reached up to a single thread of silk running along the ceiling. It stroked the web, drawing out a beautiful note. The sound reminded Ayleen of the chime from when her sword struck another crystal blade.

"I know every mother." The Fate spoke with two voices, one that her large, pointed chelicerae ground out and the other from the human lips that Ayleen prayed sounded nothing like her and knew they did. "I know them from conception... to birth..." The leg slashed at the thread with its crystal edge and sliced it in two. "...to death."

"But mine once shared this cave with you," Ayleen said, "didn't she?"

"Aydrene...Aydrene...Aydrene," the Fate stopped repeating the name of Ayleen's mother to laugh. "Life is a dream."

The uncomfortable realization that this creature's cracked head might be a metaphor for madness left Ayleen to wonder if she'd doomed herself and Dara by coming here. All she could do now was hope to get out alive. "Yes, Aydrene Torr. My Mother. You taught her to write in your language, didn't you?"

The Fate stepped closer, bringing her rear legs off the wall and back onto the water, sending ripples along its black surface. Her head lowered, and it was hard to tell if she wanted to better see Ayleen with her amber eyes or the violet one visible within the crack.

"No, no, no. I do not teach. I drink. I infect." Each word made the spider shake a little more, and her growing enthusiasm appeared more clearly in that violet, human eye as it widened. "I...shaaaare."

The beast reared back with a loud shriek of laughter, her large fangs striking against each other as its crystal-tipped legs danced on the water.

"You've come for me to share again!"

"That depends." Ayleen's sword shook in her grip as her anger warred with her fear. "What will this knowledge cost me?"

"Naughty, naughty, naughty mother... Taught her girl to run, to war, to fuck, but forgot how to share." She bit her fangs together again. Her gaze lowered, bringing that uncomfortable mirror closer to Ayleen.

Dara's hands grabbed the back of Ayleen's jacket. Only then did Ayleen realize she'd been in slow retreat, and now they'd reached the end of the path, with the crop of Ambrosia Crystals at their back. Nowhere left to go.

Ayleen's breath caught in her throat. She had to get them out of here.

"Yes!" The Fate abruptly shouted. She hissed at Ayleen as her fangs' tips scraped against one another. "Ask, ask, ask, little sister. What you wish to know. What you haven't asked. What you need to be told."

No doubt the Fate's violet eye was the one staring hard at her and taking her measure. This was like a mirror, only with the reflection flipped. The features lined up wrong.

Yes.

She knew the question. It wasn't what she'd come to ask, but she needed to know.

"Why do you have my face?"

The human lips, barely visible within the crack of the spider's head, curled into wide delight.

"Snick! Slash! Slice!" The Fate reached up with a rear leg and cut several silken threads along the wall behind her. "Those who cut the threads of life all share the same face."

"I am not a Fate."

"Fate or Fated, though the latter you can also be, the slice to make will be yours indeed. The deepest cut of all."

The mirror face within the spider glared at Ayleen. She drew closer. The stench of rotted flesh and mildew choked Ayleen's senses. The spider took deep breaths through both its mouths, each one faster and with mounting anticipation and rage. Her next words sang a familiar tune, one Ayleen had heard from her sword too many times in these past two years.

"None down...*Thirteen to go.*"

Before Ayleen could respond, the Fate lunged. Her fangs snatched Ayleen by the throat, and their tips pierced her flesh.

The venom flowed.

21.

Ayleen fell. Not her body, but her soul.

She hit the black water, and it swallowed her.

Not dead, she thought. Or was the thought her sword's? She took a deep breath, but water didn't fill her lungs, only cold air. A field of grass replaced the water at her back.

To her right, the Fate whispered numbers. The Fate's voice no longer had the spider's chitter to it, only the echo of Ayleen's.

Ayleen turned her head. Her blond-haired twin—now a truer twin, bereft of the spider's body and wearing only a human's—stared back and smiled. Ayleen and the Fate were dressed alike. They were prone upon the grassy hill with their arms stretched out.

The Fate stopped muttering her nonsense numbers. "Have you counted? No one has enough precious seconds to take the tally. I'm not so generous." She pointed up at the night sky. "Count them!"

Ayleen looked back up. Her body felt too heavy to stand, so she stayed on the grass. No clouds hid this night's stars. She saw red, blue, and yellow. A green comet trail whistled past, obscuring the rest, before it vanished over the horizon towards Ayleen's feet.

"Can you count them?" The Fate asked, her voice more insistent this time. "You won't get more than one life to do it. Perhaps you need to see it more quickly." She snapped her fingers, and the land shifted.

Ayleen grabbed onto the grass as the sky spun.

"Do you think the sky ever counts you? Do you think it has the time?"

Ayleen tried to close her eyes, but her lids refused to. "Make it stop!"

"Do you think you count!" The Fate's shout burned Ayleen's ears. An ache tore through her head and the sky turned faster, pitching on every axis.

The Fate laughed. The sound lacked any mirth, filled only with anger and contempt.

"It spins, sister. You spin, too. You stare up and miss what matters. Your matter is too grey to see the dark."

Ayleen screamed as the lights vanished, spinning out of view. Then it all tilted to bring it back.

"You see the spiral, but you aren't meant to. You're too little to know its Way. You're too little for the Galaxy to think about you, but you're on its mind. It can't stop thinking."

The Fate whispered again, running through the numbers.

"1. 2. 3. 4. 5. 6. 7. 8. 9. 10. 11. 12. 13. 14."

She kept running through those numbers, and at thirteen—always thirteen—the view pitched.

Star trails blurred. Darkness rushed at them and turned away. They hurtled through stars, obscuring all else from view and leaving burn marks in Ayleen's vision. She wanted nothing more or less than a single blink, a moment to hide the sky.

Then she saw the pattern of the stars, but it wasn't a spiral. Instead, the trails of matter, light and dark formed two hemispheres—a right and a left. At its heart, the brilliant center of it all, a stem thrust up from a spinal column into the center of a brain.

"It wants to stop, too!" The Fate screamed, and they plunged towards that brilliant center. The weight of motion pressed on Ayleen. A round speck of black appeared within the light until it filled their view. Up close, the black sphere took on more definition, as a grey, dried-up world. The Fate counted, and the sky tilted again at Thirteen. Only this time, all motion stopped.

A single, narrow stream of light flowed down from the center of the Galaxy. The light entered through the northern pole of the dead, grey world and spilled out its southern end.

Then the stream cut off, feeding only into the world, but never out.

"The Galaxy," the Fate said, as if in mourning, "has lost its Way."

Ayleen turned to stare at her twin who now stood, gazing up at that colorless orb of craters and the disrupted stream of light.

"You must unlock the Castle's Door. Go there, and make the final cuts."

Ayleen forced herself to her feet. As she stood, she realized the grass had vanished. What she stood on now was dark, dead land, a withered corpse of a world like so many she'd tread upon these past two years. Most of all, it reminded her of her lost home.

"I don't understand."

The Fate pointed at the grey planet. "Look and make this happen." The light once more spilled out the southern pole, only the light didn't stop there. It consumed the world, obliterating it and everything else.

"Find your Way, and make the cut, sister."

Ayleen turned away from the explosion. The Fate, now a whole spider with no crack to its head, lunged at her.

Everything went white.

"Find your Way."

22.

Ayleen jerked up from where she'd fallen into the water.

"It's all right." Dara grabbed her shoulder from behind. She offered Ayleen's crystal sword back to her. Thank the gods she wouldn't have to dive into these waters to retrieve it. She wondered if she'd dropped it on the path or if Dara caught it.

Ayleen no longer saw the Fate blocking their escape. Had she left? "Where is she?"

Dara pointed up to the nest. The blue and amber eyes glowed, but the rest of the spider was reduced to a silhouette.

"How long?" Ayleen staggered to her feet, fighting down the nausea burning in her gut. Her drenched clothing clung to her back. She rubbed at the ache in her neck as she glared at the beast in its nest. "How long was I out?"

"Not sure." Dara drew her sword. "Felt like an hour, but say true, might have been less. Time feels awful slow with a monster staring down at you."

The glowing eyes shifted. Ayleen felt as if the spider was smiling to mock her.

"Been up there the whole time?"

Dara nodded. "She's been counting."

The Fate whispered to herself, and as she reached thirteen, a shiver ran down Ayleen's back. She staggered and grabbed Dara to keep from falling.

The Fate stopped counting and crawled down the side of the cave a few steps. "She wants to read, but can she? Is she ready?"

Ayleen felt something slithering in her thoughts. Not a literal thing, but a series of ideas and recognition. She shook her head as if to push a hefty tome into a narrow space upon the shelf. She removed the grimoire from her pouch, relieved to see it hadn't gotten wet.

She flipped it open to the first page of letters and symbols. She felt the characters dancing on the page as each set of three consecutive characters merged into one and somehow, she knew what each new symbol meant.

Running her finger along the first line, she read the translation aloud. "A formula to induce false images into another mind." She cringed as she remembered these books contained forbidden science. Mage generals kept the knowledge for themselves, not to use, but to recognize what not to use in their own craft.

"Ayleen." Dara pulled on her arm and ran towards the way out. The Fate crawled down the wall to the right.

"Have what you need? What to read? What to do?"

She returned the grimoire to the pouch with the ambrosia crystal on her belt. "So it seems." Ayleen stayed close to Dara.

"Time to pay my price. A fee at hand. Something to pass the time."

"I never agreed to your price, Fate." Ayleen held her sword ready with both hands.

The Fate slapped at the water with her front two pairs of legs. Warm rain splashed throughout the small grotto. "You agreed the day you were born, the day you took your sword, the day you made your vow."

Another cold shiver ran through her. She knew exactly what this creature meant, and her sword whispered the vow to her.

None down. Thirteen to go.

She'd sworn to kill them no matter what.

"And what is your price?" Ayleen asked.

"An offering of time, a cut of life, one with life to spare." To make the point more clear, one of the rear spider legs reached up and tapped at the sphere of water on her back with its menagerie of dead things.

"My mother stayed in there?"

"She had the life to spare." The Fate's fangs clicked against each other in anticipation. "A life to share. Life given."

"Say true, I think I'll pass."

The spider's legs tapped against the wall and on the water. Her head tilted. "You think you have a string to cut? Precious. Adorable. Ignorant."

"What does that mean?" Ayleen pushed Dara towards the corridor leading from here to the larger grotto. If this beast meant to fight her, then so be it. She'd lost enough time. The last thing she intended was to waste another minute in this cave and certainly not trapped in the Fate's floating feast.

"Your life was cut long ago, little sister. So very long ago. Your time is already borrowed, but hers..." One of the spider's front legs lifted from the water and pointed—not at Ayleen, but at Dara. "Hers is not."

Ayleen raised her sword. "You will not have her."

The Fate screamed as she leaped at them.

23.

The Fate crashed into the water, sending up a wave that slammed against the lower half of Ayleen's body. She stayed upright, which was all that saved her as the Fate's front two legs stabbed at her. She parried both legs with her sword. The collision of crystals produced an ugly chime.

"Run!" Ayleen shouted.

Dara sprinted through the water into the narrow corridor.

Ayleen swung at the spider's head. The Fate screamed as the sword slashed between her stubby fangs.

With the Fate distracted by the cut to her mouth, Ayleen ran into the tunnel towards the grotto.

An inhuman cry of rage echoed after Ayleen and Dara. The noise cut short with a loud splash. The Fate had gone underwater.

Crystal lights swam through the water beneath Ayleen's feet. The Fate passed beneath her to pursue her true prey.

"Faster!" Ayleen sprinted towards Dara. "She's right under you!"

Four legs slashed up from the water onto the path. The Fate failed to grab or stab Dara but knocked her down.

Ayleen caught up in time to stop the Fate's next swings. The strength of the spider legs took Ayleen down to one knee as she blocked with her sword.

Kill her! The sword screamed to Ayleen.

Dara grabbed Ayleen's free hand and pulled her up. They sprinted for the grotto, but they wouldn't be safer there.

The Fate chased them down the passage. Her legs stabbed up at them, but Ayleen's and Dara's swords blocked her attacks. The little squire made Ayleen proud. She'd learned her forms well enough to draw on them in a real fight. Captain Tratella always said that in times of stress, a person reverted to their training.

Dara kept her nerve and looked pissed enough to fight. Legend claimed a Fate couldn't die. Ayleen didn't plan to stay here long enough to test if the theory was right.

"Keep moving!" Ayleen pushed Dara towards the grotto.

The lights in the water vanished. Ayleen refused to believe the Fate had given up.

They reached the grotto. The only noise came from their heavy breaths and the splashes from their footfalls along the path.

Ayleen didn't see anything moving beneath the water's surface. A fear it might strike from above drew Ayleen's gaze up. She didn't see the Fate there.

Water splashed up around them. The Fate slid out of the lake. In a smooth motion, her torso passed over them and snatched Dara with her legs.

"No!" Ayleen grabbed for Dara and missed, but she latched onto one of the spider's legs, above where the crystal tips began. Pain raged through her hand as one of the spikes cut into her palm. She took a deep breath, enough not to suffocate once she went under.

Water enveloped them. The Fate thrashed. One swing sent Ayleen's head through a strange web that formed an air pocket beneath the water. An insect the size of Ayleen's fist hissed at the intrusion. She grabbed another breath before being dragged back out.

Dara didn't have the same time to survive down here. Ayleen pushed down her fear and swung at one of the nearby legs. Her attack struck true, slicing through the portion not covered in crystal.

The Fate fled into one of the connecting tunnels, surrendering her prize.

Dara, wide-eyed but alive, raced up out of the water next to Ayleen. They emerged with loud gasps next to the path.

Somehow, Dara had held onto her sword.

"We best hurry," Ayleen paused to cough, "before she comes back for another try. Move!"

They pulled themselves up onto the path and staggered into the passage leading towards the exit.

"Say true, I'm starting to think I preferred the desert," Dara said between breaths. They both laughed at that.

Ayleen was proud of her. Dara had kept her wits and somehow grabbed enough air to survive before getting dragged under.

Webbing stuck to Ayleen's head. She pulled some off in sticky globs along with a few strands of her hair.

The passage from the grotto up to the mouth of the cave didn't appear to have any gaps in the ground, not like the one that led to the Fate's nest.

"You think she'll take another swipe at us where we came in?" Dara shouted the question without looking over her shoulder, probably more focused on not tripping in the calf-deep water.

The depth of the water slowed them, but at least the Fate couldn't attack in this passage.

"Wouldn't expect anything less of her." Ayleen ran past the girl. "Probably has another way we don't know about to reach the exit."

If the Fate was waiting for them, Ayleen would buy Dara time to get out. She'd take off all of the giant spider's legs, if need be.

Ayleen held up a hand to warn Dara back as the way out came into view. They waited near the end of the passage. She glanced over her shoulder at Dara and whispered, "You wait here until I tell you to move. Then we don't stop running until we reach the keyhole."

Dara nodded, holding her sword ready.

Ayleen sprinted into the open. Her sword sang in anticipation, but no attack came. The water sloshed about as Ayleen spun around, always expecting the next attack from the direction her back faced. None came, though. Was it possible the caves below were a prison for the Fates? She didn't think they could be that lucky, but if the Fate planned to attack, she was wasting many opportunities.

An even worse thought occurred to her, to wonder if the Fate might have a different way outside and be waiting just beyond the door.

She waved for Dara to come out. Ayleen waited until the girl reached her, and they sprinted for the exit.

Starlight beckoned from beyond the mouth of the cave. Ayleen couldn't remember when she'd more welcomed the sight of a star-filled sky.

Dara smiled at her as they passed beneath the half-shut door.

Ayleen looked over her shoulder at the rocky hill above the cave's mouth. Nothing was there.

The Fate launched out from the shadows of the cave. The spider's fangs grabbed Dara by the neck with a loud crack. Before Ayleen could swing her sword, the Fate retreated with Dara's body into its lair. The cave's door slammed down, the crash of black rock loud enough to deafen Ayleen.

She screamed Dara's name. Her sword struck the closed door with no success. She summoned its magic, warming it as hot as she could stand it. That only drew scratches into the black rock. She attempted the same on the unshaped rock around the entrance, but that produced only slightly more noticeable scratches.

In vain, she searched the next few days for another way inside the cave. Eventually, wisdom forced her to give up. She'd ignored as long as she might the truth of what she'd seen and heard. The Fate snapped Dara's neck in the grab. A vacancy had shown in the squire's eyes as her rag doll body vanished into the cave.

Dara was dead.

24.

No clouds obscured the yellow keyhole atop the hill on Lycaenidae Nine as Ayleen walked up to it. She glanced back in the direction of the cave.

Pulling out the grimoire, she rifled past the pages filled with script the Fate's venom enabled her to read. The dark sciences didn't hold her interests at this moment. She stopped when she reached the page with Dara's drawing of Sheriff Javo. She wanted so much to place the blame for Dara's life at the feet of the Thirteen.

She knew better.

She shouldn't have brought her here. Should have abandoned her back on Lagoon VII or never taken her from Midchron.

Through all her protests and screams, she'd never offered herself in exchange. That she knew the Fate would have rejected her didn't matter. Ayleen wasn't willing to give up.

She read the verse from the nursery rhyme, possibly the last words Dara ever put to paper.

> *Up and down and in and out.*
> *Bird of fire meets cold of night.*
> *Neither wins; both dearly lose.*

Thus they end in ebon light.

Ayleen ripped the page out and balled it up. She stopped short of throwing it away, couldn't forgive herself if she did. Unfolding the wrinkled page, she stuffed it back into the grimoire and shoved it back in her pouch.

She looked towards the cave. "I'll get satisfaction for our fathers."

A whisper from her sword told her the Fate probably planned some satisfaction for Dara, too. Ayleen would gladly pay that price when the time came.

She pulled the brim of her hat down in front as she turned back to the yellow sphere of light. She ignored the new emptiness in her heart and stepped into the sphere.

Her sword offered the only comfort it ever would:

Thirteen to go.

PART III

The Wolf

1.

Five months after the heartbreak on Lycaenidae Nine, Ayleen found her face staring back at her again.

She emerged from a keyhole into a cave containing two vid screens. The one on the left displayed a montage of ideal vacation stops on Kurega, which included a beach, snowy mountains, and the immense Orlander Library. The planet's name floated across the images in large, bold font for anyone who didn't know where they were. The cracks in the screen distorted the images with portions displayed in the wrong colors and marred by electric snow. She wondered how long that montage had served more as a memorial.

The second vid screen, on the opposite side of the cave's exit, cycled through a seemingly random set of information graphics that had the ring of more recent relevance. One informed visitors they could be arrested for drawing their swords in public with a minimum sentence of six weeks imprisonment for each infraction. Another image encouraged people to smile, because *"If you pretend to be happy long enough, you will be happy!"* When the next graphic appeared, Ayleen saw her face, a picture of her that certainly didn't smile.

The computer-generated composite didn't get her face quite right. The rendering made her eyes too narrow, too far apart. Her nose, forever bent to the left by the fist of her old trainer, didn't sit that straight. Got the purple of her eyes and the blue of her hair down right, though. The graphic misspelled her name as "Ahleen

Torr." The text along the bottom stated there was a sizable reward for her dead but more to take her alive.

Still alone in the keyhole's cave, Ayleen removed her wide-brimmed hat and coiled her hair up into a loose bun. She dropped her hat back on her head to hide the pile of blue hair and tilted the brim low in front to conceal her eyebrows.

The vid image charged her with larceny and multiple homicides. The crystal sword, resting legally within its scabbard, whispered to her its pride at the many lives taken.

The Thirteen knew Ayleen was coming for them. Judging from the wanted poster, the fucking traitors planned to meet her half-way. Mighty kind of them.

2.

A fierce wind slammed into Ayleen as she emerged from the cave into the city of Tarkinton. She grabbed the top of her hat to keep it from flying off. The rush of air cut into her exposed hand, dropping it a good ten degrees compared to the rest of her.

The distant skyline consisted of mountain-tall buildings, each a tilting skeleton of shattered glass and rusted beams only the most desperate fools would enter for shelter. A maelstrom of clouds swirled above it all in a dusky sky.

The part of Tarkinton the cave deposited her into still thrived in what might have once been a large park. Fields of red grass stretched for dozens of blocks in every direction. Paths of grey bricks connected the many buildings constructed from whatever materials could be cannibalized.

The steady glow of artificial light called to her from the buildings. Tall lamp posts, positioned throughout the park and along the streets that bordered it, also blazed to life with the darkening of the sky. Ayleen couldn't recall the last world she'd visited with electricity or some other power source. Gods favor her, she might enjoy a hot bath this night.

A neon sign in the window of a brick, two-story building displayed the name Niobe's Inn. The last "n" was burned out, as if the sign meant a woman named Niobe was here to meet people. The first floor didn't offer much, a long bar along the left wall and a few booths along the right, each with a cozy fit for four. Every surface was made of wood, stained dark enough to border on black.

The place looked half-full. The crowd, mostly locals by the look, met Ayleen with a suspicious stare. The ban on drawing swords didn't deter anyone from carrying them.

Her sword drew some hushed comments. One woman whispered "knight" and a man doing his worst to avoid looking at Ayleen muttered "Thirteen." The past few months had reduced most of her sword's leather grip to tatters, exposing the blue crystal. According to the limited intelligence the Knights of the Way gathered about the Thirteen before the Knighthood fell, twelve of the Thirteen also carried the crystal swords of the Knighthood. The people in this inn were mistaking her for one of those traitors and feared her for it.

She stepped up to the bar, a place near the front of the inn without anyone to crowd her.

A woman with wavy red hair, who looked only a few years older than Ayleen's nineteen, worked the bar. "What can I get you?" If she shared her customers' concerns, they didn't show in her smile.

Ayleen didn't smile back. "Need a room for the night."

"I'll have Crim ready one for you." She reached beneath the bar to produce a set of keys on a ring so big as to be impossible to lose. "Hey, Crim! Get number three put together for this lady."

She flung the keys to a boy with strong arms who'd been wiping down glasses and sliding them onto the appropriate shelves. He snatched the large ring out of the air and headed to the back of the inn to go upstairs. If Ayleen had to guess, he looked close to her age.

"Want anything while you wait?" the bartender asked.

Ayleen palmed the pouch on her belt to test the weight of her coins. A bounty she'd hunted down on Anteres III had improved her financial situation. The purses of the highwaymen who attacked her while traveling through the scorched forests on Selphus had added a little more after she'd killed them.

Deciding she had the coin to spare, she pointed to a bottle of Mithian Brandy on the wall behind the bartender. The fat, square bottle only had a quarter of its amber contents left, but it would be enough to help her forget all the dead people in her life long enough to sleep.

She exchanged a few coins for the bottle and a short, stout glass she wouldn't bother with once she reached her room. The first sip went down warm and smooth. Nice to see the drink matched the label, rare it did.

The inn's collective body heat, paired with the fire near the back, made her sweat. She resisted the urge to pull off her hat to wipe her brow.

A large blackboard covered most of the wall behind the bar. Numbers and names were written in yellow chalk. They were grouped in a manner that suggested some kind of order to it, but she was too tired to decipher it.

By the time she'd emptied her glass for the second time, Crim returned.

Ayleen saw herself to her room. Turned out to be one of the more spacious places she'd stayed. Her window looked over the street and the park. The wind whistled and battered the shutters. No one moved out in the lamplight.

She pulled off her hat, wiped her brow on her sleeve, and tossed the hat onto the foot of the bed.

The door included a lock, but she still slid the chest of drawers with a fierce shriek to block the way into her room. She set the glass on her nightstand and took a pull from the bottle of brandy while she listened for anyone to follow her upstairs. None did.

Didn't take long for the brandy to fulfill its intended purpose. With her vision dancing in pleasant circles, she slipped off her belt and scabbard. The crystal sword dropped to the floor as if to knock against the chatter of the customers below. She fell into the bed with a laugh.

The building stupor came a breath from claiming her for the night when she felt and heard a blast of mystic energy.

Ayleen leaped off the bed and ripped her sword from its scabbard. She threw open the window, and the cold wind flooded her room. A few shouts carried up to her from outside the inn. The panic and confusion in their tone eliminated any of Ayleen's suspicions they were responsible for the small explosion.

A couple ran out the front of the tavern and pointed in the direction of the keyhole. Ayleen leaned out her window. No flames or smoke. The blue energy stirred within her crystal sword's blade. It recognized the power released from one of its shattered sisters, an untamed crystal so small that it served no purpose save one.

"Cats and toads," Ayleen cursed.

Her sword's anger yearned for red, wet satisfaction drawn from enemies. The blade would get its taste soon enough. Crystals provided many uses that defied the old doctrines of science. Whoever shattered the sliver of crystal intended it to summon someone. Sure, the one summoned might be not be after Ayleen, but the Fates saw no reason to treat her with such kindness.

A fresh wave of dizziness forced Ayleen to pull back into her room and shut the window. She cursed as she returned her sword to its scabbard. Her body crumpled back into the bed. Whoever the crystal was calling here couldn't be that close. She'd sleep now and strike out at daylight. Odds favored she'd need the rest for whoever was coming for her.

3.

The first rays of sunlight dragged Ayleen from her warm bed. She fell into her clothes and shoved her blue hair back up under her hat as she had the previous night. She needed to get out of here before the Thirteen found her. Much as she was itching for that fight, she needed to delay it until she'd gotten the necessary knowledge to destroy them. The grimoire she'd found in Griffin and could now read hadn't offered any answers there, and it made the price she'd paid for the Fate's venom that much worse.

The bar sat empty with the alcohol locked up behind black, metal doors. The only light came from the pink neon sign in the window.

As she passed the last booth before the door, someone moved in the seat facing the front of the inn.

"Shite!" Crim's wide eyes crossed, focused on the tip of Ayleen's swiftly-drawn sword, an inch from his nose. He shook, but wisely didn't stand.

"Both hands flat on the table." Ayleen shifted her eyes to confirm no one else was hiding in the other booths. "Nice and slow."

Neither said a thing until he did as he was told.

"What are you doing down here?" she asked.

"Fell asleep. Please don't tell Ms. Niobe. Was supposed to make sure no one tried to break in after we closed. Everyone's on edge after that explosion last night."

He tried to look at her as he answered, but to Ayleen's amusement, her sword's threat to slit open his nose proved too great a distraction.

"I don't plan on sticking around long enough to rat you out." She stepped back and slid her sword into its wooden scabbard.

"Why—?" A long yawn interrupted his question as he glanced at the clock behind the bar. "Why you up so early?"

"Business." She took another step towards the door. "Which is none of yours."

He slid out from the booth and stretched. His fingertips almost caressed the ceiling.

"Then I hope you know where you're going," he said in a fashion suggesting he doubted she did.

"Why's that?"

"Tower bandits." He walked behind the bar and knocked on the blackboard with the names and numbers. "Folks living in the old sky-highs. They're scavengers. Some say they're cannibals, too, but I think that's shite."

He unlocked the shelves behind the bar and pulled out a bottle filled with a pale blue liquid.

Ayleen studied all of the chalk markings on the board.

"Betting board?" she asked.

Crim sipped some of the bluish drink from a shot glass. "Yeah. Every few years, time topples a building. Folks bet on which one goes next and when." He pointed to his name. "I got ten silvers on the Will's Tower. Tall sumbitch."

Ayleen didn't recognize the calendar these people used. Certainly wasn't based on the Ascension Date system the Knighthood used, but she could reason it with what was here. "You're betting on next year?"

He raised his hand and crossed his fingers in answer. "You want a guide?"

"Depends on how many coins it'll cost." Her tone made it clear she wasn't willing to offer anything else.

"Depends on where you're going."

She studied his smile, the kind that had probably suckered a few girls into his bed. "No, I'll pay you two silvers to guide me and another two for discretion."

He made a show of thinking over the offer. The tip of his index finger dipped into his drink, stirred it around, and then he licked the finger clean. "Make it an even five, and you got a deal."

She crossed her arms. Just because she was flush on coins, she wasn't going to toss them around. "Five ain't an even number."

He made a poor show of pretending to muffle his laugh. "It is if you want a guide."

"You want to be odd about it," she said, flashing a syrup-sweet smile, "I'll make it three."

For such a big boy, he pouted like a puppy dog. Only thing missing from the frown and slouch was a whimper.

"You want the four coins," she said, "then get your shite, and we leave now."

The way he grumbled suggested he didn't trust her. "I want half up front."

She slapped two coins on the counter and trapped them beneath her hand. "I said to get your shite. Make it quick, or I won't be here and neither will the coins."

They walked out the front door less than five minutes later with two silvers in Crim's pocket.

4.

The wind slapped them like a beast of burden's tail whipping at gnats.

Ayleen used a leather cord to keep her hat from flying off. The hat had come with it, but she'd never cared for the look of it. Usually kept the bit of leather in her pack for tying her hair.

"We're nearing the edge of town," Crim shouted back at her. "Wanna tell me where we're going so we don't end up adding clicks we don't need."

The edge of town couldn't be more obvious. The converted park and its surrounding streets were kempt. Beyond the town, debris from bricks, steel beams, and bones covered what remained of the asphalt. The sensation called to mind when she stepped into a keyhole on a world with a semblance of order and exited onto a planet in disrepair.

"I'm seeking the Orlander Library," she said.

He nodded without looking back at her. "That'll take a couple days. Gotta get around the Jonck Tower to get there. Collapsed back when I was two. Direct routes to the library are blocked. Lotta scavengers hole up in the Chower, so gotta avoid them."

Crim pointed towards the intersection ahead of them. A tall pole was bent so far that the side of the green sign at the end of it touched the ground. Elaborate characters provided the names of destinations with arrows showing which direction to go with numbers for the clicks to travel.

Crim glanced over his shoulder at Ayleen. "You know how to read ancient Vidian Basic?" He didn't sound like he expected her to.

Ayleen glanced at the fallen sign, considering it a moment longer before she answered him. "No, why?"

"Not surprised. People stopped using it a few centuries back. Used to be pretty common." He pointed at himself with a thumb. "Lucky for you, I'm one of the few around these parts who can read it."

"How fortunate for me." Her lack of enthusiasm coated her words in sarcasm.

He stopped to study the sign. Ayleen made her own assessment of it, waiting in silence to see which way Crim directed them to go.

"Gotta go this way." He pointed straight ahead.

As they crossed the intersection, Ayleen checked to her right and left. The road to the left went only two blocks before a tall pile of fallen glass and steel obstructed any travel. The road to the right appeared to be a clear shot for many clicks.

"About seven clicks this way." Crim pointed the way he was taking them. "We shouldn't run into many scavengers long as we stay on this road. Lotta cyber packs run along Daemon Street, night and day." He invoked the words "cyber packs" the way an older sibling taunts their kid brother about the monster under the bed.

"And those would be?"

"Metal beasts. They'll ignore us as long as we don't try to steal or break anything—two things scavengers are known to do."

Ayleen glared at Crim's back. She didn't care for the way he said the word "scavenger." He equated it with filth and excrement. Losing the Knights of the Way and her home... Was she different from any other soul living off what this decaying Galaxy vomited into their needy path? The water pack on her back was the third she'd worn since beginning her hunt for the Thirteen.

These scavengers wanted to live.

Ayleen wanted to kill.

She didn't warn Crim against his tone. Several clicks into their journey, she decided his fate.

5.

They stopped at nightfall. Crim led them to a building with its top half sheared off about ten stories up. Even without the entire building visible, she could make out the structure's unusual design that made it wider as it went up.

"One of the neighboring buildings fell when I was three." Crim glanced around them, his eyes shifted to the surrounding towers as if looking for the vacancy the collapse would have created. After a moment, he turned his attention back to her as if surprised she was still there.

He pointed to a path in the debris for them to take. Someone had gone to the trouble of pushing the glass and fistfuls of cement aside that led to an entrance. Certainly, it wasn't one of the doors, just an open frame that once housed a pane of glass.

Crim turned on a flashlight he'd brought. "Loudest damn thing I've ever heard when this building and the other went down. Happened middle of a super tornado. Ripped through here. Took out a few other towers, too. Winds swung the neighboring building like a club and decapitated this one."

"If this is suitable for us, then won't there be scavengers?" Ayleen kept her hand on her sword, ready to draw it.

"Not likely." He stopped to sweep his light across the floor's dark grey tiles and rotted red carpet. The walls of their path were formed from the fallen debris of white brick and steel beams. Some places revealed some of what this building must have been like back in its days of use. The ceiling reached high enough to be lost in shadow. Crim took them towards what Ayleen suspected was the far corner of the bottom floor.

"What's left keeps caving in." Crim turned back towards her, flashing his light on her face as if that was supposed to help her see him instead of blind her. "But don't you worry. I'm taking us to one of the more structurally safe spots."

They stopped in what resembled a hallway with a curved ceiling. Crim stood with his hands on his hips admiring the spot he'd chosen for them. "My pa says, when it comes to stability, triangles and arches are the best shapes. Figure that makes this a good spot for us."

"You figure?" Ayleen didn't voice her opinion of his pa's theory or Crim's application of it.

The pack dropped from Crim's back with a soft bounce, landing on the side containing his bed roll. "I figure it's safer than being out after dark with the cyber packs. They catch you out there once the sun's crawled under the horizon, they'll put a spike in your head. Even the scavengers have enough sense to hide by sunset."

Ayleen glanced over her shoulder into the black maw they'd traversed to get in this disintegrating behemoth. She considered leaving and taking her chances, because she didn't trust this boy. Only once Crim unfurled the blanket he'd brought with him and wrapped himself up in it, did she slip off her water pack.

"How long the charge on your torch gonna last?" Ayleen pointed to his flashlight.

"Can last a couple days, but only if we don't run it all night. I'll turn it off as soon as you get settled."

She unrolled her thin bedroll with a loud snap.

"Can get cold at night," Crim said in a playful singsong. "Can share some warmth, if you want?"

The light and shadows fell on him, making his face resemble a skull with a pinprick of light to glitter in the middle of each eye socket.

"I'll pass." Besides, she needed to see what he planned once the artificial light went away and left them in shadow.

No matter what he intended, Crim wouldn't see the morning's light.

6.

Things might have gone better for Crim if all he'd planned was to force himself on Ayleen. The most she would have done was slit his throat.

The steady in and out of somnolent breathing confirmed he'd fallen asleep right quick. Ayleen waited until enough time passed for his spirit to touch the ephemeral waters that surround the island of the dream spirit Yumenium D'sse.

She drew her sword from the scabbard she'd set on the ground next to her the way a child kept a beloved stuffed animal close for comfort. It whispered with excitement, an endless appetite whetted by the anticipation of blood.

Slipping her cover off, Ayleen whispered to the crystal blade. *"Terastrant."*

The energy within the sword awakened, bathing the confined space in its pale blue light. The confined air buzzed as the glow reached all dark corners except for the hole in Ayleen's soul.

Crim didn't stir as she neared him.

She slammed her sword through his right shoulder. His eyes popped opened as he screamed. The strike hit him slow enough for Ayleen to feel the half second of resistance from his bone, the way it cracked apart shivered up through the sword into her hands. Another jolt rippled through the hilt and up her arms as the blade buried into the floor.

Ayleen planted the heel of her boot below his throat.

When his cries paused long enough, she leaned close enough for her face to fill his vision. "Daa landee dradhain."

"What—!" he reached towards her leg to move her foot from his chest, but she jerked the sword in warning, drawing another scream from him. "What're you doing!"

"Daa landee dradhain." Her hands shook with rage. She translated each word with heavy-handed enunciation. "It's Vidian Basic. It means 'You are lying filth'."

His eyes twitched a little too long, betraying his next lie before he spoke it. "No one speaks it anymore. I can just read it."

"So can I!"

A stillness passed over him as he realized what that meant, and then the panic hit, wide eyes and shaking lips.

She twisted the sword in him a little more. He shrieked. Her sword hummed in her mind with delight, begging to make him sing more.

The street signs had pointed to where the Orlander Library should be, and he'd led her true for most of the way, but an hour before sunset, he'd done nothing but take her away from it. She'd given him enough time to see if he might correct his course, an indication his intentions were benevolent and avoiding any hazards, but each turn had pushed them down all the wrong streets. All he had to offer her was information on who'd paid him.

He didn't dare speak now, not without permission.

"How many are coming?"

"Don't know." His held up his hands in surrender. "She didn't tell me any of that!"

"She?"

He swallowed between ragged breaths. "Didn't give a name. Bounty hunter. Said there was a good chance you'd come here."

His words jolted her enough to straighten her back and ease the pressure on his throat. How in Rushiferum's Pit had this bounty hunter known?

"Did she have a sword like this?"

He shook his head, doing his best not to shift his torso around the crystal sword still shoved through him.

"She's an archer."

"Describe her."

"Humanoid. Almost as tall as me." He moved his left hand as he gestured to suggest this bounty hunter stood eye-level to him. "Got white hair with purple streaks down to the middle of her back. Silver eyes. Tanned, but not as dark as you. Looked between forty and fifty. Brown leather jacket and black denim pants. Mean thing with lots of money. Gave me thirteen silvers and promised me seventeen more if I set off the crystal near the keyhole and led you here."

Ayleen formed a mental picture of this archer as best she could. Didn't resemble anyone from the Knighthood she knew.

"How long have I got?" When he only answered with a confused stare, she added, "Before she gets here. How long have I got?"

"Swore she'd make it here in less than a day." His body shook as he muttered panicked curses to himself. "Half-expected her to be out there when we reached this place. Take you out before we got inside."

That explained the way he'd behaved before they entered this place, staring up at the neighboring buildings. Looking back on it, he'd gotten all nervous, adding some distance between them.

But for this archer to make it here that quickly…

"That's impossible." Ayleen pressed down on his chest with her boot. "How did she know I'd be here?"

"I don't know." He must have seen the disbelief in her face, because his eyes widened in panicked anticipation of the punishment she planned to inflict. "I swear!"

"Where was she coming from?"

"I don't—" His answer turned into a scream as she twisted her sword again.

"Unless you plan on sharing something else useful, don't expect me to let you live."

He laughed through gritted teeth. "Oh, cute. Like you'd let me walk away from this."

"I'm promising to let you live, but you gotta give me something."

"Said if she didn't take her shot when we got here, she'd get you at sun up."

She responded with an anticipatory stare as if to ask if that was all he had.

"I swear. Don't know anything else."

"What you told me about those cyber packs the truth?"

He nodded, as if she was crazy to doubt his word. "Kill anyone they catch out at night."

"And the bit about the scavengers?"

He grimaced. "I might have made that up. Those folks all live three days south of here where the cyber packs don't hunt."

After a moment of silence that made it clear he'd shared all he had, she nodded to him. "Deal's a deal."

She ripped the sword out of his shoulder, spun around, and slammed it down a few inches above his right ankle. Despite the blanket covering his legs, no missing the wrongness in the placement of his foot's lump compared to the rest of the leg.

He screamed loud enough to hurt her ears. By the time he'd worked his way from pain to denial, tears streaked down his face. He stammered in disbelief. "You—but—you said—"

"I promised to let you live." She used his blanket to wipe his blood from her sword. "Never said you'd walk away from this."

She packed her belongings, along with some of Crim's food and his ample purse. He hurled insults, threats, and curses at her between pained grunts. Ignoring him was simple enough. She focused on what awaited her in Kurega's streets.

Metal beasts.

An archer.

The cold.

Blood.

7.

The fallen building and the wind's howl muffled Crim's shouts. With any luck, this archer hadn't heard anything amiss, assuming she was out there.

The luminescent, gray curves of clouds formed strange beasts as they galloped in and out of moonlight. Tiny bits of glass from shattered windows twinkled as they blew down the street like fallen stardust.

Nothing else within Ayleen's line of sight moved.

If the archer was there, would she be awake and watching? Whoever she was, she'd anticipated Ayleen's decision to come here. How?

She pushed those questions aside. The most important thing to figure out was as obvious as it was complicated. Where would this archer perch?

The surrounding buildings provided plenty of vantage points. Every one of them contained glass exteriors with dozens of yawning mouths. The archer might wait several steps inside the building, concealed by shadows. She'd need to be able to see Ayleen, though. That meant she'd need to stay on one of the lower levels. Too high up, and she'd be forced to lean out the window, revealing her position. Even with those firm assumptions, the archer still had too many options.

The wind howled louder. Ayleen nodded as if to answer a suggestion in its call. Wherever this archer placed herself, she'd want to shoot with the wind, not against it. That would improve her range and accuracy. She'd want to be as close as possible. Bows and arrows provided a reach swords didn't have, but the more distance Ayleen gained, the better her chances.

That narrowed down things, but how to get past her opponent? She could limit her movements, slipping from shadow to shadow to avoid notice, but the placement of the moons worked against her. The brightest moon was directly above, leaving almost nowhere for Ayleen to hide. No, she'd need to sprint. If Ayleen ran straight at the building with the archer in it, the angle would protect her from most shots. Unfortunately, that also provided a few critical seconds for her foe to shoot her at close range.

This side of the street didn't offer any protection, not until Ayleen reached the far side of this building and turned at the intersection.

Instead, she decided to run for the far corner of the building across the street. Still a gamble, but it would keep the most distance between her and the archer and expose her for the least possible amount of time.

She worked through the distance in her mind and added in the strength of the wind thrusting all manner of debris down the street. She'd be running against that.

Half a minute. That's what she gave herself. Thirty seconds that might take her to safety or turn into her last moment.

She shoved her sword back into its scabbard. Focused her breathing—deep in, long out. Fingers flexed, clenched, flexed, clenched.

She let her hat fall against her back, the leather string kept it from falling off.

Thirty seconds, she thought to herself.

Her legs bent into a slight crouch, and then she ran for it.

8.

The screaming wind hit her in the face as she took the turn into the open. Each breath of cold night cut down her throat.

Five seconds.

Her feet dodged the ever-shifting dirt and wind-shaved bits of city stuff tumbling across the ground towards her like rolling tumbleweed.

Ten seconds.

Moonlight bathed the intersecting street up ahead in soft, blue light. Once she turned the corner into the moonlight, she'd be safe.

She pushed her legs to move faster. Her hat bounced against her back as its string hugged her throat.

Fifteen seconds.

The first arrow buried into the dirt a few steps ahead of her.

The shock of its appearance in her path slowed her, despite her strongest intent to do otherwise.

The angle of the arrow confirmed what she'd suspected, where her foe had hidden.

Her old trainer's scratchy voice warned her from some lesson in her past. *"Some of the best archers miss that first shot, because they get the distance and the wind wrong. Their second shot? That's the one that'll kill you."*

Twenty seconds.

The blue moonlight of the intersection laughed at her. She'd never make it to the corner.

She changed direction, darting straight at the archer's building as the second arrow came at her. The arrow missed and scraped across the sidewalk instead.

The archer's presence loomed, still unseen, to her left. Ayleen drew her sword.

Twenty-five seconds.

The bit of life within the crystal sword laughed with wicked merriment. Ayleen swung it, spinning her body around as she did so. The arc of the blade collided with yet another steel shaft meant for her. The deflected arrow hissed across the street's asphalt.

Thirty seconds.

The building's shadow pulled her in like a pair of comforting arms. The security of the dark ended the instant she entered it, though.

A figure jumped out of the building from the third floor. A thick rope kept the woman from plummeting to the ground. It only kept one of her hands free, though. She needed both to shoot an arrow. That didn't stop her from throwing something.

The weapon shredded into Ayleen's right shoulder blade. Freezing metal and boiling pain rippled through her back.

She turned the corner, placing her beyond the archer's reach for the moment. She searched the barren street for cover. The best option was a flying wagon on its side with no hope of ever being airborne again.

Despite the wind, the sound of pounding boots on the cement sidewalk warned the archer had made it around the building, too. The footfalls slowed but didn't stop.

No chance to reach the wagon. Ayleen answered her instincts. She turned in time to see an arrow rocket at her. Ayleen swung her crystal sword at the projectile in case her attempt to dodge it failed. The edge of the blade collided with the arrow. The steel shaft didn't break. The arrow bounced off the sword with a high-pitched chime.

The archer never slowed her advance and shot another arrow before Ayleen deflected the first. The arrowhead shaved against her left arm, easily cutting through the leather of her jacket and the shirt beneath to draw blood from her bicep.

Fresh pain. Not from the arrow cutting her arm. Something hit the weapon stabbed into her back.

She jerked her body to the right, trying to escape whatever had struck the thing in her shoulder blade. The sudden shift saved her from the archer's boot that was aimed at her stomach. The archer's momentum sent her flying past Ayleen. She landed on her feet, out of arm's reach.

The thing in Ayleen's shoulder blade shifted again. That's when Ayleen realized her hat was bouncing against it. No way to reach the damn thing to pull it out, so she swung her sword between her and the archer, giving her a second to pull her hat onto her head.

The archer pulled another arrow from the quiver on her hip. Ayleen pressed her attack, aiming for the bow and preventing the archer from nocking the arrow.

Eyes locked on the face of this stranger determined to kill her. She wasn't one of the Thirteen. The ephemeral tug that tainted all things in their paths didn't cling to her.

They traded blows. The archer blocked Ayleen's sword with her bow, angling it with calculated moves to prevent the edge of the sword from cutting through it. When the archer tried to bury her arrowhead in Ayleen's chest, Ayleen grabbed her wrist. The woman's eyes bulged in disbelief as Ayleen's grip tightened and twisted, close to snapping her bones.

A kick to Ayleen's hip forced them apart.

A ray of light from overhead blinded them before they could renew the fight. A high-pitched whoop deafened Ayleen. She raised her forearm to shield her eyes from the light, wishing she could do the same for her ears.

"Citizens!" The voice, four octaves deep, followed the series of loud whoops. *"You are in violation of curfew ordinance zero-four-one-three-point-two-three-zero and additional municipal ordinances. Cease all hostilities, drop all weapons, and present proper identification. Failure to do so will result in lethal force."*

"Shite." The archer moved in a blur. An arrow hissed up at the bright light. It struck with a clang and the light shattered, returning the street to darkness.

Ayleen blinked as her eyes readjusted. A series of smaller lights, flashing red in the sky outlined the sphere floating above her.

The archer shouted after her. "Come on!"

Had the flying sphere's voice fractured this woman's brain? Less than a minute earlier, she'd wanted Ayleen dead.

Ayleen followed, not because she trusted this archer, but because she might have the thing that brought Ayleen here in the first place: answers about the Thirteen.

The sphere whooped its alarm, buzzing through the wind in pursuit.

"Citizens, stop or you will be met with lethal force. Pacification units are responding."

The archer cursed, and the reasons marched out of the shadows further down the street. Small lights blinked on their torsos, giving their shapes definition in the dark. Each stood more than six feet tall, humanoid in shape but with four arms instead of two. A horizontal bar of light on their heads where eyes belonged blinked back and forth between red and blue. As they emerged into moonlight, the steel-grey, armored enforcers twirled long staffs in one hand. Long barrels spun at the end of the lower two arms. The human shape didn't include the heads, which resembled large dogs with long, black snouts. The heads had partially decayed with sections of their dull, white skulls exposed where their fur had rotted off. A few had lost one or both of their tall, pointed ears.

"Citizens, stand down now," the flying sphere's voice boomed, *"or pacification units will meet you with lethal force!"*

"I'd pay a hefty purse for that damn thing to shut it," the archer said, though it wasn't clear if she was addressing Ayleen or thinking out loud.

The pacification units raised their arm barrels and thick, metal spikes flew at Ayleen and the archer. The sound of the concussive blasts reached them a second slower. The spikes missed, though one came within a breath of Ayleen's thigh.

Ayleen and the archer ducked into an alley between two buildings. Before they rounded the corner, the archer shot an arrow at the flying sphere. Its angry whoops ended with a low whine, followed by a smashing sound suggesting it had crashed into one of the building's windows.

Growls and barks chased them into the alley. Ayleen glanced over her shoulder to see the cyber pack had dropped onto four "legs," with their barrel-ended arms raised out to their sides to shoot more spikes. Their staffs rested along their backs with the pointed ends reaching ahead of them like knightless horses in a joust. The damn things planned to spear them. The alley ended against the brick wall of another building. A door hung half-open to their right, so Ayleen and the archer ran inside. Spikes bit into the wall at the end of the alley with loud clinks suggesting they'd buried deep into the bricks.

Ayleen slammed the door shut behind her.

"Keep it closed!" the archer shouted as she flipped on a black, slender torch. Its luminescent beam cut through the dark to reveal a room filled with pipes. The door had a large set of bolts, five of them of differing color and design, that looked like someone had added them in an act of desperation long after this building's construction. Ayleen slid all of them into place to secure the door.

"That should hold," Ayleen turned to see the woman scrambling through the room in a desperate search for something. Before the archer could answer, the door jerked in its frame with a loud thud. Another followed with a sharp scraping noise as one of the spears pierced the steel door. The spear jerked out and loud strikes against the door suggested the pacification units planned to break it down.

The archer grabbed the end of a large metal cabinet that had fallen onto its side. "Help me move this!"

Ayleen did as asked. The cabinet was too heavy to lift. It screeched along the concrete floor. A spike shot through the hole left by the spear and slammed into the archer's thigh. She screamed and only stayed upright by clinging to the cabinet. With a last effort, in which they both shouted curses, they shoved the makeshift barricade against the door.

The cabinet muffled the thuds and the sound of other spikes that failed to breach the new barrier.

Leaning against the cabinet, the two women laughed. Then the laughter stopped. Their faces sobered. They'd removed their mutual enemy—for the moment—leaving them with only each other to kill.

9.

The archer took a single step back. The space didn't afford her more room than that to retreat. The hand the archer used to draw her arrows reached up with her fingers splayed.

"If I'd wanted y'dead, I could have shot you while y'held the door closed."

The muffled thuds of the pacification units continued.

"Wouldn't have done you much good, seeing as you needed those things kept outside as much as I did."

"I'm a fast runner."

"Not now." Ayleen pointed with an empty hand at the archer's leg.

"Seems we both have wounds to deal with." The woman's smile formed deep lines in her middle-aged face. The shadows added a few more years.

Ayleen resisted the urge to glance over her shoulder at whatever the woman had hit her with.

The archer held out her hands as if to offer something ephemeral. "Help me with my leg, and I'll see to your shoulder."

"Turn my back to you?" Ayleen's fingers itched to finish this woman. The life within her sword moaned in anticipation of the kill. "I'll manage on my own."

The archer pointed a thumb towards the blockaded door. The thuds had lessened.

"I reckon those machines know another way to reach us in here. We need to move before that happens."

Ayleen gestured away from the door, the only way they had left to go. "You first."

The archer hobbled down the corridor, placing her free hand on the wall to keep some weight off the injured leg.

They found some stairs and climbed, no easy task given the archer's wound. Ayleen fought down the urge to help her, but ignored her sword's advice to slice off the whole damn leg and leave her for the robots.

Four stories up, they stopped at the most secure space they'd seen. Whatever name had adorned the entrance was reduced to three letters, "ank." The doors were made of metal. They included an elaborate series of bolts connected to a wheel on the back of the door. Turning the wheel required both of them.

The space didn't offer much in the way of comfort. Bits of wood littered the floor, scraps that once belonged to chairs or some other type of furniture. A counter was placed near the far wall with a thick, clear plastic barrier above it to keep anyone from getting behind it but with a small space near the bottom to allow people to pass things from one side to the other. The shattered window behind the counter gaped with its jagged remains for teeth to bite anyone foolish enough to climb through it.

A metal door, less hospitable than the one they'd closed, was shut. They tried to open it, but it wouldn't budge. A square set of 25 buttons, each displaying an archaic character, was placed in the middle of the door with a black, glass rectangle above it. They pressed the buttons with the characters on them, but nothing happened.

They sat on the wooden floor, although the archer required Ayleen's help to do it. The archer rested her back against the counter. Ayleen sat across from her, in the middle of the room. Leaning back against anything wasn't really an option for her.

"What is it you want?" Ayleen bit out the words like a threat.

The archer turned her injured leg in her hands. A wide, dark stain covered a portion of her denim pants, where the spike still stuck out of her. She'd left it in her leg to limit blood loss. "A bandage would be nice."

"Nice isn't a word I'd apply to our lack of options."

The archer clicked off her flashlight, concealing her in shadows. Ayleen bathed in the moonlight feeding in from behind the counter.

"You'll like this part." The archer smiled as she tugged at her shirt's left sleeve. After several tries, she ripped it free from where the seam had connected the sleeve to the rest of the shirt. "Yank this thing out of my leg." When Ayleen didn't move, the archer added a saccharine "Please."

Against her better judgment, Ayleen grabbed the spike. The archer positioned the ripped sleeve beneath her leg, hands gripped around each end. She took a deep breath and closed her eyes. "Okay. On three."

"Sure."

"One..." The single number warped into a loud curse as Ayleen ripped the spike from the leg. Blood bubbled from the wound, widening the circle of darkness on her jeans leg. Eyes wide and breath ragged, the archer jerked her makeshift bandage tight.

Ayleen ignored the archer as she knotted her bandage into place. Instead, she held the spike up to the light. Bits of flesh clung to the tip of the spike, which had sprouted points like a miniature mace.

"Now that," the archer paused taking a few quick breaths, her bloody hands shaking at her sides. "That fit my expectations of you."

"My mother always complained I was rude to strangers."

Her body limp, the archer leaned back again. "That's what I didn't expect." The words, heavy and weary, dripped from her lips—a dirge spoken, not sung. "Still a child."

"I'm nineteen." She assumed she was. Being flung eight centuries into the future hadn't helped matters, but that wasn't what muddled the count.

"Got the look, though." The shadows hid the archer's face but not the shake of her head. "My ma called it traveler's tan. Less to do with walking in different suns, though."

Ayleen nodded back. "My parents called it a DET glow."

The archer wore the same look. Crim described her as middle-aged, but she carried more years than that. Odds favored she'd lost track of her age, same as Ayleen. Each world measured its days in different hours. Some wore their seasons as if they fell out of fashion before putting them on. Others clung to them the way one might to a lost love rediscovered. Without a stable home, age became a thing defined by how old a person felt. Ayleen didn't think she'd ever pass nineteen, not until she found a way to put the Thirteen to her sword and their final deaths.

Age hadn't stolen the steadiness from this archer's hands. She reached into her vest and removed a hand-rolled smoke, spinning it the way Dara had made coins dance between her fingers. "Want one?"

"No." Ayleen didn't hide her revulsion as the archer lit the end of her lung cookie. Captain Tratella had warned the squires in Ayleen's academy against smoking, the way it corrupted the lungs. She admonished them strongest when smoke spilled up from her mouth and a cigarette dangled between her lips.

"I need one rightly fierce." The tip of the cigarette flared as she sucked in a breath of smoke, then let it roll out. "So, what'd y'do to that boy?"

"Left him alive but shy one foot."

The archer clapped her hands together, laughing around the cigarette. "Figured you'd kill him."

"We came to an arrangement. He gave me information," Ayleen glared, "about you."

The archer nodded, as if Ayleen had breathed something profound into the space between them.

"Information makes for valuable currency." The archer looked away from Ayleen, not so much a turn of the head as an unfocusing of the eyes.

"You buying or selling?" Ayleen asked.

"Let's start with me taking my star outta your back."

"What makes you think I trust you to do it?"

"The fact I'm still breathing. Now, shut up and scoot over here."

The archer's touch proved every bit as gentle as Ayleen's had. She cursed about as loud as the archer had, too.

She mourned her pristine, purple shirt. She'd need to find someone to mend it. The shirt reminded her of Griffin, which reminded her yet again of Dara, and that forced her imagination to consider her as a dead thing floating on a spider's back. The effort to forget never worked. It only added more guilt to the till. A new shirt wouldn't change things, but that didn't stop her from hoping and regretting.

"I'm selling." The archer used the end of her one-time sleeve turned bandage to wipe the blood from her throwing star. "We can settle accounts after I share. For now, let's be starting with my name. Bonita Ferrati, but the Thirteen simply call me the Wolf."

10.

"They found me not long after I started hiring out my services. Didn't know I was working for them, not at first. Never forget the day Mera Javo sat across from me. I see you know the name. Straight up bitch that one, and she ain't changed a bit since the day I met her. Was a little older than you, coming into my traveler's tan. She offered me work, right fair amount of it, too. Wanted some alive, but most dead.

"The Thirteen made me wealthy. Made it easy to ignore what they are: walking entropy. Didn't think their taint touched me, but then I tried to get outta the game, set down some roots. Bought a ranch to raise cattle. Found a world the Thirteen hadn't corrupted and wouldn't think t'find me, a place that hadn't lost its Way. Only, it had. Didn't recognize it, because it was still higher on the slope than most worlds. As long as I'd lingered around those bastards, I'd lost the ability to suss out the taint. Y'see, selling your soul is like swimming in a pool. Y'think so long as y'stay outta the deepest end, you'll stay right fine. Only once y'get where it's over y'head... deep, deeper, and deepest stop mattering."

The Wolf bowed her head, and the smoke from her cigarette drifted up in a sad spiral through the moonlight.

"Keeping my ranch running, my people fed and cared for, ate through my blood money 'til I was digging through every pocket of every shirt, on the slim hope of pulling out some coins. Never wanted a family—still don't—but don't mean I dodged having others depending on me. I got people—good souls who don't know the predator they work for—hands only ever covered in honest dirt. None of them suss the blood on the money I give them, because it never sticks to the coins, only my hands. Right that is, too.

"Month ago, I was down to a handful of workers—folks with a family, three kids. I'd ridden into town, playing cards on the chance of bringing home more than I left with. Y'can guess how that played.

"Somewhere between the road and my house, I smelled death. One of my cattle was dropped in a bloody mess, the front and back halves parted. Only one kind of blade can carve a beast that big in a single stroke." The Wolf's eyes, catching the glow of her cigarette's burning tip, tilted towards Ayleen's crystal sword as if she could hear the pride-filled laughter coming from it. "Saw the front door sitting wide open. Candlelight burned inside, enough to see her silhouette. No question it was Mera Javo. Part of me welcomed her. Didn't matter if she'd come t'hire me or kill me. Latter sounded better at the time.

"She wasn't alone, though.

"I've stared down arrow shafts at many a monster. Men three times my size made of nothing but muscle… black-furred goonians with blood dripping from their jaws… once chased down a dragon as big as an elephant. Way people talk about Pyre Clypse, you expect the most hideous beast on two legs, and I suppose he is."

The Wolf's hand shook as she paused for a long drag from her shrinking cigarette.

"Saw him sitting at my table soon as I walked into my house. Nothing spectacular about him. Had brown hair, thinning by the looks of it, atop a round head. Pale-skinned, he was. Had some meat to his cheeks, drooping like some hound dog. Was a face made for smiling, not that you'd ever wanna see the Devil find a reason t'smile at you. Wore a dark red, velvet vest over a snow white shirt. Reminded me of what a grandfather ought t'look like—the kindly sort. He stirred in a small spoonful of sugar into a cup of coffee he'd taken from my kitchen. Looked up at me… Second those black eyes met mine, I felt fear I hadn't known in all my life.

"Think I dropped into the chair across from him. Dumb luck I landed in the seat and not on the floor.

"When you catch a person looking at you, there's always an acknowledgment, approval or disgust, amusement or hostility. Way Pyre looked at me… I didn't matter. Don't mean t'say he didn't think I mattered. Way that thing stared at me, I finally recognized my place in this Galaxy, and I was less than a drop of piss in an ocean.

"First thing he said t'me… 'You ever listen to Dreun music?'

"I laughed. Was all I could manage. Javo placed a match and a cigarette in front of me. Didn't question the offer. I just lit up and prayed for the smoke t'steady my heart enough t'not drop me dead.

"He kept talking. 'You strike me as a Dreun person. That's the music you write when all you got for ink are the few drops of blood you can wring out of a broken heart that's been stomped on one too many times by an uncaring boot.'

"Told him I'd never spent much time listening t'music. He said t'me, 'That's because you're the broken heart.'

"He didn't need t'tell me he was the boot. Felt the imprint of his soles on my spirit. Been there from the first coin Javo handed me. She didn't say anything until then. Smug thing looked taken down a few pegs compared to usual. About the only pleasant part of that night.

"Bitch said t'me, 'You never got away from us. Just knew we'd gotten our use out of you. After the first couple hundred years, we learned to accept everything—except for us—has its time. Knew you'd run months before you did it. Dark, girl, you stayed on longer than I ever dreamed.'"

The features on the Wolf's face pinched the way a person detests an ache that flares deep into their bones when it rains.

"Focusing on her—maybe more than the smoke—got my ire back. 'Then what're y'doing here?'

"Pyre sipped his coffee. Didn't bother looking at me or Javo as he talked. 'Show her your neck.'

"Oh, that pissed her off. Not the first time I'd seen her that mad, but the only time I'd watched her temper burn without a drop of blood spilled for the cause. I'm not the only one stuck under Pyre's heel.

"Until then, I hadn't given much thought t'the black scarf wrapped around her throat and tucked into her shirt. No missing what was there, though. The scar ran in a crisp, smooth line." She paused to smile down at Ayleen's sword.

Ayleen placed her hand on the hilt, felt the slight vibration as they both remembered when they'd shaved Javo's head from the rest of her and the rage and confusion when some unholy light pulled her back together.

"Woulda liked t'have seen that, but the scar pleased me plenty.

"She didn't give me the details I really wanted. Did it hurt when it happened? Does it still? Devil's rusty nails, I hope so.

"They placed on my table, right in front of me, one of those wanted posters with your face on it. Don't quite get the eyes right do it? Too far apart, not close enough to fit the predator you are.

"He planted a single finger on the paper, right above your face. He says, 'Ayleen Torr is her name. We want her.'

"I took a closer look at the poster. There's the real kicker. They want you alive—preferably.

"Pyre sips his coffee, leaving the terms t'his woman Javo. She'd already tucked her scarf back in place. You might not have gotten her head t'stay off her top, but you left a permanent mark on her pride. Good on you.

"She says, 'We don't like to make people work for us, but we can't settle for second best against this girl. She's a Knight of the Way.'

"You'd think they'd know best how t'corner you, seeing as most of them were knights. Only, I think becoming what they are—the Thirteen—changed them. They don't quite remember or get all the things that used t'make 'em tick. Money they offer me for you, they don't start low. They go high, and I still push 'em for more. If I'm going in for more money with blood on it, way I figure is that I might as well go for the whole damn bank. They don't blink an eye. The money don't matter, and that's a first.

"So I ask them t'tell me about this Ayleen Torr. Stupid fucks start by giving me everything about the way you look except your shoe size. I start getting pissed and press them for what I really need to know.

"Javo picks up on what I mean faster than that thing Pyre. No shock there. Like comparing a rabid dog to a lizard. 'She's a daddy's girl,' Javo tells me. 'Man hopped more keyholes than any other knight lived to tell. Didn't really need a map, he logged the Galaxy in his feet. Got her ambition from her momma, though. Woman rose in the ranks faster than anyone imagined. Went to see the Fates before most mage generals had hopped a keyhole on their first field study.' Said you graduated to knighthood at seventeen, a year younger than your momma managed. Science Regiment wouldn't touch you, though. All knew you were meant for a traveler's tan.

"Don't like hearing about yourself? Can't say I blame you. Hearing compliments from souls y'hate ruins the flavor. She told me plenty. Included the day y'got that unholy blade. Told me how y'made it through the bonding part without a scream—something few did. Way Javo made it sound, the lucky ones fall out early, miss out on most of the shared pain of that hilt getting fucked into submission by the metal that keeps the leather wrapping in place.

"Honestly, all the details Javo gave me. Didn't take long before I stopped listening. You aren't complicated. Y'want blood, revenge. Only you're as lost as this whole Galaxy. You've missed eight hundred years of history, and you need to fill in the blanks."

No missing her smile as Ayleen finally understood how the Wolf had tracked her down so easily. "That's right. Y'needed knowledge, so I placed eyes and ears on the few libraries left standing or close to it. There are better places for what you're after, but a woman running loose with a map of the Galaxy eight centuries behind the times wouldn't know about most of those. Someone from that time, she'd start here on Kurega with the Orlander Library.

"Figured out all that before Javo finished her biography on you. Used the rest of her rant learning about her—about Them." She pointed her cigarette, the nub that was left of it by this point, at Ayleen. "Y'got them scared. They think y'know how to end 'em. Moment I realized that, I knew my plan wasn't to hunt y'down for them. I'm here for me. I want t'know how it's done. What will it take t'wipe those fucker's off the celestial map and clean my hands?"

11.

Ayleen's stomach clenched as this woman finished her story. The Wolf wanted to work together. No, she wanted to kill the Thirteen. A canyon divided that knowledge from any partnership.

Worst of all, the Wolf had pinned her hopes on a falsehood. Ayleen had found a Fate to learn how she might destroy the Thirteen.

She still remembered the direction given to her by the Fate in the spirit dream. *'You must unlock the Castle's Door. Go there, and make the final cuts.'*

Only, the instructions made no sense. Which castle? Was it an actual castle, or was the "Castle's Door" a clever metaphor for something else? And the world she'd seen in her venom-induced dream, a grey sphere of craters with light flowing into it but never out... it wasn't a planet she recognized. As she'd shared the dream with the Fate, the light consumed the small planet. *'Make this happen,'* was what the Fate told her, but what Ayleen needed to cut to fulfill that request, to end the Thirteen, still had no real answer. At best, Ayleen hoped to find something in this planet's library to lead her to the world she'd seen in the vision. But what to do if she got there? Once the Wolf knew Ayleen was nothing but a sharpened blade without a place to strike, what then? Would the Wolf turn on her?

Her trainer's voice instructed her from the past. *"The deadliest sword belongs to a person driven by firm belief."* That's what the Knights of the Way produced, weapons driven by faith in the Way. *"Only thing near as deadly is a warrior who's lost all hope, because they have nothing left to lose, nothing for an opponent to reason with. They can achieve victory even if their enemy's destruction requires their own."*

"So what's the trick t'end their lives?" the Wolf asked. "And what can I do t'help?"

Ayleen needed to make a choice. Did she share her hopes with the enemy's hired hunter, or did she kill this woman before she had a chance to turn on her?

12.

In the end, Ayleen found herself running to the only logical answer. She couldn't risk this woman turning on her when she learned Ayleen knew nothing. Killing her outright gained her the certainty she wouldn't have to worry about an arrow in the heart or brain.

Ayleen stood and stared down at the Wolf as she played her cards. "I have no reason to trust you."

"Y'have every reason. I've already risked plenty by sitting here with you."

"You ain't risked shite. None of them know we're sitting here." As soon as the words left Ayleen's mouth, the Wolf flinched. That's when something obvious presented itself to Ayleen. She drew her sword.

"Crim used a crystal to summon you." Ayleen cursed herself for not considering this sooner.

"A little trick I learned from those bastards." The Wolf had pulled her facade back on, but it was too late. The lie was caught before she spoke it.

"The only person who could sense the call of a summoning crystal is someone with a sword like mine. You don't have one, and the Thirteen wouldn't share that magic with anyone beyond themselves."

The Wolf sighed, and when the pretense of alliance slipped from her expression, the real monster beneath revealed itself. She took one last pull on the cigarette and flicked the stub away, bouncing across the floor and up against the large steel door with the buttons on it.

Her eyes shifted from silver to a familiar shade of amber. "Aren't you the clever child?"

Demon's claws! The voice was still the Wolf's, but the inflection had all changed. The drawl shifted into something more arrogant and cold. The person talking to Ayleen wasn't the woman. This was someone else.

The name tumbled through Ayleen's lips as she withdrew a step. "Pyre Clypse."

The Wolf nodded. Or rather, Pyre made the Wolf nod. When the Wolf had told her story, she'd imitated this foul mystic. She'd come close, but her soul wasn't cold enough to match the real thing.

"You hijacked your own hunter. Does she know?"

Pyre laughed. "Of course she knows, but once the crystal chip embedded itself into her brain, it's not as if she had a choice."

Ayleen knew that was true enough. The grimoire she'd found back on Griffin detailed the profane act of possession. It also warned of the risks to the mage who performed the act, the potential damage to the soul. Something told her Pyre no longer feared such risks. Did the condition of a soul matter to an immortal?

"That whole story she fed me is shite."

Pyre shook her head. "We chose her for her skill at getting into the head of an opponent. She took some creative liberties, twisting the truth a touch for the benefit of plucking your strings. Mera wouldn't waste her sword on a mindless beast."

The sick grin on the Wolf's face told her everything she needed to know. Ayleen's next words came out in a hushed, disgusted voice. "The family working for her."

"Barely more than cattle, but yes. Laid the pieces of them out on her lawn in the shape of an arrow pointing to her door. I wouldn't think that matters to a child who so gladly butchered a town."

"I only killed the ones who raised their swords to me." She pointed her sword at the throat of Pyre's possessed Wolf.

"No, you killed them all. You forced our hands. When they dug up Mera from the mine, she was lifeless. When she revived, the town knew what she was. Can't have that. They were free labor, too distracted by their greed and self-righteous ignorance to understand for whom they really worked."

That explained plenty for Ayleen. The town on Griffin, the people living there, were mining for the type of crystal used to form her sword. "None of them knew they were shipping the crystals to you." A guess, but Ayleen knew it for a fact by Pyre's smile on the Wolf's face.

She considered trying to free the Wolf from the Thirteen's control. The grimoire she carried included the method for retrieving the crystal. Problem was the Thirteen didn't know she had the book of dark science or an ambrosia crystal. The crystal hijacking the Wolf's mind transmitted everything she saw and heard. The instant Ayleen pulled out the book or the crystal, Pyre would know. Bye-bye slim advantage, and there was no guarantee the Wolf wouldn't turn on her once freed.

"Thanks for all the useful information," Ayleen said. "Seems your strategy backfired. Now, I have a name for you, and you've got nothing new on me."

The Wolf leaned forward. Her lips curled into a sickening smile. "Oh, you've given me plenty, Ayleen Torr. "You don't know how to kill us. You've made that clear."

The Wolf's head jerked to her right multiple times as if to shake something loose from in her ear. She canted her head at an unnatural angle, and the voice that came out was once again the Wolf's, but going by her eyes, no one was at home. "I want t'know how it's done. What will it take t'wipe those fucker's off the celestial map and clean my hands?" The stiff posture melted away once the Wolf had finished repeating her earlier question. The dead expression morphed back into Pyre's smug smile. "The look on your face told me all I need to know. You haven't the answer. Why else do you think I'd reveal myself? You've removed any need to fear you.

We will hunt you down at our leisure, and we can take our time. Eternity bends to the Thirteen—to Me.

"You will age. You will tire. You will despair. Then we will crush you and flick you away like a gnat pinched flat between our fingers."

Ayleen knelt to meet Pyre at eye level. "Sounds mighty frightening, boogie man, but you've also given up something I needed to know." She stared into those amber eyes that served as Pyre's lens. "There is a way to destroy you, and the longer I live, the better the chance I'll find it and end you all."

"Best of luck getting off this dying world to make good on that threat, child. What makes you think we'd settle on one hunter to end you?"

Pyre laughed. The arrogant guttural roar of certain victory cut short as the amber light snapped back to the Wolf's silver irises. She gasped, grabbing at her chest as if she'd been drowning.

Ayleen reared her sword back to end her.

"Wait!" The Wolf reached out, fingers splayed in entreaty. "He's not lying. There are at least two dozen hired swords already here. They're not coming straight for you, though. They need to blow up—"

The Wolf's eyes went wide, the eyeballs pressing out of their sockets. The back of her head exploded. Blood, brain matter, and hair coated the counter behind her in a dripping mess reminiscent in its shape to that of a dragonfly. Her upper body, what was left of it, toppled over and planted face first on the floor. Shattered bits of blue crystal glowed in the exposed interior of the Wolf's skull.

The crystal in her brain had shattered. Pyre had sacrificed her to stop her from finishing what she intended to say. That meant whatever she was saying was true. At least 24 hired killers were waiting to end her, but there was something on this planet they didn't want to risk her finding. They intended to blow up the library before

Ayleen reached it. The only reason they hadn't yet was because they needed to hold off until curfew ended and relaxed the threat posed by the pacification units.

Ayleen couldn't risk waiting for sunrise. She needed to get past a city full of killer robots to reach that library with enough time left to find whatever might be in there to help her.

13.

Getting the door open required all of Ayleen's strength. The wheel groaned when it jerked free from its resting position. A loud set of clangs let her know the door's bolts had retracted.

She caught her breath before pulling the door open enough to slip out. Her worst fear was to find the pacification units all huddled up outside, but none of them were there. Their emotionless voices echoed through the building. The space she and the Wolf had hidden must have been soundproof.

Moonlight aided her far enough to reach the stairs, but the silken rays of light wouldn't make the turn into the stairwell to help her see her way down. She'd considered looting the Wolf's belongings. The artificial torch might have been nice, but it would force her to lose a hand for the fight, if it came to that. To see her way, she only needed the sword.

"Mirecce din kurabris."

The enchanted words whispered to her sword made it appear to glow to her, but unlike the spell she usually employed, this light only appeared for her eyes. The light wouldn't reach as far as her other spell, and she'd suffer for this later. The spell not only tampered with the spirit in the sword, but it also reached into her body. The headache behind her eyes the next day would be torture. Given her chances of living to see another day, she considered it a worthwhile trade.

Lights flickered above her. The pacification units had made it past her floor, possibly up to the seventh. She fought the urge to run down the stairs. She needed to reach the library before the Thirteen's hired swords destroyed it, but she'd get there faster with less fighting.

The robotic voices echoed down to her.

"Attention citizens, an authorized police search of this building is in progress. Under ordinance one-three-zero-three-point-zero-eight, your cooperation is required. Failure to comply will be met with..." The building's thick walls muffled the rest as the robot left the stairs.

To her surprise, she reached the bottom floor without conflict. The door at the bottom had a long, horizontal bar to push it open. She waited with her hands on it, listening for any of those robotic enforcers on the other side. Nothing stirred. All she heard came from above.

Ayleen pushed the door open, the handle clicking as she applied pressure to it.

Darkness waited between her and the far end of the lobby. She took one step out of the stairwell, and five bright red and blue lights flared to life. One of the lights belonged to a flying sphere like she'd first encountered on the street. The rest of the pacification units, more dog-faced cyborgs, spun their staffs and raised their spike shooters.

The flying sphere shouted warnings and called for additional units.

Ayleen charged into the middle of the pacification units before they could shoot her. She blocked their staffs with her sword and dagger. The robots tried to set her up for one of the others to finish her, but their synchronized movements lacked creative finesse.

She dipped in and out of their attacks. Her sword's glancing blows shifted the direction of the pacification units' attacks, but it wouldn't finish them off.

"Attadior!" Her sword blazed to life, glowing hot. She targeted their arms with the spike shooters at the end, but even with her sword burning, it wasn't enough to cut through their armor in a single swing. She left deep scars of melted steel along their bodies. The longer she let this play out, the better the chance they'd finish her or that reinforcements would arrive.

The only reason they probably hadn't shot her with their spikes was the risk of shooting each other. With her in the middle of them, they were in each others' line of attack.

Her sword hissed its dissatisfaction. The weapon wanted blood and death. The rotted dog heads atop the cybernetic units left no doubt they were spiritual vacuums.

The staffs also held up to the heat of her sword. Her arms ached, and the sustained heat of the sword threatened to burn her hand. She spotted her opening. The joints that held the limbs in place were covered in a kind of black rubber, designed to expand and collapse like the bellows of an accordion. Ayleen swung for the nearest robot's shoulder joint. The sword ripped through, and the arm slammed to the floor. The stench of burning rubber grew as Ayleen severed all of the pacification units' limbs.

A loud crash from the stairwell warned her more of the cyber pack had arrived. They must have jumped from several stories up to make that much noise. The flying sphere whooped its siren. Metal spikes fired at her. She slashed at the swift sphere and missed as she sprinted for the front of the building. A scattered pile of glass suggested the wide opening here had once been nothing but a massive window. The glass crunched beneath her feet as she raced out onto the sidewalk.

Spikes whispered after her, passing through where she'd been. More metallic feet clanged against asphalt in pursuit.

Part of her regretted not grabbing some sleep when she had the chance. The rush of adrenaline that had kept her going ebbed. Her eyelids grew heavier as pain mounted behind her eyes. The wound in her back was bleeding again, aggravated by the fight in the lobby.

The best she could do was keep ahead of the pacification units. She took enough turns to keep her pursuers off her back while keeping her path to the library as direct as possible. The ground units marched at a brisk pace, but couldn't match her speed. That kept her out of their line of fire, assuming more of them weren't waiting in her path. The flying sphere kept a spotlight on her, though. She wasn't sure if it was a new sphere or if the one shot by the Wolf had repaired itself. Either way, the spotlight narrowed her pupils, reducing her surroundings to a black cloak with faint outlines. She couldn't evade or destroy the sphere, not in the open.

Ayleen darted into a building with its windows and doors still intact. The lobby led into a narrow corridor with lifts that no longer had any power. The other side of the corridor opened into a mirror of the front lobby, leading outside to a large square of asphalt covered in white and yellow lines of chipped paint.

The sphere's light zoomed into view on the ground in the rear lot. Ayleen sprinted back the way she'd come, hoping the light belonged to the sphere that chased her in here and not a new one.

Darkness greeted her as she backtracked. She turned the corner of the nearest neighboring building, sprinting down an alley without any moonlight reaching its bottom.

The sphere's emotionless voice shouted its threats, but she'd gained enough distance to no longer understand the words.

She emerged from the alley onto a street covered in debris. The clutter came up to her knees. She considered climbing the rest of it, but the pile crumbled under her feet, and too many of the jagged edges she saw looked eager to cut her. The fastest way around ended up being three blocks over.

The sky had flipped from black to a starless purple. The first hints of pale red and orange layered into the horizon.

Sunrise.

14.

Ayleen hoped the daylight would stop the pacification units from pursuing her. She didn't think that made sense, but who knew how their damaged brains functioned. They guarded a dead city while enforcing laws from long-deceased masters.

The sun lifted into the sky in the direction she was headed. The orange-red glow half-blinded her and a magic-induced ache bloomed behind her eyes sooner than expected. She grabbed a small bottle from her pouch and swallowed some of its lavender-colored powder, washing it down with a pull from her water pack. She'd have taken more, but she couldn't risk it knocking her out.

An unseen creature screeched from above. Sounded like it might be in one of the buildings, which leaned in on her. Other creatures answered with similar calls.

She'd given up on taking random turns to keep the pacification units off her trail. At this point, the Thirteen's hired swords presented her primary threat. She'd made up the ground Crim cost her. That didn't guarantee she'd reach the library before the people hunting her destroyed it. More likely, they'd stumble along her path and kill her.

Ayleen fell into a pattern of running one block and jogging the next. The winds pushed against her, slowing her down. By the time she spotted a sign suggesting the library was only a few blocks away, the sun no longer harassed her, but it had risen along with the temperature. The wind didn't keep her from sweating.

The library came into view. The white building was shaped like an opened book with its pages flared on the side opposite of its narrow spine. She approached it from the view of the evenly spaced pages. Windows, shattered long ago, filled the spaces. A large circle, a tiled surface that dipped into the ground about a foot, surrounded the library. It was probably once a large, decorative pool, but now lacked any water.

Just a block left to reach it.

Several high-pitched whines raced up behind her. At first, she thought it might be the pacification units, but she recognized the shapes rushing in her direction. A group of wagons, like the over-turned one she'd seen the night before, were flying over the debris-filled road towards her.

The hired swords had caught up to her.

15.

Ayleen couldn't reach the library before the Thirteen's merce-naries. She ducked into the nearest building, hoping they hadn't spotted her.

The doors to the building hung off their hinges. Some daylight reached inside, but most of the stained wood floors and walls were draped in shadows.

Sword drawn, Ayleen waited to see what happened next. The wagons zipped into view. Each one had four sets of circles glowing at their bottom corners. Whatever they emitted contained enough heat to ripple the air around them, keeping each one at least six inches above the ground.

The first wagons passed her. A good sign, but the rest slowed. Ayleen tightened her grip on her sword, sparing a glance back into the lobby. She didn't see another obvious way out of here. Surely there was, but she couldn't find it in the dark, and despite being daylight outside, the risk of illuminating her sword was too great.

The last of the wagons whined into a landing past her building. Women, men, and alternative-genders jumped out of their rides and onto the street. None of the mercenaries looked in her direction. They focused on the library.

She only saw the ones who disembarked the two closest wagons. Five got out of one wagon and four from the next. There were eight wagons. If the numbers remained the same, she was facing 36 swords, far more than the Wolf's warning.

Then she reconsidered. They were supposed to destroy the library. They needed space to keep crystals for explosives. Small, untamed crystals could do a lot of damage, but odds favored they were packing extra. They needed two or three people who knew what they were doing to set the crystals in the right places to destroy everything.

That lowered the number of swords to thirty. She'd faced similar odds in the town on Griffin, but most of those people were miners, untrained. These were hired killers. Whether she went down in five minutes versus two, the end result was all that mattered. Dead was dead.

She needed to get past them and into the library.

Someone shouted. She didn't recognize the voice, but the tone, she knew. This woman gave orders often and was used to being obeyed.

"You lot! Pair up! I need at least two of you a block up from the library in each direction. Anyone spots our target, you shout for backup. Don't take her by yourselves."

Her odds of getting into the library unnoticed plummeted. She had a better chance of finding a unicorn or a giant squirrel.

16.

Time to decide how badly she needed this information.

Contrary to the Wolf's assumption, the Orlander Library wasn't the first place of stored knowledge Ayleen had tried to reach. The Xeelian Archive on Gleeman VI had offered hope, but all she'd found was ash. The destruction had looked recent, but until now, she'd assumed that wasn't the case.

More likely, they'd anticipated her move for information and started limiting her options, herding her to this planet.

That meant two things for her. This place might have some decent star charts or planetary data, the kind to help her figure out where the planet in her vision might be. Also, if the Thirteen had destroyed all the other knowledge depositories, then this was her last chance.

The hired swords dispersed. Only two, a woman and a man by the looks, took this spot. Splitting up these mercenaries to cover all the streets leading to the library was valid strategy, but it assumed they would see her in time to shout for help. If she could pick off these two, maybe she could create a diversion to draw the others here while she went around them to get into the library.

She picked up a piece of a shattered brick to fling at the building across the street. The noise would draw the two mercenaries' attention away from her. Then she could sprint out and cut them down.

Just as she was about to throw the brick, she heard a screech from the building across the way like the ones she'd heard earlier. Another screech answered. The hired swords spun in place, looking up in all directions for the source of the birdlike cries.

If she threw the brick now, there was no chance of them not spotting her tossing it out of her building. Then the screeching stopped, and that's when Ayleen realized the source of the screeches weren't animals.

Dozens of arrows rained down on the road. One of the hired swords took an arrow in the chest and fell to his back.

Scavengers. Had to be. So much for Crim's word there weren't any in this part of the city.

The surviving guard crouched against the side of her wagon, shouting for her comrades to come to her aid.

Ayleen couldn't wait. If she did, the whole lot of these mercenaries would descend on this spot and search the buildings. They'd find her, and she'd be outnumbered.

She darted out into the storm of arrows raining down. She could see the other hired swords racing in her direction. They shouted to the woman by the wagon that Ayleen was coming towards her, but the warning didn't save her from Ayleen's attack. She sliced through the woman's armored chest plate and into her torso.

Bolts from the mercenaries' crossbows joined the shower of arrows as Ayleen hopped into the wagon, which was left running. Arrows pinged against the exterior of the wagon, each one a promise that one of them would eventually reach her.

The wagon's controls looked simple enough. A stick protruded from the dashboard. It was thick at the top and curved inward, perfect for a hand to wrap around it. The stick twitched to the right when she grabbed it, pushing the wagon the same direction.

A lever on the dash, to the left of the stick, sat next to the Vidian Basic word for "Full Stop." She pushed the lever up, placing it next to the highest number.

One of the mercenaries, a tall dark-skinned woman with her sword slung over her back, grabbed the passenger side door. The mercenary jerked the door open, but the wagon jolted forward with an angry whine. The sudden thrust slammed the passenger door shut and knocked Ayleen against the back of the pilot's seat. She lost her grip on the steering stick, which sent the wagon crashing towards one of the many decrepit brick buildings.

Ayleen grabbed the steering stick. She overcorrected left, then jerked it back right to go straight at the library. The passenger door yanked open, but the correction to the right slammed it shut again before the mercenary clinging to the wagon could climb inside.

The wagon dipped with a violent shake as it reached the decorative pool. The mercenary hanging onto the wagon screamed and glared through the window.

The mercenary yanked the door open again as the wagon jumped onto the sidewalk. Ayleen pushed a second lever labeled "elevation" to go as high as possible. The mercenary got half of her torso inside before the wagon launched upwards and crashed through the library's third floor windows. The glass was gone, but that still left pillars, tables, and chairs.

The wagon bounced off of the various impediments. One of the pillars slammed against the passenger door, crushing the mercenary's torso. The door rebounded open and the mercenary fell away.

Ayleen grabbed the lever and yanked it back to "full stop." The wagon groaned, still trying to climb. The grey tiles of the ceiling shattered from the pressure of the elevating wagon and fell away into dust. Something burst, knocking the wagon to the left. Flames spewed from the front right circle. She wasn't sure if the wagon would drop if she threw the elevation lever back to zero, so she dove out. The loss of her weight helped the wagon lift, but another circle blew, and the entire thing choked to a stop. The floor creaked as the wagon collapsed, then it gave way. The wagon fell from sight, dropping with several loud crashes until it stopped.

Ayleen turned from the hole and stopped short as she was met by a pair of inhuman eyes.

17.

Only one of the mechanical eyes glowed yellow. The other stayed dark. Cracks laced through the eye and up around the rest of its metal head.

The robot stood close to Ayleen. Its right arm jerked up, bending at the elbow until it brought a long finger up to a narrow, rectangular slit where a mouth would go. The slit blinked with the same yellow glow as the robot spoke.

"Please be quiet for the benefit of other patrons."

Other patrons? "Are you a librarian?" That this robot still functioned surprised her, but then again, she'd nearly been killed by robots the night before.

"I am a personal archive assistant technician, but you may call me PAAT. How may I assist you?"

Shouts came from below, from near the hole the wagon had created. No one shouted from above, not that she could hear. A good sign, she hoped.

"Please excuse me. I should attend to—"

"Wait." She grabbed the robot by its arm to make sure it didn't walk off. "I need help finding information."

The robot jumped a little in Ayleen's grip, as if the notion of someone using the library to get information had jolted it with joy. *"I would be pleased to assist you. What information do you seek?"*

"I need to find a specific planet, but I don't know the name. All I have are some details of what it looks like."

The impression of joy vanished, judging from how the robot slumped. *"Perhaps you could offer something more specific, like the color of the book cover."*

Did this robot just sass her?

"I need this information put together, so I can take it with me."

"Do you have a library card?"

"What?"

"Only patrons with a library card are permitted to take any material away from the library."

More shouts accompanied bursts of frantic movement from below. The few words she discerned and their tone made it clear what was happening. The mercenaries weren't coming up after her. They planned to blow the building with her in it.

"I don't have time for this. I need the information now."

"The library card is mandatory. You will need identification with your image on it along with proof of your current dwelling's address."

"I don't have a dwelling."

"Oh, you are homeless."

She grabbed the robot by its pole-thin throat and shoved it up against a bookshelf. Several dust-covered books tumbled. "Yes, I'm homeless! The godsdamned Thirteen destroyed my home and killed my family. Now get me the damn information!"

"Would this information assist you in seeking employment?"

Ayleen didn't answer, because she realized the change in PAAT's demeanor.

"Would this information assist you in seeking employment?" PAAT emphasized the last few words of the question. Was this crazy robot actually trying to help her find some loophole around its protocols?

"Yes! It would help."

"Have you ever previously obtained information from the Orlander Library or any of its sister libraries or archives?"

Ayleen hesitated. She glanced towards the hole. The mercenaries' shouts grew distant. She didn't have time to play these games. What was the right answer?

"If you have, you will not be eligible for assistance."

That cinched it. PAAT was leading her to a way around the rules. "I haven't."

"Excellent. You may take advantage of a one-time exception." A panel on PAAT's right forearm blinked in a rapid pattern. *"Please be advised, formatting a disposable data pad and assembling the necessary information will require several minutes."*

"Minutes! I don't have—!"

That's when the building blew.

18.

The building imploded around Ayleen. Before she could think to escape, PAAT's limbs wrapped around her, knocking her onto her back. She'd expected the building to crush them both, but that didn't happen.

Gravity flung Ayleen down like a rag doll, knocking her senseless for a moment. When everything finally stopped, the world had turned black, save for a faint, flashing yellow light.

Ayleen tried to sit up, but her head hit something.

"Please do not move."

"PAAT?"

That's where the light was coming from. The robot's arm was blinking.

"Please do not move. I have erected a protective energy dome around us and summoned for assistance. I must limit all functions in order to conserve power for the dome."

"Are you sure anyone is coming?" This robot was following some ancient protocols, but if the help it was summoning depended on anything other than a robot, Ayleen wasn't getting out of this alive. This protective dome might be delaying the inevitable.

PAAT didn't answer. Instead, the yellow light blinked.

If the help was immediate, that might prove worse. Getting freed before the mercenaries left would simply leave her exposed with nowhere to run.

Ayleen waited. The hardest part was distracting herself from the fact she was trapped under tons of metal, concrete, and all sorts of construction materials. She avoided moving as much as possible, because she feared if she put any pressure on the inside of the barrier, it would burn out faster. Panic made it hard to catch her breath. She struggled to calm her heart, but it raced. Did her sword offer any magic tricks that might help? The sword could probably cut through the debris above her. Unfortunately, the inevitable cave-in would flatten her.

Eventually, the yellow light stopped blinking. Ayleen wondered if that meant the robot had run out of power, but surely, if that was the case, the building would have dropped on them by now.

She considered using her sword for light, but she decided against it. Her head was still killing her from the earlier magic she'd worked. Instead, she stayed in the undefined dark. At least if she didn't really see how little space she had left, she could pretend it was more.

A sob came as Ayleen's thoughts wandered to all the places she ran from every day and night. She was no stranger to facing her private demons, but rarely this sober. Memories of her mother and father joined with Dara, the last moment of the small girl's life as the Fate's fangs snapped her neck. Ayleen had doomed the girl. Even if she'd left her on Griffin, the Thirteen would have snuffed her out, along with the rest of Midchron.

For the first time, Ayleen asked herself if her determination to kill the Thirteen wasn't trading one meaningless death for another.

Sleep eventually claimed her, taking her from true darkness to the false light of dreams.

She didn't remember what she'd dreamed, but she jolted awake. Her eyes ached as they spotted a crack of light shining through the patchwork of debris above her.

How long had she slept? However long it had been, she felt rested. She'd forgotten how long she'd gone without any rest, so it was little wonder she'd managed to slumber despite her panic.

"Please do not move. Assistance is on the way."

The electronic voice didn't come from PAAT. This came from whoever—whatever—was digging her out.

The light grew brighter as the hole above her widened. The daytime sky backlit the diggers. More decaying cyborgs, but definitely not the curfew hunting variety. The shape of their heads looked familiar, but she couldn't make out any details.

What the light revealed was how PAAT's arms and legs had extended to give her a wider berth than Ayleen had originally assumed. Now that she could see her available space, she straightened her right leg. Stars above, that felt better.

While studying the dormant robot's body, she spotted the light on its forearm blinking again. This time the light was green instead of yellow. She hoped that wouldn't risk burning out the protective field before the cyborgs pulled her out.

Another light flashed on, PAAT's good eye. *"Please open the blinking panel and remove the disc inside. The requested information and more is contained within the disc."*

"But how—"

PAAT's eye went dark.

Ayleen hesitated as she touched the panel. The last thing she wanted to do was jostle PAAT's body and cause the debris above her to collapse. Her gentle tugs failed to open the panel, though. She took a deep breath and yanked the panel, which popped open.

Ayleen yelped as something fell to the ground. Then she realized it was only the disc that had been in PAAT's forearm. She held the disc in the beam of sunlight reaching her. The disc was slightly thicker than a fingernail with a blue-tinted, reflective surface.

Answers. The notion she might have found what she needed made her heart beat faster. She hoped the damn thing worked, that she could figure out how to use it.

She pocketed the disc and waited for her rescuers to pull her out.

19.

Squirrels. The heads of the rescue cyborgs were from giant squirrels.

As soon as they pulled Ayleen free from the fallen library, the protective field collapsed. She clung to the back of the rescue cyborg as it climbed back out. The debris below her shuddered as it crushed onto PAAT. How the hole didn't cave in on her and the rescue cyborg made no sense, but she decided not to argue with good fortune.

Once they neared the lip of the hole, the cyborg spoke in a deadpan voice. *"Please hang on until we reach the ground."*

"Sure thing." Her voice shrieked on that last word as her ride to safety launched into the air and the high winds pounded against them, sending them over the edge of the massive pile that had once been the Orlander Library. Wings sprouted from the cyborg's sides from beneath its arms, allowing them to ride on the wind.

She screamed out every curse she knew, running through them three times. Their flight almost smashed them into some of the buildings they were flying past. At one point, the cyborg twisted to run along the side of the building and jumped back off.

Halfway through the fourth round of her string of curses, she realized she was back on the ground.

With her legs shaking, Ayleen peeled herself off the back of the cyborg.

"Godsdamned brainless monstrosity!"

"You are most welcome." If the cyborg's voice wasn't so deadpan, Ayleen might have taken that for sarcasm. More likely, it didn't understand the language she was cursing in and assumed she was expressing gratitude.

She didn't linger. From what she had seen, none of the mercenaries had waited to make sure the rescue cyborgs pulled out her corpse. Better not to chance it.

Drawing her sword, she used it to divine the way to the next keyhole to leave this windy world. She'd gotten good at recognizing the feel of distance within the keyhole visions from her sword, and she knew this one would take her at least three weeks. Taking advantage of being rested for once, Ayleen started walking, using what light she had left in this day.

She pulled out the blue disc, and a low beep from it startled her. A bright yellow line appeared on the top and bottom of the disc, starting at the center and reaching out to the disc's edge. The line widened into what reminded her of a slice of cake. The longer she kept it in the daylight, the bigger the "slice" grew.

After two days, light covered the entire disc. She hadn't made it out of the city yet, assuming this decaying urban landscape ended. She'd come across more than one planet made up entirely of artificial landscape.

She took shelter in what appeared to have been a café. The cramped space offered only a counter shaped like an uppercase L and stools positioned along it. Whatever food had been here was claimed long ago.

Once she placed the disc on the counter, it blinked and a hologram of a humanoid figure appeared atop it. The figure reminded her of PAAT. Only, this version of PAAT came with a robe to hide all of the robot's body, except for the face and hands. This PAAT's eyes both glowed, suggesting this was how the service droid was intended to appear before this world lost its Way.

"Greetings. This is remote service disc one-one-nine-two-zero-zero-one."

"PAAT?"

"Yes, you may refer to me in that manner. All of that unit's knowledge has been downloaded into this remote service disc. Shall I take you through the tutorial for using this device?"

"First, answer a question. Did you transfer the requested data to this disc?"

"Negative. There was insufficient space on this disc to download all of the requested material."

Ayleen took off her hat and ran her fingers through her hair. If the downloaded material didn't include what she needed, then she'd come all this way for nothing.

"I have installed a remote access program that will allow you to search through all of the library's online material."

Ayleen slammed her fist on the counter. "The library got blown apart."

"Negative, that was only the primary structure. The online archive is stored in an artificial satellite that maintains a geosynchronous orbit above the primary structure—or rather above where the primary structure used to be. So long as you stay within this hemisphere, you will have access to all stored data and can download any desired data onto this disc."

She'd heard of artificial satellites. The knighthood supposedly had a few placed above certain planets, some for communication and others for spying.

Resting her chin in the palm of her hand, Ayleen smiled. Her three-week walk to the next keyhole would hopefully give her the time she needed to find the planet in her vision.

"Nice work."

"Your gratitude is welcome but unnecessary." Oh, that was definitely sass. *"Shall we begin the tutorial?"*

Ayleen's fingers slid along the hilt of her sword, caressing it as the living weapon hummed in her thoughts with delight.

"Let's get started."

PART IV

The Explorer

1.

Ayleen knelt beside the grave. Withered grass and vines obstructed what text had survived a millennium's worth of wind and rain. Ayleen had traveled three months to find Kristian Basten's resting place. She hoped to find the old lady in a talkative mood.

A mass of red clouds glowed against a dark blue sky, blotting out half of this world's twelve moons. The nights on Skimo VIII never got darker than this, so only the brightest stars cut through the veil. Seemed an odd resting place for an explorer who'd etched her place into galactic lore.

The silhouette of a bird of prey flew above her. It dove behind a copse of trees, with more shadows than leaves. A series of squeals followed. The bird launched back into the sky with the rodent-shaped loser bleeding in its talons. The bird and its prey were the most life she'd seen on Skimo VIII in the week she'd searched for this graveyard.

Of all the worlds tainted by the Thirteen's unnaturally long lives Ayleen had visited, this one lingered in its death throes the most, a dead body picking at its scabs. It reeked with the foul decay of mold and planetary puss.

She pulled the ambrosia crystal from the bag resting on her left hip. Its amber light sucked the color of life from everything around it, reducing all within its reach to its own hue. Ayleen placed it on top of the grave. The ground shivered, Skimo VIII cringing at this crystal's power.

Ayleen next removed the leather-bound grimoire. With these two things she might find the answers she needed.

Legend claimed Kristian Basten had ventured to more worlds in this galaxy's core than any other. Ayleen's history lessons as a squire had included the woman buried beneath her. She'd never forgotten *Basten's Warning,* and the ghost of that famous quote was engraved upon the explorer's headstone.

"Life can walk upon most worlds, but there are places the living should never go."

As a mage general, Ayleen's mother had carried an ambrosia crystal "and all the honors and horrors that come with it." Her mother had enjoyed that joke. With the Knighthood in ashes, Ayleen now recognized the truth buried in the wit.

Magic wasn't Ayleen's strength. Sure she knew how to make her crystal sword sharper or glow in the dark, but what she prepared to do at this grave belonged in the hands of a mage general. At best, Ayleen was an explorer forged from need.

Her hands shook as she turned the pages of the grimoire. The paper had regained its suppleness. That concerned her, because she didn't think ancient paper could cast off its brittleness. Of course, this grimoire shouldn't exist. Shame upon Mage General Honor Deus Zahn for failing to ensure its destruction upon his death, but one could argue that what Ayleen planned to do next was a greater offense.

She found the page she sought. Her eyes, now gifted by the Fates, twisted the nonsense on the page into order. The title at the top of the sheet vibrated from her thoughts into her soul.

Communing with the Dead.

A long, heavy breath filled her lungs, as if she meant to dive into deep waters.

Her gaze shifted to the headstone. "Forgive my trespass, Kristian Basten."

She started the craftwork.

2.

The spell started with a drop of blood. She'd spilled more for her sword the day she achieved her knighthood.

Ayleen used the edge of her sword to cut her fingertip. The scent of her open wound might draw this dying world's limited predators. She hoped not, because if she understood the nature of this crafting, her actions would leave her body an undefended vessel.

Her eyelids closed as she formed shapes in her mind from a single line. She cast the thin thread into the swimming, amber light of the crystal. The line attached to it represented her soul.

The grimoire provided complicated directions for drawing that line. The clinical, step-by-step process didn't prepare her. The colors changed in what seemed random places, but as the line grew longer, unexpected shapes formed from the weave.

A horned man with a spoon scooped the eyes from a child. A wolf fucked a bird while eating its eggs. Large hands wrung the blood from a small dog. A woman pissed in a man's ear. Children peeled the skin from their mother's back and tied it in knots. An unborn child strangled its twin within the womb.

An hour passed as the line of her soul formed a seemingly endless path of perversion. Each image competed with the others before it for something worse. Cold sweat, chilled by the night wind, dripped from her brow and off her nose, drenching her shirt. She continued that endless drawing in her mind's eye, but all she had to show for it was her body's stink, a hammering ache within her skull, and a stomach fit to spew its disgust.

"Ichor of the Abyss!"

She stood and flung the grimoire at the headstone. The urge to rip it apart shook her hands.

A wordless scream crawled its way out of her throat, leaving it dry and cracked.

The breeze nearly knocked her off her feet. She grabbed her water pack off the ground where she'd left it and took a long pull from the drinking tube.

Dropping to her knees, she wiped the sweat from her face. What desperate foolery possessed her to think she could manipulate a damned ambrosia crystal?

This needed to work, though, because her options decreased with each sunset. The information from the Orlander Library had failed to find the planet in her vision, but it had led her here. She required a spirit who'd ventured to forbidden places.

Ayleen cursed as she grabbed the grimoire off the ground. The book had fallen open to a page near the back where its original owner had never written.

Only, the page wasn't blank.

She dropped the grimoire as if afraid it might sting her. She stumbled back onto her arse.

The book landed open to the same page. A richly-detailed drawing in charcoal showed Ayleen with her sword standing in ankle-high water with Dara at her back. The pages fluttered but didn't turn. On the neighboring page, fresh lines added themselves. A tear ran down Ayleen's face as her fingers dug into dry grass and mud.

"Dara?"

A little girl's laughter whispered up from the ground. The lines formed the shape of a giant spider, the Fate that had offered Ayleen answers and taken Dara's life as payment.

Ayleen reached into the space between her and the grimoire.

"Dara?" Her voice cracked. A blazing heat warped the air around her searching fingertips. She screamed and jerked back, cradling her singed hand against her. No permanent injury, but the red flesh throbbed.

A nervous and paranoid tickle against the back of her neck forced her to turn, searching for the eyes she knew were watching.

"Dara?" Forming the girl's name hurt her throat. Nothing answered this time.

The pages of the grimoire flapped as the wind turned back to the necromancy spell she'd been using. Ayleen flipped back to the page with the new drawing. A vibration touched her fingers, something scrawling against the back side of the page. Muffled scratching sounds accompanied each ripple in the paper. She turned the page to find the spider's head of the Fate, complete with Ayleen's face staring out through the cracked exoskeleton. Dara's head—her vacant face locked in shock—hung limp between the spider's fangs.

"No," Ayleen whispered. "You are not Dara."

More laughter, but this time, the voice deepened to a more mature tenor. *"You'll never catch me!"*

Its laughter ran off to Ayleen's right. A dried-up bush rustled as if something had brushed against it. Some of its brittle branches snapped off.

Definitely not her squire. A demon?

Her science classes warned forbidden magic often summoned more than the crafter asked or wanted. Mage generals learned to contain such ethereal beings, but that knowledge died with the Knighthood. She searched the neglected cemetery for any movement, a sign the unwelcome thing was still there.

The ambrosia crystal waited on the grave. The light swimming in it darkened for a second as if to wink at her. Its shape looked different, longer and thinner, assuming she could trust her eyes.

Her sword contained a semblance of life. The part of her soul that swam within it allowed her to "hear" the sword. That was the only way to tame a blue crystal and shape it.

Ambrosia crystals refused to share life. A person could only touch and direct its power. Could it refuse to cooperate? She'd never considered that. Mom wouldn't bring her ambrosia crystal into their home and told Dad she'd sooner open their door to a rabid panther.

She knelt beside the crystal. Her bloody fingerprint smeared across its flat surface. She debated on whether to offer it more blood.

"I've given what's required." She pressed her hand upon the crystal. "Now, it's your turn."

She shut her eyes, fought down her nausea, and directed her thoughts to draw the line again.

3.

Ayleen offered more blood to the crystal, but not the first night. She pricked her finger again the night after. After yet another sunset, another cut drew more blood. The twilight beyond, she pondered if shoving the damn crystal through her heart would do the trick.

She'd avoided drawing out more demons. Instead, the repeated failures, the incessant effort to create that profane thread within her mind and hooking the crystal's power chipped at her ability to think.

"I don't think the mind is meant to see certain things but only so much." She paused and considered that. "Or maybe it's so little." She paced circles around the crystal as night fell, the sky shifting from yellow into dark blue. She wasn't sure if her pep talk was to encourage the crystal or herself. Was this the fifth night? The sixteenth?

"You fucking shite! What if I piss on you? What craftwork then, you lousy lying bastard!"

She clenched her hands into tight fists, because otherwise they shook.

"I've drawn your godsdamned shapes!" She spit at the crystal, but most of the sticky filth landed on her chin and what made it any further only reached dead grass. "I hate you! You worthless shite! I'd kill your dog if you had one! Worthless glass! You're worthless! This grave is meaningless! I'm sick of it! I'm tired! I'm done! I'm worthless! It's pointless!"

She jerked her sword from its scabbard. Her fingers curled hard around the hilt, lifting the weapon as high as her arms allowed. The blade pointed down. She took a deep breath, ready to plunge the blade into—

"*No!*"

The voice wasn't hers. It was the bit of life in her sword. The realization that it was shouting at her—its terror—rendered her motionless.

"Gods." The tip of her sword wasn't aiming for the ambrosia crystal. Its tip pressed against her stomach.

She threw her sword down and lurched away, dropping to her knees.

The palms of her hands pressed against her temple. Gods, those images were stuck in there. Too many nights of twisting her thoughts into a line that cornered left and then down and spiraled and widened into so many awful things. Even the undefined shapes haunted her. The line never ended, and when it seemed close to a conclusion, it rebirthed all the profanity to etch it into her brain.

"Isn't that what they call madness?" She realized the spit was still on her chin and wiped her face clean on her sleeve. "Doing the same thing over and over, expecting something different."

She charged back to the grave. The grimoire waited atop the headstone, splayed to keep it on the page with the instructions for communing with the dead.

"Why won't you work?" She flipped through the pages. Honor Deus Zahn had gathered some nasty dark science in this book. "Gods below, why did I trust a man who can't enchant his own grimoire to die with him?"

In Zahn's defense, a grimoire only collected the crafting taken from other sources. Nothing guaranteed the mage general had ever employed any of what was written here.

The book ran out of magic about halfway through, where Dara had used many of the remaining pages for a sketch book. The artwork wasn't anything impressive, but she was a child. It didn't need to be perfect, only fun. Then she reached the demon's sketches. She lingered on the one of the Fate's face and Dara's corpse.

"Dara." Her voice cracked. The Fate had its way with Dara, finishing her in payment for the information to destroy the Thirteen.

"Fucking Fate. You couldn't just tell me where to go? Wasn't Dara's life worth a little more?"

The answer, when she realized it, slammed her in the gut and dropped her back to the ground. No, Dara's life hadn't been enough. The Fate had said it couldn't take Ayleen's life, which is what it was owed. The creature had known that before Ayleen entered the cave. Dara wasn't the payment it required, and because of that, it had held back enough to punish her.

"After I kill the Thirteen, I'll go back and end you, too."

The threat rang hollow. What hope did she have to succeed? She'd severed Javo's head from her body, and she came right back from it. Wasn't beheading supposed to kill the worst monsters?

She couldn't make this spell work.

It was time to quit.

She'd nearly killed herself. Maybe that was how the spell really worked. She'd be able to speak to the dead just fine once she was one of them.

Ayleen shoved the book back into her bag. The ambrosia crystal glowed in protest as she grabbed it. Several nights of using it had eliminated any doubts each crafting was changing its shape, growing longer with one end thinner than the other.

A shiver crawled through her body as her mind failed to decipher what the crystal was changing into. No, what she needed was to figure out her next move. She needed a way to—

"Leaving already?"

She spun around, dropping her pack and drawing her sword and dagger.

The early night sky clung to its daytime hues enough to help her see the brush shifting off to the right.

"Still lurking, demon?"

It laughed. The brush rustled as if something leaped out of it. Nothing distinct appeared. A shadow that fell across nothing—a ripple of an absent darkness in the air—refused to take shape as anything other than a vague, familiar thing. It laughed as it ran to the tree, and the leaves behind the headstone rustled.

Ayleen pointed her sword and dagger towards the demon.

The crystal sword contained a piece of her life's essence. If anything might harm this ephemeral creature, her sword might. The dagger offered nothing to aid her, only a false comfort. She cursed under her breath and shoved the dagger into its sheath on her thigh.

Ayleen waited a little longer. Only childish laughter answered, a distant sound that suggested the demon had fled.

Sliding her sword back into its scabbard, Ayleen grabbed her fallen pack to go.

Less than five steps from the grave, the demon called to her from the tree.

"You don't know why."

She paused and glanced over her shoulder. The leaves of the tree shifted.

"You don't know why." The demon's tone suggested a smirk. *"Do you?"*

"Why what?"

Ayleen's mother once warned her, *"A demon's only weapon is words. Never talk with one, because that invites it into your thoughts. Once it digs a single pointed nail into your mind, it can do dreadful things."*

The space between the leaves darkened, but not because it was night.

"Why the dead woman won't answer."

The rational corners of her mind told her to grab her things and run for the keyhole, to leave this deceitful shade to hide in the brush. She didn't leave, though.

"And you know why?" Ayleen asked.

"Yes!" The branches jostled from the demon jumping on them. *"Would you like me to tell you?"*

"Why should I trust you? Demons trade in lies."

"No, we trade in truths that people misinterpret. Are you clever enough to know meaning when you hear truth?"

The back of her throat ached from holding back the request she knew she had to ask.

"Tell me why it won't work."

4.

The demon crawled out of the tree. The air rippled with heat where it walked. It grunted as its nails dug into the back of the headstone to climb on top.

"The reason you can't call the explorer's spirit is in the grimoire."

Cold rage rushed through Ayleen. "Don't toy with me!"

"Open the grimoire. The answer is there."

Ayleen jerked the leather-bound book from her bag and flung it open to the necromancy spell.

"I've followed everything here."

"The answer isn't on that page." It slithered down to the ground. *"May I turn it?"*

"Not like you waited for permission before."

In the silence that answered, she sensed the thing's smile taunting her.

She held the book so it faced the demon. "Show me."

The air grew hotter as it reached for the book. The pages turned with eager flaps. It flitted past the spells written by the original owner. The pages stopped on a picture Dara had drawn of herself.

"Dara?"

"Not the girl. Not simply that." The demon's invisible nail drew the impression of an "X" over Dara's face.

"Then what!" Ayleen slammed the book shut and put it away. "I'm done playing your game."

"Not a game!" The demon's envenomed response startled Ayleen.

"What is it you want?"

"Only a spirit wrapped in the shell of the living can travel the spheres."

Of course. "That's your price. You want to journey to the next world by possessing my body."

"Agree, and you will get your answers." This creature lived by deceit, but its hunger and need spoke the truth. These things survived by preying on the living. This world didn't offer anything of value. Ayleen might entertain it, but that was one and done. This thing wanted more.

"I'll carry you through only one keyhole and no further. I decide when you may enter my body, and you will leave me unharmed as soon as we reach the other side."

The demon hissed in anticipation, but Ayleen raised a finger to stop the demon from answering. "To be clear, I'm not agreeing—yet. I'm discussing terms."

"I cannot promise you will not suffer from carrying me. If you refuse to let me possess you, then it will hurt. Recall, you will, when you passed your hand through me. The heat. The pain. Possession would be—more pleasant."

Ayleen scowled, making no effort to hide her thoughts. "No." She wasn't shocked by the demon's attempt to con her into something more, but it smacked of a token effort. He wanted something else. This was all one big game for him.

"It must be a world with mortal life. A place that thrives. Not some wasteland with beasts and little else."

"A place with plenty of people to torment?"

"Of course."

It was agreeing to this far too easily. What opening was she giving it? Then she recognized the real threat. She acted like this thing would keep its word. The claim to not lie made it the worst liar of all, and that meant the terms it was agreeing to were all irrelevant to what it really wanted.

"There's a keyhole roughly seven days from here. It leads to Garmett Two. Word says it's dying, like everything else, but you'll find more than enough souls eager for corruption." The demon stirred from atop the headstone. Her willingness to sacrifice other lives wasn't something it expected from a Knight of the Way. "Do we have a deal?"

The demon didn't answer right away. Just as she sensed him agreeing to the terms too quickly, he must have suspected the same from her eagerness.

In the end, its hunger won. *"We are agreed."*

"What am I doing wrong?" With her sword still in hand, Ayleen spun it in anticipation.

"You draw the shape right to pull the soul of the departed to you, but your guilt directs your soul to other dead things. Those you've lost and failed."

Dara. Her mother. Her father. "I have to make peace with what I've lost before I can perform the spell?"

"No, put it aside." The demon cackled. *"You'll find it waiting when you get back."*

"Very well." Her sword hummed to her in its lust for blood, knowing she'd do whatever it might take. She gave the blade another spin, winding up to strike. "Move back to the tree, demon."

With another spin for momentum, she stabbed her sword into the dirt. Eyes closed, she whispered to the sword. *"Hogosidio wateus tanimus karaa akunibus."*

The demon lunged back. She didn't see it, but felt it. Once the invisible field of protection went up, something pushed against it in front of her.

"So unkind."

Ayleen kept both hands wrapped about the hilt as she pushed the sword as deep as she could into the ground. The scent of wet, freshly-turned dirt wafted up to her. The magic of the sword would take some of its power from the land, but most of what it required came from her. She couldn't maintain it all night, but if this went as she expected, she wouldn't need long.

She sneered at the wavy outline in the air. "You wanted my guard down, my soul distracted and my body open for you to push my soul aside once I was communing with the dead."

The demon didn't argue. His growl said plenty.

"Don't worry. Assuming this works, I'll give you your ride to Garmett Two."

Ayleen knelt, still pushing down on the hilt. She couldn't dig it into the ground any deeper, but the effort hid how she was using the sword for support as she lowered herself to her knees.

The demon laughed as it climbed back into the tree, the leaves rustling. *"With what comes next... Good luck."*

The ambrosia crystal glowed when her hand touched it and pulled it from her bag. The damn thing knew. Whatever sentience it possessed vibrated with anticipation. This time, the hook would draw in the soul she sought.

She pulled a flask from her pack. Time had worn away most of the red and beige paint on the front, but enough of the letters remained for a knowing mind to make them out as "Holy Water." She'd found the metal container in the ruins of a shop on Kurega and had refilled it on each inhabited world that followed. The last world had filled it with a sweet liquor flavored with honey, oak, and vanilla. She saved her flask for desperate nights, which was all of them.

"Forgive me." She shut her eyes and took a shot from her flask.

She rolled her head around in a slow circle until her neck cracked.

When she opened her heavy eyelids, the name that mattered to her stared back from the headstone.

Kristian Basten.

"Let's talk, old soul."

5.

The path formed as Ayleen drew with her soul. The profane acts still sickened her, but after what felt like hours, the hook connected. A sensation—slick and unliving—slid across her flesh as the forbidden line formed in her mind and pulled her within it. Distant gasps and moans echoed to her, and the decayed scent of Skimo VIII surrendered to the odor of stale water.

Ayleen stepped forward. Darkness surrounded her. Though she couldn't see it, the path she walked mirrored the line of the necromancy spell. All the horrible images sickened her more than ever, as if to walk through the spiritual sketch made her a part of them.

Light tickled the edges of her vision, and when she raised her hand to look at it, she realized the light came from her. No flesh held her soul here. Instead, amber crystal carved into her shape carried her life. A hint of blue caught her attention near her right hip. Her blue, crystal sword hovered there, only without its leather strap and steel pommel. It hovered next to her, rendering a scabbard and belt moot. A growl beckoned from the sword, as if to answer the voices of the dead echoing from the far end of the path.

A turn brought a hint of light from ahead. The moans grew into screams and shouts. Bits of names and pleas overlapped.

The path ended in the shape of an arch that emptied into a round room. Light swam in a circle across the floor. Ayleen stood on the edge of the light on a ring of brown bricks. The floor shook beneath her. She grabbed onto the edge of the door frame for fear of falling into the pool of light. Only, it wasn't a pool, but a well with beings of light crawling along its walls. Some fell and others lunged up, grabbing onto other souls or the wall. Some unseen force held them back.

A single life caught Ayleen's attention. Each soul was tinged in a different shade, but the edges of the being climbing towards her were orange. Her face looked straight at Ayleen, a hint of definition forming, along with pale flesh and blue eyes that suggested who she was in life.

"Are you here for me?" The woman screamed as she reached over the edge. Bright fingers stabbed into the bricks, leaving spider web cracks. "Please!"

"Kristian Basten?"

The tension in the arm of light vanished. The face vanished into featureless light. "No, I'm not her. No one asks for me anymore. No prayers or memories. I don't want to be forgotten!"

Was this woman connected to Ayleen in some way? Her face and voice meant nothing. "Who are you?"

"I—" The woman sobbed. "I can't remember anymore."

The hand released and being of orange-tinged light fell into the oblivion of other souls. The cracks in the floor from her hand healed, as if the edge of the well had also forgotten her.

At a loss for what else to do, Ayleen shouted for whom she sought. "Kristian Basten! I seek Kristian Basten, the explorer of worlds!"

Two hands lunged out of the pile. This soul's light was edged in violet. Like the first woman, her fingertips dug into the bricks, but they gained a deeper hold, the cracks reaching out farther.

"Kristian Basten?"

The face of light looked up at Ayleen at the name, so Ayleen spoke it again. This time, the face shaped into something familiar. Pink skin and bright blue eyes gazed out from the soul.

"I know that name." The woman's words didn't match the motion of the lips, as if something within this room took what was said and changed it to whatever Ayleen would understand. The voice came out low and scratchy, not something born of age but from too much smoking.

"Is the name yours?" Ayleen pointed her sword at the soul struggling to climb out. "Are you Kristian Basten?"

The eyes blinked—the name touching something deep within her. "Yes. I am Kristian Basten." She reached out with one of her hands, the rest of her form taking on the pink flesh tone. "Pull me free, before I fall."

The request sounded benign, but Ayleen didn't move. How could she know for certain? Yes, the face appeared similar to what the archives had recorded of the explorer, but Ayleen knew nothing of the laws over lives in this state. Perhaps the souls reflected what and who they were, but for all she knew, they could adopt any appearance.

One of the hands fell away. The soul's eyes went round in terror. The rest of her body flapped like a flag.

Ayleen reached for the soul's wrist, but her hand passed through the light, sending a faint shiver up her arm.

"My name! Call my name!"

"Kristian Basten!" Ayleen shouted as loud as she could and kept repeating it. With each repetition, the limbs of light faded into a being of strong muscle tone. The hand that had fallen back once again grabbed onto the floor. Angry and envious screams from deep in the well threatened to drown out Ayleen's voice, but she kept shouting the explorer's name. Dark blue hair spilled out from the woman's head in long waves. The soul pulled her upper half onto the bricks. A long pink leg swung up next, and with a last effort, she pulled herself free from the well. Removed from the tangle of lost souls, the bright light faded to reveal the woman Ayleen had summoned.

A shiver rippled through the explorer's body. The cries from the well lessened but stayed steady enough to drown out the heavy breathing that caused Kristian Basten's bare back to arch with each inhale.

The first thing she managed to say was a single word, uttered with a sense of awe. "Breathing." The hitch in her words added layers of skepticism and amusement.

She stood and glanced down at her body. Her hands took turns running up and down the backs of her forearms.

Ayleen stepped closer but stayed out of arm's reach. "I need to know if you're fam—"

"A moment." Her gaze narrowed on Ayleen. Without yelling, she'd cut her off in the same manner one slapped a moth into a grey smear. "Let me take it in."

She turned her back to Ayleen to glance into the well. With a slow turn, she took in the rest of their surroundings. When she looked down at herself, she sighed and scowled. "No clothes," she said to herself. "Suppose that makes sense—if not irritating."

Kristian Basten, assuming this soul before her was indeed the woman she sought, stood much taller than Ayleen had expected, at least a full head taller. She looked down at Ayleen as if the knight's eyes were level with her vibrant pink ankles and not the base of her throat.

Ayleen crossed her arms.

"What are you?" Basten asked.

"Field Knight Ayleen Torr of the Perseus Legion, a Knight of the Way."

Kristian Basten's gaze settled on the sword in Ayleen's hand before her head tilted to the left, causing her long hair to spill over her shoulder. "But what species are you? Some crystalline based race?

You certainly aren't a Mynelite from Auctiree IV or the Berynians of the Sawatch system."

She stepped closer, and Ayleen fought the urge to slap the arrogance out of her with her sword.

"I'm half-Cygnian and half-Pleiaderean." The crystalline appearance she'd noticed in the passage leading her here must have hidden any distinguishing features.

"Oh, a mongrel." Kristian Basten rolled her eyes.

Ayleen jerked back as the woman tried to tap her on the arm. She moved too slow to get out of reach, but Kristian Basten's hand passed through her. The realization prompted a grunt of interest from the dead explorer, who returned to running her eyes up and down Ayleen, as if to catalogue her.

"So, is this some new armor the Knights of the Way developed?" Then she muttered, though whether to herself or Ayleen was unclear. "Such clever tricksters. Always looking for the next innovation."

"It's not armor." The defensiveness in her own voice caught Ayleen by surprise, though it didn't merit a blink from the other woman. "I'm using an ambrosia crystal, so this is how it's projecting my soul here."

That last bit caught Kristian Basten's interest. She pointed to Ayleen's sword. "So it's true. What they say about your swords. They do contain a part of your soul."

Kristian Basten turned so her profile faced Ayleen, and she pointed to their surroundings. "Tell me, young one. Describe what you see."

"All right, Basten, I've tolerated this long enough. I need to know if you've ever been to a world with a stream of light pouring into it. The world is—"

"I've been to many worlds, but tell me what you see."

"No."

Ayleen's refusal only managed another roll of Basten's eyes. "What I'm asking will benefit me and you. Tell me what you see."

Despite the dead woman's demand, Ayleen answered with silence.

Basten's eyes glowed brighter with her anger. She planted her hands on her hips. "The shape of the room. Rectangular? Square? Triangular? Pentagonal? Oct—?"

"It's round."

The answer prompted Basten to arch one of her slender blue eyebrows. "And the floor? Bricks or marble? What color?"

"Brown bricks. What is the point of this?"

Basten paced a few steps, her eyes moving up and down Ayleen as if she could see beneath the crystal facade. "You're half-Pleiaderean. By your father? Of course. How predictable." She rubbed the tip of her middle finger against her thumb as if to grind out her analysis, leaving her index finger free to point. "Pleiadereans believe in a hall where the souls of the dead are gathered in a well." There went the index finger, pointing to the mass of light she'd crawled out of moments ago. "But your mother, being Cygnian wouldn't buy into religious nonsense, so your spiritual indoctrination was limited. Probably hindered even more by your father also being a field knight, perhaps one of the Knights of the Way's many amateur and ill-educated cartographers."

Ayleen forced herself to return her sword to float beside her hip lest she be tempted to use it on Basten's soul. "My father was one of the most respected explorers of the Knighthood, you arrogant bitch."

The declaration only managed another condescending stare from Basten, as if she found Ayleen's defense of her father both unimpressive and unsurprising. "My point is your knowledge of Pleiaderean mythology is incomplete, as is this room."

The retort that her father's religion deserved more respect than to be written off as fables and fiction burned in the back of Ayleen's throat but cooled as she realized the point being made. The room wasn't real, not as she saw it. Her memories manufactured or possibly interpreted her surroundings into something that made sense.

"And you see it the same as I do?" Ayleen asked.

"So it would seem. This world you're asking about, you've seen what it looks like?"

"Yes, I was—"

"The Pleiadereans borrowed much of their beliefs from the Pegasi Empire's fifth age." She pointed to the brick wall surrounding them. "There should be more doors. They lead to memories of those who visit this place. Make them appear. We'll see if your missing world is among them."

Ayleen required no more instruction. The thought alone, now planted within her mind, changed the room. Her memories filled in the blanks as what little she recalled about her father's religion shook away its cobwebs and moved to the front of her mind. Doors appeared every few feet, along with elaborate drawings depicting the seven goddesses of the Myrophean Faith. Ayleen wondered how much she might be able to consciously change their surroundings, but a satisfied, dismissive grunt from Basten ended that train of thought.

"Very well. We should both be cautious not to lose our way. My time to be reborn will come, but if the legends live close to the facts, failing to return to this room will trap me."

Ayleen's father once told her a bedtime story along those lines. What little she remembered was of a young priest taking a wrong door in the spirit world and spending decades finding his way back to his body only to die from old age as soon as his eyes opened. "And I suppose that goes for me, too."

"What? Oh, yes. Now, let's seek this missing world." Without a look back at Ayleen, Basten walked towards the first door to the right.

Ayleen kept a hand against the brick wall, anxious she might fall into the bright, noisy well to her left.

They reached the door. The opening revealed nothing but shadow and void. Without a word, Basten directed Ayleen to enter first.

She placed a foot over the threshold. Her toes pressed on the cold floor she couldn't see and tested that the flat plane existed and supported her weight.

Her careful dip into darkness didn't prepare her for when the rest of her body entered the room.

6.

Ayleen gasped. The change in setting startled her, but what took her breath from her was the rush of emotions.

She stood in her family's den, not as she'd last seen it, the walls marred by soot and all else reduced to ash.

Here and now, it thrived with life. The walls were painted in a bright shade of eggshell. Maps collected by her father and tapestries of ancient battles hung on the walls. Her feet, back in her uniform's pristine boots, stood on the circular red, blue, and grey rug covering most of the room.

"The keyhole to Astes IX has turned green."

Her father's voice! She turned on her heels and saw him sitting at their dining room table.

Tears threatened to drown her as she saw his face. His blue beard was freshly trimmed, the way he always shaped it upon returning from a long exploration. Mother loved the way his beard looked on his tanned face. Ayleen did, too.

Mother sat next to him. Unlike Father, still in his morning robe, Mother wore her uniform. Five silver bars decorated her collar, the mark of her rank as a mage general. She sipped from her favorite mug, decorated with stars and galaxies of every color swimming in a dark blue sky. Judging from the scowl on Mom's face, she was only on her first cup of coffee.

"Intentional, no doubt," Mom said. Ayleen remembered that happening to several keyholes, their caves being flooded to cut off the Knights from interfering with those worlds.

"They're tired of being left in the dark, Mother." The words belonged to Ayleen. She'd spoken them against her wishes. She wanted to run to her parents and hug them, but something trapped her to the spot with one hand resting on the hilt of her sword, still within its scabbard.

Mother rolled her eyes at Ayleen, and the manner in which she did it reminded her of—of someone. Someone she'd known. No, wait. It'd been recent. Someone she needed to find? Was it her old trainer Captain Tratella? Yes. No. As the need to remember struggled within her, she thought she saw someone out of the corner of her eye.

"Then they're fools." Mother paused for another sip of coffee, and then cut off Father before he could add his opinion. "The proposal to gift certain worlds with our crystal technology is madness. Once these savages harness that kind of power, they'll bring about their own ends—wars that will wipe themselves from the celestial maps. They'll make the apocalyptic legends of Kalle-Al look like pleasant fairy tales."

"They're already unlocking the technology." Ayleen considered slamming her fist on the table. Taking a deep breath, she calmed herself. She hated it when Mother talked to her like she was some ignorant toddler, but she'd learned years ago that a calm, rational argument got under Aydrene Torr's skin a lot more than any tantrum might. Still... She carried her own crystal sword, charted worlds, and had passed every challenge the Knighthood offered. Gods above and below! She'd killed people in the course of her duties. She'd also spared lives, but none of that proved anything to her mother.

"The Thirteen are organizing these people and disseminating crystals to them," Ayleen said. "If we don't offer a sign we trust our own allies, they won't trust us. I've seen enough worlds in revolution to know that if they don't know how to tame the crystals or fashion them into swords, they know enough to turn them into a threat."

Without a glance in Ayleen's direction, Mother stabbed her fork into the half-eaten pile of scrambled eggs on her plate. "The Thirteen are a fiction and one best ignored. We need to confiscate the crystals these worlds have somehow harvested. It's for their own good."

Father pushed his empty plate away from him as he leaned back in his chair. "I'm not so sure about the Thirteen being propaganda. The uprising on Ostice is real enough. They claim three knights and a man in a dark green robe led a mob into the president's castle, killed everyone in there, and walked out without a scratch.

"I also find it interesting this claim there are Thirteen of them. Our intelligence suggests no one has seen them all together. Still..." Father shook his head as he considered something in silence before he continued. "Didn't you once say thirteen is a powerful number within the dark sciences?"

Mother rubbed her forehead, hiding for a moment the deep purple eyes Ayleen had inherited from her. "Can we please discuss something else? I'm already sure to waste enough time today in pointless meetings going over this same nonsense."

"Sorry." Father reached over to take her hand. "We should go for a ride tonight."

Mother managed a smile. "I'd like that. Maybe we could do it earlier. I'll try to get free after lunch."

"Whether the Thirteen are real doesn't matter." Ayleen crossed her arms, refusing to be influenced by their desire to dismiss the rumors. "These less-advanced worlds are catching up to us. That's the reality, and if the Knighthood doesn't start to guide them instead of holding them back, they'll turn against us. The Thirteen might be manipulating these people, but we're doing enough damage ourselves..."

"Enough, Ayleen!" Mom's glare pushed her back a few steps. "Aren't you supposed to be training the new recruits today?"

Ayleen groaned. Yes, she'd agreed to help put them through their sword lessons and take them on a scouting trip to Regan Five as part of their training.

"It's important." Mother leaned towards her while still holding Father's hand. "Don't let the recruits run behind schedule. You and those children need to be out of here before the sun reaches its zenith. You don't want to upset Captain Tratella."

"Yes, I know!"

Ayleen stormed out into the hallway. No one else was out of their quarters yet. Still too early.

"Wake up, young one!"

She stopped at the unexpected voice coming from her left. A tall woman with pink skin stood there. She was naked!

What was—?

Wait.

"Wait." She shook her head. The woman. "Basten?"

"You've gotten lost in this memory. None of that was useful. Although, I'm intrigued by these Thirteen."

Behind Basten, in the wall of the hallway was the door leading back to the well. She forced herself to walk past Basten and through the door. As soon as she passed through the doorframe, her body collapsed to its knees.

She stared into the well. Were her parents in there? Could she summon them as she had this woman?

"We should try another door." Basten stared ahead at the other doors, ignoring Ayleen's struggle to regain her control. "It might help if you focus on the memory we need."

Ayleen sobbed. No tears came, though. In this place, she was nothing but amber crystal.

"Oh, please." Basten crossed her arms. "This drama is wasting time. And for such a banal memory."

Passing from that moment into the present left Ayleen's heart as raw as if she'd just lost her parents again. A sharp pain coiled beneath her breastbone, doubling her over.

"It was the last time I ever saw my mother."

The Thirteen's forces flooded the Citadel before Mother and Father could leave for their ride. If the attack had come a little later, all three of them would have been away from Mount Hawkken.

The difference of an hour had orphaned her.

7.

Ayleen got better at extracting herself from the memories before they grabbed hold of her. One door revisited the moment the Fate leaped from her cave and killed Dara. She managed to get out before she could see the vacant look of death in her squire's eyes, not that she'd ever remove the memory from her mind.

Another door led to her first ride on her takert when she was ten. She'd clung to Ziggy's long neck without a saddle, her legs gripping tightly to his scaled, reptilian back.

There was also the day she confronted her boyfriend, a fellow squire who'd been cheating on her. That one still burned, more from all the things she wished she'd been clever enough to say to him before she'd punched him. She'd indulged in throwing the punch for a second time, though. That part had felt damn good even if Basten had yawned her impatience.

The more potent the memory, the harder it was to pull out of it. The one with Dara had taken all of her will to escape.

The doors offered no pattern Ayleen could discern. They came at her out of chronological order, as if her life didn't flow in a straight line. On the twelfth door, she entered a room she'd never forget.

The bottom-most place in the Citadel wasn't a part of the structure. A door from the back of the Citadel's amphitheater connected to a natural cave. A winding corridor, too narrow for more than two people to walk side-by-side, led to a small grotto. The floor, what little there was, reached out from the mouth of the tunnel to the center of the cave with the rest of the floor a deep pool. The water connected with Lake Kurter.

Four torches—two by the entrance and the others on the center island—provided the only sources of light.

This was the Forge. Swords were made here, not steel blades—only crystal.

Captain Tratella stood to Ayleen's right. "Lie face down on the table, Squire Torr."

One of the knighthood's mage generals stood on the far side of the table, garbed in a ceremonial cloak to hide their identity. All Ayleen knew was that whichever mage general it might be, it wasn't her mother. Mother had paled at the notion of it and assured Ayleen she'd understand why after the ceremony.

"No!" Ayleen flung herself back the way she'd come, tearing herself out of the memory. She fell out of the door back to the Well of Souls and collapsed onto the brick floor.

"What was that?" Basten stormed out of the memory door.

"It's my sword forging ceremony." She gestured to the sword on her hip. "It's how our swords are fashioned from the crystals. Survive that, and you become a knight."

Basten stared into the darkness beyond the door with her arms crossed. "I would have liked to have seen that."

"Find another knight to take you, because I won't go back to that."

"It's that traumatic?" The question lacked any empathy, only a deep-rooted curiosity.

"You know how people speak of the kind of pain you forget?" Ayleen forced herself back to her feet and met those glowing blue eyes. "Well, that's the kind you never do."

Basten rubbed her fingertip against her thumb as she stared back through the door. "Then why do it?"

"Because I wanted to be a Knight of the Way."

Ayleen brushed past the explorer's spirit towards the thirteenth door. When the doors had formed, she'd taken count of them. There'd been eight, counting the one she'd used to enter. The path seemed to never circle back on itself with a new door always waiting past the previous.

"Thirteen," Ayleen muttered to herself at the edge of the door frame. The number tickled at her mind, not because of the murderers she sought. Instead, she remembered what the Fate had spoken in her drug-induced hallucination counting from one to fourteen again and again, the fever dream spinning each time the count reached thirteen. She started counting as the Fate had, running through the numbers each time and punching out the number thirteen with all her conviction.

"1. 2. 3. 4. 5. 6. 7. 8. 9. 10. 11. 12. *13.* 14."

Basten stepped up to her, staring at her face with confusion. "What are you—?"

She ran through the numbers yet again, but this time, on the number thirteen, she flung herself through the doorway.

8.

Ayleen fell into herself. She lay flat on the ground as the sky spun above. Prone next to her, in this remembered fever dream, the Fate pointed up at the sky.

Star trails blurred. She fought down the panic induced by the shifting universe, but a part of her chuckled at how this paled compared to the nausea induced from the crafting she'd done to reach the Well of Souls.

"It wants to stop, too!" The Fate screamed, and they plunged towards the brilliant center of the Galaxy. The Fate counted, and the sky tilted again at Thirteen.

The world with the light streaming into it appeared.

"The Galaxy has lost its Way," the Fate said, staring up at the floating, grey orb of ugly craters and the disrupted stream of light.

"You must unlock the Castle's Door. Go there, and make the final cuts."

Ayleen forced herself to her feet. The grass had vanished. She stood on withered land, a corpse.

Before she could tell the Fate she didn't understand what she was telling her, another voice interrupted, shaking Ayleen back into the realization she was only watching what had already happened in the past. The Fate here couldn't offer any better knowledge than she had the first time around.

"So this is the world? No wonder I didn't remember it. You never said the light had come out the other pole."

"It doesn't," Ayleen pointed up at the small world above. "Look. Something stopped its flow."

The Fate pointed back up at the grey planet. "Look and make this happen." The light spilled out the southern pole again, only the light didn't stop there. It consumed the world, obliterating it and everything else.

"Find your Way, and make the cut, sister."

Ayleen turned away from the explosion of light to find the Fate, as a spider, lunging at her.

Then it all went white.

9.

When Ayleen lowered her arms, she found herself back beside the well.

Basten stared into the empty door frame. She whispered to herself. "Life can walk upon most worlds, but there are places the living should never go."

Ayleen scrambled to her feet. "You saw it. You know it?"

"I do." She walked past Ayleen towards the way they'd come.

Ayleen chased after the dead woman. She caught up to her outside the door that led to her forging ceremony. Reaching out, she grabbed Basten by the arm and forced her to turn around.

"What is the name of that world? Where is it?"

"The world is Dosquam." Basten's gaze was lost to her own memories. "It orbits no star. I found it on the other side of a red keyhole hidden in a cave beneath Paladin Castle," she hesitated, "on Cephei VI."

Basten grabbed Ayleen by her forearms. "You say these Thirteen are immortal? Had I a body to return to..." She shook her head.

"Basten, thank you. I cannot repay this."

"Actually, young one, you can." Basten smiled down at her and tightened her grip on Ayleen's arms.

"Wait." Since when had Basten's spirit been able to touch her? "How?"

"I realized it earlier, when you brushed past me." Basten's hands jerked Ayleen towards the door. "I wish I could join you to study your memory, but I want my second chance at life."

Basten flung Ayleen through the door and back into her forging ceremony.

10.

Captain Tratella tightened the straps with Ayleen lying on her stomach. Her head hung over the edge of the table. She struggled but the bonds held tight. It was as if the memory had kept moving without her.

Blue light blinded her as the mage general removed a long, slender crystal from a box on the floor. The mage general placed it in a stand within reach of her bound left hand.

"You must hold the crystal tightly." A male mage, judging by the voice, one of the older ones.

Panic gripped Ayleen, and she grabbed the crystal. She'd heard stories about this part. If a squire's hand slipped, they often ended up catatonic. The Knighthood gave those unlucky souls three months. If there wasn't any improvement, they euthanized them.

Her hand was sweating and she wished she could wipe it off. The crystal, in its raw shape, didn't offer a comfortable grip.

A wave of déjà vu overcame her. Her fear had distracted her from… She couldn't remember. There was something—someone?—else. She needed to stop this, get her mind back. It was important.

More important than getting her sword?

Was she mad?

Before she could ask anything, Captain Tratella knelt beside her. "You'll need this," she said in that rough voice of hers.

The captain slid a bite guard into Ayleen's mouth, muffling any protests.

The mage general gestured towards Ayleen. "Who offers this squire for entrance into our Knighthood?"

The captain answered with a simple, "I do."

"She is worthy?"

The captain placed a cold hand on her bare back. "She is."

"She is willing to place the welfare of the Galaxy before her own?"

"She is."

"She is strong enough for her soul to share a second place in the Galaxy?"

"She is."

"So be it."

Captain Tratella stepped back.

"Squire Ayleen Torr, we will pray the Fates share your captain's judgment." He turned to the captain again. "You may leave us until we are ready for your assistance to finish her sword."

Ayleen heard the captain's boots click against the stone floor, stopping beyond the mouth of the grotto.

The mage general knelt so his eyes were level with Ayleen's. "When the sword is fully formed, you will hear its voice. Offer it your name, and it will answer with its own."

But I already know its name, she thought to herself, but she couldn't recall it. No, she didn't know the name. How could she? She hoped it would be one like her father's which was named *Pasufator* which meant "Pathfinder."

With a small dagger, the mage general drew three quick cuts along her forearm. She hissed at the swift strikes to her skin, but the pain passed quickly. The table was angled so the end with her head and arms was lower than the other end. This meant the blood flowing from her arm ran in tiny streams down her hand and along the blue crystal.

The mage general pulled out another crystal, only this one was about a foot long and slender. Most remarkable of all, it wasn't blue like every other crystal she'd ever seen. This one was amber. He placed the ambrosia crystal so it touched her hand and the blue crystal.

"Kattondeo Kanius Tanima," he whispered. The amber glow flared brightly enough to obscure the blue crystal.

Her breath caught. An icy sensation entered her body through the cuts. She tightened her grip on the blue crystal, fearful of slipping and losing her mind.

The mage general repeated the words he'd spoken until he'd spoken them thirteen times. With each syllable, the sensation of unwelcome cold slid deeper into her body.

When he finished, the sensation of ice pressing against her flesh covered her entire body.

The mage general stepped back and stared down at her. Had something gone wrong? Why was he staring at her? Oh, gods! Had it failed? Had the crystal rejected her, deemed her unworthy of the Knighthood?

"Hold tight, Squire Torr."

She tightened her grip on the crystal, and something shifted. A scream, a cry of pain. Then she felt it. The crystal changed. It stretched half an inch higher. As the crystal grew, pain filled her body. A sharp crack thundered through her as if she were the finger on a much larger hand and someone had snapped that finger back until it formed a right angle in the wrong direction.

The crystal grew taller and more slender. Each time the blue gem thrust a little taller, another "finger" cracked.

Its glow blinded her, but she no longer needed her eyes to know the crystal was transforming.

An invisible razor-thin needle stabbed into the center line of blood running down her forearm. It stabbed in hard until it struck bone, scraping against it. More needles buried into her forearm. It started with the lines of blood drawn by the mage general and then bloomed across the rest of her body, as if those unseen needles intended to peel back all of her flesh and rip it free in long, bloody strips.

Phantom flames consumed her next. Dropping her in a pool of molten rock would have been kinder.

"Hold tight." The mage general repeated the command to her several times. She could scarce discern his voice above the wails from the crystal as it bent and stretched.

The crystal shook within her death grip, but she couldn't tell if the shiver came from her or the crystal. That's when she realized she wasn't being broken. The crystal was changing, and she shared its suffering. A hilt formed, a perfect fit for her slender hands.

"Hold tight."

She gagged. Snot and tears rolled across her face and past her lips to drip off her chin. The crystal snapped and popped. Through the blur of her wet eyes, she recognized the sword resembled a katana.

Her raw throat forced her into silence. She'd reached a point where the pain numbed all her brutalized senses.

That's when she recognized the sword's voice separate from her own. The agonized moan resembled Ayleen's voice the first time Captain Tratella had stopped going easy on her, breaking both her arms and her nose.

"Well done." The mage general stepped back to take in the sword held within Ayleen's blood covered hand. "Now tell it your name."

She spit out the bite guard, a ruined mess from her chewing through it. "I am—" She stopped realizing she didn't need to speak it aloud. Thinking the words was all that was required. *I am Ayleen Torr.*

A gasp answered. It was as if the sword had always been there, but forever alone. This was its first time meeting the spiritual gaze of another. It whispered its name to her.

"What?"

Ayleen shook her head. She must have heard it wrong, but then it whispered its name to her again. Her heart pounded in denial.

"What is its name?"

Ayleen jerked her sweat-coated face up towards the mage general. She didn't dare share the name. Instead, she said the first word that entered her thoughts.

"*Shyritas.*"

The mage general smiled to her, recognizing the word she'd chosen from the dead language of the *Mui Vanum.* "Truth? A most honorable name for a sword."

He reached over and took the sword from her. She whimpered, not wanting to surrender it.

"We must finish it for you." The mage general said this as if to beg her forgiveness. At first, Ayleen thought he meant an apology for parting her from her sword, but then she remembered. *Oh gods! The hilt isn't finished!*

She struggled against the straps, but for all her convulsions during the first part of the forging, they still held her tight. The mage general acted oblivious to her desperate grunts as he waved the captain back into the cave.

Ayleen stopped as the mage general moved out of view. A contradiction hit her harder than with the name of the sword. She knew the addition of the pommel would overwhelm her with more pain than anything the forging ceremony had hit her with up to that point. But she couldn't possibly know that. The Knighthood forbid discussion of the ceremony. Only those who had gone through it were allowed to speak of it and only then among others with like knowledge.

"This isn't real."

The knight captain knelt in front of her again, holding a fresh bite guard for her.

"Captain Tratella, you have to let me go! Please! You have to—!"

"Just a little longer." She shoved the bite guard into Ayleen's mouth, acting as if Ayleen hadn't spoken. And she hadn't, not when this first happened.

She bit down and clenched her fists trying to focus on pulling herself out of this memory.

She screamed, but then she felt the leather strip wrapping around the hilt.

The hammer came down on the pommel, giving it enough dig to stay in the crystal.

Ayleen's head flung back. Pain bloomed within her brow and her vision failed her. The room hazed over in a brilliant white light.

The pommel screwed into place with slow turns. Each turn set her eyes aflame, as if watching daggers thrust into her eye sockets and twisting in place. This time, she didn't scream. The pommel dug into the hilt deeper, trapping the wrapping in place and it was as if someone had flooded her lungs with ice water. She fought in vain to catch her breath.

Flakes of crystal shaved off, surrendering before the bond with Ayleen's soul was complete and rendered the sword indestructible. One shard proved especially stubborn. She felt as if a pair of pliers had grabbed onto the tip of a fingernail and tugged.

Turn.

Tug.

Turn.

Tug.

The nail ripped from her finger as the pommel buried into the hilt. Another nail jerked, fighting against the tug until the pommel screwed into place.

Sweat covered her body. Her vision wavered. The first time around, she passed out at this point.

She didn't dare do that this time.

The explorer. The pink woman. That deceiving heifer!

It's not real, she told herself.

The memory went dark. Ayleen's body jerked back, free of the bonds that vanished.

She landed on her arse along the brick walkway circling the well. She scrambled back on all fours from what was hidden within the shadows past the door, less fearful of falling into the pit of howling spirits than of repeating that memory again.

Stopping at the edge, she looked at her hands to make sure she still had her fingernails, same as she had when she'd awakened from passing out at the end of the ceremony years ago. Only these hands were amber crystal.

Her present dilemma rushed forward. She looked right and left. There was no sign of Basten.

Ayleen puzzled over what Basten hoped to gain from distracting her with that memory. Thinking on her forging ceremony brought back the pain of the imaginary needles stabbing into her body to flay her. The pain—all of it—always lingered, an echo of memory seeking sensation in the void where that detached part of her soul no longer dwelled.

She screamed as she forced it from her thoughts, focusing on her anger.

What had Basten said before throwing her into the memory? Ayleen whispered the words to herself. "Had I a body to return to…"

Basten had her wish. A body, short one soul, waited at the end of that profane path Ayleen had drawn.

11.

Ayleen ran around the well, hanging as close to the wall of memories as she dared. Her mind ached from reliving the forging ceremony. If she fell into another memory now, she wasn't sure she could pull free.

The spirits waiting for their next lives howled and laughed and screamed and pleaded. The noise dug into her heart. If her mother and father were in there, would falling into the pit with them be the easier end to all this?

Yes, surrender was always easier, but all the shrieks of the dead couldn't drown out her sword's angry whisper that giving up always cost too much.

She harbored a fool's hope she'd catch up to Basten before she reached the crack in the wall leading back to her body. The pink-skinned deceiver wasn't there.

Ayleen plunged into the ebony passage and ran as hard as she could. Her hands pressed against the walls she couldn't see. The inky surface clung to her crystal fingers as if to pull her back or cover her in filth. Perhaps both. She ignored it as much as she could. Even in reverse, this disgusting line of corruption threatened to sicken her. Surely she couldn't vomit in this form, but that didn't stop the nausea.

The path felt more cramped than the first time, but at least this time, she knew where it led. That kept her pushing forward.

A wail echoed through the dark path. The sound rippled through the walls and pulsed against Ayleen's fingertips.

Basten hadn't known what Ayleen suffered to get here. The horror must have settled on her, but that also meant she was close to the end.

Ayleen sprinted, bouncing into the wall at its sharpest turns. The viscous surface pulled on her. Her physical body waited at the end of this path. Whether it was imagined or not, she felt her soul's true home calling her into its embrace.

She neared the last turn, but she'd yet to find Basten. Had the walls consumed the bitch? Gods let it be so.

Panicked grunts came from around the bend. She rounded the last turn and spotted Basten. Her body glowed more white than pink now, closer to the near-featureless soul that had clawed its way out of the well. She staggered down the path towards an even brighter light at the end.

Ayleen feared she'd never catch up in time, but then she remembered how she'd summoned this woman from the Well with her name.

"Kristian Basten!"

The shout stopped the woman ahead of her. She shook, going rigid for a moment.

When Basten regained her senses, she turned to face Ayleen. "I won't go back!"

"You'll never be reborn, if you don't!"

"Reborn to what? A life where all my knowledge is lost to me?" She pounded her fist against her chest, not that it produced any sound. The light of her hand melted into her torso. "I've seen so many worlds and wonders. I wish to keep it and add more, not to be reduced to a tabula rasa."

"Kristian Basten!" Ayleen drew her sword as her call produced another stilling shudder in the spirit. "Kristian Basten, I call on you to stop!"

Ayleen charged forward, sword at the ready.

Basten screamed as she plunged ahead. Ayleen swung her sword, but the explorer's soul dodged the attack. Instead, that hand of light wrapped around Ayleen's wrist and flipped her to her back.

"I won't go back! There won't be enough time left for another life, if I let you free."

What was she talking about?

Ayleen shouted Basten's name again and grabbed her ankle to trip her onto her face.

They struggled down the path. The light of the exit drew closer. The call of her body distracted Ayleen like a hymn of forgiveness to a lost soul.

Ayleen lost her grip on the woman. Basten dove for the light at the end of the path, and Ayleen plunged after her.

They both hovered there in the light. No wind or noise disturbed them. Like a drain, that seems slow to empty at first, the light then dragged them down and shoved them against one another until they stopped.

12.

Ayleen opened her eyes, and jerked back to her feet. She stumbled. Her legs didn't answer right. They weren't supposed to be this short.

She spotted her sword and grabbed its hilt before she could fall to the ground.

"Back! The knight returns." The demon cackled from the tree. *"And not alone. Better!"*

She was on Skimo VIII. Vertigo threatened to knock her over. Her eyes fixed on her headstone. Ayleen looked up to the sky as anger filled her.

"Skimo VIII? Lying bastards!" She'd died here, bitten by an insect, a dokenum wasp. The group she'd brought with her had vowed to take her body back home to Caspenia XII. "You didn't even have the dignity to give me the stars!"

What the Dark was she on about? Ayleen grabbed her forehead. Pain split from behind her eyes and through the center of her brain.

"Oh, gods." Ayleen shivered, not from cold but from an unwelcome heat. She was burning from within. A fire with too many coals...too many souls.

"We can't last like this, Basten. You'll kill us both!"

She jerked her sword from where she'd stabbed it in the dirt. She couldn't cut the bitch out of her, not without ending herself.

"We can do this, young one. I swear it." Basten's haughty accent on her lips sickened her. She vomited a puddle of bile on the woman's grave. When she stopped, she laughed. She'd defiled the bitch's resting place.

"Silence! I won't be treated in this manner."

Ayleen glared at the headstone. "You're nothing but a parasite! This body is mine."

She wiped the spittle from her lips and laughed. "Parasite or not, you can't kill me without killing yourself. Despise me all you like, we are bound together from this breath to the last."

Ayleen ignored her for now and returned her attention to the demon hidden in the tree. "You ready for your ride, demon?"

"More souls to play with? Garmett Two? We go now?"

"You made a pact with a shade?" Basten jerked their body back, stumbling in terror from what lurked in the tree above them. "You're mad! You think me a parasite?"

"Stop it!" Ayleen screamed. "We can't fight for control and survive. It's my body, Basten. Give it to me. All you hunger for is knowledge and fame. You can gather knowledge in silence. Let me have my body."

"Very well."

No sooner had the pretentious tone left her lips than the tension fled her limbs. Ayleen collapsed to her knees.

"Demon?" Ayleen sheathed her sword. The leaves rustled and the shadowy void of nothing dropped to the ground.

"Now?"

"I've not forgotten our pact. Nor should you."

She heard it jumping in place and laughing.

13.

The seven days of travel Ayleen had estimated from Basten's grave to the keyhole for Garmett Two stretched into ten.

To Basten's credit, she honored Ayleen's demand to cede control of her body. That didn't keep her silent. The quickened explorer's mind worked at every moment. Bad as it was in the day when Ayleen needed to mind her surroundings, the nights turned worse.

Her dreams left her restless. Memories stirred, many not her own. Having crossed back into the mortal plain, Basten's knowledge took shape in whatever space Ayleen's mind provided.

More than once, Ayleen opened her celestial map and studied what was there. She would scribble notes onto the map about worlds she'd never been to. In some empty spaces, she drew in worlds the Knighthood had missed. Much as Ayleen rankled at Basten's disrespect for her father, she better understood the woman's frustration as she filled the gaps in her map.

The demon seethed at their delays, kicking up clouds of dirt.

Basten's disruptions to her sleep didn't end with her own memories. The knowledge-hungry witch searched through Ayleen's life. She dredged up one memory after another. Ayleen sensed her parasitic partner hungered for something specific, and she fought against the woman for as long as she could.

Their last night on Skimo VIII, Ayleen surrendered the memory. All too many nights, she dreamed of her forging ceremony. Most knights did.

Ayleen's heart quickened with Basten's excitement as she witnessed what none outside the Knighthood ever had. The thrill of discovery died—replaced with horror—as Basten heard the first thing the sword ever said to Ayleen.

14.

She jerked awake to that bright sky. Night offered stars on most worlds, but not this one. She'd deserved those stars over her resting place. Caspenia XII would have offered a glorious view with a long arm of the Galaxy reaching through the heavens—countless stars clustered to resemble a thick trail of gas. That's why she'd made it her home.

"Gods of blood and fire." Ayleen grabbed the sides of her head, her blue hair snarled within her fingers. The line between her and Basten was blurring. They both knew it, and Basten's willingness to give up control of their body was growing less so.

"You lied," Basten said. Her panic had Ayleen's heart pounding hard within their chest.

Ayleen got to her feet. "As did you."

They'd settled in for the night, which was only half gone, on a hill overlooking the remains of a city. A black sign with brightly colored symbols and numbers indicated the keyhole sphere waited for them in the city. Its name had vanished with its inhabitants.

"*Awake.*" The grass shuddered a few feet away where the demon had waited. "*Twice the minds get half the rest. Can we go?*"

"Silence, you foul thing!" Basten answered before Ayleen could.

The demon hissed. Not that the demon cared for Ayleen, but he despised Basten more.

"Yes, young one, I lied, and well I did. You will doom us all."

Ayleen laughed as she paced beside their bedroll. "You're as corrupt as the Thirteen. You'd see everyone suffer, so you could live a little longer than the rest."

"I've tasted the horrors of the afterlife. I find it lacking."

Ayleen reached down to pick up her sword belt. Her arm resisted. "What you want is pointless. Your life ran its natural course."

"As with this galaxy." Her heartbeat skipped to a faster beat every time Basten took control to speak. "Your lust for blood is just, but if you kill the Thirteen, your revenge will destroy everything."

"Paladin Castle!" Ayleen grabbed the front of her own shirt as if to drag herself forward. "Where is it?"

Basten resisted thinking on the answer.

"That's right, you lying bitch. My father taught me well enough to read a map. There is no Cephei VI."

The half of her brain crowded in by Basten shouted random numbers. Ayleen screamed aloud and slammed her fists against the ground. Even prodded into thinking on Paladin Castle, the dead woman proved too clever to think the planet's real name.

Ayleen grabbed her bed and rolled it up.

"We go now? Finally?"

"Yes!" Ayleen wanted to sleep, but she couldn't risk it. Each time she closed her eyes to rest, she woke up a little less of the woman who'd gone to bed. The only comfort was how much she sensed the same fear in Basten. Given time, they'd both lose this fight. They'd become someone else, assuming the struggle didn't rip their body apart.

15.

The sun rose as they reached the keyhole cave's entrance, a path leading into the ground. The white brick walls pressed in on them as they descended the spiral path. Lights lined the ceiling, but they didn't work. Ayleen used her sword's magic to see where they were going.

The sphere for Garmett Two glowed a welcome yellow.

The demon's invisible talons echoed on the concrete floor as it danced.

"Taking him with us is madness." Basten's fear stopped them short of the sphere.

"I made a bargain. I intend to honor it." Ayleen narrowed her eyes on the shifting hint of shadow off to the side. "Are you ready?"

"Yes!" It shrieked. *"Ready to play with lives, old and young!"*

"Remember your bargain with me." Ayleen lent every ounce of her malice to the warning. "Try to cheat me, and I'll cut you down."

"Yes, yes. I'll be true." It drew closer, the air rippling where it stood.

"Climb in, and we'll go."

Ayleen meant to lunge at the sphere the instant the demon crawled inside her, but pain flared within her left leg, where the demon entered her. Imaginary flames licked up the inside of her calf and thigh. Instead of lunging into the sphere, Ayleen collapsed to the floor. Two lives was bad enough, but the demon was a black hole of fire radiating through her. The agony reached her stomach.

Both Basten and the demon shouted to get up and leap into the sphere.

The notion to let the demon take control tempted her. A possession would make the pain stop, but she didn't dare. Once it had control, the demon would never honor its promise to leave her on the other side, if they ever made it.

Fighting against the pain as it pushed up through her heart, Ayleen dragged herself upright. Both legs shook. Sweat covered her. Dizziness threatened to fell her, but Ayleen reached out as she fell forward into the keyhole.

Its gentle tug offered a second of comfort against the growing invasion of the demon. Reality blinked for an instant, as it always did, offering the briefest of reprieves from their agony.

They emerged into a neglected cave on Garmett Two.

They screamed, the pitch switching between the three of them.

"Now, demon!" Ayleen shouted. "Your bargain is with me, not her!"

"No!"

"Yes!"

Those fiery talons reached deeper into her body.

"Deceitful child! No!"

The pain peaked as the demon crawled its way out of her. It started as a gasp and morphed into an agonized cough. Gagging, Ayleen hunched over, her body shaking as if to vomit, but nothing visible escaped.

Basten's screams grew distant. The dead woman hurled every curse she knew, most in languages Ayleen understood less as their union spewed up and out her throat.

Once expelled from her mind and body, Ayleen rolled onto her side. She couldn't stop. She needed to move, but whatever she'd expected to be able to do at this point proved a gross overestimation. Instead of pulling on her reserves to stand, she closed her eyes as her mind shut down for an overdue rest.

16.

When Ayleen woke, a slow ache chastised her body and spirit.

A little rested, she got her first true look at this cave. The floor was flat dirt, not paved or tiled. Her mind no longer felt crowded and noisy. She laughed to herself.

"The knight of lies awakes."

The demon's voice startled her and sent her scrambling to her feet. Her panic pushed her enough to stand, but once she got there, she realized her body lacked the energy to stay upright on her own. She stumbled to the left and reached out a hand for the wall. That kept her stable enough to stand. If she'd had the strength, she'd have drawn her sword, but she didn't dare.

"Surprised you're still here." She glanced around the part of the room she could see. An exit was set off to the far side of the room.

The hint of light that came from the corridor fluttered enough for her to know the demon was near the opening's arch.

"You lied."

Ayleen's smile widened. The demon had known. It wasn't talking about her game to betray Basten. Ayleen had prepared the demon, reminding it throughout their walk that the deal was with her and not the dead woman.

No, the lie the demon spoke of was her original intent to draw her sword on the demon and banish it with a single strike once they got here. She'd kept her intent buried, not wanting to risk her or Basten letting that slip during their journey.

"Yeah, I planned to finish you off once we got here. Never promised to do otherwise when we made our pact," Ayleen said. "Not that it matters now. You get to go free, after all."

"Free to play so many games." The demon's snicker cut short. *"Seems I couldn't take her all, the arrogant one. Still a little left in your face."*

Ayleen didn't get to ask what that meant. The waviness in the air disappeared with the echoes of its steps.

She let out a long sigh. Clinging to the walls, she followed the demon's path to the surface of Garmett Two.

By the time she reached the end of the corridor, she'd broken into a cold sweat. The way out of the corridor was blocked by a collapsible, metal gate. Its crisscrossed metal bars formed dozens of diamonds, each a little too small for her head to fit through.

Beyond the gate, the corridor was replaced with a set of steps leading up to a platform. The walls, floor, and steps were covered in pale pink tiles. Lights flashed across the tiles in fast-moving rectangles, followed by a furious rush of air that built to a ground-shaking crescendo before fading.

She sliced the gate open with her sword. The gate parted to the right and left with a rusty creak.

At the top of the steps, she found a type of guard house blocking half of the corridor. Next to it was a pair of waist-high towers. Most of their green paint was chipped off. Three metal poles jutted out from each tower to block her path. The poles appeared to rotate, and when she pressed herself against one of the poles, they turned with metallic clicks to let her through.

Beyond, a platform overlooked a long, fat, steel rail that ran the length of the tunnel. Another loud hum built up before a train rushed past, generating a powerful wind and sending her hat and hair flying. The hat landed behind her by the guard house.

She walked back to retrieve it after the train disappeared. The bottom half of the guardhouse was a reflective metal surface, and as she knelt to pick up her hat, she saw her reflection.

Ayleen jumped back, landing on her arse.

Her eyes didn't match. The right eye stared back with the same deep purple as always, but her left… The iris had turned a bright blue, the same as Basten's.

That's what the demon meant. He'd said some of Basten's soul was still in her.

"Paladin Castle." She said the name of the place, and the words stirred memories that didn't belong to her. She imagined a grey stone castle. No, she remembered it on an island with a sun setting at its back, casting it in silhouette. The name of the world popped into her thoughts.

"Witbrom VI." Not Cephei VI. Ayleen laughed as she leaned back against the tiled wall. The risk had paid off. After two years of wandering from one keyhole to another, she had a final destination.

Her head turned to look back at her reflection and her laughter stopped.

That blue eye—Basten's blue eye glared back at her. She struggled to grab onto the memory from the Well of Souls, the last time she'd seen her mother and the way both of her mother's purple eyes took her in from across the room. Despite reliving it a week earlier, the memory felt fuzzy. She looked back at her reflection and turned her head to the left until her profile hid the blue eye.

Her sword laughed—whether at her or Basten, she couldn't say. Maybe both.

Until today, no one else had ever known the name of her sword.

Kalle-Al.

The End of All Things.

When the sword whispered it to her after its forging, she lied with the first thing that entered her thoughts.

Shyritas.

That she'd answered with "Truth" had always troubled her, but for the first time, it filled her with an impulse to drop her sword and spend the rest of her life running from it.

Instead, she gripped Kalle-Al by the hilt and held it close. It was the only living thing left from her life before the Galaxy lost its Way.

PART V

The Castle

1.

Ayleen stepped off the elevator into one of the lowest levels in the underground city of Veil. A series of atmospheric catastrophes about seven centuries earlier forced the residents of Witbrom VI to live within enclosed cities. Considering Sub Floor 103 stank of piss and oil, an argument for risking the surface could be made.

The 103rd provided a place of commerce and assembly for the city's lower income citizens. As was typical for these floors, the ceiling sat low, only reaching seven feet high, but floor 103 offered a little something special compared to the other levels in the lower third of the city. Instead of an upward view of pipes and dark grey cement, most of the ceiling was made up of a massive display screen. This late in the evening, the view offered a clear, starry sky which included a spectacular rendering of the nearby nebula. The remnants of a supernova drew blue and purple veins across a crowded field of stars with the brightest star of all, Cygnus L2, positioned behind the nebula.

The busy crowd bustling from taverns and other shops paid little attention to the artificial display. One exception was a little girl—a green-skinned Fillian with big, black eyes—pointing up and shouting excited grunts. Her father held her other hand and dragged her along.

Ayleen stopped in the corridor, watching the father and daughter pass. When she was a child, she'd hoped to one day map the Galaxy with her father, but she only traveled with his memory. Would her parents approve of why she was here? She planned to avenge them, but part of her suspected they would be disappointed.

The false sky above her included the names and logos of businesses on this level with glowing arrows to point the way. Finding Efram's Pub didn't take long. She heard the pub's obnoxious, electronic music before she saw it. At the end of a corridor that branched off from the main one, she reached the door to the pub. The hexagon-shaped room offered a little more headroom since it didn't include the ceiling display. The only light came from small lamps on the tables and a few rectangular lights embedded in the walls. Customers crowded around the well-stocked bar set along the back wall. Ayleen ordered a drink and took it with her to a booth off to the right.

She adjusted the thin, black trench coat to keep it closed enough to conceal her crystal sword. Counter to her dark disposition, she wore a vibrant pink shirt. She bought it on the world before Witbrom as soon as she saw it, using the money she'd earned from helping a group of smugglers deliver some contraband data tablets, among other goods. Seemed good swordfighters were hard to come by, and her skills had earned her way across several planets where money was as vital as breathable air.

At the time, she wasn't certain what made her desire for the shirt so strong until she got up the next day and pulled it on. The color of the shirt was a near perfect match of Kristian Basten's skin. Five months had passed since the dead woman's soul had possessed her, and her left eye remained a vibrant blue. Basten's influence hadn't ended there. Her appearance mattered to her more. What frustrated her most was that seeing her take the extra time to brush the knots from her hair and keep her clothes tidy would have thrilled her parents. Father would have teased her while Mother danced in celebration.

The pub's music shifted to a familiar tune. Ayleen couldn't place the name, but most of the crowd shouted and wailed along with the lyrics. One stumbling, fall-on-his-arse, off-key drunk felt the need to mimic the guitar solo instead. Their voices peaked as they shouted, *"You are the fugitive kind!"*

During the half hour she spent waiting through one song after another, people floated in and out of the pub. By the time she was drinking her third pint of cider, a woman waddled up to her table and blocked her view of the door with a pronounced belly that left no doubt she was drinking for two, possibly three.

The pregnant woman stared down at Ayleen with an amused tug on her lips. "Now, I get it."

"Excuse me?" Ayleen fought the urge to reach for her sword. She'd noticed more than one person in here carrying swords despite the ban on such weapons, but none of them were dumb enough to be obvious about it. That didn't include this stranger, though. The only thing this lady was packing was a scowl.

"Why my son sounded so smitten when he told me about his latest recruit." She struggled to slide into the booth, pushing the table up against Ayleen's chest in order to make room for herself.

"You're Mack?"

"Mackenzie James." She slid off her hat and set it on the table. "My son conveniently left out how pretty you were when I demanded to know why he'd smuggled someone into Veil for half of what I usually charge."

"What makes you sure you have the right person?"

Mack pointed a fat finger at Ayleen's face. "The eyes. One blue, one violet."

Ayleen hid her irritation at the reminder about her eyes. Curse Basten's soul!

"He said you wanted to talk business, that you're looking to do a little sightseeing."

A server, a woman who looked a little older than Ayleen with long, haggard hair falling into her face, placed a brown mug in front of Mack. Steam wafted from it with the delightful scent of coffee. The closer Ayleen had gotten to Witbrom, the better the amenities had gotten.

"Anything else, Mack?" the server asked.

"Yes." Mack pointed at Ayleen. "She's paying for this and for a beer I'll enjoy after it's eviction day." She patted her belly as she said the last part.

"Sure thing."

The server never looked at Ayleen to see if she'd agreed to that. Only added confirmation to what she'd heard about Mack. People in Veil knew better than to question her.

Witbrom VI wasn't lawless, but that didn't mean the lawless didn't have a place in it. Mack had supposedly shoved enough of the competition out of airlocks to claim a monopoly on the smuggling trade.

"I'd like to visit a place most tourists don't get to see," Ayleen said.

Mack grinned. "What place you got in mind?"

"Paladin Castle."

Mack leaned back as far as she could manage in the cramped booth. The fake leather cushions of her seat creaked. Her eyes narrowed on Ayleen as if to find something she'd overlooked.

"Let's pretend for a minute it's possible to smuggle you in there. Tell me why."

"I don't see you really need to know why, just that I'm willing to pay."

Mack no longer looked amused. She leaned back in towards Ayleen. Her voice lowered with an edge that left no doubt she was irritated.

"When they built the train system above ground to connect the cities, three tracks were constructed for Paladin Castle. Two supply trains make weekly trips from the cities to the castle. Guards search each train top to bottom before each trip. That includes cracking open each crate, and you have to go by train, because the surface is uninhabitable—the air's too thin to breathe.

"But let's assume you can get past the inspection teams and make it into the dome covering the castle." She waved her hand between them as if to sprinkle magical dust in the air, suggesting how realistic she considered the possibility. "A hundred guards defend the place. They all know each other, so it's not like you can dress up as one and pretend you belong there. On top of that, they're zealots—true believers in the divinity of the Thirteen. Plenty of people would love to see the Thirteen cut into little pieces—especially in the Far Reaches—but not those boys and girls. They'd slit open their mammies and pappies' throats without a tear of regret if the Great Lord Pyre Clypse ordered it."

"Not an acolyte of his?" Ayleen hadn't missed the sarcasm Mack had given Clypse's honorific.

"Doesn't matter what I think. The Thirteen can't die. Every summer solstice, they empty the prisons by publicly executing all the convicts with their swords, and then they run through one of their own to show the same weapons that can kill us can't harm any of them. They're gods."

"They aren't gods!" Only the music kept Ayleen's voice low enough to not be heard. "If you despise them so much, help me get into that castle."

"And if you get caught?"

"I won't be."

Mack shook her head. "Not good enough. I don't know you, so I don't trust you. If you get caught—and you will—I don't want your wagging tongue landing me in a prison cell, certainly not with the summer solstice less than three weeks away." She scooted out of the booth and forced herself to her feet.

"What if I offered to pay twice the asking price and all up front?" Ayleen knew it was a desperate offer, but she needed to get into that castle and the keyhole beneath it.

"Money can't buy my trust. You have to earn it. Something tells me you aren't willing to wait to make that happen."

"I've spent the past month working with your son. My sword has made you plenty of money and kept him alive."

Mack slammed her fist on the table as she fell into a fit of laughter that didn't end until she was wiping a tear from her eyes. "Let's dispense with the candy-coated shit. You've worked all of three jobs for my people. What you've done for the past month is warm my son's bed."

The accusation brought a flush to Ayleen's face. She hadn't expected Mack to know, not that she and Kelvin had made any secret of what was happening between them.

"You're already tied too close to me and my people, and especially to my boy." Mack downed the rest of her coffee. "I'm half-tempted to turn you in right now, but knowing my fool-headed son, he'd get himself caught trying to break you free."

Ayleen didn't say anything, not when she knew the woman was right. Kelvin had a good heart, the kind she no longer believed she deserved.

Mack slammed down her empty mug on the table. "Thanks for the drinks. Breathe easy."

Little chance of that. Each breath she took felt like borrowed time. The Thirteen still believed her dead, thanks to their hired swords back on Kurega, but that would only last so much longer now that she was hiding in the heart of their empire.

She felt the presence of the Thirteen here, stronger than ever. At least one of them had been on the world prior to Witbrom, but whichever traitor that might have been, they'd managed not to cross Ayleen's path or sword.

Whenever one of the Thirteen was near, reality felt wrong. At first, she thought their presence alone was what provoked the decay of the worlds she'd found, but as she drew closer to Paladin Castle, she realized that was only half-right.

The Galaxy was crumbling, collapsing in on itself. She saw the signs in this pub. The way the shadows of the patrons painted the floors and walls didn't work right. Did any of them notice? She suspected they did, but they'd none of them known the Galaxy when it hadn't lost its Way. To them, this was normal.

Mack's silhouette filled the pub's entrance as she shuffled out into the corridor. Little wonder she'd refused to help. The Thirteen were simply the demons she knew. Why would she risk trading them for a devil she didn't?

Ayleen finished her cider and settled up at the bar, gladly paying for Mack's coffee and postpartum beer. The smuggler wouldn't help her get into Paladin Castle, but she'd provided her with plenty of information on the obstacles she faced. She mulled over those challenges as she headed for the room she'd rented up on level 78.

2.

Veil contained 113 levels. Only the top three existed above the outer crust of Witbrom VI. They were called the Upper Crust levels.

The wealthiest citizens of the city lived on the top two levels. Rumor had it the only people with windows to look out on the barren scenery of the surface opted to spend most of their time substituting the view for video displays of more scenic surroundings, images of mountains or oceans that no longer existed.

No one lived on level three. The floor housed a large public park and the train station that connected Veil with other cities.

A wall across from the main elevators displayed a massive screen of a map of the train station and a constantly updated schedule of arrival and departure times. Ayleen studied the layout of the tracks.

"You enjoying the sights?" The deep voice came from over her left shoulder, and she recognized it.

Ayleen turned and smiled to Kelvin. She stood a few inches taller than him, but he packed plenty of muscle. He smelled of leather, thanks to his dark blue jacket which covered an off-white t-shirt with a v-neck.

"Can't say I've found anything I'm all that interested in yet," Ayleen said, with a playful lilt to her words. Kelvin had that effect on her. At first, she'd feared her interest in him might be another symptom of Basten's soul, but from what little she remembered of Basten's memories, she'd enjoyed her men taller than herself. Given Basten's stature, there weren't many options for her.

Kelvin laughed as he lifted his tan, wide-brimmed hat and ran his fingers through his hair. His wavy, dark green mane reached down to his shoulders where it curled up a bit in a way that invited a girl to run her fingers through it. "I'll try not to take that personally."

"Nor should you." Ayleen glanced behind him at the rest of the crowd on the platform to make sure no one was with him. "Not that it isn't nice to see you, but I thought you were going back to Ryjal II."

"Yeah..." He gave the word the kind of extra emphasis that added a few syllables to it. "I was before my boss found out I'd given a pretty lady a hefty discount to smuggle her into Veil."

Ayleen cleared her throat. "Sorry. I suspect that had more to do with the business proposition I took to your mother last night."

"Ya think?" Despite the thick sarcasm, he couldn't hold back his smile.

He stepped around her to offer her his left arm. The boy remembered she liked to keep her left hand free to draw her sword, if needed. He played things a bit too chivalrous for her tastes, but that didn't stop her from hooking her arm through his. She remembered watching her parents walking arm-in-arm through the passages of Mount Hawkken with her skipping ahead of them when she was about five.

"What say," Kelvin said with a comfortable drawl, "we go looking for some sights you might find more to your liking?"

"Scenery already seems to be improving. Lead on."

3.

The view he led her to didn't provide a look inside the train station. Instead, they stopped in front of a long window on the west end of the city.

The maudlin sight of the horizon reminded her of her home world of Teikorium. Not the world she'd grown up in, which had offered yellow skies and a horizon covered in waves of blue grass. This reminded her of home as she last saw it: barren and hot.

A soft vibration ran through the floor and up into Ayleen's legs.

"That would be the 10:50 train to Justice," Kelvin said before the train burst into view, cutting a straight path towards the edge of the horizon.

The train moved too fast for its lines to gain any definition beyond a blur of white and bright orange streaks against the dark brown sands. Its metal surface reflected the pale yellow rays of light peeking out from beyond the cover of grey and black clouds. A thick steel rail provided the track for the train and offered the only sign of life along the surface of Witbrom VI.

"Reaches speeds of 225 clicks an hour."

Ayleen let out a low whistle. "Hover technology applied to a controlled route."

"Um... Honestly? I have no damn clue how it works." He shrugged and offered a dopey grin. His manner bespoke a life of little hardship. Should have angered her, but Kelvin's smile had a way of evaporating her rage. The idea people like him could still exist in a galaxy that had lost its Way made no sense to her. The only lives that had mattered to her since the fall of the Knighthood were the ones she'd lost and the others who'd taken them.

"Don't worry." Her playful tone matched his. "I wasn't assuming you brought me here for a lesson in train technology." She jutted her chin in the direction of the now distant 10:50 to Justice. "So how does this help me get to Paladin Castle?"

"I'm not sure anything will get you in there," he said with an apologetic tone. "Some things will get you closer, but to make it inside and survive..." He shook his head.

She considered reminding him of the police ambush on Ziltra II when they'd been forced to fight their way out of the warehouse. His friends had argued against her advice for the best way out of the city, and he'd opted to put his trust in her. Her sword killed more than three dozen compared to his three by the time they'd made it into the surrounding forest and holed up in the cave where they'd chosen for everyone to rendezvous, a meetup his friends never reached. Kelvin knew how to use a sword, but his heart got in the way with no real love for a fight or the kill.

"Humor me," she said.

"An hour out from here, there's a substation. Only people who live there are the workers. The trains stop to refuel and switch tracks." With a gentle tug of her arm, he led her back onto a grass-covered path through a grove of trees that took them back into the wide, open field of the park. "One track goes straight to Paladin Castle."

"Don't suppose I could hop off the train there and walk the rest of the way."

He shook his head. "Atmosphere's too thin. A breather mask would make up for that—and yes, I could find you one—but if you got caught out there with the sun up... *Poof!* Like an overcooked bird in an oven."

"Do you have birds here?" She gestured to the park around them. Birdsong played throughout, but it was a prerecorded loop. Whoever put the audio track together had forgotten to include the sound of wings fluttering, and nothing moved in the trees.

"Only the imported, prepackaged variety. Air's too valuable a resource to raise any kind of livestock here."

Ayleen gestured for them to head back towards the lifts to the lower levels and the screen with the railway map and schedule on the platform. "So how much trouble did I really get you into?"

"Honestly?" He laughed. "Not much. Well, not yet. I know my ma, and something tells me she grounded me here hoping I'd talk you out of whatever it is you're planning to do."

"How's that working out for you so far?"

"What say I take you somewhere for lunch and see how I'm doing after that?"

Gods above and below. This guy's smile hit her in the sweet spot. Her mother had told her what it was like when she'd first met Dad. The idea of not being with Dad sucked the air out of her. For Ayleen, kissing Kelvin hit her like a double shot of oxycodone straight to the brain.

"I'm staying on level 78."

"There's a café on 79."

They joined the group of people clustered around the lift for levels 60-89. Their arms were still hooked together. His hair smelled like mint, probably from whatever he used to wash it.

The public address system announced the latest arrivals and departures, cycling through four of the most common languages in this region.

"Passengers now boarding on platform eight for the 11:30 train with service to Gidion, Meercroft, and Windsor. Allow passengers to disembark before boarding, and please mind the gap between the train and the platform."

The crowd shifted with some people rushing to catch their train while new arrivals jockeyed for a good position in the lines for the lifts.

A deep chime announced the arrival of their ride. The doors opened and an arrow pointing down lit up bright blue. The noise in the waiting area doubled as people rushed out and others shoved their way inside lest they wait another twenty minutes. A woman wearing a grey uniform worked the controls. She shouted above the crowd in a tone as bland as her clothes.

"This is a lift for levels 60 through 89! Please let exiting passengers off before boarding! Mind your belongings, and please keep your hands and other appendages to yourselves!"

Ayleen and Kelvin made it on board before the door frame lit up yellow, which was met with groans from those still on the platform. The driver held up a hand to stop anyone else from boarding. "Stand back! We're full!"

The doors hissed as they slowly closed. More new arrivals added to the crowd of people waiting for rides down. One man with yellow, reptilian skin stood above the others. Ayleen would never forget the face of her father's murderer, and her sword screamed for blood.

On instinct, Ayleen grabbed the hilt, but stopped short of drawing it. The cabin door shut as the Khymeran looked her way. Had he seen her?

"What's wrong?" Kelvin whispered without his usual humor.

The last time she'd seen that Khymeran bastard's face, he'd been racing up behind her and the squires during the Thirteen's attack on Mount Hawkken. Only one thing was different about him. He'd had two green, slit eyes then. Now, he only had one. A brown leather eyepatch covered the right socket.

He was one of the Thirteen, and her sword screamed for his cold blood the entire ride down.

4.

Ayleen and Kelvin skipped the café. Instead, they went straight to her room on level 78. She planned to tell him why the sight of the Khymeran had startled her and almost sent her launching out of the elevator to attack him. Kelvin knew the Thirteen had killed her family, but that wasn't an uncommon story in the Galaxy. She meant to share what happened to the Knighthood and how she'd crossed centuries to kill them. There was so much she'd held back from him that he deserved to know, and she wanted to share it all with him.

Only, once the door to her room closed, Kelvin kissed her.

She'd never expected to have another moment alone with him after their last night on Ryjal II. Revenge had driven her for the past few years, but Kelvin possessed the unique talent for making her rage vanish. She should have stopped him so they could talk and plan. Instead, they ripped off their clothes and fell into the bed.

Being with Kelvin wasn't a battle or a dance. The best part of making love with him was how much she didn't need to think at all. Until Kelvin, everything in her life had demanded careful planning, precision, and ruthlessness. With him, she could simply exist.

When the moment passed, they collapsed onto their backs, struggling to breathe. They lingered in silence and traced lazy, curving paths across each other's naked bodies. When Mother had told Ayleen about sex, she'd said Father had called it a bedroom supernova. Now that she'd met Kelvin, Ayleen wasn't sure she agreed with the description. Supernovas were the deaths of stars, but being with Kelvin made her yearn to live.

Taking a deep breath, she looked away from him at the ceiling. "The Khymeran with the eyepatch..."

"Ysil Leesp."

The Knighthood had three Khymeran captains, a fact she didn't bother sharing. She'd never met any of them before the day the Thirteen's army invaded the Citadel, but she always suspected the traitor was Leesp. "He had a reputation within the Knighthood. Damn good with a sword. Had to stop giving him apprentices, though. Was too hard on them. Had a real hate for warm bloods."

"Still does. I've seen the way he executes someone. Wait!" Kelvin sat up. "How'd he lose the eye? People have placed bets on that for ages, but no one's ever found out."

She cursed under her breath. "Last time I saw him, he still had both eyes. Was hoping you might tell me what happened. I sliced off Javo's head when I fought her back on Griffin, and she still pulled herself back together with only a little scar. Far as I can tell, they can heal any injury they receive."

"That's why everyone has placed bets on it forever and a day. That and it's fun to make up ways that insufferable snake got shamed."

The best Ayleen managed was a faint smirk. She needed a way to injure these immortal traitors, especially when her next encounter was all too likely to include more than one of them.

A noise resembling a klaxon came from where Ayleen had tossed Kelvin's jacket to the floor.

"Aw, shit." He climbed out of the bed and snatched up his jacket. A rectangular screen embedded in the right sleeve, above the cuff, was blinking red.

"What is it?"

"My ma."

"What? No, I mean, what is that—" She didn't get to finish asking what the device on his jacket was. She'd never seen him use it back on Ryjal II.

"Where are you?" The way his mom barked the question, even Ayleen sat up to attention. She could make out the moving image of Mack on the screen, although Kelvin was doing his best to keep his mother from seeing Ayleen.

"Level 78, " he said. "What's the problem?"

"The police are doing a floor-by-floor search. They started on Level 60 and are working their way down."

Ayleen didn't wait to hear more, she scrambled to get dressed. She muffled her shriek as her bare feet hit the cold, metal floor. As soon as the sensation passed, she grabbed for the nearest article of her clothing.

The Thirteen believed she was dead, but Leesp still recognized her. How in the blackest hole had the bastard known who she was?

"Are you with that godsdamned girl?"

"Uh…"

"Shove me out an airlock! Brainless boy! They've already reached level 76. Stash her somewhere and run."

5.

Ayleen had gotten as far as to pull up her pants, but she still hadn't found her bra. Where had Kelvin flung it?

"In the future," she said as she dug her bra out from beneath the bed, "we need to place our clothes in easy-to-find piles."

He laughed.

She scowled at him. "I'm serious."

"Oh, sorry."

A minute later, they were put back together. Ayleen didn't bother tucking in her shirt, but she piled up her hair to hide it in her hat. "Where to?"

"The lifts." He slid open her room's door. "Gotta get off this level before they reach it."

They marched out into the corridor. Ayleen grabbed him by the wrist to keep him from launching into a sprint. "Don't run. Best not to stand out."

"Security cameras might be active, too. They usually don't use them to conserve power, unless the stubs are chasing someone."

"Stubs" were what these people called the law on this world on account of the gladius each of them carried. The stubby swords worked well for the city's cramped spaces.

Two boys ran past them. Going by the panicked look on their faces, they knew about the search. One of them almost collided with Ayleen as they dove into another room.

"Gotta flush our stash before the stubs—" The door shut, cutting off the rest of whatever he was saying.

The lobby for the lifts was packed. People cursed and took turns trying to summon a lift, as if the first twenty folks pounding the up and down arrows had done it wrong.

"Dammit." Kelvin pulled her towards the other end of the lobby. "Maybe the stairs are still—"

Before he could finish the thought, they heard a man shouting and pounding both fists on an orange door in the direction they were heading. The man stopped assaulting the door long enough to glare up at a camera pointed towards him and made a locally-recognized offensive gesture as if to choke himself.

Kelvin stroked his beard stubble as if he might rub an idea loose.

"No lifts and no stairs," Ayleen said. "What next, smuggler?"

"Back to your room." They walked much faster this time.

"There's no place to hide in there."

"No obvious place." He stopped as they reached the hallway where the two boys had run into their room.

"What's the hold up?" Ayleen stared back at him as she thrust a hand in the direction of her room.

"Which room did those guys go into?"

"What?"

"Which room!" His normally deep voice managed to jump up an octave. When she pointed to the door in question, he marched up to it and hit it as if to knock it down. "Open up! I need to score!"

Ayleen gaped. Surely, he wasn't doing this for a hit. She'd never seen him smoke. He hit the door in a rapid-fire style with both hands and threw his shoulder against the door. "Open the gods-damned door!"

The door slid open with a loud shriek of steel on steel. A hand shoved out with a pale green plastic bag. "Fuck you! Take it all! Good luck explaining this to the police when they find you."

Even excluding the drug dealer's spiked hair, he still stood a full head taller than Kelvin. That didn't help him as Kelvin grabbed him by the throat and shoved him inside. Bodies banged around inside the room, but Ayleen waited outside. She knew from their time on the run together that Kelvin could handle this. He'd earned some extra money for them one time by winning an underground cage fight. His size, compared to his opponent, had left him with some steep odds. He convinced Ayleen to bet all they had on him. Kelvin took down his opponent in less than five minutes.

The door opened back up. "I only want enough to party by myself," Kelvin said. "What you do with the rest is your problem. You got it?"

Kelvin stormed back into the corridor with his fist wrapped around three poorly-rolled smokes.

"Let's hustle." He didn't look back to see if the drug dealers were chasing them.

"Oh, now you want to hurry," she teased him.

An alarm sounded, cutting off their banter. The hallway lighting doubled in brightness. No chance of hiding in the corridor's shadows, because there weren't any. The booming voice of a woman followed the alarm.

"Citizens, law enforcement are conducting a room-by-room search of your level. Your compliance is mandated. Failure to allow officers entry into your home or business will result in an immediate arrest. All citizens are required to present their identification or travel visas upon request."

The voice on the sound system repeated the announcement two more times, stopping as they reached Ayleen's room.

Kelvin grabbed the door, but it wouldn't budge. "Oh, choke me blue!" He turned to her. "Did you bring your—?"

She answered him by waving her room key in front of his face. "Yes, I brought it with me."

"Probably should've asked you sooner."

"I trust you're planning something better than getting high or offering these to the police." She placed the key in front of the sensor, and the door slid open. "Right?"

"Bright side of being a smuggler is that I see potential hiding places everywhere." As soon as they got inside, Kelvin grabbed the bed. "Turn on the shower as hot as it'll go while I move this."

She ran straight into the bathroom. Turning the knob, she had the shower raining hot water at full blast. In seconds, steam covered the mirror.

Looking back into the room, she saw the bed leaning at an angle against the wall, blocking the door to the corridor. Kelvin yanked off his clothes, pausing to point towards her feet.

"There's a seam in the floor at the door to the bathroom. Think you can slip the blade of your sword in there without leaving a mark? On the floor, I mean. I know that sword is super—um, whatever..."

"Yes." She drew her sword and rewarded him with an amused expression. "You have it exact."

She understood where he was going with this and whispered the incantation to make the blade of her sword paper-thin. *"Suaret."*

The blade slid into the space easily enough.

"Careful," he said. "If they see it's damaged, they're gonna know what we're up to."

She glanced up from the floor to smirk at him. "This would be easier to do if you weren't distracting me by standing there with your shirt off."

"I promise I'm only stripping in self-defense."

Using the sword as a lever, she lifted the floor panel up enough to get her fingers into the space. The panel only reached halfway into the bedroom. The bed, in its original position had rested on both panels, which was why Kelvin had moved it.

"So I'm hiding under here?" The memory of Kurega, when she was buried beneath the library drowned her along with a ringing noise that reminded her of how the blast had briefly deafened her. Her mouth went dry and left her unable to speak for a second.

"Yeah, I know it's not pretty." Kelvin wasn't looking at her as he said it, too busy lighting up one of the smokes he'd taken from the drug dealers. "Once you get in the crawl space, make your way towards the shower and get close to the pipes."

Forcing herself to take a deep breath, she fought down a wave of dizziness and stepped down into the crawl space.

Her nose scrunched up in offense to the smoke wafting over from his direction. "That smells mighty foul."

"I'm counting on it." He mumbled the words through the smoke dangling between his lips.

Fists pounded on the door to the neighboring room, followed by official sounding shouts.

"Shit." Kelvin pulled the smoke from between his lips. "Time's up."

6.

Ayleen tasted mold in the stale air of the crawl space. Her sword, free of its scabbard offered enough light to see. A simple spell would have brightened the light from the sword, but she didn't dare risk it.

Something cracked beneath her back as she crawled towards the sound of the shower's spray hissing against the tiled floor. Trying not to decipher what might have made that cracking, pop-like noise worked about as poorly as one might expect, with her imagination providing a myriad of unwelcome insects and arachnids to explain it.

The bed landed back onto the floor with a thud. Kelvin was putting it back where it belonged to keep the officers from realizing

Ayleen was under the floor. Steam soaked her. She closed her eyes to keep her sweat from dripping into them. The space required her to keep her head turned to her left. Otherwise, her nose was right up against the metal sheet of the floor above her.

She tried to distract herself by counting, but when she hit thirteen, she realized that wasn't helping.

Every muscle in her body screamed to move and thrust up on the floor panel. She couldn't rock her body as a way to burn off her fear. The best she managed was to fidget with her foot while making sure not to kick anything that would give her away. Most of all, she needed something to distract her.

The Galaxy provided in the most unusual of fashions.

Music pounded within the room above. The catchy tune featured a piano with strings, percussion, and brass.

Over the vocals, Kelvin's off-key wails drowned out what might have been an otherwise enjoyable, soulful song.

"Don't you tell me no truths! I forget the other lines!"

She felt certain those were not the lyrics. Kelvin pounded his feet on the floor of the shower as he shouted and cursed in the hot spray. He really needed to move elsewhere, because she could feel the floor shaking between them—felt it in the cheek she had turned up to the floor.

The police knocked on the door. The music drowned out any definition of what was said, but the tone made it through clear enough. Kelvin sang a little louder. He'd abandoned actual words and opted for nonsensical grunts in the appropriate places.

After a few more grunts and shouts, the sound of the door sliding open startled her. She hadn't expected it to be louder in the crawl space. How she kept from yelping her surprise, she couldn't fathom.

"Anyone else in here?" The woman barked at Kelvin as she struggled to be heard over the music.

"Whua?"

"Turn off the music!"

"I'm sorry, occifer, but I can't hear you over the music."

"I said turn off the music!"

"What?"

The music turned down to a soft hum as the officer shouted as loud as her alto allowed. "I said turn off the godsdamned music!"

"Why? I can hear you fine."

A man, probably another officer, coughed. "Gods, boy. This room reeks."

"Just having a lil' party for one is all."

"Show me your ID," the first officer said. They sounded like they'd made it deeper into the room.

There was a pause and then some muttering. What stood out much louder were the heavy footsteps shaking the floor above Ayleen. She went as still as possible, stopping her foot from fidgeting. The officer's steps shook loose what she hoped was dust and not bugs falling onto the side of her face. The shower handle creaked and the water raining above her stopped along with the hiss of the pipes beside her. Something beeped in a steady rhythm above her, something the officer was carrying, probably the male, because she still heard the first one talking in the bedroom.

"Kelvin James?" No missing the surprise to her voice. "As in the Mack's second born?"

"The one and only!" The flourish he gave his response almost made Ayleen laugh. Gods, she did not want that to be her epitaph.

'Here lies Ayleen Torr. Died laughing.'

She bit her bottom lip to hold it all in, especially with Lawman Heavy Feet pacing above her.

Kelvin kept his slurred mess of a show going. "Well, being her second born, I guess that actually makes me the two out of the three. Or would that be the third out of second? Two? Um, one? What was the question?"

An electronic sounding voice interrupted. *"Radio to Officers Kensington and Feng, your timer is going off."*

"Feng, you got anything in there?" the first officer shouted.

Feet pounded from Ayleen to the bathroom door. "Nah, just a bunch of steam, and two more party favors Mack Jr. here hasn't lit up yet."

"Radio, we're fine. Moving to the next room." There was a pause with the radio squawking something back to her. The officer talked over it, addressing Kelvin. "Only reason we're letting you walk is because we got bigger problems than a fuckup all lit up on dratang. Next time, you won't get half this lucky. You hear me, boy?"

"Clear as loud, ma'am. Yeah. That."

"Gods, the future is fucked."

The door slid shut. The music started up again, but not quite as loud this time. She heard Kelvin walk back into the bathroom.

"Knock twice if you can hear me?" he whispered, and she could tell his lips must be close to kissing the tiled floor.

She knocked twice.

"Give them a few minutes to make sure they're gone, then we'll get you out."

She answered with two knocks, but the wait tested her nerves. With the immediate threat of the officers gone, her imagination was granted free reign to consider all the filth and exo-skeletal life trapped in here with her.

As soon as the bed scraped against the floor, Ayleen crawled back to the seam. This time, she didn't need the sword. Once Kelvin's footsteps crossed the threshold into the bathroom, she pushed up on the floor with both of her hands. She gasped a greeting to the free air. Kelvin held the floor up as she scrambled out the rest of the way.

Every inch of her body itched from imaginary insects crawling on her.

"Nice performance." She waved her hand in front of her face. The officer wasn't off, complaining about the stench of the smokes Kelvin had lifted off the dealers down the hall.

"Thanks." He made for quite the sight, too. He'd stripped down to his boxers, which clung to him, every inch of his body drenched from the shower.

He pulled her close. She meant to tell him to dry off first, but then he kissed her and the complaint fell away.

When they stopped, she realized his pupils were dilated. "Oh, so not all an act."

He shrugged with a dreamy grin. "Not used to that stuff is all. Little goes a long way, I guess." The words slurred off his tongue, though he was clearly making an extra effort to enunciate. "Had to sell it, so they wouldn't question the shower going. Was counting on the heat from the water and steam to foul up their scanners so they wouldn't detect you in the floor."

She remembered the beeps from the second officer while he was in the bathroom. Must have been whatever device Kelvin was talking about.

"When does the next train leave for the substation?"

He let go of her and snatched his jacket up off the floor. Using the device attached to the sleeve, he slid his fingers over it, pressing at times. "That's the 6:20 to Avremore. You seriously think you're gonna get on that train?"

"When the floor-to-floor search for me fails, they might lock down this entire city. Can't risk being trapped here."

He rolled his eyes and sighed, letting out a long, low "Lousy stubs."

"Sorry," she paused to kiss him, "but whatever it takes, I need to get on that train."

7.

When Ayleen stepped out of the elevator onto level three, the same place she'd seen Leesp, she and everyone else exiting the elevator were met by a makeshift checkpoint. No one was allowed on or off of the platform with the railway map without coming face-to-face with an officer to present some form of picture identification and stating where they were coming from and going to.

Thanks to Kelvin, a few of his mother's illicit workers helped him and Ayleen under the agreement all parties would never speak of it to Mack. This meant Ayleen stepped up to the officer with her blue hair hidden beneath an expertly made wig of real hair. Makeup made her eyebrows look as black as the wig. A fake card identified her as Kyla Arunfar from Sylon of Ryjal II. Kelvin explained faking an ID card from Ryjal II was easier than one for Witbrom.

The officer glanced at her face and her card, each for less than a second. Based on what Kelvin had told her, the trains ran a tight schedule because of the limited number of tracks and the few sub-stations where they switched tracks. That meant the police could only hold up the trains for so long.

"What's your destination and business on Witbrom?" the officer asked, already looking at the next person in line behind her.

"Heading for Avremore to meet some friends for a party." She tossed in a snarky grin as if to say, "Don't you wish you were going?"

A female officer patted her down, checking for weapons. They didn't find any, because Kelvin's friends had already smuggled her belongings onto the 6:20 for Avremore. She didn't say anything to the officer searching her and avoided eye contact. She wore a pair of brown contact lenses to hide her mismatched eyes, but better not to draw attention there, in case they noticed and asked her to take the lenses off.

Kelvin, who'd gone ahead of her, had floated through the checkpoint much faster than Ayleen. The police knew they were hunting for a woman. Most of the men got waved through without a body search.

Ayleen took the stairs down to the loading platform for the trains. Kelvin's green hair made him easy to spot.

"You really shouldn't go," she said as she took one of the ticket cards from him.

"You don't know where the cargo is kept on the train, and there's a trick to opening the hidden compartment on the crate."

He chose this moment not to sell his opinion with a flashy smile. This time, he was playing the "I know this stuff better than you" card. In this case, it pissed her off mainly because it left her without a legitimate argument for keeping him safe. No matter what, she refused to let him end up like Dara.

"When we reach the substation and I get my belongings, that's it." Her voice cracked at the last part.

"Let's get something straight. I'm not going because I'm drunk on love. I owe you, more than you know."

She started to protest that he hardly owed her for saving his hide on Ziltra II, certainly not after what he'd done to hide her from the police twice over now. Then she realized he meant something else.

"What are you talking about?"

"Once we get on the train and get outta here, I'll tell you."

An announcement over the public address system ended the discussion.

"Passengers now boarding on platform three for the 6:20 train with service to Avremore and Ostice. Allow passengers to disembark before boarding, and please mind the gap between the train and the platform."

She took his hand and squeezed it. "Seems we have a train to catch."

8.

The 6:20 to Avremore consisted of twenty-three cars. Most of them were devoted to passengers with the front car serving as the engine and the rear six set aside for luggage and commercial goods. Ayleen heard her sword's whispers coming from the back.

Thirteen to go.

At least it made it onto the train. What disturbed her more was that she could also sense the ambrosia crystal, a low hum like a choir of deep voices holding the same note for eternity.

Their tickets placed them in car eight. The cabin had two seats on the left side and a single seat on the right. Not surprisingly, Kelvin had gotten them seats together on the left side.

"You want the window seat?" He waited in the aisle to see what she did.

"No." If someone attacked, she didn't want him caught in the middle. "Thanks, though."

His insistence on being a gentleman was endearing, but she also recognized it now appealed to her more because of the bit of Basten's soul in her. Basten had loved to manipulate people into bending over backwards for her.

Monitors on the front and rear of the cabin came to life a few minutes before the train's scheduled departure time. On the screen, a woman in a blue uniform lacking any military function smiled way too much as she discussed the procedures for passengers. She started with how to buckle up and why passengers should wait in their seats with their buckles fastened until the driver turned on the sign indicating it was safe for passengers to move about the cabin.

From there, she mentioned what to do if the train derailed or if the cabin was breached and lost oxygen. The lady in the monitor explained how the ceiling would open to drop breathing masks for passengers with additional masks kept in compartments behind each monitor screen.

Ayleen noticed the video didn't mention anything about what to do if they had to leave the train while the sun was out. Apparently, the train makers trusted passengers to know how to die without an instruction guide.

"So," Ayleen said as she drummed her fingers on the armrest, "what's going on that you think you owe me?"

He sighed as he rubbed the bridge of his nose. "I knew my ma was gonna refuse your request. I didn't realize how dangerous that would make things for you."

She was about to point out he wasn't his mother's keeper, nor hers, but he didn't strike her as the type to manufacture pointless drama. "What made you so sure?"

He kept his eyes directed towards the floor of the cabin. "I knew if I let it slip into the right ear that I'd let you only pay half to get into Veil, they'd tell Ma. She'd dig, and she'd freak. I'm sorry. I wanted more time for us."

Ayleen knew she had every right to be angry, but she wasn't. She'd also wanted more time, and she was grateful they'd gotten it. She turned his face to look at her and kissed him.

"You're an idiot," she whispered, "but you're a romantic idiot."

A hum rippled through the train. It started from the front and grew more noticeable as it worked its way to the back. When it reached the car in front of theirs, their car jostled with the front end pulled up as the car in front of it floated off the track. Their car lifted with a vibration rippling through it.

Every seat was occupied in their car, and the two women in the seats in front of her each took a deep breath, grabbed the arms of their seats, and leaned back.

Ayleen expected a slow acceleration, building up to the 225 clicks an hour it could travel.

The train shot out of the city. The pressure knocked her back into her seat.

Kelvin laughed with a strain to his voice. "Like a punch to the lungs, ain't it?"

Once they'd adjusted to the speed, she sat up. "Can't say I find it to my liking."

The monitors displayed a message in white text on a green field: *You may now move freely about the cabin. Bars are open in Cars Two and Seventeen.*

The track they were taking was the same as the one they'd watched from the observation deck earlier this morning. The direction they were traveling was slightly northwest, placing the sunset to the train's left. The sky shifted from a milky grey to a pale blue around the sun as it settled in for its nap. The moon wasn't pressing into the horizon yet, but the first few stars were starting to appear.

"Let's get my gear."

"Yeah." The way Kelvin said that word made it clear he meant "no." "Let's get a drink first."

9.

Night was settling in when they reached the last of the passenger cars. Kelvin pulled open the door and let her go inside to the bar. This car included tables with seats facing each other with tables for two on the left and tables for four on the right. The room was already packed with people eager to drown their day in booze. The bar was placed against the far end of the cabin, and the wall behind it included a versatile selection of liquor, including Ohmejan Tequila. What were the odds Sheriff Javo was the reason the train bars stocked it?

Kelvin pointed to the door in the very back, behind the bar. "That connects to the first storage car where the bar's extra stock is kept. It requires a code to open it and there's always a guard on it."

Ayleen kept her voice too low for anyone other than Kelvin to hear her. "Lots of people in here to raise the alarm, too."

"Our best bet is moseying back to our seats and waiting for the train to stop at the substation. Then we can slip outside the train and walk to the back while it isn't moving. Nobody'll notice."

He turned to go until Ayleen grabbed him by the arm. "Where are you going?" she asked.

Kelvin took a second to answer, and when he did, it wasn't with much confidence. "To our seats?"

"We came all this way to a bar, one with Ohmejan Tequila, so I'm not leaving without a shot."

Kelvin's eyes widened. "You are on the run from the Thirteen, with your face plastered on every screen in Veil. You could land smack into a fight with odds stacked as high as a small mountain, and you want to do it drunk?"

The thought he might have a point flitted through her brain, but the second she realized it was Basten's influence, it only clinched her decision.

"You know damn well a single shot won't do much to me, and it was my mother's favorite drink." There was also the fact it might be the last drink she ever had. That same sense her time was running out was part of what rendered her incapable of resisting Kelvin's charms when he'd first flirted with her.

"Besides," she said, "weren't you the one high on whatever that foul-smelling shite was earlier?"

He raised a finger as if to make a point, let it float out there in silence, and then pulled it away. "I don't have a good argument for that—yet."

She grinned at him and stepped up to the bar.

10.

One shot of tequila later, they headed back for their seats in car eight.

"My mom used to call it 'the Good Stuff'." Ayleen savored the subtle burn to her throat from the shot. Two shots would have felt much better, but she knew better than to press her luck that much.

"I don't have a stomach for it." He'd refused to partake. "Last time I took a shot of liquor, I spent most of the night puking up half my vital organs. Now, ale…I'll drink you and anyone else under the table."

"I've seen you do it, too."

The screen in car fourteen displayed a map of the rail they were traveling with a red dot to note their current location. The dot looked close to a blue square identified as Substation Three.

The public address system clicked on before Ayleen and Kelvin could open the door to exit the car they were in and enter the next.

"Passengers, we will arrive at our first stop at substation three in approximately ten minutes. At this time, please take a seat and buckle up until we come to a full stop. There will be no exiting the train while we refuel. Our layover time will be twenty minutes, and the bars will remain open during the layover."

A soft seal connected each car to the next, with walls resembling the inside of an accordion.

"How do we get off the train?" Ayleen asked within the privacy of the soft seal connection.

"You're standing in it." He pointed at the collapsible walls. "We cut through the seal in these compartments and use the same trick to get inside one of these connectors between the luggage cars."

Ayleen considered that, running her hand over the wall. While the material gave a little to her touch, it felt thick. That wouldn't challenge her sword, but if she had her sword, she wouldn't need to cut her way out of here.

"They won't notice the cabin has been compromised?" she asked.

He shook his head. "Not while we're in the substation. Only once we pull out, are they gonna know. And before you ask." He raised a hand for her to wait and then turned his back to her as he pulled up his shirt. "I've got the cutting utensil covered."

A knife, in its sheath, was taped to his back. Ayleen had to confess she was impressed. "That's what they get for only patting down the women."

"Damn right." He dropped his shirt back down to hide the knife. "And you heard the driver. We'll have roughly twenty minutes to get it all done. Plenty of time." He snapped his fingers.

Ayleen opened the door to car thirteen's cabin, which was a lot more crowded than when they last went through it. Four officers stood in the aisle looking over people's identification and their tickets. Behind them, standing a good head taller, was Captain Ysil Leesp with his one good eye locked on Ayleen.

11.

Leesp shouted orders at the officers with him. Ayleen lost a second wondering why Leesp would be on this damn train before sense kicked in and she slammed the door to the car shut.

"Run!" she shouted at Kelvin as they retreated into the previous car.

Dammit! She needed her sword. The crystal blade screamed for release from the box they'd stashed it in before leaving Veil. Before they could reach the door to the next car, the one behind them was flung open. The closest officer charged on them and shouted for them to stop. Anyone who hadn't gotten out of Ayleen and Kelvin's way wasted no time in dropping back into their seats and out of the path of the officers.

The first two officers reached them before they could go out the other end of the car. The uniformed men had drawn their short swords, each resembling a gladius.

Kelvin reached around Ayleen, trying to move her out of the way. She responded by turning him around, snatching the dagger from his back, and shoving him towards the exit to the next car. "Get the doors!"

The closer guard thrust his sword at Ayleen. She'd already dodged the blade, though. His body language had betrayed the move long before the attempt.

Ayleen got in close and slit the wrist to the officer's sword arm. The officer stumbled back and dropped his weapon. She grabbed him by his uniform's jacket and flung him at his partner. The two officers didn't fall, but they got tangled together as the second officer struggled to keep them both upright without cutting his partner.

Ayleen snatched up the fallen sword and buried the gladius into the second officer's gut.

The passengers shouted. Those closest scrambled away as best they could in the cramped compartment. One man climbed over seats and other passengers to escape.

"Move!" Leesp shouted as he appeared in the door.

"We're gonna run out of cars real fast!" Kelvin was already through the door and grabbing the next one.

Leesp passed his men and hit a full sprint. His long legs made quick work of the distance. He'd made it within a meter of them by the time Ayleen entered the next car.

"Faster!" she shouted. "Get the next doors ready for me."

More passengers shouted. They didn't know what was happening but quick to recognize Ayleen was armed with a dagger and a sword dripping blood.

"Get the doors!" She shouted when Kelvin hesitated. His attention was more on Leesp, as if he wanted to fight this giant instead of run.

She'd stopped halfway down the aisle when Leesp emerged into the cabin.

"Captain Leesp." She offered him her most snark-filled smile. "I used to think your face couldn't get any uglier. Seems I was mistaken."

He took in a deep breath as he stalked towards her. His crystal sword had forged into a different blade than Ayleen's. While hers resembled a katana, his blade curved and swelled closer to its tip in the style of a falcata, a perfect weapon for a brute warrior.

Training kicked in, and Ayleen met brawn with finesse. She didn't risk blocking his swings. They came at her with the might of flying hammers. She deflected the attacks, nudging his sword off course. A direct hit from his crystal weapon would shatter the metal sword she'd borrowed.

He kicked into her stomach hard enough to send her flying back. The breath expelled from her lungs as pain crushed her stomach, and that was with her already retreating from him to lessen the blow. If he planted his foot with all his strength, her rib cage would cave in like dry branches.

Leesp seethed as he pointed to his eyepatch. "I owe you, human."

"What?" She didn't so much say the word as gasp it.

"Ayleen!" Kelvin's shout brought her to her senses. She scrambled to her feet as Leesp marched on her.

He slammed his sword down, burying it in the floor where she'd been less than a second beforehand.

As he jerked it free, she ran for the door Kelvin was holding.

"Get the next door open and grab my belt!" She turned around within the accordion walls of the soft seal connection.

Through the narrow window of the connecting car's door, Leesp glared at her, his forked tongue hissing out in a threatening manner. He ran for the door as he saw Kelvin pull open the next car's door.

Ayleen felt the tug on her belt as Leesp reached the door. "Pull!" she shouted as she swung the sword at the accordion walls. The wind hit the blade as it was exposed to the open air of Witbrom VI and jerked it from her hand. The sword slashed a savage hole. Hot air screamed and bright light from the setting sun hit her. A loud alarm sounded. Her throat burned as she gasped for air. Screams from the next car competed with the warning alarm and the wind. She fell into the cabin and blinked away phantom blobs of retina burn from her vision.

The door slammed shut, cutting short the rushing wind and the alarm. The door frame was outlined in a red light warning the door was sealed.

Ayleen got to her feet and stared through the window in the door. Leesp glared at her from behind the other door, also outlined in a red light. A wide row of sharp teeth ground at one another. He slammed a fist into his door, shaking it but not breaking it loose. He splayed his fingers for her to see. She got the message.

Ayleen grabbed Kelvin by the arm. "We've got five minutes."

Five minutes to get into the cargo containers, retrieve her sword and belongings, and get off this train.

12.

They reached the bar in car seventeen with roughly three minutes left until the train stopped.

The guard on the door behind the bar had already drawn his weapon, which wasn't a sword or any type of blade. Tiny lightning bolts danced around a small, silver ball at the end of the metal stick he held.

"You just—just stand down, little lady. You and your fella there."

A half dozen passengers remained in the bar's cabin. They'd buckled themselves into the seats at their tables. None of them dared to move. The bartender sat at one of the tables now with a drink of his own, a tall glass with red ale.

Kelvin's dagger danced in Ayleen's hand. "I'm giving you three seconds to drop the stick and open that door." She pointed at the door behind him with her free hand. "Three. Two. One."

The guard stood his ground.

Ayleen had expected him to cave. Just her luck to get a glorified, low-paid bouncer who believed his life was worth defending cases full of booze—none of which she wanted.

She snatched up the tall glass mug from in front of the bartender and threw its contents in the guard's face. The guard screamed, blinded for a split second. He stabbed at the space between them with his stun stick. Ayleen grabbed him by the wrist, held it firmly against the wall, and kicked him in the side. Her next move sent him down onto his back behind the bar, and she slammed the back of his head on the floor.

When she stood, she made a show of wiping off the dagger with a cloth. While there wasn't any blood on it, no one watching would realize it. They'd assume she'd killed the guard.

Ayleen focused on the bartender. "Your turn. Three seconds to open the door."

She didn't get past "two" before the bartender was scrambling behind the bar to punch in the code.

13.

To Ayleen's surprise, none of the doors beyond the first one behind the bar required any codes. Now that they were in the rear storage cabins, Ayleen let Kelvin take the lead. She'd never seen the container in which her sword and other belongings were stashed.

They scrambled through the cars in the back of the train. She hoped they weren't going too fast for Kelvin to spot the container. Only when they reached the next to the last car did she know they were in the right place.

"There!" Kelvin pointed to a large, cube-shaped box strapped to the floor that came up to Ayleen's waist. He knelt beside the blue steel box. Text was painted on the side with the bottom line identifying it as "Freight Container #100347-370130." He pressed on all four zeroes, and a panel on the bottom of the box popped open.

He pulled the sword out first, perhaps guessing her need for it, and handed it to her as he reached in for the rest of her belongings.

The crystal sang with joy as her hands wrapped around its hilt.

"Thank you, Kelvin."

She closed her eyes, using her sword to reach out for a sense of where the castle with the keyhole she sought might be. The answer came, and it wasn't the news she'd hoped.

"What is it?" Kelvin asked as he handed her the rest of her gear. She slipped on her uniform's jacket, the water pack and the leather pouch containing her few belongings, including the grimoire and the ambrosia crystal.

"Paladin Castle," she said without finishing the thought.

They were flung towards the front of the cabin as the train's momentum slowed. They collided with a stack of containers similar to the one they'd used to smuggle her belongings here.

They'd reached the substation.

The instant they slowed to where they could move around again, Ayleen swung at Kelvin, planning to hit him hard enough to knock the sense out of him. He spotted her fist fast enough to dodge it and jump back.

"What kind of sun-baked craziness is that?"

"If I leave you here for them to find, they'll think I forced you to help me. After this, there's no turning back for you."

He reached out to wrap his hand around hers. "Think we reached that station a lot further back. For certain, after Leesp saw me with you. I'm in for the full ride."

She shook her head. "The full sprint. We have to jump and run before they close the outer doors to the station."

They grabbed four breather masks from the box above the door at the rear of the container. Ayleen cut their way out through the accordion wall connecting the two rear cars.

The entrance the train had used to enter was closing. The doors slid in from the right and the left. If the doors closed before they reached them, they'd be trapped.

Kelvin reached the doors first with enough room left for two people to fit, but it narrowed more as he waited for her.

Ayleen slipped off her water pack to carry it in her hand when she realized their exit might get too narrow for her to get through with the pack on. Kelvin stepped out before she reached the doors, and she collided with him as she flung herself through the narrowing opening and out onto the surface of Witbrom VI.

14.

Bitter cold replaced the blistering heat of day the instant the sun set. If Ayleen and Kelvin had started out earlier, they would have died. In that sense, their timing couldn't have been better.

They'd buttoned up their jackets. Ayleen had thrown on her pale green poncho. For lack of anything else, Kelvin wrapped himself in Ayleen's bed roll.

Ice collected on the edges of scattered boulders and other rocky formations less than an hour into their march towards Paladin Castle, but the breathing masks ranked higher than the cold on Ayleen's list of complaints. The masks only covered her mouth and nose. The strap wrapped around her head over her ears to hold the mask in place and dug in tight enough to give her a headache.

What little conversation they had was limited to hand gestures and meaningful gazes. They could talk, but with the breathing masks on, they had to shout to be heard. She needed no words to see Kelvin regretted he'd followed her.

You waited too long to cut him loose, she told herself. She should have blown him off the instant she saw him at the train station platform. No, better to never have tackled him into bed when she met him.

She blamed Basten. She'd suffered more than a week as she shared her body with Basten's soul, but once she'd excised her, Ayleen felt the void she'd known for two years suffocating her. Kelvin couldn't have come along at better or worse time. She'd never met anyone as comfortable in their own skin as him. The only thing she hated about him was how they met. That they'd met playing a card game in a tavern sounded so pedestrian.

She had to do right by him, find him a way out. Only, where could he go? By now, the authorities in Veil had to know he'd been with her on the train, so going back wouldn't work.

All she could do now was drag him along, but where they were going…Basten had gone to the world in Ayleen's vision. Basten only shared the name for the place where Ayleen assumed the Thirteen were made immortal, Dosquam—one of the few details she hadn't lied about. What that world might be like, if there were other key-holes available to leave it, she didn't know. Basten hadn't hidden that from Ayleen so much as she hid it from herself.

What worried Ayleen most was how convinced Basten was her quest would kill more than the Thirteen. She'd insisted her revenge would destroy everything. Up until Kelvin, Ayleen hadn't given a shite about the consequences.

She glanced over at Kelvin, and he caught her looking. The crinkle of his eyes let her know he was smiling at her. If it came to it, could she sacrifice Kelvin in order to kill the Thirteen? She'd already spilled an ocean of blood on account of those traitors, but she wouldn't add Kelvin's life to that red sea.

The sky darkened as the few stars visible disappeared. The first sign morning light wouldn't be long off.

Pulling out her sword, she stabbed it into the ground and lowered herself to one knee.

"Mitsukate."

The sword provided an intuition for finding the keyholes on a world, as if the crystals were connected in some way to the intergalactic passageways. The tunnels were formed from the dark energy connecting the universe like a circulatory system. The command she spoke provided a more direct answer to where the next keyhole was. The brief vision tugged on her spirit. Reality sped up, the distance between here and the castle blinked past, but it also showed her the passage of time that would take place and the path she would need to travel to reach it.

Ayleen scrambled to her feet, shoving her sword back into its scabbard.

"Run!" Her filtered air struggled to keep up with her increased need.

They'd made good time since leaving the substation, but they were still six hours out from the castle with sunrise upon them.

They either reached shelter within the next half hour, or they died.

15.

The vision provided by her sword revealed more than time and distance between her and the keyhole she sought. The view provided an elevated flight which revealed the terrain. Despite flashing by in a blur, her mind captured all of the details in that mystical shift from here to there.

She ran as hard as she could. A rock formation protruded on their left, reaching up into the sky in the shape of a giant hand with its fingers splayed. Their path to Paladin Castle would take them under those arching digits. What they needed was buried within the palm of the stone hand.

Sweat froze on her face, mostly on the tips of her eyebrows. What slid off collected on the front of her poncho.

The run kept her warmer than she would have been otherwise. Her chest ached, partly because the filter made it difficult to pull in enough air. The cold muscles in her legs also protested the sprint, threatening to tear.

At their backs, the base of the horizon turned bluish-grey.

Kelvin kept pace, out of arm's reach to her right.

Set within the base of the rock formation's palm was a slit, as if the end of a long cut that started in the wrist of a person eager to die.

Ayleen saw her shadow stretch out ahead of her. The sun warmed her back. After the long night in the dark, the warmth was welcome. A pity it promised too much of a good thing.

Their footfalls kicked up grey dust at their backs. She noticed the dirt cloud they created hung in the air a bit longer than would have been normal back on her home world. The corner of her mind belonging to her father noted the sign that the gravity of Witbrom VI wasn't as strong, though it didn't feel much weaker than the norm.

She clung to the brim of her hat, pulling it low each time it threatened to fly off. To her right, Kelvin shouted curses from several languages.

The morning light was warming the air to the point where it hurt. The long night's cold wasn't enough to stave off the burns to come.

Ayleen ran into the cave with Kelvin right behind her. The cave, shaped like the inside of an egg, didn't go as deep as she would have hoped, only about ten feet.

"Ayleen, this won't be enough to protect us!"

She flung off her hat and poncho and then tugged off both gloves. "I'm on it." Digging into her pack, she pulled out the grimoire and the ambrosia crystal and threw them to the ground.

"Ayleen."

"Not now!"

She dropped to her knees and sifted through the pages of the grimoire. She drew her dagger from the sheath on her right thigh.

"Ayleen, it's important!"

The air in the cave offered shade, but no real protection from the heat. She guessed they had only a few minutes before they started cooking.

"Ayleen!" He grabbed her by the arms, turning her to him.

"What?" She struggled against his grip but stopped when she saw the sadness in his copper eyes.

He cupped her face in his hands. "I love you. I don't want this to end without telling you."

"Kelvin..." She paused, struggling to catch her breath, and placed her hand against his chest. She felt the pounding of his heart. "You're gonna love me even more in a moment."

She pulled away from him. Dagger in hand, she made a small cut her right palm and then wrapped her bleeding hand around the ambrosia crystal.

Her breath caught the moment her open wound touched the crystal. The world changed from grey to amber.

"*Mayulusk.*"

She repeated the word as her mind formed the shape, a line drawing of a vast fire. Flames reached high and far. Then she carved out the center of the flames.

No sooner had she finished the craft, than the dark energy of the crystal filled her. A pain-filled ache pressed upon every muscle in her body, and she savored every moment of it. Her body jolted as the magic formed, knocking her away from the crystal and onto her back.

Her eyes fluttered as she rode it out, writhing on the ground until the tension in her body passed. A last moan whispered out of her as the connection between her and the ambrosia crystal dimmed but didn't vanish. She "heard" it almost as well as her sword.

Before she opened her eyes, she knew the spell had worked. The cave felt cooler.

Kelvin stared down at her.

"What?" Her concern and confusion drew out the word. Had she grown a second head or something?

"You okay?"

"We're not burning up, so I'd say we're doing mighty well."

"Oh, because the way you screamed, you were either hurting really bad or feeling really good."

Her stomach ached as she laughed. She got up onto her knees. "It's a defensive spell against fire. Was gambling on it working against the heat outside the cave. Might have worked out in the open, but I figured our chances were much better in here."

"Good." Kelvin dropped to the floor of the cave beside her. "Because I really would have hated to have done all that running for nothing."

She wanted to kiss him, but the cocoon she'd woven with the crystal wouldn't do anything for the air. In its place, she settled for leaning in close and nuzzling against his neck, careful not to dislodge their breathing masks.

"Let me get my belongings packed again before we sleep." Gods knew she needed the rest.

While he spread out the bed roll, she crawled over to the grimoire and the ambrosia crystal. A chill ran through her flesh at the sight of the crystal. It had changed again. The length of it was roughly short of her forearm. The top two-thirds of it had narrowed into the thin blade of a dagger and a perfect fit for where she normally kept the steel one on her right thigh.

16.

Ayleen woke to a sharp pain in her chest and a mind full of aimless panic. Her breathing mask had stopped working. The unfiltered atmosphere bit into her lungs with the force of an army of feral rabbits. She shot up, reaching for anything that might help and not sure what would.

Kelvin came up behind her and grabbed her by the arm. "Here." He ripped off her breathing mask and pressed one of their two extra masks up to her mouth and nose.

Tears ran down her cheeks as the filtered air crawled inside her. The pain didn't lessen right away.

"Like swallowing a mouthful of sandspurs, ain't it?" He cradled her against his chest while she recovered. "Mine crapped out about a half hour before yours."

A headache bloomed behind her forehead and through her sinuses. She fought back a whimper as she slid the strap for her breathing mask into place. With her hands now free she cradled her temples in her hands.

"I'll be fine." Her words croaked out of her as she sat up.

"So good news and bad news," Kelvin said. "The good news is these things work as long as advertised. If we hadn't been walking and running all night, they might have lasted a few more hours. The bad news is once we use up our spare masks, we're dead."

She waved her hand side-to-side in what was meant to be a reassuring gesture. Probably looked more like "Leave me alone."

"I've got some good news and bad news of my own," she said once she was sure she could say it loud enough for him to hear. "Good news is we're only a few hours away from Paladin Castle."

One of his eyebrows shot up in confusion. "And the bad news?"

"We're a few hours away from Paladin Castle, and they're probably waiting for us."

"Was kind of hoping they'd figure we're dead by now." He pointed to the bright sky beyond the opening of the cave. Despite the cocoon Ayleen had created, the cave had gotten plenty warm during the day, and what little clothing they were wearing was soaked with sweat to prove it.

"They dropped a building on me a while back. That didn't take. Now they know, so they won't settle for anything less than my cold corpse." She picked up the breathing mask she'd used to get to the cave and tossed it aside. "If we don't show, they'll come looking."

The hatred boiling within Captain Leesp left her without any doubt he'd hunt her down.

Why had he been on the train? Had he known she'd be there? Out of all the trains she might have used to get out of Veil, he'd managed to find the right one.

"Shite!" She didn't realize she'd said that so loudly until she noticed the puzzled look on Kelvin's face. "Leesp knew I'd be on the train. He assumed I was heading for Paladin Castle and the keyhole below it."

Kelvin got a distant look in his eyes as he nodded. "Then maybe we do what they don't expect. Backtrack to the substation."

"I'm not worried about the Thirteen's soldiers." From what she'd learned, most of the Thirteen didn't often stay on Witbrom VI. She suspected they didn't care for each other or for being under Pyre's rule any longer than necessary. "The Thirteen weren't expecting me until Leesp spotted me yesterday. So the others might not be at the castle yet, and they're the real threat."

Kelvin shrugged. "Yeah, at the Summer Solstice executions, they never have all of the Thirteen there. The ones who attend it don't usually stay on Witbrom for long."

"I have to strike now, before more of them can return to the castle, but you don't have to go. If you go back to the substation—"

"Save it. I meant what I said. I'm with you the rest of the way. Besides, we both know they won't buy any story I give them about you forcing me."

She took his hand into hers and squeezed it.

The sky outside the cave was darkening. They took several drinks from her water pack as they dressed for the approaching cold.

They'd reach the castle in the middle of the night. With any luck they'd catch the guards at the moment they'd be most tired, some having been up all night and others just waking. If Ayleen really believed all that, she might have shared the notion with Kelvin.

17.

Finding Paladin Castle required little effort. Most every window shined with artificial light, and floodlights swept the terrain around the castle. The place shined so brightly that the low-hanging clouds above it glowed.

Ayleen and Kelvin got their first view of the castle from a cliff overlooking it. The entire area occupied by the castle looked man-made, as if it had been carved out of the rock.

People in Veil claimed the castle was kept in a protective dome. The truth was a little off, as with all things relating to the Thirteen.

A pole reached twice as high as the tallest tower. From the top of the pole, a translucent tent that leaned in on itself flowed to the ground. The design limited the amount of breathable air required for the castle compared to what a dome would demand.

What resembled a small canyon surrounded the castle, but upon closer inspection, Ayleen realized the space had once been a moat. The protective tent included the moat within its boundaries. A small train station was positioned in front of the castle. A tunnel of the same translucent material as the tent provided safe passage between the station and the castle.

"There are four entrances, in addition to the tunnel from the train station." Ayleen pointed to the doors placed at the corners of the tent.

"We already knew the place was crawling with guards," Kelvin said, "so what's really got you worried?"

She pointed to the surroundings. "The way the land has been altered to accommodate this castle makes no sense. Look where we are. Any enemy with the firepower to reach the castle from here is placed in a perfect position to obliterate it. Catapults could do it, especially given the low gravity."

What she wouldn't give for a catapult right now, and an army to operate it.

"As if anyone could get out here?" Kelvin laughed.

"The Thirteen didn't build Paladin Castle, did they?" Ayleen realized Basten had known the name for this place, claimed to have visited it before her death, but that would have been centuries before most of the Thirteen were born. Basten's vague memories of Witbrom VI suggested this planet had been habitable with a breathable atmosphere. "What caused Witbrom's atmosphere to degrade?"

He shrugged. "Was more than seven hundred years ago. It's how the Thirteen got their hooks into the planet. People were pissed off, because no one in the government was acting fast enough to do anything about the air problem. Thirteen led a revolt, but was too late to fix anything by the time they were in charge. That's when the underground cities got started."

"Sounds like the problems with the atmosphere worked out twice as well for the Thirteen. Put them in charge and made the one place they would want to protect above all others pretty much inaccessible to their enemies."

Kelvin laughed. "You sound like one of the atmo conspiracy theorists. Only all of them think the Thirteen messed up the atmosphere to control the rest of us, trap us in our cities. Paladin Castle is usually one of the reasons no one buys into the conspiracy, because of how inconvenient it made getting to this place for the Thirteen."

"Could be coincidence, but I doubt it." Ayleen's grimoire mentioned ways to manipulate the weather, but that spell above all the others warned against its use. Cast the spell wrong, and you could end up with—well, Witbrom VI or worse. The damage might not show itself the first day, maybe not in the next month, year, or decade. Eventually, the changes would show, though.

Ayleen gripped the hilt of her sword, resting impatiently in its scabbard.

"Let's go knock on the door."

18.

Paladin Castle offered a frustrating challenge for any small force invader. The key problem focused on the number and position of its guards. Each of the four direct entrances into the tent had at least six guards to it with two patrols of four circling the perimeter of the tent, which made it impossible to cut through the tent's advanced material and sneak inside. If an invader entered that way and took out one of the patrols, the guards on the other entrances would descend on them before there was a chance to get near the castle's gate.

The guards weren't dumb enough to waste their manpower patrolling the land outside of the protective tent. That might have allowed Ayleen and Kelvin to ambush the guards and steal their uniforms. The ruse would be discovered quickly, but they might get deeper into the castle.

Worst of all was the central tower and the guard on its parapet. The guard there could see in every direction without obstruction. Paired with all the spotlights, the guard could sound the alarm to warn the ground forces of anyone approaching—with one notable exception.

The train station, though tiny compared to the one in Veil or the substation, was tall and wide enough to enclose an entire train. The guards recognized the vulnerability, because the tunnel connecting the station to the open gate of the castle was patrolled by no less than ten guards.

As for how many might be inside the station was anyone's guess, because it didn't have any windows. The large doors trains used to enter the station were closed. Next to them was a smaller door intended for people to use. Ayleen didn't doubt the guards would know the instant they entered, but that didn't change it from being the best of the many poor options left to them.

The doors looked as though they might have once been white, but centuries of dust storms had aged them to a dull grey.

"Let's see how serious they are about keeping us out of here." Kelvin pulled on the handle placed into the wall next to the door. To Ayleen's surprise, the door opened, sliding to the left. Fans clicked on, circulating the air to remove what came from outside and filling the room with something more breathable.

Less shocking was what came next. The handle to exit the airlock and enter the station refused to budge.

Kelvin smirked. "Looks like it's time for your little friend to do its job."

"Little?" She drew her sword and whispered. *"Attadior!"*

The sword flared to life, glowing as heat emanated from it. She thrust the sword through the airlock door and carved a hole in it. A kick knocked out the carved piece of door.

The glow to the sword faded as Ayleen stepped into a narrow hallway with six armed guards.

19.

Less than two minutes later, Ayleen stepped through the collective puddle of blood from all six guards. Red bootprints followed her and Kelvin until they reached the turn leading into the translucent corridor connecting the station with the castle's tent.

"Looks like I counted wrong." Ayleen drew the ambrosia crystal dagger from the sheath on her right thigh.

Twelve guards were gathered inside the corridor. They converged on her and Kelvin. None of them showed a hint of concern for the six men they'd lost. They were zealots, as Kelvin's mother warned.

Captain Tratella had counseled her and her fellow squires about people like this and the danger in being one.

Always be willing to die for a cause, but never take pride or joy in it. All that does is make you more willing to die, and no cause will ever die for you.

"Kelvin, let me know if any come up from behind, and any of them I knock down who aren't dead yet, finish them."

He didn't answer. He didn't need to.

The closest pair of guards reached her. They approached her from opposite directions. When she deflected both of their swings, their sense of strategy died. A few swings later, they died with their throats slit open.

Her sword thrilled at the taste of their deaths dripping down its blade.

Eight down, so many more to go...

Unlike the hallway leading out of the airlock, this corridor provided a space too wide to limit their numbers. Instead, she rushed at them. They'd spread themselves out in pairs in the corridor in case she had cut her way in somewhere in the middle. The faster she cut down the closest guards, the less likely she had to face more than two at a time.

One guard tumbled when she slit open the inside of his thigh. His last breath belonged to Kelvin, armed with both his dagger and Ayleen's old steel one.

More guards flooded into the far end of the corridor. None of them wore a breathing mask. She ran to the left side of the corridor and slashed up through the translucent material with her sword. A rush of wind sucked out some of the breathable air, but only for a few seconds. The damage healed itself.

Ayleen cursed. The move had cost her time, enough to increase the numbers she faced. She'd hoped the breathing masks would give them an advantage, but she'd underestimated the castle's defenses.

The guards forced her into a retreat.

"Give me room!" she shouted over her shoulder to Kelvin.

She blocked a sword, lunged in, and slammed her fist into the guard's throat. Slitting his throat would have been easy, but keeping him upright and stumbling in the way of his fellow guards helped her more for the moment.

Other guards she finished off or left for Kelvin to do the deed. She turned the rest into more living barriers.

The ambrosia crystal thrummed with a single note of joy with each life it took. The dagger glowed brighter with each kill.

More guards rushed into the end of the corridor.

Whether it was the bloody path of their fallen comrades or the murderous hunger in her eyes, she wasn't sure, but the guards turned and ran for the castle's gate.

"Come on!" Her shout at Kelvin was met with a wide-eyed stare, but he followed. He lacked any enthusiasm for this work. His life belonged to quiet resistance, and she hated that the gravity of her revenge had pulled him into her violent orbit.

The guards sprinted across a narrow, stone bridge to the raised gate. As soon as the last guard crossed the threshold, the steel portcullis started to bite down. Its teeth creaked towards its bite marks in the dirt. The bridge retracted at the same pace, too slow for the guards' liking and too fast for Ayleen's.

She reached the edge of the moat and leaped across the widening gap. A glance down revealed the hole in the ground surrounding the castle wasn't as empty as she'd first thought, but the water, a brownish grey soup, only reached about a quarter of the way up. She landed on the edge of the retracting bridge, and Kelvin's boots hit the stone surface a second later.

The guards descended on Ayleen and Kelvin as they slipped beneath the gate. The space beyond was filled with stairs and weapons. In an extravagant display of power, the round ceiling was covered in swords from throughout time. What little of the ceiling remained exposed by the gaps between the blades and hilts was lost in shadows.

Elaborate murals covered the walls near the start of each set of stairs. Levers were placed within the walls next to many of those murals.

She took in the details of the vast greeting hall as she carved her way through the guards who stood their ground. The castle's other defenders fled into different parts of the building, like children running to their parents for protection.

What captured her attention was painted on the far wall to her right, next to a set of stairs leading down. A red sphere hovered in mist above a blue sea. The lever next to it pointed down, the way she intended to go.

The guards sensed the change in her attack. They placed themselves in her path. Their desperation mirrored hers. She severed arms, beheaded one guard, and carved another open from navel to neck.

A man and a woman emerged from the stairs leading up from a mural of a great feast. That sense of wrongness flowed from them, as it did for all of the Thirteen.

The slender, muscular man had already drawn his sword, a double-edged blade the length of his legs with a long hilt. His pale, hairless skin and his four yellow eyes stacked in pairs marked him as a Zelthan from the white sands of Kaestro. Not many Zelthans belonged to the Knighthood, and the name tickled at her memory. Were she not occupied with parrying swords and ending lives, she might have recalled it.

The woman, though... She knew Field Knight Ulé Ontré-vas. Ayleen's father had gone on survey missions with her. He'd described her as ruthless and uncompromising, though whether as compliment or insult depended on the day. Ulé's sword waited within its scabbard on her left hip. As she sauntered down the stairs, she slipped on a pair of gloves. What offended Ayleen most was how Ulé had the audacity to wear her knight's jacket, as if she still swore allegiance to the Knighthood.

Ayleen slit open the throat of the last guard who challenged her before the two traitors had reached the floor of the greeting hall.

"Come on!" She shouted for Kelvin to follow her as she descended the spiral staircase. The narrow steps limited how fast she could go.

From above, the Zelthan's bored voice called after her. "Yes, do run if you like. We've no reason to rush when you're as good as caught."

The casual taunt lacked any hint of a bluff. She didn't share the thought with Kelvin, but he was probably thinking the same.

"Where's the one-eyed, scaly bastard?" Kelvin asked.

The artificial lamp at the bottom of the stairs was a long, vertical bulb that flickered. The hallway was curved and so narrow it only allowed enough room for one person. Any more cramped and it would have rendered her sword near useless.

Ayleen ripped off her breathing mask as she found the answer to Kelvin's question. Standing beyond an open door on her left was Leesp.

"Nowhere left to run." He lumbered backwards, but it didn't have the manner of a retreat. Leesp wanted her to see something.

A damp, musty odor choked the hallway. As she reached the open door, Ayleen risked a glance through it. The turn led to a set of descending stairs, but she could only see the top three steps. The same brownish grey water she'd seen so little of in the moat flooded everything below the first step.

Ayleen remembered the lever by the mural. She'd misinterpreted the image. The sphere wasn't hovering over the water. The mural indicated what the lever did. Up meant access to the sphere. Down, as it had been, meant the entire cave was flooded.

"Your breathing masks can't turn water into air," Ulé said in her clipped voice.

Ayleen glanced over her shoulder to see both Ulé and the Zelthan standing there with their swords out.

"Ayleen…" Kelvin didn't need to say anything else. The panic in his voice shared his thoughts well enough. They were surrounded.

The best attack she could make was limited to a thrust, and she wouldn't chop off a head or a limb doing that. They were flanked in a corridor with their best exit sure to drown them.

Her sword howled. *Kill them all!*

They wouldn't let her live. That made Ayleen's choice simple.

She lunged at Leesp. Her katana met his falcata, pinning his sword to the wall. Before he could counter, she thrust her amber dagger deep into his throat. His tongue lashed out rigid in pain with his one good eye wide.

The strike didn't drop him. Instead, he stumbled back and bright light flared from the wound and healed it. She didn't wait for it to finish. She slammed her foot against his torso to knock him onto his back. Only, Leesp didn't fall.

She'd expected him to be incoherent and weakened for a split second of false death.

His fist, the one wrapped around his sword's hilt, slammed into her face. Everything blinked. She'd been standing, but the next thought found her on her knees. Somehow, she'd managed not to drop her weapons.

Something hot and wet landed on the back of her neck. She turned her head and looked up.

The curved tip of Ulé's single-edged dao stuck out the center of Kelvin's back. His body didn't move for a moment. His arms remained tensed, having used his daggers to block the Zelthan's longsword.

More blood dripped off Kelvin's lips as he turned his head to look down at Ayleen.

He smiled. "Like I said… the full ride."

Ulé jerked her sword free, and the life vanished from Kelvin's eyes, which rolled back. His body crumpled next to her.

Ayleen struggled to stand and fight. She never got one foot planted flat on the floor.

"Warm bloods die too easy." Leesp hissed as he slammed the flat of his sword against her temple.

20.

When Ayleen woke, she found herself in a small, square room. The only light, little though it was, came from the crack at the bottom of the door.

She couldn't track time, because the light beyond her cell was artificial.

The only comfort the room offered was a hole in the floor near the back of the cell. Didn't take her long to figure out two things about the hole. One: it wasn't big enough for her to crawl into it to escape. Two: the only purpose for the hole was pissing and shiting.

They fed her enough to keep her alive. Didn't bother her much. She knew hunger on a first name basis, having experienced it on one too many of the worlds she'd walked to get here.

Her sword's screams for blood never stopped. She heard it and her amber dagger, but she couldn't sense where they were. They'd taken everything she'd had except for her clothes and her hat.

All the worlds and all her struggles ended up meaning nothing, because at the last turn, the one that mattered most, she'd dropped like a first year squire not worth trusting with a wooden sword.

What hurt her soul most was Kelvin. When he thought they were going to die in the cave, he said he loved her. She'd answered with a joke.

Tears ran easily enough. Didn't stop the pain, not even when her eyes dried.

A slender flap in the top half of the door opened each time before her guards would slide her meal through a slightly bigger panel at the bottom. Only reason she hadn't tried to escape yet was because she hadn't figured out a way to do it. She also didn't understand why they hadn't killed her.

She wasn't sure how many days had passed when the top slot once again opened. After her vision adjusted to the light, she recognized the eyes staring in at her.

"Long time no see, girl."

Ayleen stood and stepped closer to the door. "Tell me, Javo, how's your neck looking these days? Still hiding my sword's mark under pretty little scarves?"

Sheriff Javo chuckled. "You hold onto that sense of humor. Enjoy it while you can, because once Pyre gets here, he's gonna break you every way he can until he gets his answers."

Ayleen crossed her arms. "He'll be wasting his time."

"Oh, I know." Her voice quivered. "And I'm gonna love watching. Every. Fucking. Minute."

Javo slammed the flap shut and whistled a cheery tune as she walked away.

At least now Ayleen knew why they kept her alive. They wanted to know how she was alive after eight hundred years and if she'd really figured out how to destroy them. All she knew was where to go to destroy them, not what to do. Once they broke her enough to admit that, Pyre and his lot still wouldn't believe her.

21.

Another long stretch of time passed. Ayleen's instincts assumed Javo's visit was three days ago. She'd considered killing herself to spite Pyre. Hanging was out of the question; the room didn't have anywhere she could tie the opposite end of a makeshift rope. Most every method she considered went beyond her ability to carry out.

One of the moments where she started to drift into slumber, the upper flap to her door flung open and blinded her with the light from the other side. She raised her hand to block the light. A woman's voice whispered in disbelief. "Heaven's cunt!"

The door to the cell ripped open. The unexpected rush of light burned Ayleen's eyes. When they adjusted enough to see, all she could discern was the silhouette of a woman in the door.

"You finally get the stones to come and kill me yourself, Javo?"

Something heavy hit the floor of her cell, producing a pair of loud chimes.

Recognition hit, and Ayleen snatched up her sword and dagger. The crystal weapons shook in her weary grip as she stood.

Ayleen narrowed her eyes, trying to see the woman's face. Definitely not Javo.

The woman stepped away from the door, and the light of the corridor revealed her face. Ayleen stumbled back until she hit the wall of her cell.

No, it wasn't Sheriff Javo or Ulé Ontré-vas, but she was without question one of the Thirteen.

"Mom."

PART VI

The Three Names

1.

Ayleen raced behind her mother up the stairs to the greeting hall. To get this far unnoticed, her mother must have killed most of the guards and hidden the bodies.

They paused short of the greeting hall. Mom held up a hand to keep Ayleen waiting until she deemed it safe.

Ayleen's sword whispered to her. *There's blood waiting. Lives for taking!*

She wanted to shove her sword through her mother's back and rage through this castle taking every soul in her path. Gods knew she owed Kelvin that much. She'd tried to make her peace with his death in the dark of her cell. The best she'd managed was the knowledge she'd join him soon enough. Her mother had delayed that penance.

Ayleen glanced past Mom. The wooden lever still pointed down, indicating the keyhole room was flooded. She wondered how long it would take to divert the water back into the moat.

The placement of the lever, keeping it so far away from the actual keyhole room, was a subtle type of security. If she'd flipped it before she and Kelvin raced down the stairs, Ulé Ontré-vas or the Zelthan could have flipped it back before following them.

Mom waved for them to move. Ayleen kept close but with enough distance between them to use their swords without striking each other. The clicks of their boots on the stone floor announced their approach.

They stopped at the lever. When Mom didn't push it up, Ayleen reached past her for it, but her mother grabbed her wrist and shook her head. "The castle notifies the guards anytime the lever changes position. I need to disable that first."

Ayleen looked up the stairs Ulé and the Zelthan had descended from last time. She half expected to see them and a line of guards. The front gate was raised and the stone bridge extended. She noticed another lever on the wall next to the entrance she assumed worked the portcullis and bridge.

"Keep watch." Mom leaned close to the opening in the wall, closing one of her eyes so the other could better focus on the lever's inner workings. She slid her broadsword's blade into the narrow slot. "This is how I was able to slip by them last time I used the sphere. With any luck, we can make it onto Dosquam with half a day's head start, maybe even—"

A loud klaxon ended any optimism.

"So much for our head start," Ayleen muttered.

2.

Mom jerked the lever up to empty the water from the key-hole room.

Ayleen ran for the bridge and portcullis. At least five guards, who'd been patrolling the perimeter of the castle, ran to confront her. She slammed down the lever by the opening to the courtyard, and the stone bridge retracted with a harsh groan as the portcullis bit down. Both features to the castle's entrance moved too slowly.

To Ayleen's surprise, the guards hesitated for a breath as they saw what she'd done. They must have expected her to run for the train, not stay in the castle.

Only two of the guards made the leap into the castle in time. They landed in front of Ayleen. Her sword parried the pair's attack and plowed through them.

Ayleen turned to see her mother fighting another pair of guards. Whether they'd come from the direction of the keyhole or the stairs leading up into the interior of the castle, Ayleen couldn't say. Mom's broadsword sliced open one of the guard's stomachs and severed the sword arm of the other. Before the guard could retreat or take up his sword with his remaining hand, Mom pulled her ambrosia crystal from her jacket. The crystal had also taken the shape of a dagger but different from Ayleen's. Where her dagger was double-edged and short, her mother's resembled a pointed spike with no edge to it. She buried it in the guard's chest. His life's sacrifice set the dagger ablaze with light.

Mom pointed the bloody end of the dagger at the wide frame atop the stairs. *"Hokuina!"* The structure rumbled as cracks formed within the walls and floor. A half dozen guards, some half-dressed in their uniforms spilled out through the collapsing door frame.

Ayleen slashed through the stomach of the closest guard, who'd leaped down to the floor. Mom took a place on the opposite side of the steps from Ayleen, making it impossible for any of the guards to get past them without engaging them in a fight, and both crystal swords provided a longer reach than the short gladius each guard carried. Bricks rained behind the guards as the wall and ceiling collapsed. The rear-most of the six guards took a large chunk of bricks to the back of the head before getting buried. The others tried to parry Ayleen and Mom's attacks, but they eventually dropped to the floor in a lifeless pile.

Mom grabbed the lever to the keyhole room. "Run!" She threw it back into the down position to flood the keyhole.

"Attadior!" Mom's sword blazed alive with heat. She slashed through the lever and stabbed into the mechanism hidden in the wall.

They sprinted down the passage to their escape. As they neared the turn to the keyhole's entrance, a hint of red stained the stone floor. The reminder of Kelvin's death fueled Ayleen's attack as she met the two guards standing by the door. One guard hesitated as Ayleen charged at them and screamed. The other responded, but fear made his response shaky. In two swings, both men's corpses littered the floor.

Mom ran past Ayleen and down the steps to the keyhole.

The room was shaped like a large cylinder with the red sphere glowing at its base. Dark, frigid water had entered from the moat and covered all but the top quarter of the sphere.

Without a word of warning or command, Mom leaped from the steps that spiraled down the wall of the room and vanished into the top of the keyhole.

Ayleen plunged into the sphere's light a few seconds behind her mother. Gravity vanished. All she was, body and soul, launched for the world where none were meant to walk.

3.

Despite the speed at which she'd hit the sphere, Ayleen emerged on the other side with a gentle push from the dark energy tunnel to land on her feet as always. Mom stood a few feet away, giving Ayleen a quick look up and down.

She turned away from her mother to see the sphere pulse as it changed from yellow to green, indicating it was now submerged on the other side.

Dosquam greeted them not with a cave, but a star-filled sky. If her vision from the Fate was right, then this was a fully-formed planet. That meant it should have four other keyholes, but as she reached out with her sword, she sensed only the sphere behind her.

"We'd best hurry." Mom waved for Ayleen to follow, and they ran down the side of the hill.

An ever-present sensation of wrongness pervaded Dosquam. The impression resembled what she felt from all of the Thirteen, including her mother.

As she followed Mom across the grey, lifeless terrain, *Basten's Warning* echoed to her.

"Life can walk upon most worlds, but there are places the living should never go."

As the emptiness in the air filled Ayleen's lungs, none of Basten's memories stirred. Whatever happened here, Basten had never forgotten it. Rather, she'd chosen to never remember this barren planet.

Only one thing about Dosquam showed any movement, and they were running towards it. The thread of light spilling down from the heavens pulsed into the distant horizon. If she tilted her head just so, the light seemed to vanish.

Each fall of her feet into Dosquam's grey dust sent an angry warning up into her nervous system screaming to leave this place now.

They couldn't turn back, though. So she followed her mother towards the thread and prayed their head start would be enough for them to end the Thirteen.

4.

An hour into their run, Ayleen and Mom stopped. They shared from the water bottle Mom carried.

Ayleen's hands shook and her lungs ached. Unwelcome and unavoidable thoughts, sharp as daggers, stabbed their way to the forefront of her mind. Every time she met her mother's assessing gaze, everything in Ayleen insisted this woman couldn't be here.

She wondered if Mom's thoughts mirrored hers, refusing to believe her daughter was here. Mom was hunched over, gripping her legs above the kneecaps for support.

"You haven't asked." The words came out angrier than Ayleen intended, not that she wasn't pissed. She wanted to sound calm and in control. Letting her anger show felt like handing Mom a victory she didn't deserve.

"What did happen to your eyes?"

The question startled Ayleen into standing straight. She'd managed to forget about that. "I spent ten days sharing my body with another woman's soul."

Mom frowned as she diverted her gaze to the ambrosia crystal resting in the sheath on Ayleen's right thigh.

"Why would you do something so reckless?"

"Kristian Basten explored more worlds than any other traveler. I needed her knowledge to find Dosquam."

Her mother shook her head in disappointment. Ayleen remembered how mother's long black hair flowed down her back, the way it shifted when she shook it. The hair she now had was trimmed short and shifted only a little as she moved, part why Ayleen hadn't immediately recognized her.

"Wasn't my eyes I was talking about." Her temper flared, the words burning their way up her throat. "Pyre Clypse was itching to torture me to find out how I'm still breathing eight centuries later. I'm your godsdamned daughter, and you don't give a shite how I'm here!"

Mother took a step back, her body swaying as she did.

"I haven't asked, because I already know the answer."

"What shite is that! I don't fucking know! How would you?"

Her anger didn't provoke her mother. Instead, Mom's lips curled into a satisfied smile. "Took you long enough."

"What is that supposed to mean? Long enough for what?"

Mom pointed at her. "Long enough to ask a question that really matters."

"Enough!" Ayleen ripped her sword free of its scabbard.

"Or you'll kill me?" Mom chuckled. "We both know you can't, not yet."

"Oh, I've thought it through, Mother. I know it won't kill you, but it'll hurt a whole lot."

Mom's humor vanished with a long sigh. "Do you want answers and revenge against all of the Thirteen, or would you rather waste time carving me up for fun until we're ambushed and you die—again?"

"Again?" Ayleen lowered her sword.

"I buried you. You and your father. I put you both in the ground next to Lake Kurter."

"I didn't die. I mean…" She stopped short as she pointed to herself, the only evidence she felt was needed.

Mom stepped closer, and Ayleen realized they were finally the same height. Only took her eight centuries. A pity Dad wasn't here to see it.

A light flashed in the corner of her eye, drawing Ayleen's attention back to the yellow keyhole. Yellow, not green.

"Shite!" Mom's curse came before Ayleen could speak her own. She didn't move, though. Instead her mother muttered numbers, counting each time the sphere pulsed to indicate another arrival. She stopped counting by the time she hit twenty, but the sphere continued to pulse.

"Damn fools are running scared," Mom said.

"They'd have reason to be, if I knew what it is I need to do to kill them."

Mom didn't respond. Instead, she ran in the direction of the thread of light.

They had a head start, but not nearly enough to give them the advantage they needed.

Ayleen followed. Their shadows, faint lines along the grey sands, grew a little darker and more pronounced the closer they got to the thread of light. The shadows didn't line up right.

5.

They ran until they reached the edge of a large crater.

"Get a good look at the sky. Might be the last time either of us sees it." Mom didn't bother looking up as she said it, though. "From here on out, we'll be traveling beneath the surface, and there are things you need to know about Dosquam before we do."

"We're losing time." Ayleen glanced over her shoulder. She didn't see movement in the distance, but she felt the rest of the Thirteen and however many others they'd brought with them closing the gap.

"We're about to make it up." Mom pulled her grey hat down in the front, hiding her eyes as she stared into the crater. "We're trading one threat for a bigger one, though, and that mess of fools coming up behind us will only make it worse."

Ayleen looked back and forth from the direction of the key-hole and the crater's dark center. "Is there a point where you start speaking sense again, because I'd prefer not to die?"

"This is a dream world, and it's why the sphere to it is red. It's because where we now stand isn't as real as the rest of the Galaxy. It's a weak point where we can see the line between dreams and reality."

Ayleen had never heard of the like in her training, and it was unexpected from her mother. Between her parents, Dad was the one who always tutored her on all that made the Galaxy strange, wonderful, and horrible.

Mom stepped up to the edge of the hole. "Dosquam means 'the hunter in the night.' That same hunter still troubles all of us. Only, we call it 'nightmares.'

"Nothing lives on or beneath this world." She glanced up at Ayleen. "But down there is what gives Dosquam its name. Our worst nightmares will manifest. Some will be yours. Some mine. And anyone else's on this world. When I said the Thirteen are running scared, it's because they know everything I'm telling you. The more of the living you bring to this planet, the worse things get, and knowing that hasn't stopped them from bringing every guard they have left."

"Well," Ayleen said as she knelt next to the hole, "guess it's a good thing we killed as many guards as we did."

Mom grunted. "A pity we didn't kill them all."

As she pulled out her sword, Mom whispered, *"Terastrant."* The broadsword glowed. Holding her hat in place with her free hand, she stepped into the hole and disappeared into the darkness.

Ayleen took a second to wonder what waited for her down there and how much worse it could possibly be than the Thirteen and their small army.

She drew her sword, its eager whispers for satisfaction having never ceased since coming to this world, as if knowing how close they were to the Thirteen's weakness, whatever that might be.

"Terastrant."

The crystal katana brightened within her grip. Mimicking her mother, she held onto her hat and stepped into the hole.

6.

The drop turned out deeper than Ayleen expected, somewhere close to twenty feet. The gravity on this small world wasn't as strong as she was used to, though, so she hit with less of an impact than expected.

Mom stood off to the side. She'd stabbed her sword into the floor of the cave so it would stay upright. Its glow bathed her and their surroundings in its blue light.

The cave they found themselves in didn't look particularly ominous despite its uneven walls and scattered bits of rocky debris. A path formed within the cave's floor, with a half dozen branches leading out in different directions.

"Doesn't look so bad," Ayleen said, despite the creeping sensation crawling along her back.

Mom laughed, a grunt without any humor to it. The look in her eyes warned it would get worse. She pointed into the branch she was standing in front of. "Get in there. I'm gonna buy us a little time."

Ayleen stepped into the tunnel as her mom pulled out a slender case from a breast pocket inside her coat. She opened the case, and blue light spilled out. The interior was lined with a foamlike material and held five small pieces of the same blue crystals that were used by the Knighthood for their swords.

Mom pulled out one of the crystals, then snapped the case shut and slipped it back into her trench coat.

"Start running."

Ayleen raced into the tunnel. She saw her mother's movements from out of the corner of her eye. Mom's arm swung up, sending the crystal flying up to the crater's hole.

The next sounds she heard were Mom ripping her sword free of the cavern's floor, pounding feet behind her, and then the blast.

Debris shot past them and what didn't get past them pounded at their backs. Dust flowed through the artery and dug into Ayleen's exposed flesh.

The rumble of falling rock only caressed her ears as soft thuds buried within the thrum of a long whistle born from the blast.

They stopped once the cave settled.

Mom coughed into her hand. "Should keep them off our backs for a little while."

"There's not another way in?"

"Plenty of other options, but they all require them to go out of their way to get in the tunnels."

Ayleen raised her glowing sword to offer a better view of the cave-in. "Where'd you get the crystal fragments?"

"Stole them from Pyre's stockpile before sneaking into the castle to free you. He's spent the past eight centuries tricking people into mining them for him. They're getting harder to find. Weren't the most abundant resource to begin with."

Ayleen remembered the town of Midchron back on Griffin, the people mining the crystal. Sheriff Javo had made sure the only people they traded with would be working for the Thirteen. "He's been hoarding those crystals."

"Yep." Mom led them deeper into the cave, with her sword for a torch. "The crystals power Pyre's castle and the cities and about everything that requires energy back on Witbrom VI. He's turned that sad world into his personal paradise in Hell."

Ayleen stopped and stared at her mother's back, which was fading into the dark of the cave. "How could you let yourself be a part of that?"

When Mom realized Ayleen had stopped, she turned around. The position of her glowing sword made her more shadow than human. "I'll tell you more when we stop to rest. We need to push ahead while the way is easy. If you haven't sensed the shift in the air since we got in here, you'll notice it soon enough. Things will get worse."

"Tell me while we're walking. If you have the answers I need, then quit leaving me in the dark." Ayleen's grip on her sword tightened. That she still didn't know how to kill the Thirteen frustrated her, and she was tired of waiting.

Mom rounded on her. "Do you have any idea what it's taken to get you here?"

Ayleen moved in closer, her face inches from her mother's. "No, I have no idea, so fucking tell me already."

She expected her retort to really set off her mom, but it had the opposite effect. All the anger emptied out of Mom, and the glow from her sword emphasized all the sad wrinkles on her face.

"I have spent a miserable eternity walking from one mistake to another. Now, the Fates have given me one chance—my last—to make things right. That's not something I mean to do without all my focus on the task. I don't know how long you've waited to hear my sins, but I've had eight centuries to prepare my confession. Not yet sure it was enough time."

Ayleen answered with silence.

Mom held her gaze for a moment, then turned and continued her march through Dosquam's bowels.

Ayleen followed without voicing more protests, but all she could think as she followed her mother was how it's rare the truth requires thought.

But lies?

The deadliest ones require time to craft.

7.

The dark kicked up Ayleen's paranoia. Didn't take long to recognize her growing fear was more than simple dread.

"People talk about the five senses, but we come packed with a lot more than five. Some of us are equipped with more than others," Mom said as they paused hours later for stale water and nutrient bars that tasted even worse than the name suggested. She'd sat on the ground with her pack beside her. "The reason most people don't notice the others is because our brains haven't evolved enough to properly translate the information. Doesn't mean they aren't constantly at work and affecting us."

Ayleen wiped the sweat from her brow with a blue, paisley handkerchief she'd gotten from Kelvin a few days after she'd met him on Ryjal II. She'd avoided thinking of him, but being trapped in the dark again, as she'd been in her cell in Paladin Castle, quickened the memory of his death.

"Is there a point to this? Can't say I'm in the mood, if you're just reliving old times as a science instructor."

Mom scowled at her. "The point is that the Galaxy talks to us. We aren't capable of processing the exact message, but we react to it on a subconscious level. We hear the Galaxy all the time, and its message is carried to us through what we call CBR. Science has listened and studied it for eons."

Ayleen held up her hands in surrender. "Cosmic Background Radiation. Yeah, I remember this lesson. Basically, the temperature of the universe which for the most part has been getting colder ever since the Big Bang." She chomped off a large chunk of her nutrient bar.

"What you were taught was wrong," Mom said. "The CBR isn't getting colder anymore. Everything is shifting in the opposite direction. Started before either of us was born."

That got Ayleen's attention. "The Knighthood fed us lies?"

"In your teachers' defense, they didn't know. Only the mage generals and a handful of others realized this. Your father knew it, too."

"So what has that got to do with anything now? Clearly, reality is taking its sweet time dying."

"That's just it. None of us should be here now. The universe was sending out a simple message that all living things can understand and recognize on a primal level: *I'm dying.* For a monster like Pyre who spent all his life chasing after immortality, there's nothing more terrifying. He was racing against time for a way to slow the process."

Ayleen's brain ached as she absorbed that shift in her reality.

Mom continued, not willing to wait on her to catch up. "The message is strongest here—on this small world where reality is so thin—and it magnifies our fears, gives form to them. That's what you're feeling."

Yes, that fit. Not only did it make sense for here and now, but everything in the past few years took on new meaning.

Mom stood and slid on her pack. "We should get moving again."

Ayleen didn't move right away. She wrapped up what was left of her nutrient bar. "But if everything is dying, then what's the point of immortality? You and the rest of the Thirteen are on borrowed time, same as the rest of us."

"If you were told you were going to die months from now, what would you choose? Savor the tiny time left with friends and family? Or would you fight for a chance to share in the entirety of your loved ones' lives and more?"

She didn't wait on Ayleen or say anything more. She turned and walked deeper into the cave. Ayleen followed.

The sensation of something stalking her grew stronger.

8.

The cave brightened, and not because of their swords.

An orange glow appeared against the wall where it turned a sharp left before making a slow curve to the right, as if forced to go around something round before correcting its course.

The orange light came from around the curve.

Ayleen's suspicion was heightened by how much warmer the cave had gotten. The cave opened into an underground canyon. Lava flowed out of fissures in the walls like bright orange and red waterfalls feeding into a molten river hundreds of meters below. The path they stood on narrowed to a bridge no wider than two inches that crossed the chasm and disappeared into the shadows on the far side.

"Well, someone has a serious fear of heights," Mom said.

Panic crushed the breath from Ayleen's lungs. "You think?"

Mom turned to look at her. The confusion on her face changed to recognition. "Oh, sorry. Didn't realize this was you."

Ayleen pointed at the lava below. "Can't say I'm fond of burning alive either."

"Well, yes," Mom pointed to the path ahead them, "but if it's not this, then it's something else."

Without waiting for Ayleen to respond, Mom slid her sword back into its scabbard on her right hip and started across.

"For what it's worth, I've more reason to fear the lava down there. I don't die, so I'd suffer a damn long time."

The thought of stepping onto the bridge suffocated her. Ayleen edged closer, and everything beneath her breastbone twisted. This might not be her worst nightmare made real, but that didn't stop it from scaring the piss out of her.

Mom, who didn't spend a day trapped in the remains of an imploded library and then was yanked up through the air on a giant fucking squirrel, moved along fine.

Ayleen looked back into the tunnel that led them here. They hadn't come across any other turns. Going back would mean going all the way to the crater and digging their way out and probably getting killed by the Thirteen or by initiating a cave-in on top of themselves.

Accepting this was the only way, Ayleen slid her sword back into its scabbard and stepped up to the edge.

Her mom had already made it halfway across.

Ayleen wiped her brow with the back of her hand. She pulled out her gloves, but then debated on whether they would ruin her grip if she fell and had to grab onto the rocky bridge. She finally decided they might improve her odds of surviving and put them on.

She took in a breath, but it didn't get her to take the first step. Instead, she whispered a long string of curses.

"Ayleen," Mom called to her without looking back, "you can do this."

Maybe if she crawled? Only, with the bridge so narrow, that might be worse. At least her boots were flat with treads. Her knees and toes were rounded and with little traction.

"Shite! I can't do this!" She could drain a well of ink listing half the reasons not to.

"Listen to my voice and follow." Mom's slow, reassuring tone did nothing to lessen the terror of this height and the fiery hell below.

Before Ayleen could protest again, she heard another voice.

"Ayleen…"

Not from her mother, but from another whose voice she'd never forget.

"Aaaaay-leeeen…"

Not from ahead, but behind. The sound of something too big for the cave scraped against the cavern's walls as it squeezed its way through.

Despite the heat below, a cold shiver started in her core and shook out into her arms and up through her flesh.

"Aaaaay-leeeen…"

A massive, shadowy shape emerged from the tunnel into the light.

"Life… is a dream."

The Fate—her spider-like form, with a crack in its head that revealed Ayleen's twin face with blond hair—grinned at her.

Its mandibles clacked together in hungry anticipation. The spider's long legs, tipped in blue crystal, slashed forward.

Ayleen ran out onto the bridge.

9.

Ayleen's body reduced to two functions: putting one foot ahead of the other in a straight line and producing as much sweat as possible without turning into dust.

She whispered under her breath. "Right. Left. Right. Left." She maintained her mantra and did her best not to think on falling or being speared by a crystal-tipped spider leg or trapped with all the living and dead things in the giant ball of water on the Fate's back.

Heavy ticks vibrated through the bridge. The Fate's legs tapped against the rock much faster than Ayleen's footsteps. Little shock there. It could walk on threads. Ayleen glanced up. She hadn't made it a quarter of the way. She'd never reach the other side before the Fate reached her, and she lacked the grace to turn and fight on this narrow path.

"Moira!" Mom shouted, already on the far side of the canyon.

The Fate hissed its reply, and its legs stopped ticking their way across the bridge. Mom's distraction bought Ayleen a few more seconds. She forced her feet to move faster as the Fate cursed her mother.

"Deceiver! Thief! Thirteen! Thrice damned!"

"I've given you your due and more." Mom drew her ambrosia crystal from her jacket. Reaching towards her throat, Mom hooked a finger on a thin, silver chain and pulled out a tiny corked bottle of blood. "Ayleen, run."

She didn't know what attack her mother planned, but she knew well her mother's glare. Without protest, Ayleen muttered her "Right! Left!" mantra as fast as she could. Her breathing sped up enough that she might as well have been sprinting.

"A life owed! A life promised! A life to devour!" The clicking of the spider sped up, too.

"Faster!" Mom shouted.

She dipped her dagger's tip into the bottle of blood. *"Funsidam!"*

A loud crack sounded a few steps behind Ayleen. She didn't need to look. The word from the dead language *Mui Vanum* meant "shatter."

The cracks grew louder, but the click of the spider's legs stopped. Probably unsure whether to retreat or leap.

"Don't slow down." The amber glow threw unpleasant shadows on her mom's face.

Ayleen's mantra for "Right! Left!" changed to "Yes! Yes!" with more than half the distance covered. The Fate howled at her back, but the threat meant nothing when it wouldn't risk going forward.

She was going to make it.

"Ayleen, don't let her keep me!"

That voice.

Not Mother.

Not the Fate.

The words echoed from the water on the Fate's back... Dara.

Ayleen stopped. Her mind shouted to her this wasn't real. That this Fate, despite having physical form, was nothing but a nightmare vision given substance.

But she had to see.

She had to know.

Mom screamed. "Ayleen!"

The bridge cracked past her feet.

She turned her head to stare into the massive drop of water suspended upon the monster's back. The same collection of life and death she'd seen so many months ago still resided there, but now it consisted of one thing more.

"Don't leave me!" Dara's head floated at an angle with a bit of her spine sticking out her torn neck. The worst part was her eyes. Although she spoke, Dara's eyes never moved. They stared out as dead as she'd been in her last moment, when the Fate ripped her away.

Mom's shout tore her gaze from the horror on the spider's back. "Run!"

The cracks reached all the way to the far side of the chasm. The Fate screamed as it lunged.

Ayleen ran on the narrow strip of crumbling rock. Tiny slivers of the bridge flaked off.

The Fate cried out. Its crystal legs stabbed into the space behind her. The bridge shivered beneath their combined weight, forcing the Fate to stop short of the kill. Its breath blew Ayleen's blue hair around her head and into her face and filled her nostrils with the stench of rot.

Her boots slid. She overcorrected her balance to the right. Arms flailed with nothing to grab.

She ran three more steps before the bridge shattered.

10.

The rocky wall and its bright falls of molten rock blurred past Ayleen. Hot air pushed up against her but failed to slow her fall. The side of the chasm curved in halfway down, bringing it within reach. She grabbed her dagger. Both hands wrapped around the hilt and stabbed forward.

The amber blade jerked in her hands as it struck the rock. It bounced off, but on the second strike, the dagger bit into the rock and held. Pain screamed within her shoulders, but she held true and stopped her fall.

The Fate's scream continued a second longer. Ayleen didn't sing praise or joy when the creature's shriek stopped short. All she heard was Dara's scream, begging for Ayleen to save her. Her attempt to shout "Please!" and never finishing the word.

Ayleen screamed and channeled all her anger into her hands and arms. She needed to hold on long enough to get her footing.

The tips of her feet slid against the wall. Each miss threatened to shake her hands loose from the dagger.

Mom shouted down to her.

Ayleen studied the wall in front of her. Close to her knees, the wall jutted out enough to where she might get half of her feet on there if she turned them sideways.

The foothold was closer to her right, so she focused on that foot first. A thick layer of smoke flowed up in slow motion. The tainted air tickled the back of her throat as she breathed deep and she erupted into a fit of coughs as she was trying to pull her foot up.

The ache in her hands and arms shifted into agony.

She pulled her right leg up. The edge of her boot scraped against the rock until she felt certain it had established enough of a hold on the narrow surface beneath it. She put her weight on it a little, enough to be sure. Using all the strength she had left, she pulled her body up to get her left foot on that jut of rock.

The pain subsided from her arms as the focus of her weight shifted from her arms to her legs. She didn't ease the grip of her hands, though. The move had brought her face level with the dagger embedded in the side of the chasm.

"Mom?"

She sobbed Ayleen's name in reply. Her voice was choked with relief and panic.

"Mom." Ayleen leaned her forehead against the rock as she caught her breath. "Is there some craft I can do with this dagger to fly me up there?"

"No."

Ayleen sighed. Of course there wasn't. Between her and her mother, they had two grimoires, and neither one of them contained shite to help her out of this.

She looked around to see if she could climb over to a nearby opening in the wall to try to reach Mom by way of a connecting passage. No such luck.

That's when she realized her hat had fallen off, the last thing her father had ever given her had blown away in the fall.

"I lost my hat." Her voice cracked as she said it.

"Not quite."

Ayleen looked up. Mom waved the dark brown hat over the edge of the chasm for her to see it.

"The wind blew it up here."

"Would've been nice if the wind had offered me the same kindness. Gonna have to climb my way up." Ayleen studied the rocky wall for the best handholds to lead her to the top. "Try pretending to be scared of rope. Maybe it'll trick the planet into manufacturing some we can use to get me up faster."

Mom called down to her. "Save the jokes for after we get you up here."

We? Seriously?

Ayleen climbed and prayed the gods didn't decide to seek humor at her expense by letting her drop just short of the top.

11.

Climbing to the top of the chasm required several hours of effort. For want of a second dagger, the climb probably took twice as long as it would have otherwise. Her metal dagger was lost back in Paladin Castle. She remembered it dropping out of Kelvin's hand as he collapsed to the floor. At this moment, she wanted the dagger more than him, and she despised herself for it.

The Ayleen who pulled her body over the edge of the wall carried more guilt and self-loathing than the one who'd fallen.

Mom hugged her and cried. Ayleen leaned against her mom too tired to move her arms or legs.

"Please get me out of this place."

Mom put Ayleen's hat on her and then lifted Ayleen's arm over her shoulders. Ayleen's breath caught in a flash of pain.

"I'm sorry." Mom pulled her towards the entrance to the tunnel leading away from the lava chasm.

They made it about ten steps into the tunnel, when Ayleen's feet gave out.

"Wanna stay here for a bit."

Mom nodded and lowered her to the ground. "We can't stay too long." She raised a hand against any protest Ayleen might voice. "A few hours to let you sleep. But too long, and the Thirteen will get ahead of us."

"Can't sleep yet. Not yet." Ayleen's words came out as little more than a weary gasp as she rolled onto her back. If she closed her eyes now, she'd go back to that vision of Dara's head floating on top of the Fate. She'd hear her scream, the look of betrayal forever frozen in place. Gods... she wanted to be done. She wanted Dara and Kelvin and Father all back. If the price was her life, she was more than willing to be done and have the reward she'd never get to enjoy.

Mom brushed Ayleen's hair out of her face. "You need rest."

"Why the fuck did you do this to us? Was Dad awful? What in the Heavens did I do to you that was so wrong?"

Mom sat across from her. She leaned against the opposite side of the wall with only the orange glow of the lava chasm to let them see one another. "The only mistake you and your father ever made was giving me a reason to love you both."

When she spoke again, she didn't look at Ayleen. Didn't take long for Ayleen to realize Mom couldn't bear to see her reaction as she explained why she threw her hat in with the Thirteen.

12.

"The short answer is easy enough." Mom stared out towards the light from the lava. "I was going to die. Chaemtiale, the silent erosion. Best estimate I got was two to five years. Couldn't bring myself to tell your father, because letting him know was too close to accepting it was real. At least, I told myself that was the reason. Looking back, I think even then I already knew I was willing to sell my soul to change my fate.

"You'd turned twelve, and there was still so much of your father in your face. I went into the village near Lake Kurter. There was a tavern the knights would visit, but I'm sure you got plenty familiar with The Bent Blade after you earned your sword and first assignment."

Ayleen knew it better than her mom suspected. She'd lost her virginity in one of the rooms on the second floor. The ale was cheap and the cards were always played fair. You got caught cheating, they'd never let you back in the place. What Ayleen wouldn't give right now for a tall glass of a Baron Arnold's Red Ale, not that she had the energy to raise a glass.

"I ran into an old friend." No missing the disgust she gave those last words. "Mera Kaillavo graduated within my academy. We'd drifted apart. I worked my way up the ranks of the science regiment while she made a name for herself in defense and enforcement.

"By then, I already knew I was going to be promoted to mage general. Everyone knew, but no one beyond my personal healer had a clue how short a time I was likely to hold onto the post.

"Got drunk that night. I'm talking the kind of drunk that gets you loose in the lips and makes everything twice as funny and every action four times as bold and brilliant as all the gods in Altifany.

"I told Mera all the shite burning a hole in my heart. I'd never get a chance to make my mark in the Knighthood. What good to be the youngest person ever promoted to mage general when my time would be cut short? My daughter would grow into an adult, but only after my eyes were rotted black and my body buried. My husband? Damn me for a jealous woman, but the idea he'd live so long as to later marry again, no matter how much he might doubt he ever would..." Mom shook her head, then hid her face behind her hands and groaned. "I believed your father's gods had cheated me, turned me into a butt for a cosmic joke.

"Mera came to me again a few days later. Told me she knew a way to beat the odds, to heal what the best mage generals in the Knighthood couldn't with all the forbidden science they knew. She arranged for me to meet Pyre Clypse. If I hadn't been so desperate and so sick, I'd never have bought into his snake oil. His sales pitch was perfect. They were this close—oh so close—to achieving the one thing our mage craft forbids we ever seek: Immortality."

Mom's head slumped as she gave voice to the code of the Knights of the Way, the creed she'd betrayed.

"The Way is an arrow as true as time.

"Arrows are only so long. Narrow and small at the tip, stretching out just so, then flare out in beauty at the end.

"All lives have an ending. All things conclude, but I wasn't ready to.

"So I lost my Way." Her voice caught. "The plan—that was all Pyre. He'd sussed out a way to live forever, but there was one thing he didn't know, and that was where to find the Fates. That's why they needed me.

"I made them the Thirteen. They couldn't have done it without me. I gave them what they needed, helped Pyre perform the ritual, and walked away never guessing what Pyre would unleash on the Knighthood and the Galaxy to protect our secret. They didn't call themselves the Thirteen until we parted ways, but something in me suspected from the first field report that named them.

"For a time, the deal seemed mighty fine. I saw you turn seventeen, and I shouldn't have. My husband and I still made love in our bed when my resting place should've been a grave. Only I never saw my daughter finish growing into a woman, and I didn't share my bed with my man into our old age.

"Five years. My 'best odds.'

"We didn't get a sixth year, because I buried you both in the fifth. At the start of the assault on the Citadel, bastards sent a suicide attacker to my office who set off a crystal the size of my arm. By the time my body pulled itself back together, it was all over. I dug your bodies out of the ruin of Mount Hawkken and interred you in the ashen fields in front of the lake.

"No gods had pranked me. I'd set myself up for all of it, the butt of a joke I didn't know I was telling."

Mom fell silent. She stared out at the past, seeming oblivious to Ayleen and the cave around them.

"But I'm not dead," Ayleen said.

Mom jerked her head out of her memories and back into the moment. "I'll explain it, but for now, get some sleep. The rest can keep another night."

Ayleen wanted to protest. Instead, she closed her eyes. Sleep came all too easy to her along with all the nightmares she'd wanted to avoid.

13.

Ayleen woke to her mother's screams, the high-pitched choir of thousands of tiny feet, and a rising heat that had her sweating as if she was next to the sun.

"On your feet!" Mom tugged Ayleen's arm. Any harder and Ayleen thought her arm might rip free.

A wave of fire filled the cave, top to bottom, crawling towards them. She thought the lava was flowing into the cave, but then she saw the fire for what it was. The flames billowed about the shapes of thousands of small, black beetles.

"Gods!" Ayleen jumped to her feet and ran with her mom at her back.

Keeping ahead of the beetles wasn't difficult, but no matter how fast they ran, the fiery wave kept coming. At best, they gained enough ground to put five meters between them and the fire.

Something about the path of the corridor ahead looked wrong. For a moment, Ayleen thought the tunnel might be a dead end.

Ayleen drew her sword and shouted. *"Terastrant!"* Her sword glowed bright, revealing the way ahead wasn't a dead end.

"There's a split up ahead! Right or left?"

"Left!" Mom shouted the word several times.

When Ayleen glanced over her shoulder, Mom held her ambrosia crystal. She grabbed the vial of blood from around her neck, but then she tripped on one of the rocks.

They screamed at each other. Ayleen struggled with Mom, grabbing her beneath her arms to get her back on her feet. Mom snatched up her dagger, but fought against Ayleen's pull trying to find something else.

"I dropped the blood!" Mom's voice turned shrill.

Ayleen pulled hard on her. Fresh pain shot through her sore shoulder as she jerked Mom to move. The wave of fire bugs made up the ground between them.

"Shades of the Abyss!" Mom cursed. As they took the turn to the left, Mom grabbed Ayleen's arm, pulling her to a stop. "Wait!"

Was she mad? They had seconds before the wave of fire beetles hit them. Ayleen turned to shout at her to run, but the words morphed into a scream as Mom stabbed the crystal spike dagger into her right palm.

"Mayulusk." The magic command shrieked from Mom's lips. The spike dagger glowed bright and a flash of amber light slammed up against the opening to the tunnel. A handful of fire beetles dropped to the floor, but the rest raced along the protective barrier thrown up by Mom and down the other passage.

"Kill them!" Mom stomped on the beetles that made it in before the barrier formed. Ayleen's feet joined her mother's. They made quick work of the beetles. Their bent and flattened carcasses burned only a few moments longer.

Once the bugs were all dead, Mom started to say, "I'm sorry."

She didn't get all of the "sorry" out before Ayleen punched her in the face. Mom toppled to the cave's floor. She held up her free hand to beg off another attack.

"Next time, you use your own damn blood, or so help me, Mother, I'll run you through."

Mom glared up at her. "I can't."

"I've used my own blood plenty enough with my ambrosia crystal. You can damn well do the same, *mage general.*"

"I don't have any blood for craftwork." Mom focused on putting her dagger away. "Losing your blood could kill you. Makes it a suitable sacrifice. Even if I had blood, spilling it would mean nothing."

Ayleen fought down the urge to bury her dagger into her mother's throat. About the only thing that stopped her was how insanely wrong this moment was. How many times had Mom been the "in-control" one? The "thought-before-action" one? Mom had brought order to their home with solutions to all problems, but now, she was the chaos. Perhaps she had been all along.

Ayleen dropped onto her arse. She knew enough about the crafting her mother had done to know the protective barrier formed a sphere around them. They couldn't go out the other side of the sphere without collapsing the whole thing, so they had to wait for all of the fire beetles to skitter by them.

"We better pray that branch," Ayleen pointed to the wave of fire beetles racing over the barrier and then down at their feet, "doesn't circle into this one, or we're fucked."

Mom didn't respond. She leaned her head back against the wall and stared off into oblivion.

Mourning for her mother still hadn't ended for Ayleen. Having discovered Mom was alive didn't change anything, because the woman she'd assumed was dead wasn't the one sitting here.

Minutes passed, but the wave of fire beetles continued. Mom shook her head and let out a long, bone-ass-tired sigh. "Might as well put the time to good use." Her gaze turned away from Ayleen to the fire. "I've told you why I joined the Thirteen, but I haven't told you why they so desperately needed access to the Fate's cave."

14.

Mom pulled out her spike dagger. The smooth, rounded blade bent the firelight into odd shapes and colors across the floor and up into Mom's face as if to burn the past free from her mind.

"You know how rare ambrosia crystals are. Every few hundred years, one might grow within the Knighthood's crystal farms, and when they did, we always took them to the Fates for safekeeping. Their connection to the dark energy of the Galaxy runs deeper than with any other crystal. They're dangerous, which is why the Knighthood went to great lengths to keep them out of the hands of anyone who might use them for ill purpose. The Knights of the Way fought wars to stop worlds from abusing that power.

"Pyre Clypse was born from the last of those conflicts, the War of the Centaur's Arm. And yes, if you're startled by the math, that means he was already two centuries old by the time I made my pact with him. What seduced him into his quest for immortality was the most enticing fruit of all—curiosity. You wouldn't think it possible for someone as cold and disconnected from the Galaxy as he is, but for some, the burden of ignorance only worsens with the more we learn. Every decade brings greater understanding of the universe we inhabit, but for each advancement, we're still left with galactic mysteries that no single lifetime can hope to solve.

"He couldn't accept a life that ends without all the answers, and so Pyre began his descent. The War of the Centaur's Arm started with the genocide of Deltsag VIII, a billion souls butchered to give Pyre a second century and make certain each year was filled with vitality. He's a true parasite and a wasteful one. A billion lifetimes cut short, and he only gained a century from ingesting all those spirits. Wasn't enough, so he slaughtered five more worlds and countless souls. He snuffed out a star, plunging its orbiting worlds into eternal darkness, and that still failed to give him what he craved.

"The Knights of the Way hunted him and his followers. We believed him wiped from the celestial map, but it was all a lie. He turned a handful of the knights charged with his demise.

"Armed with access to the Knighthood's knowledge, Pyre eventually found this world. The thread of light that runs deep into Dosquam used to run out the other side.

"He learned the most inconvenient of truths, the answer to why parts of our galaxy defy reality's fundamental laws."

Mom looked back at Ayleen. "Remember your science lessons in the Knighthood, how the human brain has a hundred billion neurons? That's roughly the same number of stars in our galaxy. Do you really believe that's a coincidence?

"The thread of light you saw is a single thought. Not a simple one, but a grand one. All this—our galaxy and all that exists within it—is a dream. Pyre realized the dream was nearing its end, that when the Galaxy woke, his bid for immortality would mean nothing. He'd vanish into oblivion along with everyone and everything else, but if he could bind the thread, trap the Galaxy within its dream, that would change everything.

"Pyre puzzled out a way to tie down the dream, but he needed access to the Fate's cave. I refused to divulge the location. Instead, I agreed to steal what he needed. After my months floating on Moira's back, I'd learned where to find all of our life threads. I stole all Thirteen of them and delivered them here on Dosquam where we all gathered. Pyre and I used our ambrosia crystals to wrap our life threads around the light running into this world. We're now tied to the dream, merged with it. We are the dream, and the light I'm sure you saw when you cut off Mera Kaillavo's head comes from the Galaxy's dream. The dream binds all thirteen of us to the Galaxy and this nightmare without an end. We've forced it to maintain this construct beyond its intended time. Might seem like his plan worked, but Pyre only achieved immortality for himself and the rest of the Thirteen. Doesn't preserve anyone else. We'll live forever, but what waits for us is a destiny of dusty, lifeless planets we'll share in mutual loathing. The others don't see it yet, or maybe choose not to. The truth is we're trapped, because we can't undo the knot we tied. Only a Fate can cut the threads of life."

The light from the fire running along the barrier vanished. The darkness dropped over them with only the faint glow from Mom's ambrosia crystal.

"We're not real." Ayleen said. The words tasted of vinegar and harsh citrus.

Mom laughed. "Out of all I told you, that's what you take from it?"

Ayleen heard her mother draw her sword and whisper *"Teras-trant!"* The blade glowed to life.

"If we're only a dream, doesn't that mean we're figments in a made-up reality?"

"No, we're all too real." Mom stood and with her free hand, slapped away the dust from her coat. "Real enough to stall the process of creation from its natural course. We defied God, and we're suffering for it."

"I don't think Dad would have thought it possible." Ayleen stood and walked deeper into their artery of the cave.

"Achieving immortality?"

"No, you finding religion."

"What can I say? The Galaxy is full of miracles." Mom's words were tinged with a bittersweet tone. "You're one of them."

Ayleen stopped to look back at Mom. Her declaration lacked any sentiment.

Mom, her sword aglow, stepped around her. "We'll get to that before we reach the dream thread."

Ayleen stared after her, and for the first time, she realized Mom was avoiding something. As awful as everything she'd told her was, something worse waited.

Mom paused to look back at her. "We need to stay within sight of each other."

"Why?" Ayleen didn't move.

"Because I need to be certain the you I see is the actual you and not a nightmare."

The notion she walked her mother's nightmares flattered her, but she wasn't sure she wanted to see it firsthand.

Ayleen drew her sword. *"Terastrant!"* The glow of her sword joined Mom's and they pushed deeper into the caves to find the next terror in the dark.

15.

The caverns grew more difficult to walk. Razor-sharp stalagmites littered the cave's floor. They sliced a path through the rocks. The task wasn't difficult, but each time they were forced to hack at rocks, they lost time. If the Thirteen got behind them, Ayleen and her mother were making the way easier for them.

A low buzzing sound filled the air. At first, Ayleen thought her hearing was damaged from the earlier explosions, but the buzzing got loud enough for her to recognize what she was hearing. Voices whispered from ahead and behind.

"I can't understand anything they're saying." Ayleen stared back the way they'd come.

"Not sure we're meant to." Mom grunted as she sliced at a patch of spikes. "If you understood them, would they be as frightening?"

"Depends on what they're saying." Something about the whispers tickled her memory. Were they plucked from her nightmares?

Another grunt and swing from Mom sent stalagmites clattering to the floor.

"You said having more people here makes things worse." Ayleen stepped past Mom when she waved her forward to swap out.

"Yes." Mom paused for some water. "More minds to draw on means more terrors."

"But it's more than that, isn't it?" Ayleen swung a few times. "Been thinking about the Fate we saw."

"Yes?"

"That came from my nightmares." Swing. Slice. "But the Fate knew things about you that I don't."

Mom sat while Ayleen cleared the path. "The fears we share have a greater chance of taking form. While it might be a natural thing, I'm not sure that's the case."

"You think it's malicious." Ayleen gritted her teeth and fed her anger into her swings.

"Sensed that, huh?"

"Yes." She turned to look back at Mom. "It's as if whatever forms these things is angry with us."

Mom nodded. "Not sure if it was always that way, but I have to think if it ever worked in a benevolent way, people would have swarmed here."

Moments passed and they eventually reached a stretch of cavern clear enough to rest their sword arms. They'd walked a good while without speaking as Mom led the way. Ayleen wished the inside of her head was equally quiet. Bad enough she had the disembodied whispers of Dosquam pestering her from without, but Basten's voice was running wild somewhere within the back of her brain. Sometimes she tossed out dates or counted one to a hundred. Basten wouldn't shut up. The piece of her soul still clinging for life within

Ayleen sensed Dosquam all around them and refused to give her nightmares any chance to rise up for this cursed rock to haunt her.

"I've seen your father every time I've come here."

Mom's admission pushed all the other voices away. Ayleen suspected if her mother had turned to look at her, she might have absolved her of everything, no matter how foolish that notion might have been. Every few minutes, she caught herself falling into the old habits of their relationship before the Galaxy lost its Way.

"Seen you each time, too," Mom said. "Not this time, though."

Something in the way she admitted that made a few things click into place. "You saw him," Ayleen said. "While I was sleeping."

"Yes."

Mom's earlier warning they should stay together, within each other's line of sight, took on clearer meaning.

"He didn't like that I didn't let him cut me up this time. Your shadows have both taken their pound of flesh from me. At least, they've tried."

The admission ended their conversation. The silence between them chipped at Ayleen's sanity in a manner that the deadest of worlds she'd walked had failed to.

The whispers grew louder and clearer. If Mom noticed, she said nothing. Nor did her body betray anything when Ayleen heard the words she could discern.

"Trust."

"Betray."

"Kill."

The dozens of voices jumbled together. No, that wasn't quite true. Not dozens of voices. Ayleen listened closer and realized it was one voice, but that didn't prevent the speaker from stepping over herself. What troubled her most was that she knew this voice.

The voice shouted five times all at once. *"Don't trust her!"*

Ayleen cursed as she tripped on a rock. She grabbed a low-hanging stalactite to keep from falling.

"You all right?" Mom stopped to look back at her. The voice shouted again, but Mom's face didn't flinch. "Ayleen?"

She waved off her mom's concern. "Tripped."

Mom stared, looking unconvinced. She definitely hadn't heard the voice. Otherwise, she'd have said something, because what the voice told Ayleen was a warning.

"Mom plans to kill you."

That's when Ayleen also recognized the voice. She'd heard that woman for years now, ever since she'd matured enough to lose the shrill tones of her youth.

The voice Ayleen heard was her own.

16.

Ayleen's warnings to herself echoed from ahead and behind in the cavern. She considered telling Mom, but instead, she watched her with greater caution. Even if the voice wasn't true, her mother had earned her distrust. She'd betrayed her and her father. Her actions, however indirect they might be, toppled the Knights of the Way and fractured the Galaxy itself, and all that by her own admission! What if the lie wasn't in the confession but the guilt?

And the voice was hers.

Mom had waited to admit to seeing Dad. Of course, Ayleen assumed Mom had told the truth about that. What if it was only a ploy to tug at Ayleen's heart? It worked when she'd said it.

The whispers continued to overlap. At times, her voice shouted. *"Kill her! Cut her down before she kills you!"*

The shouts slammed into her temple above her left eye, making her wince. She rubbed at the pain as if she could really work it out of her head.

"How much longer?" she asked.

Mom turned to look at her. Only when Ayleen saw the quizzical look did she realize two things: she hadn't specified "until what" and the demand had come out harsh.

Ayleen cleared her throat. "Until we reach the dream thread."

Mom drew her dagger and closed her eyes. The glow to her sword lessened as the dagger brightened.

"Less than a day." Mom opened her eyes and slid her dagger back into her trench coat. "That's assuming the way doesn't turn on us more than I expect."

"Why can't I feel it?" Again, Ayleen was surprised by the harshness of her tone.

"Your life thread isn't tied around it."

Ayleen nodded, but all she could think was how convenient that was.

"Don't trust her!"

Mom was working against the Thirteen. That much, Ayleen felt certain of. Only, that didn't ensure she was working with Ayleen.

Another noise joined the cacophony of whispers: a howl. The call came from ahead. It wasn't an animal, though. The howl never paused for breath. A wind slapped at them. It grew strong enough to make Mom's long coat flap like a cape.

Their branch of the cave led them to a large junction. The space that greeted them was massive and round with a large hole at the center of it. The ground surrounding the hole was barely enough for them to walk around it. Along the wall were seven other doors. The place reminded Ayleen of the Well of Souls, only no light and life existed within this hole.

"The Well has run dry!" Her voice screamed over the wind's endless cry. *"No life left! None in all the Galaxy!"*

Ayleen winced again, and this time she couldn't hold in a grunt of pain as she rubbed at that pounding above and behind her left eye. Her left eye… the one turned blue by Basten's soul.

"So which door do we take?" Ayleen asked.

Mom gritted her teeth. "I have no idea."

17.

They discussed options for figuring out the best door to take. Mom's ideas all boiled down to going a little ways into each one and see if one might eventually straighten out. Ayleen considered that gamble a waste of time, but she didn't have any better ideas. What worried her most was that all the doors might lead nowhere.

"I've been here before." Ayleen pointed into the dark hole before them. "Sort of."

Mom hit Ayleen with a sideways glance. "What is it that haunted you about this place?"

"Don't tell her!"

Ayleen shook off the advice with a twist of her head.

"It resembles the Well of Souls. It's where I met Kristian Basten."

"What's different about it?"

Ayleen pointed to the well. "There should be a vast well of light, the gathered souls of the dead waiting to be reborn. I guess Dosquam can't duplicate that for some reason."

"Duplicate the essence of life?" Mom grunted. "Despite appearances, none of what we've encountered is truly alive."

"I'm worried how well it might duplicate the rest." Ayleen explained how the doors to her past memories had worked. "If we're lucky, Dosquam can't duplicate that either. No way to know until we try, but it's the other thing about the well that worries me. We see only eight doors, including the one we came through. In the real Well of Souls, you could circle the well seemingly forever without passing the same door twice."

Mom kicked a pebble off the brick path circling the well. If the pebble hit bottom, they never heard it.

"Falling forever and mazes are common fears in dreams." Mom knelt next to the well, staring into it. "Perhaps this is Dosquam combining nightmares again, drawing on the layout of this Well of Souls to heighten our fears."

"Either way, we need to know if it's an endless circle, like the Well." Ayleen headed to the right. "Stay put."

Ayleen walked the full circle, and she blessedly ended up back at her mother's side. No endless loop.

"That's a comfort." Mom headed for the first door to their right. "Let's see what happens this way."

"Wait!" Ayleen's shout echoed.

Mom ignored the warning. She crossed the threshold and turned back to Ayleen with a quizzical arch of an eyebrow.

Ayleen took a step forward to follow. The setting didn't change into some mindscape from her memories. "Gods be praised," she whispered under her breath.

Mom raised her glowing sword to stare deep into the corridor, which was still too dark to see if it curved anywhere nearby. She waved for Ayleen to follow. "We need to move quickly."

Ayleen didn't follow her. "No, I think I have a better idea."

18.

Ayleen led Mom to the door directly across from the one they'd used to enter the Well.

"You can sense the direction of the dream thread, right?" Ayleen pointed into the passage they stood in front of. "Does this one lead that way?"

"It does, but there's no guarantee it won't turn and lead us away from where we need to go. I think it's likely this nightmare would trick us with that."

Ayleen nodded her agreement. "But what if they all lead the wrong way?"

"That's a risk we have to take."

"Maybe not." Ayleen walked through the door and headed down the passage with her sword glowing again.

"Ayleen, look." Mom pointed past her with her own glowing sword. "You can already see it takes a sharp right up ahead."

"Yes, but we won't go that way."

Ayleen stopped as she reached the wall at the turn. Glancing to their right, she could see how the cavern turned again after that, leading back towards the Well.

"We already know there are eight passages leading out of that junction," Ayleen said. "They'll likely twist and turn close to each other in order to be as confusing as possible. Also means the walls between them are thin."

The tension vanished from Mom's face. She stepped up to the wall blocking the direction they needed to go. "Close enough to cut our way into the next tunnel? Let's see if you're right."

Mom gave her broadsword a spin, winding it up for the swing, and whispered, *"Attadior!"*

The blade's glow grew more brilliant, changing from blue to white. Ayleen felt waves of heat ripple through the air around it. Mom plunged the blade into the wall. It resisted for a second, but then the sword sank up to its hilt. She forced the blade to move, carving out an opening large enough for them to go through.

She shook the sword a bit, the way one might put out a match. "Clever thinking," Mom said. "I'm impressed."

Ayleen smiled. Mom was always stingy with compliments. The disembodied voice only Ayleen seemed to hear ruined the moment.

"You can't trust her!"

As luck would have it, they only needed to cut through two more walls. Mom paused a few times to check they were going the right way.

Ayleen lost track of time as they walked in the darkness. Mom eventually raised a hand as if to feel the air. "We're getting close," she said. "A few hours out, I think."

Ayleen struggled to hear her mom. The chatter in her head had worsened. Gods, wasn't Mom hearing any of this? How could she pretend not to?

"I still don't know what I'm supposed to do once I reach the thread," Ayleen said. "You said only a Fate could cut the Thirteen's life threads."

Mom stopped in the middle of the cavern. When she turned towards Ayleen, her eyes didn't look up. The amber crystal dagger in its sheath on Ayleen's right thigh held her attention.

The whispers fell silent. The air in the cave pressed in on Ayleen, trapping her in place.

When Mom looked up at her, Ayleen couldn't retreat.

"You still had my eyes." Mom's lips trembled. "And your father's hair."

Mom reached out as if to touch her but pulled back. Her fingers curled into a fist.

"She took all the rest, and my shame is that I begged her to do it."

Ayleen didn't answer. She didn't understand what her mother was saying, but the way fear twisted every line on her mother's face left Ayleen certain she didn't want to know.

Taking a deep breath, Mom wiped away the emotions that had broken through what Ayleen now realized was only a mask of certainty. Mom started to speak again, but a loud roar erupted from the darkness ahead of them. Into the blue glow of their swords, the massive shape of Ysil Leesp rushed at them with his own crystal sword raised.

The Thirteen had found them.

19.

Ayleen knew better than to counter Leesp's attack. Mom seemed to, as well. They both scattered in opposite directions as he slammed down his falcata.

More boots pounded along the ground behind Leesp. Before they emerged from the shadows, Ayleen counted four more attackers, all armed with crystal swords. She recognized only one of the others, the pale-skinned Zelthan with four yellow eyes.

They were all immortal like her mother. She couldn't wound them enough to slow them. Leesp also packed three times her mass. The best she managed was to knock his swings off target enough to dodge them. He could no more shatter her sword than she could his, but he might knock her sword from her hand or shove the edge of her blade into her chest or face.

Ayleen retreated. "We've got to get past them!"

Even if she got around Leesp, she might trap herself between them all. Little chance she'd survive that.

"Can't do it!" Mom threw her entire weight into a swing at Leesp's neck. The attack forced him away from Ayleen.

He hissed, his tongue snaking out before he jerked it back into his mouth to speak. "Witch!"

Mom jumped back as he swung his sword parallel to the ground. The blade caught her trench coat, but only managed a small cut. She reached into her coat's breast pocket and flung the slender case she kept there to Ayleen. The box hit the ground past Ayleen. She snatched it up and flipped it open. The crystal shards still inside added to the glow of their swords.

"Mom, now!"

Mom turned to run, leaving Leesp to swing at air. Ayleen threw one of the shards towards the ceiling over Leesp. The shard hit with a flash of light that she saw from the corner of her eye as she turned to run, but she already knew she'd waited too long.

The heat wave slammed into her back before the cave collapsed.

20.

The first cough hit Ayleen as soon as she moved to get up on all fours. The dust she'd inhaled coated the inside of her throat like hundreds of tiny talons clawing their way down to her lungs. She reached behind her for her water pack's drinking tube and cursed when she remembered she didn't have it.

Her coughing fit refused to abate.

She avoided the worst of the cave-in, but a large rock had smashed against her sword hand. She'd dropped her sword and the glow was gone. She didn't think it had been buried, though.

"Terastrant." Despite not touching her sword, she could activate its magic. It flared to life about two feet ahead of her. In the pale, blue light, she saw the lines of blood running down her hand. Despite the pain, she didn't think anything was broken.

More coughs joined hers. Mom was on the ground behind her and cried out, unable to move. Ayleen ignored the sharp pain in her right thigh as she crawled close enough to grab her sword and raised it for a better look.

A wall of fallen rock blocked their path to reach the dream thread. With any luck, the cave-in had trapped all five of the traitors.

Six down, seven to go, her sword whispered to her with joy. She cursed at the sword, realizing it counted her mother in that number.

"Mom?"

She held her sword closer. The rocks, some as big as a large dog, covered her mom up to the waist.

"Can we pull you out?" Ayleen asked.

Mom coughed out a laugh. "Better chance of crystals growing out of my arse."

They still tried. Ayleen cleared what rocks she could. She freed the right leg, but one of the dog-sized rocks pinned the calf of Mom's left leg with a cow-sized rock on top of that.

"We're losing time."

Ayleen studied the rocks pinning her mother down. "I can try to cut the rocks into smaller pieces."

Mom slammed her fist on the ground. "Leesp wasn't far behind me. I can feel him stirring back there. You start cutting those rocks, you might free him, too."

Ayleen feared the same, but she didn't like the odds that left her against the rest of the Thirteen.

"I wanted to be there with you." Mom bowed her head. "It's why I've waited to do this."

"Don't trust her!" Even before the warning from the disembodied voice, Ayleen had taken a step back. She remembered what her mother had said before the attack.

"I need to let you in on a long-held secret of the mage generals."

21.

"Most knights are akin to cats, because they have three names." Mom offered a sympathetic smile, and her gaze turned up to Ayleen's sword. "I'll explain that in a moment, but we need to discuss why you're here, why it has to be you."

Ayleen knelt beside her mother. Her attention was divided, no matter how important what Mom had to reveal might be. The danger of the Thirteen digging their way out remained, and there were at least seven more left, including Sheriff Javo and Pyre Clypse.

"It took me four centuries to build up the courage, but I journeyed back to Lycaenidae Nine to face Moira.

"I went with nothing but a guilty conscience. The information I thought I could offer her was nothing she didn't know, and she laughed at me. I begged for her to journey to Dosquam to cut the threads, but she refused. Claimed she couldn't make the journey. Before I could ask, she cut off part of a leg, the lower half covered in the same blue crystal we use for our swords.

"She let me bring the limb here to Dosquam and try to make the cut myself."

Ayleen remembered a leg the Fate had avoided moving more than the others, the one with the crystal reaching higher than the other seven. That extra crystal was to fuse it back to the rest of the leg.

"Noticed the lame leg? Yes, that was why.

"Was easy enough to get the spider leg past the rest of the Thirteen to bring it here to Dosquam. Most of us avoid each other when we can.

"I didn't understand why the Fate would surrender a piece of herself like that, not until I returned it to her. The point was that it must be a Fate who makes the cut. Me using a piece of her to do it wasn't enough."

Mom shook her head. "Moira offered me a choice that would bind my offspring to the Fates. I assumed she meant I would give birth to another child, which I couldn't imagine. None of the Thirteen can produce offspring. She added her blood to the mix within my womb, only the taint didn't travel with me when I left Lycaenidae Nine. For a time, I thought it failed or that maybe the Fate was toying with me. I gave up hope until I saw the wanted posters with your name and face on them.

"That's when I realized the truth. The Fate's blood traveled backwards to the moment when you were conceived. Moira used her blood to take you from the past and pull you forward. You might say Moira is as much your parent as your father and I."

Ayleen stumbled back and fell on her arse. The face within the spider's exoskeletal head had resembled hers so much. "Those who cut the threads of life all share the same face." Ayleen whispered the words and felt a wave of nausea double her over. "That's what the Fate told me when I asked why her face looked like mine."

"When I escaped from the Fate's cave the first time, she chased after me. She screamed that I would see her face again and much sooner than I expected. At first, I thought she intended to pursue me to Dosquam where I planned to meet the Thirteen. Eventually, I got home, and you ran into my office. You have no idea how close I came to attacking you with my sword.

"The blood of the Fate had touched your conception. It hid within you. I swear, I think it waited for the moment I was gone to press forward and reshape your face.

"The Fate prepared you for this day. That first touch of her blood wasn't enough, but now you have an ambrosia crystal—your dagger. We have to bind you and your sword to it. It will probably seem like having a third voice in your thoughts, along with your own and your sword's voice, if you can imagine that."

"She'll betray you!" the disembodied voice answered. Ayleen laughed. She definitely understood the sensation of a third voice in the mix.

"Help me up onto my knees." Mom was already pushing up with her hands.

Ayleen's sword protested with a hiss, displeased by the thought of sharing her soul with anything else.

Once Mom was up on her knees, she took a few breaths with her hands on her waist to steady herself.

"We—I mean the mage generals—often quipped that most knights have three names. There's the name they're given by their parents, the name their sword tells them," she hesitated and wiped her brow, "and the lie they tell when asked to share their sword's name."

Mom lifted her sword. "My sword is not named Akara."

Ayleen had always known Akara's name meant "bright." She found a strange comfort in knowing her sword was not the only one with a false name.

When Mom spoke again, her gaze was lost in the past and her voice cracked. *"Hitlum."* She cleared her throat and continued. "And as my sword promised, I have been 'alone' for a very long time."

She reached out and cupped Ayleen's face in her hand. The hand felt cold, and the voice that had harassed her with doubts about her mother was silenced. "You're not so different as you think. I've always known your sword wasn't named for truth."

"Shyritas…" Ayleen shook her head, lost in memory. She'd answered the mage general who performed her forging ceremony with the first thing to enter her thoughts. Seems they all did this. "I don't understand."

"The sword takes a part of your soul. In a crystal, it's not clouded by the biases of the mind and linear time. When it spits out a name—it's a true one." Mom winced, and it was hard to say if it was because of pain from the rocks pinning her leg or from the truth she was sharing. "You see, it's not the sword's name it's telling you. It's giving you your name, and that's a truth most of us are ill-prepared to face."

Mom reached for Ayleen's sword. She stroked the hilt. "The name your father and I gave you means 'light.' I don't think we were far from the truth, but before we part for the last time, I'd like to know my daughter's true name."

The request hollowed out Ayleen's heart, because she'd never willingly shared it with another, because too many people would recognize what the name meant.

"Kalle-Al."

Mom nodded. If the idea of a sword—no, a daughter—named for the End of All Things bothered her, nothing in her face or her touch revealed it. If anything, the sparkle in her eyes suggested nothing but pride.

"The Galaxy has lost its Way, my beloved Light, and it's long past time this dying spiral gives way to the next."

Mom pulled her close. Ayleen answered her hug in kind.

22.

The next few moments were spent with Mom instructing Ayleen in the craft for the sharing of a soul with a crystal.

"Why couldn't you do this for yourself?" Ayleen pointed to the bulge within Mom's trench coat where she kept her dagger.

"Ambrosia crystals are the first stage of a Fate's eggs. As a Fate nears the end of her life, she imbues it with her life force over the span of an eon. In your case, we're going to connect it with you, shaving off a part of your soul into the crystal as with your sword. A small bit of the Fate's blood flows in you, and that will allow you to place a part of your soul within the ambrosia crystal. If anyone else attempted this, they'd die."

"She lies!" The damn voice had returned, but Ayleen ignored it. She kept reminding herself it was nothing but another illusion created by the thin reality of this planet. She wished belief was enough to silence it.

"Do you mean I'm about to do the same as the Fate, giving life to this egg?" Ayleen stared into her ambrosia crystal, trying to see any hint of the potential Fate within it. All she saw was the amber light. She suspected what resided in the crystal was the metaphysical building blocks for a soul. That perhaps explained why it could perform such miraculous craftwork.

"No, you're merely connecting with it. It's..." Mom stopped and sighed. "I'm not sure I could ever explain this well enough, even if we had another eight hundred years."

"Don't trust her! She'll betray you!"

"There's one last thing you'll need." Mom removed a small steel flask from a pocket in her coat. She unscrewed the top and tossed it aside. "This contains the Fate's blood."

"Moira?" Ayleen couldn't imagine how the Fate had drawn the blood from herself, nor how it had been funneled into this flask. Wasn't sure she wanted to know. "What do I do with it?"

"I'll poor half of it onto the dagger, letting it join with your blood for the crafting."

"What about the other half?"

Mom's eyelashes fluttered as if to blink away something uncomfortable. "You'll drink it. If you don't, you'll die."

"It's a lie!"

Ayleen fought down her fears and took the dagger in her sword hand. She placed the edge of the dagger against the open palm of her right hand.

"This will bind you," Mom said, "as close to the Fates as we can possibly bring you. Only then will you be able to cut the threads. You might even be able to injure the Thirteen, but I can't be certain."

Ayleen took a deep breath. Wasn't like she hadn't ever cut herself, but the prospect of joining herself to an ambrosia crystal and to the Fates daunted her. "Probably should have done this sooner."

"Would you have trusted me enough to do it?"

"No, I suppose I wouldn't have."

"Don't!" the voice shrieked. *"Don't trust her!"* Ayleen winced from the spike of pain behind her left eye.

Mom poised the flask over Ayleen's hand. "I'll pour it onto the dagger for you and keep it ready for when you need to drink it."

"How will I know when?"

The laugh from Mom sounded more like a grunt. "You'll know."

Ayleen decided against sharing how much that answer failed to comfort her. She closed her eyes and sliced across her palm with her dagger.

The amber crystal brightened with the drawing of her blood. As Mom had told her to, she turned the dagger around, gripping it by its hilt. Her blood shown darkly upon the bright crystal blade. Mom poured the black blood from the flask onto the blade.

The Fate's blood ran off the dagger and onto her hand. It pushed and ripped its way into her open wound. She almost dropped the dagger, but she didn't dare. Instead, she drew the shape in her mind that her mom had instructed. The shape resembled the key-hole spheres they used to travel from planet to planet, then she cut a piece of the sphere away as she spoke the words thirteen times, same as the mage general had for her forging ceremony long ago.

"Kattondeo Kanius Tanima!"

On the thirteenth time, Ayleen gasped as light flared in her eyes. When the mage general had performed this command for her sword's forging ceremony, the pain had started slow before it peaked. This time, agony hammered into her like a million barbed-tipped nails driven into her all at once. No, not nails. She knew what ripped into her soul and her mind—a million spider legs.

"Hold tight!" Mom shouted to her. "Hold to that shape in your mind and don't drop the dagger!"

Ayleen screamed. She'd managed to stifle her cries when her sword was forged, but this was like someone scooping out her eyes with dull-edged spoons.

Her body shook. The light from the spell craft flooding her eyes faded, but what she saw wasn't her mother or the cave but a spinning sky of stars. She spun away from the stars until they formed the spiral of the Galaxy. She gasped as she hovered at its edge. The spin of reality paused.

"Hold tight, daughter." Mom's fingers wrapped about her right hand. Her voice echoed within Ayleen's thoughts, as if she'd waited on the far end of the Galaxy for those words to reach her. "One more thing before the blood."

Ayleen croaked, struggling for the next breath. She couldn't find any air.

"Hold tight," Mom seemed to whisper. Her hands crushed Ayleen's fingers. "Hold tight."

A furnace of pain bloomed within her chest.

She found that missing breath, and it rushed back out in a scream as the spiral spun faster than ever, sucking her back into the cave in another flash of light.

"I'm so sorry." Mom's voice cracked.

Ayleen felt the pain in her chest more sharply than ever. Only when she looked down did she understand the source of her agony. Mom's hands, still wrapped around her right hand and the dagger's hilt, rested against her chest. The blade of the dagger was buried in her heart.

Mom's tears dripped onto their hands.

"I'm so sorry," Mom said again, but the look on her face wasn't sadness, only determination.

"I warned you!" the disembodied voice screamed.

23.

Ayleen fell back to the floor of the cave. The crystal dagger slid out from her chest and slipped from her grip. It chimed a perfect note as it landed next to her.

She gaped up at her mother as she raised the flask and held it above Ayleen.

"I'm sorry, but the rest isn't for you to drink."

She tipped the flask until the thick, black blood spilled onto Ayleen's chest.

The pain she'd felt in her hand was nothing compared to this. If the blood had dug into her hand, then this was on par with scalpels slicing each atom of her skin and sculpting the bloody remnants into something else.

Reality blinked, and the Fate's voice echoed within her ears.

"Wake, Kalle-Al. Wake!"

The simple act of inhaling filled her chest with a dreadful ache, but she was still breathing. She hadn't expected a next moment.

"Ayleen?" Mom brush a strand of Ayleen's blue hair back behind her ear.

She swatted her mother's hand away, but it was a weak swing that bounced off Mom's forearm with little impact. In that same moment, she realized the hand she'd injured in the cave-in was healed.

"Why?" The single word burned Ayleen's throat.

"Because the blood would have taken too long to get into your system the other way."

"She lies!"

"Yes, she does," Ayleen said to the voice only she seemed to hear, "but not about this."

The admission didn't stop her from glaring a death wish at her mother.

She recognized the expression on her mother's face. She'd seen her study a page of ancient text while seated in her favorite chair at home with the same look.

Ayleen crawled away from her until she knew she was out of her reach. The brief moment of connection she'd felt with her mother minutes ago was banished back into the distant past. She belonged more to the Fate now.

"You're ready," her mother said.

Ayleen sat up. She lifted her dagger in her right and her sword in her left. They sang a darkly beautiful chant to her. The song held a single lyric.

Thirteen to go.

24.

They parted without another embrace. They each offered a tense "I love you." Her mother's words were warm with need and Ayleen's were as cold as dead steel.

A strength born of purpose kept Ayleen moving. She sensed the dream thread with a clarity greater than her mother had. The bright and terrible thought that couldn't reach its end spoke to her not because of a connection to it, but because of the life threads of the Thirteen wrapped around it.

She not only sensed the direction to go, but she saw the path as if the light emanating from it formed a loose string with the faint glow of dying embers.

The walk took the better part of a day. Her sword and dagger, the bits of her soul within them celebrated their union with her and one another. They drowned out the annoying, false voice that had taunted her leading up to her forging with the dagger.

Her heart beat faster as she neared the dream thread. She believed without question she was meant for this, but that didn't take away her doubts. That same certainty had failed her on Witbrom VI when she'd gotten Kelvin killed. If not for her mother, her quest would have ended in the dungeon of Paladin Castle.

Even if she reached the dream thread before Leesp or the others dug their way out, that left seven of the Thirteen. She knew to expect Pyre who was more of a science mage than a fighter. Among the six others, she only knew two of them: Ulé Ontré-vas and Sheriff Javo.

If the Galaxy could offer her any kindness, it would be to make Ulé suffer for killing Kelvin.

Her desire to kill Javo ran as deep. Dara might have died in the maw of the Fate, but Javo had created the circumstances that forced Dara to leave Midchron.

The other four were just bodies to kill.

The first sign she was near the dream thread was when the cave brightened. She stopped the enchantment that made her sword glow. This part of the cave had taken her deeper into the planet and made it all the more clear why they couldn't have walked up to the thread on the surface and blasted a hole to enter the cave where the Thirteen's life threads had bound it in place.

As she neared the end of this artery, the silhouette of a woman stood with a hand resting lazily on the hilt of a sword still in its scabbard.

"About damn time, girl. Been looking forward to our rematch."

Sheriff Javo.

Ayleen gave her sword a slow spin. "Feeling's mutual."

25.

Sheriff Javo grinned at Ayleen but didn't draw her sword. Instead, she turned and walked back into the cave she'd been guarding.

The cavern this corridor led her to was a wide open space. Her eyes went first to the thread of light pulsing at the center of the cave. It looked at least a meter in diameter. The land curved out from it with sharp stalagmites scattered about it in a random fashion. The bottom half of the cave reminded Ayleen of a giant anthill, but when paired with its mirror above, she decided it more resembled an hourglass.

"Seems Aydrene didn't make it," Sheriff Javo said as she climbed halfway up to the dream thread.

Ayleen counted at least a dozen guards standing at the bottom of the cave. Scattered around the top half of the hill were the seven members of the Thirteen not buried back in the passage where she'd left her mother. At least Leesp was still taking his dirt nap.

She spotted Ulé with the other traitors to the Knighthood, a few familiar faces but none she knew by name. Perhaps she'd passed them in the halls of the Citadel or noticed them at larger gatherings within the amphitheater. They all looked human with the exception of a purple, leather-skinned Qualtaen, who traveled on four limbs but could as easily stand on two and use any of the appendages to wield weapons.

Up at the top, standing next to the thread was Pyre Clypse. At first glance, he wasn't much to see. He looked more like a surly grandfather. His lips curved into a wide, toothy smile, but the look forced his wrinkles into paths that didn't fit right on his face. He wore a white button-down shirt that ran over a stomach which half-covered the buckle of his belt and tucked into his tan slacks.

"Ayleen Torr," he said. "Pleasure to finally meet you in the flesh."

The way the Wolf had channeled his voice left no doubt this was Pyre. There was no imitating the icy lump of inhumanity in his core.

"I'm mighty glad this'll be the last time," Ayleen said.

Sheriff Javo barked a laugh and turned to look up at Pyre. "You're wasting your breath with this one."

Pyre glared at Javo. "There's always room for common ground." His forced smile returned as he looked back at Ayleen. "Just need enough time for the decent conversation of better men to prevail."

"Common ground?" She hated to agree with anything out of Javo's mouth, but she'd hit this one on the mark. "What you've done—all of you, including my mother—has left this galaxy to suffer for your survival."

"Every soul alive, all the worlds of the living you've encountered, wouldn't exist if not for us. We've preserved their lives." He pointed to the weave of the silver strings of their souls wrapped around the dream thread, stopping it short of the hole in the ground beneath it. "You're the one who plans to kill them all."

She strolled closer to where the mortal guards waited on the hill.

"And what about all the life that comes after? The lives you're denying by keeping this Galaxy spinning?"

"Tell me you don't have a soul you care for here that won't be lost." He crossed his arms.

"A week ago, your threat might have had some teeth for the bite, but Ulé there," Ayleen pointed her sword at the woman who'd speared Kelvin's heart, "she ruined any chance of that."

"So you'll damn your own mother." Pyre shook his head. "Shame that. Wasteful given all the years she's kept going. Could make up for lost time."

"Until I die of old age, and she's alone again? No."

"And what if you didn't have to die?" He threw out the question as if it trumped all others. "Did you ever consider why I included twelve others? Wasn't friendship. One life thread wasn't strong enough. Would've ripped a single life apart. But thirteen? One of the most significant numbers in mage craft? That did the trick." He unfolded his arms and reached over to the intricate pattern of life threads and flicked one of them with his fingertip. "There's room for one more, but this is the only time I'll make the offer. After this, we'll kill you and be done with it."

Ayleen wasn't surprised by the offer. Seemed Pyre's style.

"I'll pass."

Pyre glanced at Javo who shrugged. "That's the problem with youth," he said. "Think they'll live forever anyway."

"Just long enough," Ayleen said.

Pyre abandoned his feigned smile. "Kill her."

26.

The Thirteen's guards were willing to give their lives for their gods. Ayleen accommodated them.

These zealots didn't offer enough imagination to spot her weaknesses and take advantage of them. They didn't understand their real purpose. No matter how swiftly she might dispatch them, the display would offer the Thirteen insight into her style. Only two of them had seen her fight before this, Javo and Ulé. Making her exert herself against the guards would make her an easier kill for them. There was also the slim chance the guards might kill her.

The steep angle of the cave's floor hurt Ayleen's footing, but she braced herself with the stalagmites. The more clever guards did the same. The fools died.

Within less than a minute, bodies littered the hill. Blood, spilling from cuts to thighs and throats, ran downhill in complex trails.

The guards' short swords served them well in their enclosed cities on Witbrom VI, with their narrow hallways and cramped spaces. In this setting, the limited reach worked against them. Before they drew close enough to thrust at her, she slashed at their legs with her katana.

Realizing the mistakes of their fallen brothers and sisters, the four remaining guards coordinated their attack. Two drew her up the hill, keeping out of range of her strikes. The other two split up, going wide to her right and left to get around her.

Ayleen rushed left and relied on her momentum and footing for a controlled slide down towards the guard trying to get behind her. The guard stopped, likely realizing he wouldn't reach an advantageous spot to strike at her before she got close enough to attack. He kicked at her feet, but he moved with caution, giving her time to dodge. She drew in close, parrying his swing, and buried her dagger in his thigh. A shove sent him onto his arse, sliding down the hill.

The other three synchronized their attack with one coming up behind her. Ayleen pivoted out of her way and sliced off her left arm. Despite the guard being right-handed, the shock of losing a limb caused her to drop her sword. Ayleen buried her dagger in the woman's stomach and shoved her up at one of the two men racing down towards her.

With a swing that ripped open the guard's stomach, Ayleen dispatched the first of the remaining pair.

The last unwounded guard charged. Ayleen ducked to avoid his thrust. A sweep of her sword severed the bottom half of his right leg. He grabbed the top of a stalagmite to keep upright and lunged at her. His sword aimed for Ayleen's throat. She spun out of the way of his attack and buried her dagger into his lower back. She directed his fall, nudging him to his right. He screamed before a stalagmite speared him through the center of his chest. A few labored gasps replaced the scream.

"Seen enough?" Ayleen asked the Thirteen before she buried her sword in the back of the woman who'd lost her arm.

None of them said a thing, including Pyre with his infinite love for the sound of his own voice. Sheriff Javo shook her head with an admiring smile.

Ulé blanched. She hadn't really crossed blades with Ayleen when they'd faced one another in Paladin Castle. Ulé had been too busy killing Kelvin.

"You!" Ayleen pointed her sword at Ulé. "We have unfinished business."

Ulé's face turned from worry to smug confidence.

"So do we, warm blood." The threat didn't come from Ulé. The words came from behind Ayleen, from the entrance to the same passage she'd used to get here. The loud hiss that followed warned her who was there before she turned to look.

Ysil Leesp emerged from the passage's shadows.

27.

The Khymeran's clothes clung to him in tatters. He'd lost his eyepatch, exposing his sunken, right eyelid. The exposed injury heightened the menace in his glare.

He stalked up the hill.

Ayleen turned away from him, ready to run up towards the rest of the Thirteen. She stopped as she realized keeping Leesp as a threat behind her was suicide, so she charged on him.

His one good eye widened in surprise, but Leesp stood his ground, digging the talons of his feet into the dirt. No chance existed he'd slip or fall. He raised his falcata, not bothering to hide he intended to pummel her with his opening swing. The reptile's tongue snaked out, cracking like a whip.

At the last second, Ayleen dropped into a slide. She deflected his downward swing with her sword. Normally, she'd never be able to stop his strike, but he'd expected a higher target. Ayleen slammed her dagger into his kneecap, burying it up to the hilt.

A scream ripped out of his wide mouth as his body crumbled to the ground. She ripped her dagger out and scrambled out of his reach.

He struggled, trying to get back up, but his right leg was worthless. A dark hole exposed the damage she'd inflicted, and it resembled the injury to his dead eye. No blood flowed from it. No scab formed. No brilliant light shone to mend the damage.

Frustrated and pained hisses rippled from his throat. His entire body shook as he used his remaining limbs to turn and face her at all times. He held out his falcata in a threat.

Ayleen parried his panicked swings, slipped around his attack, and sliced off his sword arm. His scream drowned out the sound of her kicking his falcata out of his reach.

She spit on his face. "That was for my father."

She'd expected her crippling of Leesp to cower the rest of the Thirteen. She turned to face them and ask "Who's next?," but they were already descending on her with swords drawn.

28.

As the six traitors converged on Ayleen, a split second of panic crushed her heart. She'd fought multiple opponents at once many times. Her training as a Knight of the Way prepared her for being outnumbered, but it didn't include fighting a half-dozen other knights who'd received the same training.

The long-limbed Qualtaen reached her first. He leaped over her, taking a swing as he passed overhead. The move amounted to a feint, but she only realized it right before Javo reached her. Javo thrust forward with her broadsword. Ayleen darted to her left with a wild swipe of her sword to defend herself. The edge of Javo's long blade hissed against Ayleen's side, getting through her jacket to draw blood.

The six coordinated their assault better than their guards. They trained long ago to fight with their fellow knights at their sides. They took turns setting up openings for each other to attack. The efforts were obvious, though, because they were out of practice fighting as a unit. Ayleen used all of her energy to defend herself with no chance to take the offensive. The best she managed was to keep moving and avoid getting surrounded. If that happened, they could kill her with a synchronized thrust of their swords.

From atop the hill, Pyre's voice whispered over the symphony of crystal swords chiming against one another. Ayleen didn't make out what he said, but she recognized the results of his craftwork. The ground slid out beneath her feet. A quarter of the hill's face crumbled. She leaped back, counting on the lower gravity to help her on the landing. A rough fall still offered better odds than to stand there and get skewered.

Halfway down, a wind from another of Pyre's enchantments pushed her back up and flung her against the far wall of the cave. Her back slammed against the rock, knocking her senseless for a split second.

The knights slowed their approach to give Pyre more time to rough her up with his magic. As she got back to her feet, a wave of rocks launched towards her.

Ayleen pressed her crystal dagger against the cut in her side to get some blood on it and shouted the command *"Ridaigere!"* while drawing the shape of the curved barrier in her mind. The wall she created didn't just protect her from the flying rocks. The rounded shape of it flung the debris at her enemies as they ran down the hill towards her.

As fast as she reacted, the barrier went up too slow to stop all of the rocks. The first few made it through, hitting her in the right shoulder and left hip. The blows knocked her to the ground again. She dropped her dagger, but that didn't dispel her barrier. That required a mental command from her.

She pushed aside her pain and grabbed her dagger as she scrambled to her feet. The barrier blocked the six traitors, but it didn't completely surround her, Sheriff Javo and a man in a grey hat with an extra-wide brim were the first to get around the invisible wall.

Javo came at Ayleen with her broadsword, using fast and calculated moves. She did little to set up openings for the others. That left the man in the wide-brim hat struggling to find a place to join the fight. He lunged in on Javo's left, fooled by his partner's feint to the right. Ayleen took the opening, getting past his lunge and sliced open his throat with her dagger.

As with Leesp's knee, the wound didn't bleed or heal in a flash of light. The man dropped to the ground with a desperate gasp. He reached for his throat trying to keep his breath from escaping through the gash.

The rest of the swordfighters split up with three coming around on Ayleen's right and a woman with black and orange striped hair on her left. Ayleen parried Javo's attacks and got past her to the woman with the striped hair, choosing the one-on-one fight as opposed to the three-on-one odds in the other direction.

The woman with the striped hair wore a black cloak with its hood lowered. Her scimitar, held in her right hand, slashed with fast, efficient moves. Ayleen deflected her swings with her sword and turned in time to block Javo's attack with her dagger.

She dropped the barrier, and many of the rocks that had stopped against it rolled downhill between her and the Thirteen to create a new obstacle for them.

Ayleen sprinted up the hill. Getting to the top and cutting the life threads mattered more than dismantling these traitors, no matter how tempting the idea might be. She leaped over the corpses of some of the fallen guards. One of the Thirteen, a bald man wearing a black shirt and a white vest, caught up to her before the others. She turned in time to parry his katana. They traded three more swings before she severed his head.

The round hairless ball of flesh tumbled down the hill as the body collapsed. A faint glow appeared where she'd cut him into two parts. The head stopped rolling when it came up against a guard's prone corpse. With his face leaning against the guard's thigh, the traitor couldn't see, and his headless body crawled about in blind confusion, attempting to retrieve his head.

When Ayleen beheaded Javo back on Griffin, the head and body had flown back together. The blood of the Fate in her prevented that from happening this time, but she wasn't certain the two parts wouldn't still rejoin when they reached each other. Even though Leesp's knee still appeared a carved up mess, his severed limb used its fingers to crawl along the hill towards his body.

Before Javo and the four-armed Qualtaen reached her, Ayleen used her amber dagger's magic to break loose a half dozen of the stalactites from above and drop them on Pyre. He muttered another spellcraft to erect a protective barrier. His ambrosia crystal resembled a slender, gnarled branch from a tree.

She hadn't expected the attack to kill him, but if he was focused on defending himself, then he had fewer opportunities to attack her.

The effort to sideline Pyre left her open to the Qualtaen's attack. He reached her before Javo. He somersaulted around her. She tried to slice off one of his limbs, but he dodged the attack and came at her with his sword, a bizarre design with hilts on each end and another place to grab it in the middle to spin it like a staff, if he wanted.

She parried a few strikes from the Qualtaen before Javo swung at her. Ayleen jumped back and to her right, placing Javo between her and the Qualtaen. The worst thing Ayleen could afford was to let that spinning monster get behind her.

Javo glared from beneath the brim of her hat as they traded swings. This had gotten personal for her, and that worked to Ayleen's advantage. Javo would gladly sacrifice the others for a chance to even the score.

"Tsukamus!" Pyre shouted.

Ayleen didn't know that one, but she spotted the volley of rock-formed spears flying at her from the far wall. She parried a swing from Javo and sprinted towards the Qualtaen. She turned, swung her sword and struck most of the spears, splitting a few in half. The other spears caught the Qualtaen from behind. His sword dropped as three of the spears impaled him and flung him across the cavern to pin him against the wall.

She wouldn't last much longer. Exhaustion was setting in, making muscles and lungs all burn. A swing from Javo sent Ayleen sliding downhill on her feet for about a meter.

Ulé and the woman with the striped hair caught up to Javo. The three women worked together. Javo pressed her attack on Ayleen. That allowed Ulé and the third woman to split up and come at her from the right and left.

Ayleen retreated before the three could trap her. She ran straight towards Pyre and flung her dagger at his throat. No sooner had she thrown the dagger than she jerked to her left, back towards the dream thread. Pyre shouted a panicked craftwork to erect a barrier against the dagger. With him focused on protecting himself from her dagger, Ayleen swung her sword at the Thirteen's life threads.

Her single-edged sword glided down at the bright, silver threads. The tip of the blade was lined up perfectly to catch the top of the complex knot.

Something collided with her. Arms wrapped around her waist, one hand grabbing her by the belt with the other still holding to a scimitar. The tackle from behind by the woman with the striped hair took Ayleen's katana off target. She missed the top of the life thread knot.

But she didn't miss completely.

Her sword flashed a bright blue light as it caught the middle of the threads. A loud series of snaps sent half of the threads flying off in all directions.

The striped-haired woman and Ayleen tumbled down the far side of the hill. Ayleen landed face down. Rock and dirt scraped up her nose and left cheek. When they stopped, the traitor was on top. This close, the other woman's shorter scimitar had the advantage. The killing blow never fell as Ayleen fought to get out from beneath the traitor, whose body had gone limp. The woman was dead.

Had it been enough? Pyre had said the knot required all thirteen threads.

Off to the side, she spotted the dark mage's body facedown on the side of the hill. She struggled to get to her feet and stared at Pyre's form. The side of his face was withered and wrinkled. His dehydrated flesh clung to his skeleton enough to see the difference between each bone's slender middle and fat, rounded ends.

Her sword's song swelled, but the victory hymn stopped short as Pyre's body shifted. The arm moved as he got up onto all fours.

She looked up at the dream thread, still halted short. A few of the Thirteen's life threads fluttered in a manic dance. Both Javo and Ulé met her wide-eyed gaze with grim expressions that vowed she'd taken her one and only swing at ending them.

Pyre, still on all fours, coughed and hacked before he spoke in a mangled voice. "Did you really think we'd go down that easily?"

29.

Ayleen took a quick count of her enemies. Leesp still struggled on the side of the hill, his knee ruined and his arm severed, though he held it in place, trying to force it to rejoin his body. Javo and Ulé looked in perfect health. The Qualtaen, the beheaded bald man, and the man with the wide-brimmed hat and slit throat were all reduced to lifeless, withered husks. The woman with the striped hair had collapsed into a pile of bones and dust beneath her cloak.

Then there was Pyre. As he struggled to stand, he turned to face her. His left side was savaged into the same kind of emaciated corpse-like form as the ones killed by her cut. His right was unchanged, save for a weary look in his only remaining eye.

"It's only a matter of time now." Ayleen marched towards him, giving her sword a spin. "You don't have enough life threads to maintain it."

The exhaustion in Pyre's lone eye turned to rage. "You think we can't find more! We have time, and how many do you think will turn down immortality?"

Ayleen sprinted at him with her sword raised.

He scrambled back, reaching into his vest to pull out a vial of blood. The ambrosia crystal, in its wand shape, flared in his emaciated hand. He bit the cork off the vial and poured its contents onto the wand.

"Barrice!"

Her sword slammed down onto a shield protecting Pyre from her attack. The force of her swing was flung back at her, knocking her to the ground.

She cursed herself for going after him at all. As enjoyable as cutting Pyre into tiny pieces might be, she needed to get the rest of the life threads. Preventing him from launching craftborn attacks would have helped, though.

Unlike Ayleen, Javo and Ulé hadn't lost focus on what mattered. They stayed atop the hill to guard the wounded knot obstructing the dream thread.

"Time to die, girl." Javo walked a few steps down the hill.

Ayleen smiled up at her. "Try not to slip this time. Would be a shame to make things too easy for me again."

Javo's lips curled into a snarl.

A scream ripped out of Ayleen as she sprinted up the hill. Pain ached through her legs' muscles. Her sword hung low at her side. She swore to get past these two women, finish the job, and free everyone and the Galaxy from them.

Ayleen and Javo's swords chimed against each other. Kalle-Al hissed in her thoughts. *Three to go!*

Javo pushed her back. Ayleen slid down the hill, her boots unable to find any traction until she grabbed onto a tall stalagmite.

She'd stopped her slide, but she wasn't braced in time for Javo's attack. The traitor rushed down on her, sword raised. Ayleen scrambled to her right, surrendering her hold on the protruding spike of rock. Javo slammed her sword down and missed Ayleen's left arm.

Javo chased her around the hill, what was left of it. Ayleen spotted her fallen dagger on the ground a few feet from her. If she could get enough distance between her and Javo to grab it, she might be able to throw up a protective barrier or launch an attack at her.

Ayleen feinted the opposite direction, but Javo didn't bite on it. Instead, Javo brought her sword down on Ayleen as she was in mid-lunge for the dagger. Ayleen threw up her sword's blade to deflect the attack, but without any leverage, Javo's broadsword caught Ayleen on the back and drew a horrific cut running from below the right shoulder blade and down to her waist.

She was close enough to get the dagger, though, and reached for it. Her fingers bounced off a barrier. No wonder Pyre hadn't attacked her with any craftwork, he'd been too busy cutting her off from her own ambrosia crystal.

Javo slammed her sword down at Ayleen's outstretched arm as she jerked it back. The crystal broadsword took off three of her fingertips. Hot pain shot through her right hand from the trio of stumps.

Ayleen cradled her wounded hand against her stomach as she rolled away from her opponent. Javo grinned as she pressed her attack, a shark frenzied at the scent of her prey's eminent defeat.

Blood spilled onto the ground to mark Ayleen's path of retreat in dark red spots. Tears stung the cuts to her face from when she'd been tackled.

Coherent thought came in limited flashes, except for one memory of Captain Tratella's wisdom while training her. *The hunger for the kill can blind an enemy, especially when their victory seems closest.*

Ayleen forced herself upright. Javo swung at her torso. They parried blows to the angry ring of crystal swords crashing against each other. Javo wanted to beat her into submission, so Ayleen gave her an opening to swing down on her. The broadsword slammed down, but hit empty air. Ayleen spun around the attack and sliced through Javo's right thigh, sending her tumbling to the ground in two pieces. Javo screamed in denial and agony as Ayleen's next swing severed her sword hand.

"Don't worry." Ayleen flung Javo's sword to the bottom of the hill. "You won't hurt much longer."

She glared up at Ulé. *Two to go.*

Ayleen didn't run at her, though. The air stirred in the cave as more craftwork sent stalactites flying down at her. The ground shook as the large pointed rocks speared into the ground. One sent Ayleen's crystal dagger spinning out of the invisible barrier Pyre had erected around it. The dagger slid down the hill. Ayleen snatched it up and struggled to keep hold of it in her damaged right hand. The hilt brushed against her fingers' stumps. Her blood dripped onto the dagger, giving her crystal the fuel for craftwork.

"Hyave!" The command gathered up all the condensation in the cave, flung it up at the top of the cave, and froze it. Icy pellets rained down. With any luck, the small ice storm would distract Pyre from forming a counterattack in time.

She ran up at Ulé.

The traitor expected Ayleen to attack with her sword and dagger. Instead, Ayleen parried the woman's swing without slowing her charge. Too late to realize Ayleen's intent to plow her down, Ulé tumbled back towards the dream thread behind her. She wished Kelvin could have seen his murderer knocked onto her arse.

Ayleen raised her sword and dagger.

A shout came from Pyre, trying to form an attack with his wand. Before the command could finish leaving his half-rotted throat, Ayleen's two blades sliced through the pulsing threads of silver. The threads shredded, not just from her weapons, but from the rush of the now freed dream thread.

Light thundered down into Dosquam's mantle. Ayleen turned away from the blinding glow and saw Leesp's decomposing body, his face a death mask of hatred for her with the old wound to his right eye still visible.

The dream thread filled the cave and buried them in a symphony of hammer on anvil strikes that ripped the land out from beneath Ayleen's feet.

30.

The Galaxy didn't end for Ayleen, not in a flash of fire. Instead, she felt something familiar. Her body floated up as when first drawn into a keyhole. Then momentum asserted itself. An invisible wave slammed into her, hurtling her much faster than the typical journey along a dark energy tunnel.

She'd experienced this same thing only one other time: the day the Thirteen had attacked the Citadel and she'd leaped into the keyhole beneath the Knighthood's mountain.

The light ended with her body flung out the other side.

She collided with several bodies rushing towards her. She took a moment to make sense of where—and when—she was.

Screams sounded from all around her. She was startled to see she was back beneath the Citadel. The last time she'd been here, the ceiling had been caved in with a pack of fire hoppers chasing her. Only this was the Citadel restored to its glory days. No, its last day.

More screams went up as a crystal sword swung down at the young squires. A loud, angry hiss asserted itself above the squires' cries and the sound of metal swords shattering against the superior crystal blade that Leesp possessed.

Leesp—alive and breathing and with both of his eyes.

She was back on the day when and where the Knighthood died, the moment that had flung her eight hundred years into the future.

Squires ran into the glowing yellow sphere to escape.

A squire grabbed her arm, a boy with panic dripping down his face in two salty rivers. "Knight Torr, we have to run!"

"Go!" Ayleen shook him off.

She charged towards the closest man armed with a steel sword. He swung at her, but compared to the knights she'd fought on the dream thread's hill, he moved with all the speed of a drunken turtle. She sliced open his throat and kicked him away.

"Leesp!" She pointed her sword at the yellow-scaled captain. He glared down at Ayleen and ran to meet her. Their swords sang as they collided. Blows were parried.

Each strike knocked Ayleen back, unable to compete with Leesp's power. With each strike, a new thought would drop into place for her.

The Fate had said her string was cut long ago.

Her mother swore she'd buried her.

And Leesp had glared at her back on Witbrom, hated her, swore he owed her as he pointed to his ruined right eye.

Crystal swords chimed as they battled for the first and last time. All thought paused as his falcata impaled her chest and bit out her back.

White-hot agony stunned her. She stared up at Leesp, and his smile faded into confusion.

She wasn't dead. Not yet.

She dropped her sword and grabbed the bandolier wrapped around his torso.

"Take a good look." She paused, blood spilling out of her mouth with pain-filled coughs. "Because you're never gonna forget my face."

She buried her dagger into his left eye. He screamed as he fell back. She dropped to the floor with his falcata still sticking out of her chest and back.

She didn't move, fighting through each fast, ragged breath. The Fate had planned all this somehow, having the Galaxy pluck her out of this moment only to send her back in time to die.

A laugh dripped out of her blood-filled mouth as Leesp bellowed. He struggled to pull the dagger from his left eye socket.

Ayleen paused, her heart slowing as a numb, cold sensation flowed out of her chest and into the rest of her body.

His left eye…

Hadn't his eyepatch been on the right?

Then it all fell to shadow.

The last thing she heard was Kalle-Al's words reverberating in her mind with a dreadful hunger.

Thirteen to go.

Afterword

When Sheri and I started dating in high school, the first book she ever lent me was Stephen King's *The Gunslinger*. The book blended the Wild West with dark fantasy, and it was unlike anything I'd ever read or seen in film or television. I spent a lot of my early writing efforts trying to mimic some of what King did in *The Dark Tower* series, and most of those stories should never find their way to a bookshelf.

In 2017, I found myself between projects and unsure what I wanted to write next. I decided to experiment, starting a story in a similar place to *The Gunslinger*. I held onto the Wild West motif, made the main character a young woman, and stripped away the guns to turn it into a story about swordfighters.

On September 2nd of that year, I wrote a very loose outline for a six-act story, and three days later, I wrote the first 575 words of Ayleen Torr's adventures. I poured into the story a lot of my anger at what was happening in America at the time, especially towards women.

West of Apocalypse started as simply something to write. It didn't take long to realize I was working on a passion project and that it was the story I'd been waiting all my life to tell. My skills had finally reached a point where I could try to follow the lead of a book that was formative for me as a writer.

In many ways, this book is a love letter—a damn weird one—to Sheri. I couldn't have asked for a more perfect creative partner, and I was lucky to find her so early in my life. I never would have found my Way without her.

Acknowledgments

Most of all, I have to thank my wife Sheri. She's supported and inspired me as a writer for more than three decades. This book wouldn't have happened without her.

Sheri got us involved in James River Writers when they held their first conference here in Richmond, Virginia. Yet another thing I'm grateful to Sheri for, because I don't think I'd have seen the success I've had as a writer without getting involved with JRW. Writers need a community to thrive, people who will push them to improve their craft and keep working through all the tough times of the journey. JRW helped make Richmond my home.

Thanks to Katharine Herndon and Phil Hilliker. Not only are they two of my best friends, but they encouraged me through the journey to get this book published. They also helped keep me sane during the tough times along the way (there were too many to count). Phil also created the beautiful cover to this book.

This is my first real dive into indie publishing. Even with all the writer events I've attended during the past two decades, I still faced a lot of unknowns during this process. Writer and consultant (and one of my best friends) Kristi Tuck Austin, author David Kazzie, and Fountain Bookstore owner Kelly Justice provided a lot of helpful knowledge and support when I've needed it along the way. Authors J.C Kang and Jennifer R. Frontera also provided some helpful connections and advice as I made the journey towards publication day.

Thanks to Trudy Hale for the Porches. I've written tens of thousands of words for this book (and many others) at her writers retreat. I cannot overemphasize what a wonderful place it is. I'm grateful for the times I've shared there with Sheri, Katharine, Phil, Kristi & Adam Austin, Mike & Shawna Christos, Leila Gaskin, Denise Golinowski, Eric Smith, and many others.

I've no doubt there are others I've forgotten here (sorry!). Writing and publishing are always best accomplished with the support of others, whether its feedback on craft, kicking around story ideas, or the business of connecting with readers. Writing can be a lonely art, but thankfully, it doesn't have to be.

Trigger Warnings

While I had a lot of fun writing this book and hope you will enjoy reading it, be warned that this is a dark ride. With that in mind, here's a list of some trigger warnings.

- Alcohol Consumption and Abuse
- Buried Alive
- Confined Spaces
- Death by Fire
- Death of a Friend
- Death of a Parent
- Decapitation
- Demons
- Dismemberment
- Drug Use
- Gore
- Knife and Sword Violence
- Murder
- Police Brutality
- Possession
- Sex
- Suicidal Ideations
- Terminal Illness

I've tried to include everything I could think of, so if I've missed anything, please feel free to contact me via my social media and let me know. I keep a mirror list on my website's page for this book, and will update that with additional items, if needed. If there are future editions of this book, I will update those, as well.

ABOUT THE AUTHOR

Bill Blume's love for the written word started in high school with an addiction to comic books that was later hijacked by novels such as *Franken-stein* and *Dragonflight*. His short stories have been published in many fantasy anthologies and ezines. Like the father figure in his *Gidion Keep, Vampire Hunter* series, he's worked as a 911 dispatcher for more than 20 years.

To learn more about Bill and his books, visit his website at www.bill-blume.net.